The Price of Forever

The Bad Boys of Wall Street

Ember Leigh

The Price of Forever © 2024 by Ember Leigh

All rights reserved.

No part of this book may be reproduced in any form or by any electronic or mechanical means.

This book is a piece of fiction. This book is licensed for your personal enjoyment only. This book may not be re-sold or given away to other people.

Published by Ember Leigh

EmberLeighAuthor@gmail.com

Cover Model: Maca

Photographer: Reggie Deanching

Cover art: Covers by Combs

Editing: Elisabeth R. Nelson

Contents

Content Warnings

Mentions of drug usage
Mention of sexual assault
Mentions of past assault

CHAPTER ONE

JORDAN

"Outta my way, bitch."

The hunched man threw his shoulder into me before storming past on the sidewalk. I barely stumbled—I had a lot of practice keeping my balance under pressure—and didn't offer a response. By now, I knew better than to take it personally. Or maybe I *should* take it personally, since he seemed to only regularly snipe at me. Like he knew me and loathed me, just from sight alone. He said the same thing to me whenever I made the morning commute to my coffee shop job.

A poetic way to start the day in NYC. It was one of the many things to expect in this grand and gritty place—getting harassed by the unwell on the street. Along with eating delicious thin crust pizza. Being regularly boggled by prices and the sheer diversity of human life throbbing around you. Buying a hot dog off the street. Finding a prized Pokémon on your commute to work.

I hoisted my backpack strings, needing to readjust the contents since my eight-inch heels were currently stabbing the middle of my back. My regular hard-sided backpack broke unceremoniously last night after my shift at the club; this soft drawstring bag was the only thing I'd been able to find last minute this morning. Not a great bag for stripper heels.

I resettled everything, weaving through pedestrians as I beelined for Columbus Park. I had about five minutes of leeway this morning—early for my tardy ass—and I planned on taking full advantage it. I pulled out my phone, loading the app to see if there were any new Pokémon this morning. I usually hunted them in the fringes of my days, like now. On my way to or from work, since that was the main reason I left my apartment. That and goddamn delicious rice noodles.

As my account loaded, I scanned the plaza, looking for any red flags, creeps, or other signs I should move the fuck on. Even half past seven wasn't too early for fucked-up shit to happen. I knew from experience. Nobody stood out save a few early risers playing mahjong along the edges of the sidewalks, and a few more practicing Tai Chi on the grassy part. The mid-September mornings and nights were getting chillier, but plenty of people still gathered outside in the crisp air. By four p.m., New York would collectively be sweating—but I wouldn't have to worry about my makeup melting off because I had stripper-grade finishing spray.

I rolled my shoulders back, checking out a loner near the huge bronze statue of Dr. Sun Yat-sen in the center of the park. He pinged my radar for some reason—seemed familiar. It was the red hair, the curved shoulders as he hunched over his phone. He turned slightly, and that's when my stomach twisted.

Fuck. *Dustin.*

I didn't have time to talk to Dustin this morning. I didn't really *want* to talk to him, even if there was time.

I lifted my backpack again, the damn heels still scraping my vertebrae, and tried to spin slowly, without looking like I was running away from him—which I was.

Before I'd finished swiveling on my heels—which surprisingly was *not* easier in regular old black tennis shoes than the eight-inch mama jammas in my backpack—I could feel Dustin's attention prickle over me. I was barely two steps in the other direction before his gruff voice broke the calm morning air.

"Jordan!"

He thudded up to me a moment later, a goofy smile on his face. "Jordan. Hey."

I offered a tight smile, waving my fingertips at him. "Sup, Dustin? Looking for the Snorlax, huh?"

"It was here earlier," he confirmed. I started walking toward the main sidewalk. My Pokémon window had officially closed, and I hadn't even gotten to hunt like I'd wanted. "But it's gone now. Were you looking for it too?"

"Yeah. Bastard keeps escaping me." I heaved a sigh. Pokémon Go had been one of the main things that kept me from spiraling into a complete mess as my life unraveled around me through middle school and high school. Now, it was one of the small comforts I had in my life. I was an orphan—a single girl drifting through the boroughs of New York. No attachments. No roots. No *nothing*.

Except a space to call my own and the lure of the Snorlax.

To be honest, I didn't want to change a thing.

Mostly.

"I've heard from some of the other guys that it's been showing up around three," Dustin said, his words coming out smashed together, like he couldn't get them out fast enough. His elbow bumped into me as he followed me into the throng of pedestrians. I walked quickly as I resumed my commute. "You wanna meet here and we can team up? Throw a lure?"

"I've gotta work all day," I said.

Curious gazes swept across us as we walked. I had the trifecta of attention grabbing—clothes like a nerd, face like a stripper, and a guy who looked like he might still live in his mother's basement. I adjusted the backpack again—*these fucking heels!*—and Dustin shouted with something like glee a moment later.

"Whoa there! What's that?"

I stopped mid-stride, twisting to follow his gaze. My backpack. I groped blindly behind me, hand connecting with the actual spike of my work heels. I sighed, swinging the bag around front to assess the situation. In doing so, a translucent eight-inch heel went tumbling to the cement. I swore under my breath and scooped it up as quickly as I could, stuffing it back into its home.

Maybe Dustin didn't notice. But as I looked sheepishly up at him, his saucer-wide eyes told me there was no getting out of this one.

"Are those *shoes*?"

No, I wanted to say. *They are weapons, and they will kill you if I'm provoked.*

"They are shoes. I don't have time to explain. I have to go." I picked up my pace, but Dustin kept stride.

"You can *walk* on those?" He snorted, and an unpleasant waft of body odor reached me across the cool, humid morning. "Did you have to take classes or something?"

"It's not really important."

"Something like that kinda makes you look like a stripper," he said.

I grimaced. I *was* a stripper. No *kinda* about it. An actual, real-live, full-on stripper.

"So do you dance in these?" he barreled on. His elbow jostled mine again, and my annoyance was breaking through to resentment. We'd been Pokémon buddies. That was it. He didn't need to know shit about my life, and I didn't talk about things I wasn't ready to share.

I pushed my stride as fast as I could. Luckily, I was toned as fuck, and Dustin was huffing soon enough. These were the benefits of becoming a serpent on the pole two to three nights per week, as well as walking the equivalent of five miles each day—and in eight-inch heels on occasion. I hadn't even broken a sweat. Dustin was *flushed*.

The sign for my subway station loomed up ahead. Canal Street. I popped a hand up—"Bye, Dustin!"—and took the steps two at a time, my footsteps echoing off the damp walls.

"We should really hang out more," Dustin called, peering down the staircase. His voice became softer as I sped away. "I can help you find that Snorlax and we can chill after!"

Oh, right. Snorlax and chill. Honestly, it sounded like my dream date. But not with Dustin. Not with *anyone*.

I didn't know who I was truly fit for in this world. It seemed like the answer was *nobody*. And maybe my role in life was just to become okay with that.

I raced through the tunnels to the waiting train and skated through the doors just before they closed. I grabbed the nearest pole and stayed put—no spinning this early, thank you very much. It was a quick morning ride. I popped my earbuds in, though I wasn't listening to anything. It was more of a *fuck you I'm busy* warning to anyone who tried to talk to me.

It didn't matter how dressed down I got. How hunched I became, or how much I tried to blend into my surroundings. The creepers always arrived, the men sniffing for something more. The weirdest part was that these guys didn't even know I worked as a stripper at night.

What was the tip-off? My immaculate eyebrows? The falsies I had in place for tonight's shift at the club? I couldn't tell, and it irked me.

All I wanted was to be left alone.

The train rumbled through one stop before I got off at the next station, unapproached on the train. *Score.* My morning job, barista at Black & Brewtiful, was filed away in the Regular portion of my life. It's what I did to feel normal. *Why yes, I can hold a regular job interacting with the public!* Based on the money I made stripping, I didn't *need* this job. But it was smart to have savings in the city.

I had nobody else looking out for my ass. Only me. I needed to be not only smart, but ahead of the game.

I breezed through the doors. The blast of coffee bean and mocha coated me in a pleasant bubble, bringing a smile to my face. As soon as I crossed the threshold, my coworkers' faces lit up.

"Hey, Jordie!" Mitchell tipped his head toward me as he steamed some milk.

"Jordan's here, the party can begin!" Lillith announced to the person she rang up, winking my way.

A few regulars beamed at me as I glided toward the back room, waving at everyone. It was almost eight on a Thursday morning; a hefty line meant I needed to drop my things and clock in fast. Once I'd stowed my things and punched my time, I paused by the swinging doors to give myself a once-over in the mirror. I pulled my dirty-blonde hair back into a quick ponytail, checking that my morning makeup still looked good—a simple lip gloss and basic eye-liner to make my blue-gray eyes pop. They reminded me of Kaylee's eyes—it was one of the ways I still felt connected to my big sister, even though she'd passed away a decade ago. I entered the fray, scanning the coffee shop to see who was here.

But this time, it wasn't because I feared for my life every second inside these walls. It was a safe spot for me. At least, it *had* been.

Until my brothers Axel and Damian showed up last week, along with the older guy Trace they *also* called a brother. Well, I hoped they never expected me to do the same.

Every shift I worried they'd come back.

I squeezed Lillith's shoulders as I sidled past her, snapped Mitchell's apron string, then busied myself at the espresso machine. We fell into a quick rhythm, cranking through customers more quickly with three of us. I had a quip and a smile for every person I saw. New York was chaos and volume, which I thrived on. No, *required*. It was one of the only ways to get my thoughts to quiet down. I needed to be busy, or I needed bass thumping so loud I couldn't think about all the shit that threatened to drag me under.

My brothers might not drag me under now, but they had certainly never thrown me a life preserver when I fucking needed it most.

Time melted away as the three of us took orders and served coffee. I bumped hips with Mitchell, laughed raucously with Lillith while grinding beans. I barely noticed the door jingle each time a new arrival came in anymore. Except for one newcomer in particular, right after the morning rush started to die down.

"Oh, he's back," Mitchell murmured, wiggling his perfectly sculpted eyebrows my way as he tipped his head toward the front door. Then he ran his tongue along his top lip. "Mitchell likey."

I laughed, my gaze sliding to the newest arrival. He walked deeper into the coffee shop, his fists bunched as he scanned the room. Brawny, tall, impossibly built, which was obvious in a way I couldn't even explain. I just *knew* that if I tore off his button-up shirt and black slacks, I'd find pure steel beneath. Hills for biceps. Thighs with muscled cliffs. His dark, nearly black hair was clipped short at the sides, almost buzzed, and longer near the top. Though he was dressed like an office worker, the squareness of his shoulders suggested something far different than office work.

A shiver raced through me. I gulped. His head moved like the Terminator as he looked around the shop. He came toward the line, finally sliding his hands into his pockets and relaxing a modicum. Veins popped along his forearms, sending a very hot spiraling sensation through my core.

Haven't felt that in a long time.

"I'm gonna need to be on the register now," Mitchell hissed, bumping past me.

Lillith shot him a look that said *you're crazy.* "I'm logged in!"

"It's time for your break," Mitchell said.

Lillith huffed but conceded. After seeing his forearms, I thought maybe I should be on the register.

But no. As a rule, I disliked men. Heterosexual men, at least. Physically speaking, they were all I was attracted to. But my track record left a lot to be desired. Men were to be avoided—as partners. As interests.

They could pay me. They could exist near me. But that was it.

The line slowly moved forward. I didn't even need to look up to know that Mitchell had finally begun waiting on his hottie du jour.

"Oh, hello there," he said, extra sugar in his voice. "Now what can I get started for you today?"

I bit back a smile; he was laying it on thick. The vocal equivalent of preening his peacock feathers.

I forced myself to focus on my task—cleaning the milk containers—as the Terminator ordered. He ordered an Earl Gray tea, no sugar. His voice came out like rough velvet—gritty and lower than I expected. I was so surprised by the order—I'd pegged him for a red eye kind of guy—and unnerved by the way his voice echoed inside me that my gaze slid back to him.

And found soulful brown eyes already looking at me.

Heat zipped through me again, and I buried myself in my task. While Mitchell tried to make small talk, I started brewing the tea. An easy order. I had it ready for the likely robot practically by the time the guy stepped to the far end where the orders were picked up. I flashed him a breezy smile, steeling myself to meet his gaze again. This time, though, I noticed the eyelashes.

Fuck. They were far too long and luxurious for someone so *beefy.* Terminators weren't supposed to need an eyelash curler. I almost choked on my words. "Earl Gray for..." I double checked the name. "Sven?"

He cocked a smirk. "Close enough."

I handed him the insulated container, my fingers trembling as his hand came near. Energy surged between us; this felt far too momentous, practically preordained. Why could I almost hear angels singing? The ridiculousness of my bodily reaction to this man made me falter. My fingers relaxed just as he reached for the tea...and the cup crashed to the countertop.

Hot. Tea. Everywhere.

Heat flooded my cheeks, and I clamped a hand over my mouth. He stepped back quickly. Didn't even look surprised, much less perplexed. And somehow, that was even more mortifying.

"Oh my god. I'm so sorry. I thought you had it. I'm so, so sorry."

My cheeks had to be the color of apples. I grabbed a rag and started mopping up the countertop. I couldn't even look in his direction. I hadn't dropped a drink since my first week on the job two years ago. "Did any of it get on you?"

"All good," he responded smoothly.

My heart thudded in my chest. "Just give me a second. I'll make you another one."

As I faced the hot water dispenser, Mitchell sidled up to me. "Too hot to behold in the flesh, isn't he?"

"Shut up," I hissed. "It was an honest slip."

"He came in earlier today. I hope he becomes a *regular*." Mitchell bumped my hip before returning to the register. I took a deep breath and popped in the tea bag and lidded the insulated cup. Round two. I could do this. I would not even *look* at this man until his beverage was securely in his hands. I would walk up to him with my eyes pinched shut and some sort of protective suit on, so his testosterone didn't *get on me*.

Jordan, when was the last time you were attracted to a man?

I couldn't remember. Probably back when I was naïve and dumb, in my late teens. Life had sure beaten the naivete out of me. A little too hard, I'd say. I made sure the lid was *extra* secure before stepping back toward the counter and offering a glossy smile.

"Round two. No spillage. Have a great day."

His lips parted like he might add something, but instead he nodded. He strode off, leaving a pleasant waft of his cologne, which settled over me in waves of pure male and cedar.

Goddammit, the cologne was always the fatal final blow.

I drew a deep breath, feeling like I needed to fan myself. Was this how the men felt at the strip club every night? I put on a damn good show, I knew that much, but I was wearing heels with my ass cheeks hanging out. Different ball game. This man was fully clothed and just *ordering tea*.

Maybe the tea was the sexiest part so far.

The possible robot retreated to the far side of the café and sank into a seat at a table for two. He uncapped the drink, blowing gently on the liquid. I watched intently—if he drank it instantly, that would confirm his Terminator status. If he didn't, well, maybe he really was a mere mortal. People crisscrossed the shop, obscuring my view. After a moment, Mitchell began clearing his throat. *Loudly.*

"Ahem! Earth to *Jordan.* I said two small drips black, thankyouverymuch." Mitchell's annoyed tone was overridden by the humor in his eyes. He knew who I'd been staring at. And I hated that he knew.

"Heard. Making." I busied myself, vowing to forget about the coffeeshop hottie. I saw any number of attractive men each day in here. Sometimes even a celebrity or two. But none of them came close to affecting me the way Close-Enough-Sven did.

And that meant I needed to stop looking at him and never think about him again.

As if on cue, a big family came into the shop. Raucous, clearly tourists, bickering amongst each other as they drifted toward the menu boards and fretted over who paid for the last coffees. I smiled as I overheard them but tried not to let myself get sucked in.

Families that like only reminded me of what I didn't have. I'd fought this tightening in my chest my entire life. I needed to be happy with what I *actually* had, which was myself, an apartment, and enough money to feel like I was making it. My coworkers at both jobs were the closest thing I had to family. And between all those factors, it felt a lot like stability.

The one thing I'd wanted my entire life. *I had it.*

And I didn't need any other goddamn thing.

Especially not my brothers.

CHAPTER TWO

SEVEN

There was one thing I liked less than onboarding a new protection client after I'd vowed to step back from personal close protection.

Onboarding a new client who wasn't even fucking aware that she was my client.

I checked my watch, almost finished with my third root beer of the night. Sitting at a bar for six hours and only drinking root beer wasn't exactly my definition of fun, but on day three of tailing Jordan, I needed to get creative about staying in the shadows.

Her strip club was across the street. I had a perfect view of the long, black awning lining the front door that she went into around seven p.m. Now, at almost one a.m., I was dying for her shift to end. You could only drink a root beer so slowly and use the restroom so many times before the bartenders started to wonder. From my initial scope of the property, the only back entrance led to an alleyway accessible from the front of the building. I should have seen her if she'd left. But there was always that possibility she was long gone already and I'd somehow missed her.

This is why setting up formal security checks with a willing client is preferred.

I knew this. Axel knew it. Damian knew it.

But Jordan didn't exactly want a relationship with her brothers. And her brothers weren't exactly willing to let their recently discovered sister wander the streets of New York without someone looking out for her.

After spending the past ten years thinking she was dead or had been abducted, discovering her mere miles away from their home base had been the surprise of their lives. Of course I had to say yes when they asked me to check things out and make sure she was safe.

I just wasn't sure how much longer I could remain undetected. Jordan didn't seem like the type of little sister to take kindly to an unwanted close protection officer.

"You need anything else?" The buzzed-head bartender jerked his chin toward my drained glass. I liked root beer, but not this much.

"I'm good. Just gonna hang out here for a little bit longer, see if my friend shows up." I slid him another hundred dollar bill. His eyebrows arched, and he quickly accepted it, nodding.

"Sounds good to me. Take your time."

The Fairchilds paid well. Handsomely, even. Especially for a job like this, for someone so loved.

A sister they thought was dead or missing, resurfacing alive and well.

I couldn't even fathom. There'd been a time in my life I wished for such a surprise discovery. But my loved one—not my sister, but my fiancée—remained dead. Life didn't have a miracle in the cards for me. Eight years later, I could think about it without emotion stirring. Sometimes I worried that meant I'd become an unfeeling monster. But then I remembered that had been the plan all along.

I kept an eye on the strip club across the street. She had to be coming out soon. She worked eight to two at the coffee shop, and now seven to after one at the club. The girl's schedule was intense.

I'd know, because I'd been trailing her to every activity and planned to continue until I could identify all the security risks in her daily life.

I'd already identified enough for a goddamn multi-page list. I knew where she slept, where she worked, the times she transited, the routes she took. Her apartment complex could win a gold star in subpar security—I'd walked right into the foyer the other day while she was at the coffeeshop, and then into her actual fucking apartment. Everything was unlocked. Not a single set of eyes or camera to see me.

Abysmal. And already highlighted in my report.

The front door of the strip club opened and two girls strode out, laughing. A platinum blonde—not my charge. And the other? I squinted, trying to see through the murky shadows of the sidewalk. Dark blonde hair pulled into a sleek top knot. A black leather jacket, halfway zipped, with dark leggings and black boots. It was the boots that tipped me off before I made out her face. *Jordan.* They started walking along the sidewalk but paused a moment later, gesturing toward the bar.

I groaned inwardly as they crossed the street and headed this way. Spending even more time in this bar was not the goal, and now this opened me up to being spotted in another locale she frequented. I sighed and flagged the bartender for another root beer.

From my seat, I could see the main doors. The girls came in, attracting plenty of looks. They weren't dressed provocatively by any means, but I'd quickly found in the past three days that Jordan attracted looks wherever she went. Whatever she did. She had a magnetism I'd personally felt when she almost gave me a third-degree burn at the coffee shop. And being the subject of attention, wanted or otherwise, was yet another security risk.

But as far as I could see, she couldn't help it. The woman was perfection in physical form. I hadn't seen the inside of that club yet or what she did in there, but there was something about her that satisfied a deep, primal urge for aesthetics. Her gray-blue eyes had nearly rendered me mute earlier that week at the coffee shop. Judging from the way her co-workers and customers interacted with her, she had a little extra sparkle for everyone. And hell, if she wasn't the client's sister, I'd try to find out if she had a little sparkle for me, too.

But there was nothing more off-limits than a client. Especially one ten years my junior.

Besides, I didn't go sparkle hunting anymore. I was an unfeeling monster who couldn't even relate to his former self, since losing my fiancée eight years ago.

I didn't let people in. I observed them. I protected them. And I went on with my life.

"We're gonna need two gin and tonics." The blonde's order rang above the din as she leaned over the counter to speak to the bartender. Jordan pressed in at her side, nodding along. About nine people separated us. I prayed that would be enough to blend into the faceless mass of people inside the bar. I snuck a glance at Jordan just as her gray gaze snapped my way.

Our gazes connected in a gut punch.

Fuck. Clients weren't supposed to make my balls do that scrunchy thing.

I pulled out my phone and tried to look busy. Bored as fuck. Whatever drunk people did at bars when they were trying to zone out. I swiped into my messages and looked at the last texts I'd sent Damian: *Visual confirmation at her second workplace, I'll stick around until she leaves and heads home.* Their plan was to slowly reconnect with her before launching the big question: would she accept a full-time bodyguard, or any amount of protection, while they navigated this media shitstorm and SEC prosecution?

From the edges of my spatial awareness, I felt someone approaching. I swiped my phone off and sipped my drink. Jordan was at my side a moment later, wedged between me and the occupied barstool to my left.

"Why do I keep seeing you?" Her voice came out low, almost lethal. This wasn't a come-on. Or maybe it was, and I was just out of the game.

I took an extra sip before responding. I cleared my throat. "Because you have eyes."

Her chin dipped, something equal parts furious and amused circling in her expression. "Hard-hitting dad joke there. Are you following me?"

I worked my jaw back and forth as I mulled over my response. I hadn't expected her to confront me like this. Hell, I hadn't even thought she'd connected the dots. But she wasn't supposed to come inside this bar. I'd backed myself into this corner, in all possible senses.

"You've been to the coffee shop every morning this week."

"Is that a crime?" I asked, because something inside me was begging to poke her a little. "I like the shop. It's cute." I liked the view of her from this close. She was the same as Barista Jordan, but with a full face of makeup and a brazen attitude that couldn't give a fuck about customer satisfaction.

She snorted. "Cute." But she softened. Call something cute to a woman's face and it'll get them every time. "But that doesn't explain why you're here. Right outside where my *other* job is. Absolutely nowhere near that cute little coffeeshop."

I could have blamed it on coincidence. But that would never fly for the remaining portion of my security risk assessment. She'd surely spot me again. I needed to fess up. Immediately.

"You're right. I'm actually a close protection officer."

Her eyes narrowed. "You a cop?"

"No."

"Then what the fuck are you doing following me?"

"I've been tasked with assessing your security risks."

Her eyes shrank to slits then, and I could see the gears turning in her head. "That sounds like some made-up bullshit."

I reached for my wallet, thumbing through the cash and credit cards until I found the business card I needed. *The Showalter Agency.* I'd worked for them in Louisville, where I'd crossed paths with Trace. I wasn't with them anymore, since my goal was to start my *own* company now, but it had my name on it, my credentials, and it looked professional.

She plucked it out of my fingers, holding it between two magenta-polished nails as she studied it. "Seven. Not Sven."

"Correct."

"Well, I think you've got the wrong girl." She slipped the business card into the pocket of her leather coat. "I didn't hire you for a security assessment, so you can move along now."

"Somebody hired me. And I'm doing the job I was hired for."

She lifted her chin, staring at me in a way that made the thing with my balls happen again. There was something about the hipster clothing paired with the stripper makeup and the no-fucks-given conversation that had me short circuiting. Jordan was an anomaly. One that had me deeply intrigued.

"Who hired you?" Her question landed like a knife.

"Axel and Damian Fairchild."

At this, her eyes fluttered shut and she visibly crumpled. Her jaw flexed and she pressed her magenta-tipped index and middle fingers to the center of her forehead.

"You have to be fucking kidding me."

"They want to ensure your safety, which is no laughing matter to them."

She laughed, but it was brittle. "Oh, I'm sure they are very concerned about my safety. Now that they remembered they even have a sister."

I wasn't ready to wade into that family dynamic. I knew the Fairchilds' side, and couldn't even claim to know the whole picture. But the whole picture didn't concern me. I was only invested in the picture I was hired for.

"Why don't you just go home now?" she went on. "I'll buy your drink. You can stop wasting your time." She leaned in closer, inspecting my soda. "What the fuck are you even drinking?"

"Root beer."

"Odd choice for a Saturday night in Manhattan, but whatever." She pulled out a bifold wallet from her backpack and thumbed through the fattest stack of bills I'd seen in recent history. Whatever she did inside the club walls, it paid well. She pulled out a twenty and patted it against the bar. "Okay? You're dismissed."

"Do you typically take the subway at this hour or do you call for a private ride?"

A cocky grin curled her plump, pink lips. "Why the fuck would I tell you?"

"You don't have to. But the way you get home has degrees of risk that would be helpful to assess. Including your level of intoxication."

"I'm a single girl in New York City. You think I don't know about the fucking risks?"

"Do you carry pepper spray?" I asked.

She blinked once, tipping her head. "I'm not an amateur. I have three different ways to defend myself on my body at all times, including eight-inch heels that double as harpoons. I hear they work best on close protection officers. They'll touch your brain Egyptian-style. Are we done here?"

I lifted my palms, trying not to show my amusement. A prepared woman was absolutely an aphrodisiac. Not that she'd ever hear that from my lips.

"And don't follow me," she added. "If you even try, I'll make sure you know just how risk aware I am."

"Noted."

She sent me another long, level look before pushing off the bar and heading back to her friend at the opposite end. Jordan popped on a bright smile and received her gin and tonic. She settled into a chair, clinking glasses with the other woman before taking a sip.

This was my cue to leave. But after seeing those soulful blue-gray eyes up close, it was hard to leave. Even though she'd come over with fangs bared, she still managed to sparkle. But I couldn't stick around to see anything else.

The unconventional approach to the security assessment had failed.

I left the rest of my root beer untouched, along with Jordan's twenty, and wove through the crowded bar for the front door. Jordan's eyes scorched a hole through my back as I left the bar and paused on the damp sidewalk outside. I twisted to look back through the window, and her gaze flicked away from me.

She was smart. Vigilant. Good qualities for a twenty-five-year-old to have. But she could do so much better. There was no way in fuck I should have been able to waltz right into her apartment building.

She needed upgrades or at the very least, someone to show her where the rotting joints of her existence were.

I booked it to my M5 parked in the corner garage. Nights like these, I didn't mind driving through the city, when I knew the traffic would be calmer. Normally, though, I took the Fairchilds up on their offer to send a vehicle. I had no problem bathing in the luxurious life they offered, like handing off annoying city driving to someone else; I'd come to prefer it, even. But sometimes, a man just needed his BMW.

As the car hummed with power and the cold leather seat beneath me warmed, I sent a text to Damian.

SEVEN: She took a detour after the club and ran into me at the bar across the street. She recognized me from the coffee house and approached me. Didn't go terribly well.

DAMIAN: Fuck. Where are we at now?

SEVEN: I told her you and Axel contracted me for a security assessment. She asked me to stop following her. I'll swing by her apartment later and stick around until I see she's home. Then I'll reconfigure the plan tomorrow.

DAMIAN: Thanks. How'd she approach you? Mad?

SEVEN: She threatened to stab a heel through my skull.

DAMIAN: Okay. I guess that answers my question.

SEVEN: She'll likely reach out. Be prepared.

DAMIAN: I'll wear a helmet. You warned us this could happen. I just don't understand why she doesn't want to talk to us.

I stared at his message for a few moments, mulling over what she'd said to me. I didn't understand it any more than he did. And with the way things were progressing with Jordan, I might not ever.

I stored my phone and pulled out of the parking lot. First stop, some late-night pho. I had time to kill before I staked out her apartment, since I had an inkling Jordan wasn't just a one-and-done girl when it came to a night out with her girlfriend. As I accelerated down the street, heading for Chinatown, my mind drifted back to Jordan.

Those stormy, gray-blue eyes that doubled as a whip. The take-no-shit attitude that begged me to dive deeper.

But I wouldn't go deeper with her. That wasn't the M.O. The game plan was, and always would be to stay focused. Don't open up. Just remain a brick wall. Complete the job. The rest would fall into place.

In a way, Jordan's resistance to the assessment was a blessing in disguise. I didn't want to be anybody's close protection officer again for some undetermined amount of time, and I certainly didn't want to be glued to the side of someone like *her*.

Because I already knew that Jordan would make the focus and brick wall portions of the job worse than difficult.

She would make them impossible.

CHAPTER THREE

JORDAN

I awoke with a gasp the next morning, drawing deep gulps of air. Seconds before, I'd been drowning. But as soon as my eyes popped open, the nightmare faded into wisps and shadows like it always did.

Until I couldn't even remember what I'd been fleeing from or fighting.

The familiar setting of my bedroom sank into me. Cars honked in the distance and the undertones of an argument drifted up from the floor below. A plate smashed a moment later. It had to be that old couple in 3C. They only fought around lunchtime. I glanced at my phone: 11:56. Like clockwork.

I yawned and folded myself forward over my legs, opting for some bed yoga. My head pulsed lightly as I bent. Thanks, gin and tonics. I'd drunk more than I meant to—partly because I hadn't been out with Roxie just the two of us in a while, and partly because I'd been desperate to forget about *Seven*.

The memory of him shuddered through me, and I melted into my forward bend. Why were his chocolate eyes so unforgettable? His handsome face felt like a deep, cleansing breath. And I couldn't lie—I'd wondered on a few occasions last night what it would feel like to be wrapped up in those thick, strong arms. The man could probably crank out fifty push-ups as a warm-up.

I groaned into my kneecaps.

Reminiscing about Seven reminded me of the anger simmering beneath the surface.

Why the fuck had my brothers ordered me a stalker?

I didn't go into it with Roxie last night. She didn't need to know. In fact, nobody knew about my history. Where I came from, what happened with my family, that I was even related to Axel and Damian Fairchild, even though our last names were different now. It was just easier that way. The most I'd give up was that I came from Kentucky.

But as far as I was concerned, Kentucky was a graveyard for my former self.

I moved my body around, trying to cleanse my thoughts, but I couldn't stop thinking about what transpired last night. Seven's good looks were a red flag. Attractive men like that only led to bad outcomes, if our nation's famous sociopathic history had anything to say about it. Eyelashes and beefy bicep combos like that? Yeah, couldn't be trusted.

But really, his good looks were just the icing on a red-flag cupcake. I couldn't believe what Axel and Damian had done. *Hire a stalker? Just because they ran into me at the coffee shop? What a bunch of psychos. I deserve to live my own life, without them intruding. It's been ten years since I last saw them. What right do they have to know anything about my life now? Much less follow me and snoop into every last corner.*

My thoughts went from spinning to hurricane. After a few more minutes, I knew relaxation was completely off the table. I hopped out of bed, my heart thudding and cheeks hot.

They couldn't do this to me.

And I needed to make sure they knew just how inappropriate and outlandish they were being.

I snapped up my cell phone and raced toward the kitchen, pacing back and forth as I struggled to remember where I'd stashed Damian's number. He'd given it to me on his second visit to the coffee shop, about two days after their first visit with Mercedes. He'd begged me to call him and Axel, to at least put his number somewhere safe. In case I ever needed them or wanted to connect. I'd saved the business card—only after digging it out of my work's trash.

If I connected with them for anything, it was going to be to ream them new ass holes.

Through my panic and frustration, I remembered I'd tossed the card in a pile of junk mail on my bookcase. I rummaged through the stacks, mail flying to the floor as I hunted the matte black card. Finally I found it, looking worse for wear.

The Fairchilds.

I scowled. They'd been born Haynes, just like me and Kaylee, but completely forgot about us once they changed their names to their foster-turned-adoptive parents' name.

Was I slightly salty they'd lucked out on the foster front? Of course. Especially when Kaylee and I had lived through nightmares for years on end. And Kaylee hadn't made it through to the other side alive.

My throat tightened as I looked down at the floor. If Kaylee were here, she probably wouldn't let me call them. She'd died resenting them. And every last bit of resentment that she wasn't able to carry on, she passed to me.

I ground my teeth for a moment, mulling my options. Anger won. I swiped my phone on and called Damian.

It rang a few times before he picked up. "Hello?"

"Damian."

A pause. "Jordan?"

"That's right." I tugged at my upper lip with my bottom teeth, suddenly at a loss for words. I was still mad, but I hadn't planned out my speech. What the fuck was I supposed to say now? I'd blanked.

"How are you?" he asked.

"Furious." The pieces came crashing back, and I suddenly remembered what I had to say. "You sent a stalker to follow me?"

Damian sighed gently. "He's not a stalker—"

"What gives you the right to *send someone* to hunt me down and follow me all over fucking Manhattan like I'm a mouse to be caught? Do you know how fucked up this is?"

"Jordan," he said more forcefully this time, "he's a protection expert—"

"I don't care if he's an expert in saving babies from treetops. You don't send a stranger to track me like a serial killer. How do I know if this guy is really on my side or not? How do I know to trust him? I don't, Damian. That's the thing."

"But *we* trust him. We would never send someone untrustworthy—"

"And do you think I trust *you*?" I asked, my voice coming out a shriek.

There was the first thump of silence between us. "I would hope so."

"Well I don't," I spat out. "You two might be my brothers, but I don't even *know* you. So why would I just welcome this strange man into my life?"

Damian sighed again. Finally he said, "You're right. I'm sorry."

I took a few deep breaths. My chest was practically heaving from getting all those thoughts out of my head and heart. Fuck, I felt *lighter* now.

"We should have approached you before we went ahead with the plan," Damian went on. "But you didn't reach out, and we didn't want to leave you vulnerable. There's a lot you don't know. A lot we want to protect you from. And that's all this is about—protection. Now that we know you're alive, we want you to stay that way. Because whether or not you know us, you're still our family. Our baby sister."

I scoffed, but my throat clamped before I could say anything.

"We never dreamed this day would come—finding you alive. So now that our wildest dreams have come true, we just...want to make sure you're okay."

"Why the fuck wouldn't I be okay?" I asked. "I've made it four years in New York on my own, perfectly fine. Not to mention the absolute hell I survived for almost twenty years before that. I think I can handle continuing my daily routine."

"There's a lot you don't know about yet. And I'd love to tell you more about it. I'd love to see you. Can we meet sometime?"

The hopefulness in his voice sliced through me. God, it was easy to believe that tone. The words. But I couldn't. Not after everything Kaylee and I lived through.

"Why do you even care?" I forced the words past dry lips. "Kaylee's gone. You're a Fairchild now. You've spent the last ten years fine without me. You can keep doing the same, you know."

"Jordan. Don't be ridiculous."

"I'm being realistic."

"I care because you're my little sister." The hardness in his voice made me grit my teeth. "We've been trying to figure out what happened to you for the past ten years. You think now that we found you, we're just going to walk away? You're out of your mind."

"Well you might have to keep on walking," I told him, drifting toward the front window of my living room. I sniffed hard, peeking past the burgundy curtain to the afternoon activity. Cyclists and cars clogged the street, and pedestrians milled along the sidewalk. A normal Chinatown Sunday. I looked for my trusty buddy, Ranger—a black tabby cat that I'd found mangy and starving a year ago and nursed back to health. He visited me regularly since I'd saved him, and I liked to think that we'd become family in a way. I made sure to leave food and water out for him on the fire escape. "I'm not sure I want to reconnect like you and Axel do."

Another wallop of silence. This time, I could practically feel how my words had served as a punch to his face. I was glad for the separation of the phone call. When Kaylee and I had found out that Axel and Damian had dropped the Haynes name and become *Fairchild,* it had felt like a slap in the face. One that I'd never gotten to talk to them about, because they simply...left us behind. Moved to New York after graduating from high school and never spoke to me again.

Until last week.

"Can you at least accept the security assessment?" Damian finally asked. "There isn't much left to it. All we want is for you to be as safe as possible. That's it. You won't have to worry about anything, and we can rest a little easier too."

"I don't know."

"I promise you, this man assessing the risks in your life will only be a benefit to you. Even if you decide not to continue with him."

"There's no way in fuck I could afford something like that," I snapped.

"You'd never have to pay for anything," Damian said with a smug *duh* tone. "That's what your brothers are for. Trust me."

I didn't trust him. But I did see the opportunity to get free stuff. And I loved free stuff.

"I'll think about it," I told him. "But no guarantees."

Damian agreed, and we hung up. I sat in the throbbing quiet of my apartment, staring out the window for what felt like an hour. When I spotted Ranger prowling the fire escape stairs, I pushed my living room window open, calling for him.

"Here, sweetie." I held out the tray of food I always had ready at the window. He leapt my way, slinking inside the apartment. I pulled the window closed and sat back on my heels, starting a quick inspection of his fur as he munched.

"You look pretty clean and happy," I murmured, stroking his fur once I determined he wasn't injured or infested. "Have you been having fun since I last saw you?"

He wiggled his butt as he settled in to eat, purring loudly. I took that as a yes.

"Well, what do you think about this? Some real-life human brothers of mine showed up, wanting to reconnect. They want to send a bodyguard to look after me. But we all know your opinion is the only one that matters. What should I do?"

Crunch crunch crunch. Ranger didn't even look at me as he scarfed the food.

I heaved a sigh, watching my adopted feline family member eat while my thoughts began spinning once more. Then I reached for my phone and texted Damian.

JORDAN: I'll take his number. But that's it.

Seven's phone number was in my contacts list a moment later. My heart raced as I initiated a new text message. Why the hell was his name Seven? There was no way his mother named him that. Unless he was raised in some cult-like enclave. Maybe he had no legal last name. I hated how curious I was about him.

I stared at my empty New Message screen, debating my words. By that point, my stomach was growling. It was after one p.m. and I still hadn't eaten. I headed into the kitchen to make avocado toast and some coffee. As the bread quickly turned golden in my toaster, I sent the message.

JORDAN: Do you know who this is?

I stared at the phone so intently I accidentally burned my toast. The toaster had been a free find on the side of the road and tended to burn things unless you paid strict attention, but otherwise it worked fine. Once a thick layer of mashed avocado and chipotle sauce had been drizzled on top of the crisp bread, I took a triumphant bite.

Still no response.

I got to work making drip coffee—nothing fancy at home for me—twisting to look at my phone every few seconds.

Nothing.

Once my toast was gone and the coffee brewed and I was ready to never entertain the notion of a security assessment ever again, Seven wrote back.

SEVEN: Of course.

JORDAN: What's my name?

SEVEN: Jordan Marie Haynes.

JORDAN: Knowing my middle and last name hardly makes you a security expert.

SEVEN: Do you need me to prove that I'm a security expert?

I bit back a grin. It felt a little too easy to snipe and banter with this one. I thought back to his eye-rolling response when I asked him last night why I kept seeing him everywhere—*because you have eyes.*

I'd almost laughed out loud. But I needed to force him out of my life, not engage with him.

But it's hard not to engage with a man who has such luscious eye-lashes...

JORDAN: Kinda stupid that you're supposed to be assessing my risks but I don't even get to assess whether you're qualified or not.

I barely breathed as I waited for a response to that one.

But none came.

I couldn't tell if I'd poked the bear. Or maybe Seven was just running to Damian to complain that I was uncompliant. Maybe he wouldn't rise to the occasion whatsoever. After all, the likelihood was that Seven was just a dumb bodyguard with too many muscles and not enough brain. That's what I decided to believe. It would just make things easier, neater.

Still, though, I peeked out my front window one last time before leaving the living room. Just to see if he was lurking somewhere on the sidewalk.

All clear. Which meant I needed to get on with my day.

I drifted toward the bathroom, humming to myself as I thought about the day ahead of me. No coffee shop today, just a pick-up shift at the club from five until ten. At least I wouldn't be getting out super late. Monday was my off day across the board and usually served as my recovery day. Doing my routines on the pole—in those heels—for too many nights in a row really took a toll on my hips and calves. If I made enough tonight, I'd treat myself to a luxurious spa day on Monday. But only if I was able to hit my weekly savings goal first.

I took a quick shower, my thoughts stuck on Seven—remember-ing the way his biceps filled out his silky black button-up. The way he'd shown up at the coffee shop with the cuffs of his shirt rolled up, his forearm veins bulging.

His dark, neatly trimmed hair and olive skin tone did something to me that didn't really happen anymore. Just looking at him turned me on.

When I felt a tingle of excitement between my legs, I decided that was enough. I was not going to sit here and fantasize about a hired stalker. I had better, more important, things to do with my time. And I would certainly not think about him if I just so happened to find my vibrator in my bedroom.

I huffed as I stepped out of the shower and grabbed my towel.

Jordan, what on earth is wrong with you?

My feet padded softly over the thin rug that ran from the bathroom to my bedroom as I toweled off my hair. I planned on lush curls for tonight's short shift, so I'd start with a quick blowout in my bedroom. I crossed the threshold into my bedroom and froze.

A tall, shadowy male figure stood tucked near the window, his back to me, peering through a slit in the curtain.

Panic zipped through my veins, icy hot and consuming. I stumbled backward as I fumbled to cover myself with the towel.

"What the fuck?" My voice came out ragged. I bumped into the doorframe, *hard*.

The man turned toward me slowly. And that's when I noticed the neatly clipped dark hair. The black stubble along his jaw, the silky black button-up straining at his biceps.

A smirk curled at Seven's lips as he faced me fully.

"If I were a sexual predator, I'd already be taking what I wanted," he said, his deep voice coming out like smooth velvet. Excitement prickled across my shoulder blades, and I tried to shut it down immediately. I should not be aroused by this man breaking into my bedroom. Even though it put him in an incredibly useful position for what I'd been thinking about during my shower...

"How the fuck did you get in here?"

"Oh, you mean this time? Or are you asking how I broke in the first time, last week?"

I swallowed hard, trying to school my reaction.

"You need a new apartment. *Badly*. The first time I got in, I literally walked inside. The front doors were open, and you didn't completely lock your door. Easy. This time, I claimed I was your boyfriend. The super showed me into your apartment with a smile."

I opened my mouth, eager to retort with something that might absolve myself.

But I had nothing.

"Everything about this building is a red flag. I conned your super. There are no security checks, no cameras, not even a neighbor looking out for you," Seven went on. He never moved from his effortlessly cool position, leaning against my window frame, as he picked apart my entire living situation. "It's my job to identify these weaknesses and improve upon them. But there's no improving on shoddy, rotting structures. You need to find a new place to live."

I swallowed again, tightening the towel around my chest. I'd been so proud of moving in here. Did he know how hard it was to afford a place on your own in this fucking city? "It's the only thing in my price range."

"What about roommates?"

I shook my head. "I don't want to live with anyone."

"What if it would keep you safe? Keep you alive?"

"I'm not living with anyone ever again," I repeated forcefully. "I'll just...I don't know. Find a way to make more money, I guess." I ground my teeth, pressing a palm to my forehead.

"Why don't you want to live with anyone?"

"Would you want to live with someone, day in and day out?" I challenged him. "A girl needs her space. I don't want people up in my business. What more reason do I need than that?" I didn't want to tell him the truth, because I told no one the truth about what I'd lived through in the foster system. That every night before I went to sleep as a kid, I used to think to myself, *Someday I'll have my own place and nobody will be there to hurt me.* That was true, living on my own. I didn't plan on that changing.

Seven straightened with a curt nod. "That's fine."

"Well I'm glad you approve of my rationale," I muttered. "Am I going to have to prove every last bit of my life to you or what?"

"Just the parts that affect whether or not you'll make it through the day unscathed."

"Well here's a little news flash—sometimes it's the ones you live with that do the most damage." I headed back to the bathroom, grabbing the hair product I forgot I'd needed. When I returned, I said, "How long are you going to be around, anyway?"

"Depends on how dangerous your life really is."

I sighed. "Well, do I have permission to get dressed? Or do you need to assess the risks inherent in that before I move forward?"

That cocky smirk returned. "Get dressed. We can talk more about the details when you're done."

He sauntered past me, leaving me feeling more like a stranger in my own bedroom than I liked. I shut the door behind him—locking it for good measure—and let my towel crumple to the floor. *What the actual fuck?* I'd learned something today—don't provoke the probable ex-CIA agent to prove his worth. But damn, it was hard not to poke and prod this man. I wanted to learn more as much as I wanted him to disappear and never return.

I took my time getting dressed—sports bra and mesh shorts, my standard attire for getting ready for a shift at the club—and when I opened the door to continue the conversation, I already had my hair prepped for a blowout.

Seven sat on one of my wooden barstools at the small island in my kitchen, looking hulking and comically out of place. I came around to the other side of the island to face him.

"Can I get you an Earl Grey?"

A genuine smile ghosted his lips. "Not now, thanks." After a beat, he added, "I didn't bring spare clothes if you decide to spill it again."

I narrowed my eyes, crossing my arms. "So how long is this assessment supposed to last?"

"If you grant me full access, I can have the rest of your risks drawn up and detailed within another couple of days." He shifted, the stool creaking beneath him. If he was worried it would break under his weight, he didn't show it.

"And then what happens?"

"Once the assessment is complete, that's when we talk recommendations." He rested his elbows on the island, lacing his fingers together past big, bulky knuckles. "Based on what I've seen already, there's a lot you need to improve on. I'll likely be recommending a daily close protection officer. Among other things."

"Like a new apartment I can't afford."

"That's right."

I sighed, drumming my fingers along the countertop. "So what happens once you have your recommendations? It's not like I'm legally required to follow them, right?"

"It's all up to you, of course."

My escape hatch was opening. I could see through to the other side. "So what if we just plan on you finishing this assessment? You can give me the recommendations. I'll take them into consideration, make improvements where necessary…and…" I shrugged. "And then we go our separate ways. That's it. You get paid by my brothers, I'll be slightly wiser, and everyone's happy."

He tipped his head to one side and shrugged. "That could work."

"Great." I popped on a bright smile. "Now, does the stalker committee approve me getting ready for work? I have a lot I need to get done before I leave for my shift."

"Approved."

"Will you be accompanying me there as well?"

"Of course." His *duh* tone grated on me. "Go get ready. I'll be waiting out here and we can leave together."

"Oh." My smile dropped. "You're *staying*?"

"You have an unsecured building and countless unknown predators within a half-mile radius." He flashed a humorless smile. "I'm staying."

I narrowed my eyes at him again but had no retort. *Because he's right…again.* Fuck. It bothered me that my brothers had a point. But I might as well bilk them for some free security services while I could. And then in a couple days, Seven would be gone.

And everything would return to normal.

"I guess make yourself at home," I called over my shoulder as I walked into my bedroom. "If you can even relax with so many predators swirling around."

Seven said nothing, or if he did, I didn't hear it before I shut the bedroom door. Working at the club required a certain level of *preparation*—both physical and mental. I was an introvert by nature, so I needed to transition myself for several hours before stepping into that interaction-driven den. My shifts at the coffee shop usually accomplished this, thanks to all the customers. But if I wasn't working at the shop beforehand, then I needed to get myself ready the only way I knew how: loud-ass, thumping electronic music.

"Hope you like my music," I muttered as I cranked the volume on my Bluetooth speaker. Once the rhythmic thumping filled the room, I rolled my shoulders back and reached for my phone. I had one important piece of business before I got to work on my hair.

Asking my super, Michelle, WTF.

JORDAN: Why did you let this random guy into my apartment today? He's not my boyfriend and he scared the shit out of me. Don't do that ever again!

MICHELLE: Shit, girl, I'm sorry. He looked like someone you'd date! I thought I'd seen him with you before. My bad.

I frowned at my phone before tossing it aside. An honest mistake—that could have ended very differently if Seven were anybody else. One that I could take the building owner to court over. And I hated the other important piece of what Michelle had said: he did look like somebody I'd date. Which was potentially the most unsettling aspect of all.

Just a couple more days. I turned my blow dryer on high and brushed through my dark blonde tresses. I could last a little longer with this unexpected stalker companion, then take his recommendations and run.

And then life would continue as normal. I wasn't about to let some prime number manhunk and barely-there brothers disrupt my hard-won stability.

In just a couple more days, Seven and the Fairchilds would be out of my life forever.

CHAPTER FOUR

SEVEN

The electronica, bass-thumping remix of "Hey Mickey" threaded through me as I wound deeper into the black carpeted paradise known as Gemstones. I'd already read up on the establishment—one of the classier affairs in SoHo, with plenty of so-called champagne rooms, VIP lounges, and some of the most gorgeous dancers the city had to offer.

I followed the most gorgeous one of all deeper into the sultry labyrinth. Jordan looked over her shoulder at me, eyes twinkling. "Remember, you're my friend."

She smiled over at a bartender, who shouted out "Hey, Sapph!" as she strutted past. A half-dressed dancer slunk by, squeezing Jordan's shoulder.

"Right. Your friend. Who's Sapph?"

"Sapphire. That's me. Stage name."

Which explained why as soon as we'd stepped into the building, something came over her. Like she was playing a part in the show. She still wore simple leggings and the black leather jacket, but she moved with the importance of someone who knew she was about to get up on that center stage shortly and command the entire fucking room.

And I didn't want to admit how excited I was to witness it.

I looked around the spacious warehouse illuminated by sensual purple and blue lights from above. It sure didn't feel like four thirty on a Sunday in here. Scantily clad women wandered the club—some wearing body suits, others in skintight dresses, and some in mere thongs and bras. Every last woman was toned, busty, and beautiful.

I wasn't supposed to be itching at the chance to see Jordan strip down. But I considered this a secret perk of the job.

"I have to go back there," she said, leaning in to speak into my ear. She jabbed her thumb toward a door that stated GEMS ONLY. "You can hang around. Get a drink if you want. Just try not to look like Bodyguard Ken, okay? Be friendly. Don't stare like a Neanderthal."

I flexed my jaw. "I've been to a strip club before."

"Just thought you might need a refresher." She pasted on a fake smile and patted my shoulder. "And who knows, maybe you could try to have fun? If, you know, it's not too much of a risk."

She winked at me before she disappeared into the back room, leaving me secretly amused and distantly horny. I appreciated her wit, as well as her ass—not that I'd ever let her know that. I rolled my shoulders back, scanning the room to understand the layout a little better. Between all the butt cheeks and gyrating bodies, this place was sensory overload. I roamed the main room, pausing to watch whatever erupted around me—one girl giving a surprise lap dance to a solo gentleman; a busty waitress who trailed a finger along my bicep while purring about snacks.

The main stage lay silent and dark. Jordan's shift was only five hours, which was plenty of time for me to get a feel for how risky this job was. While she was in the back getting ready, I strolled as much as I could of the thousands-square-foot club. I made note of all the exits and entrances to private areas—the champagne rooms, which were partially visible to passers-by with low, backless couches around a central, tiny stage, and the VIP lounges, which were fully closed off rooms that I couldn't look into. A few different bars stretched along the perimeter of the main area, decked out in glossy wood and glittery, brightly colored floor-to-ceiling shelves stuffed to the brim with liquor bottles.

I mapped out the bathrooms, even peeked into the women's restroom just to make sure there wasn't an unexpected point of egress. I'd killed almost forty-five minutes by the time I returned to the main area—all my notes and questions for later logged on my phone—and plopped down into an overstuffed leather chair facing the stage. Almost all the other chairs were full, not to mention the uncounted men roaming the club floor. The place was far more bustling than I'd expect for a Sunday, but apparently horniness never slept in a city like New York.

The music shifted then, going a bit quieter. Spotlights flooded the main stage. Someone was about to perform.

Please be Jordan.

I needed to see her as much as I didn't want to. In the deepest part of me, somewhere between my balls and my gut, I already knew the truth. Jordan could ruin me. She'd break me apart and show me something new. Something I didn't fucking want or need in my life.

A different, lower-tempo electronic music filled the club, with modulated moaning forming part of the background. Out of nowhere, someone began sliding down the silvery pole. Huge, translucent heels were strapped to her feet. Creamy thighs led to the sharp V of a black bodysuit.

Jordan descended the pole in a slow, calculated spin. She dropped her head back as she lowered, a spray of lush curls cascading below her. Her body was all lean muscle and sensual curves. I'd seen women wearing bodysuits before, but there was something special about what Jordan chose for tonight's performance. I coughed into my closed fist as she touched the ground in her sky-high heels. Her bodysuit was cut scandalously high. Smooth, creamy skin glinted everywhere I looked under the bright lights of the stage.

As expected, Jordan was pure perfection.

She sank to her knees, gripping the pole above her head in a needy, submissive pose. Electricity snapped through the air, and it seemed like every man in the room was transfixed by her, leaning in closer. My cock twitched as I watched her. *Fuck.*

Her full lips were painted deep burgundy. Every inch of her looked provocative and sexy. She arched her pelvis toward the audience, gyrating in a slow, sensual move that made my fingers curl and my cock go from *thinking about it* to *hard as a rock*. I sank back in my chair, hardly daring to blink as she mesmerized the audience with every movement.

Jordan traced her tongue along the outline of her lips along with the music, dragging one hand down the front of her skin-tight suit and between her legs. Men drifted closer to the stage, hollering as she mimicked pleasuring herself—a little too well. Dollar bills began flying as she responded to their encouragement. Then the music tempo switched, and she popped to her feet and began scaling the pole.

She spun and humped and damn near fucked that pole, legs spread and tongue out. Everyone with cash crowded the stage, showering her in a rainstorm of money. A genuine smile broke through on occasion as she winked at someone.

I knew that hard-ons and titillation was the fucking point of a strip club—I just didn't expect to get hard pretty much immediately upon seeing the crease of Jordan's pussy through her bodysuit.

This didn't bode well for our protector/client relationship. In fact, it made me hope Jordan made good on her promise to take the recommendations and fuck off afterward.

I wasn't sure I'd be able to withstand working alongside a stripper as sexy as her.

A waitress approached me as I watched the show. I ordered a root beer—drinking on duty was a no-no, as a rule, but *especially* in a situation where even slightly lowered inhibitions could lead to me saying or grabbing something I shouldn't.

Other strippers milled around, trying to engage individual members of the audience. I only had eyes for Jordan. While she was in the room, I couldn't spare the attention. This could be my one chance to see the show.

Jordan made the pole her bitch. I'd seen my fair share of pole dancers, but her performance could only be described as Cirque du Soleil with less clothing. For her final move, she did a backbend off the pole and onto the ground. The entire club lit up with cheers as she held up the peace sign with both hands and strutted down the side staircase and onto the club floor. She was a celebrity, swarmed by men. I surged to my feet just as the club security stepped in. I was supposed to be her friend, not her bodyguard. I smoothed the front of my shirt and sat back down.

I watched as Jordan coyly entertained a middle-aged man. Couldn't tell what he said, but it must have been good because she followed him, hand in his, to one of the champagne rooms. A few other guys followed, all of them eyeing her like fresh meat.

I tapped my closed fist against my mouth, unsure what to do with the conflicting urges inside me. Fucking the client was obviously the biggest faux pas in the personal protection business. Especially as I was aiming to start my own company and begin raking in the millions as the boss, instead of the day-to-day grunt.

But what about when Jordan's express work goal was making men want to fuck her?

I'd fallen into the trap. Luckily, I was strong. Desiring from afar was one thing. I'd certainly never act on it.

No matter how much I couldn't get the vision of the tight V of her pussy out of my mind.

I took a sip of my root beer, adjusted my pants, and headed for the champagne room. Over the half-walls that encircled their semi-private area, I saw the men gathered around her on the couches while she shook a champagne bottle then uncorked it, laughing hysterically as the cork popped and bubbly sprayed her guests.

"Can I lick it off you?" one man asked.

"I want to see you lick it off yourself first," she purred. He obeyed, looking like he was in heaven. "You're a good boy, huh?"

He nodded eagerly, his imaginary tail wagging.

Jesus Christ.

I lingered outside the champagne room, trying to look like I wasn't keeping tabs on what was happening inside, though really, I was logging every bit of activity within. Did sex acts occur? How far did Jordan and any of these men go? Who was there to stop them if they pushed it past the limits? Had that happened before? Was she worried it would happen again?

All questions I needed answered ASAP. While I knew how *some* strip clubs worked, I needed the insider scoop on how *this* strip club worked.

The champagne room session lasted about an hour. But as soon as she finished, she was whisked away to another booking. From what I could tell, her one dance set her up for an entire evening of private performances. Smart, and likely lucrative from the way I saw these guys slip her twenties, fifties, and hundreds as they got their time with her.

This time, she was escorted into one of the private VIP rooms by a bald man in a designer suit. He could easily be the CEO of some *Fortune* 500 company. Hell, some of these patrons were likely D-list celebrities and I had no idea. I saw one group that looked like a rapper and his entourage, dripping with bling. On the opposite side of the room, a man who must have been in his seventies with a blond bombshell on his arm. There was an immense amount of wealth in this club. I had to hand it to Jordan—if she wanted to make a living, she'd come to the right club.

Once the door shut behind them, I decided to test the boundaries. I waited a few moments, then I strode up to the door and turned the knob.

The door swung open, revealing Jordan sitting with her legs crossed on a huge velvet couch, leaning into the man. The entire room was bathed in sultry red lights with black, velvety walls. Everything screamed sensual delights. A small stage and pole took up the middle of the room, but the couches in here were much wider—more in tune with lying back, stretching out, and *seeing what happened.*

Both sets of eyes turned my way. Jordan looked surprised, but Mr. CEO was just pissed.

"Hey! I paid for time *alone* with her—get the fuck out!"

"You okay?" I asked Jordan, offering a thumbs up.

She nodded quickly, sending me a grateful look. I retreated, lingering near the door to listen for sounds of foul play. It was just the two of them in there, and on my brief sweep, I hadn't seen any cameras. That didn't rule out the possibility of some other type of surveillance. It didn't appear the door could lock from the inside *or* outside, which was a plus. If there were locks, Jordan could get trapped in there by some sick fuck and get taken advantage of—and nobody would ever hear it over the loud music.

They were in there for an interminable amount of time. All I could do was lean against the wall and try not to imagine what I'd be doing in there with her. Or back in her bedroom in Chinatown. Or even, impossibly, back in my king bed in my Tribeca bachelor pad.

I imagined a hundred other men were having similar thoughts, now that she'd teased us beyond belief with her amazing skills on the pole.

I ground my jaw as I tried to corral my thoughts. The club was effective, that was for fucking sure. I considered myself a rigid man of honor. In here, I was one sexy look away from asking Jordan for a half hour in the VIP room. It had to be the lights. Or maybe the relentless ass cheeks. Whatever it was, I was just as much as victim as the next guy.

I definitely need to end this contract as soon as humanly possible.

I checked my watch. They'd been in there for almost two hours. I'd left once to piss, and another time for water. She had to be making good money—or maybe they were just having good sex.

I didn't like that last thought.

When the door flew open, Jordan bolted out, tossing her hair over her shoulder, a fat wad of bills stuffed under the clear ankle strap of her heels. The man came out a moment later and heaved a sigh. He spotted me there, his eyebrows went up.

"You been waiting this whole time?"

I shrugged. "Nothing better to do."

"Sapphire's worth the wait," he confirmed, then he staggered off. I couldn't tell if he was alcohol drunk or sex drunk. My stomach twisted at the thought of it being the latter.

I spotted Jordan across the club, entertaining a small group of guys with a lap dance. On the main stage, another dancer used the pole, but she wasn't nearly as captivating or skilled as Jordan. Half the audience engaged with different girls or chatted amongst themselves. I cut to the bar along the far wall and ordered another root beer. The bartender, a brunette with pigtails and volleyball-sized tits smushed together in a sport bra, lifted her brow at me.

"Again?"

"It's all I drink on nights like these."

She filled my glass with a wry grin. "I'm gonna call you the Root Bear."

"Bear?" I considered myself pretty trim, not nearly as bearlike as some gym rats could become.

"It has a good ring to it, for a stage name." She pushed the glass my way across the countertop. "You're a big guy, you could get away with it. You trim your body hair or no?"

I hefted with a laugh. "I do."

"Mmm. The trim Root Bear. Gotta get you on the stage sometime, sweetie. We do get women in here, and they'd eat a guy like you alive."

"Thanks for the offer." I lifted my glass in a salute. No way in fuck I'd ever get on a stage or anywhere near a pole. But a woman could fantasize about whatever she liked. I wouldn't stop her.

I settled into the plush seats to while away the rest of Jordan's shift. She moved from lap dance to lap dance. Men ate her up, and fuck, she looked sexy with every glance, breath, and dip. By the time she wrapped up with the lap dances, she breezed past me, patting my shoulder.

"I'm off to change. Meet me by the doors in twenty, okay?"

She didn't wait around for my response. Every inch of her skin glistened with sweat under the lights. She'd spent the last five hours in those heels, which seemed like a physical impossibility, much less moving with grace and sensuality at every turn.

I texted Legs to let him know we'd be needing him outside soon. Once I'd paid for my drinks and left a hefty tip—"Don't be a stranger, okay?" the bartender purred as I handed her the fifty-dollar bill—Jordan was heading for me in leggings and her black leather jacket, clutching the straps of a new backpack.

All traces of the incredible performances were gone. save the luscious deep lipstick, winged eyeliner, and her curls, which were pulled back into a low ponytail.

"Oh, he's your friend?" the bartender asked, jerking her chin in my direction.

"Sure is," Jordan said with a tight smile, slapping my shoulder.

"I named him the Root Bear," the bartender said, her Brooklyn accent revealing itself.

"Aww. You like that one?" Jordan pushed onto her tiptoes to pinch my cheek. "You're a cute little root bear."

"All he drank was root beer," she went on. "What else am I gonna call him?"

"Root Bear, meet Joss." Jordan gestured behind the bar and Joss grinned in return. "Stage name is Jade. She's the best damn bartender in this entire club. Her Manhattans will knock your socks off."

"Nice to meet you," I told her. "Do you all have gemstone alter-egos?"

Jordan laughed. "Most of us."

"I also told him he needs to get on that stage a time or two," Joss added.

"Oh, now there's a thought." Jordan eyed me from head to toe.

"Not gonna happen," I confirmed.

Jordan and Joss shared smiles and goodbyes before Jordan led the way out of the club. We hit the cool night air, and Jordan strode off down the sidewalk. I paused under the club's black awning and took a deep breath. Clarity flooded me now that I was away from the seductive lighting and bare bodies.

"What are you doing?" Jordan stopped about five paces away and looked back. "The subway station is this way."

"I called for a car," I told her. "He'll be here any minute."

She smirked. "I don't use private cars to get home."

"At ten o'clock on a Sunday night, you should."

Her smirk turned into a sneer. "Thanks for the advice. The subway is perfectly fine, and it's better for the environment. Anything else?"

"I'd like to review what I found inside the club tonight," I told her. "I'd rather do that in a private space than in the middle of a crowd with uncounted strangers listening in."

She bored a hole through my head with her gaze. Finally she said, "Fine. Guess it won't hurt to experience your life of luxury just once before you're gone forever."

The shiny black Fairchild SUV rounded the corner, pulling up to the curb in front of me a moment later. The hazard lights blinked, and I gestured toward the tinted windows. "Ready?"

She trudged toward me, and I opened the door to the back seat, waiting patiently for her to climb in. I couldn't pry my gaze off the flex of her ass as she stepped in, only able to see the bare half melons she'd been flaunting for the past five hours.

This assignment definitely needed to end. I trusted Jordan to follow through on her promise to fuck off once I handed over the final report.

Once we were both settled into the backseat, Legs waved from the driver's seat.

"Hey there." He twisted around, eagerness shining in his dark eyes. "I can't believe I'm lookin' at ya."

Jordan's brows scrunched together, and she glanced between Legs and me. "Do I know you?"

Legs thrust his hand between the front seats. "Name's Legs. I'm a Fairchild driver."

She received it hesitantly. "I'm Jordan."

Legs let out a sharp laugh. "Don't I know it! You're all my guys have been talking about for the past two weeks. Can't believe I'm seein' you with my own eyes."

Jordan shifted in her seat, nodding slowly. "Nice to meet you."

"Have you seen the building yet?" Legs asked.

"What building?"

"The one they named after ya!" Legs laughed as he pulled ahead, merging into the flow of traffic. "You gotta see it. It's a real beaut. You and Kaylee are on there."

Jordan dipped her chin, saying nothing as she examined her nails. A dark cloud seemed to descend over her.

"We'll be showing her sometime soon, I'm sure," I offered. "Legs, I've got some things I need to go over with Jordan before she gets home."

"All right, all right." He waved me off. "You do your thing, I'll do mine."

Legs cranked some music in the front of the SUV. I cleared my throat, running through the mental snapshot of my list before I spoke.

"Okay. So your club has pretty good security. We didn't pay to get in obviously, but is there typically a cover charge or any limits to admission?"

It took her a moment to look away from her nails before she shrugged. "They offer corporate packages sometimes. Free entry with the purchase of however many VIP rooms or something like that. Typically it's $50 to get in at the door. They have a dress code, too."

I nodded. I'd noticed that the entire place stayed classy. Not a ballcap in sight. "What happens in the VIP rooms?"

She hefted with a laugh. "Whatever you want."

My stomach executed an unnatural squeeze. "Are you fucking people in there?"

"Me? No."

"Do men expect it?"

A coy smile graced her lips. "They all want it. But they don't get it. That's how we make our money."

"But if you turn them down and they get aggressive? What happens then?"

"They're usually fine. We have a reputation for being a classier joint. Nobody *really* expects to get fucked in the VIP room. Though they push the limits whenever they can."

"Are there cameras?"

"Not in the VIP rooms."

It wasn't quite enough for me. There were too many risks. "So what's the escape plan when a group of men want to take what they think is theirs?"

Her mouth opened and closed a few times before she deflated slightly. "There's a panic button. That's it."

I cleared my throat. "Which I'm sure you couldn't reach in ninety-nine percent of emergency scenarios. Great."

"It's a risk we take for the job," Jordan shot back. "The money is worth it."

"Do any of these men ever follow you out of the club after your shift? Can they track you down?"

"I never give out my real name or number. They know me as Sapphire, and I have both a plan B and a plan C for men who push for my number."

"You didn't answer the rest of my questions."

She lifted her chin. "Some have tried to follow me."

"Jordan. This isn't good."

"What do you want me to say? It is what it is. And if your report is going to recommend I quit this job, well, you can fucking keep it to yourself."

I rubbed my palms together, trying to strategize what a long-term game plan might look for her. The only thing I could think of was daily, on-the-scene protection—*inside* the club. But lord above, I wouldn't survive an assignment like that.

I'd be putty in her hands within a month, tops, if I had to watch that performance multiple times per week.

I ran through the last few questions I had for her—mostly logistical things and layout concerns regarding the areas I'd never have access to—and we finished just as Legs pulled up to her apartment building.

"Couldn't have gotten here a second sooner," Jordan muttered, halfway out the door. "Thanks for the ride, Legs."

"Send me your schedule for tomorrow as soon as you can," I ordered her.

"We'll see." Then she slammed the door shut and strutted up to her apartment.

I watched her go, heaving a sigh.

"Sounds like another Fairchild firecracker," Legs murmured, more to himself than to me. Thank God Jordan hadn't been around to hear herself linked to that last name. She might have socked Legs in the face for it.

Once she was inside the building and the light of her apartment had flicked on, I relaxed into the back seat.

Tonight's shift was over.

And if Jordan made good on her word, only one more to go.

CHAPTER FIVE

JORDAN

Seven is taking off his shirt, thick fingers undoing each button on his expensive, black button-up. It falls away, revealing every last inch of those bulky muscles beneath. I run my hands over his chest, relishing every groove and dip in his defined abs. He watches me with the most heated gaze I've ever seen as my hand trails lower. I can already see the outline of his cock in his pants as my hand nears. I'm dying to hear him say something. Anything.

"Talk to me, baby," I whisper into his ear.

He opens his mouth. My entire body prickles at what he'll tell me next.

"NNNR. NNNR. NNR. NNR."

My eyes popped open and I gasped, completely disoriented for what felt like a full minute.

And then the pieces drifted back together. My alarm blared. I had a pillow stuffed between my legs, which I'd been humping in my sleep. I was *not* about to fuck Seven. I was alone in my bed.

Wonderful.

I groped for my phone, made contact, and silenced it. I flung myself onto my back and sighed.

Ten a.m. and my off day. Since I hit my money goal last week, I planned to haul my ass to the spa. I sat up and reviewed my phone quickly. There was a slew of texts, but a couple stood out:

SEVEN: Need that schedule.

SEVEN: Now would be good.

AXEL: Hey little sis. You wanna grab lunch with me today? On me. Your pick.

I groaned, unsure where to focus first. My entire body tensed thinking about what I'd say to Axel, so I started with Seven.

JORDAN: Off day. Might head to a spa later since I fucking earned it at my high-risk, completely unsafe job.

SEVEN: What spa, what time?

JORDAN: I don't know yet. I'm seeing where the day takes me.

I went to the bathroom to pee and wash my face. Once I was clean and slightly less bleary-eyed, I checked my phone again.

SEVEN: Need details.

JORDAN: I'm wearing panties and a tank top. I haven't had breakfast yet. I just brushed my teeth.

SEVEN: Not that kind of details.

JORDAN: I weigh 125 lbs and I love avocado.

SEVEN: Jesus Christ.

JORDAN: If you're the security guy, aren't you supposed to just naturally intuit my next move? I thought you were linked in telepathically by now. If you're not able to tell me where I'm heading next, I don't want your services.

SEVEN: Quit being a brat. I'm heading over.

JORDAN: I'm not putting pants on.

SEVEN: Whatever you're wearing is probably more than you had on last night. I'm sure I'll survive.

I narrowed my eyes, a weird heat circling in my belly. I desperately wanted to follow this thread further. But he was irrelevant, since he would be gone soon. I didn't have time for him, or any of my brothers, at this stage of my life.

Which reminded me...Axel's text.

I set the phone down as I prepared my standard avocado toast and coffee. I had no idea what to say to my brother except *no*. Though part of me wanted to say *yes,* especially after what Legs revealed in the car.

What would Kaylee think if she knew that you opened up to them and let them into your life?

I scowled as I finished off the spicy chipotle drizzle then took a big, crunchy bite. Avocado toast could cure a lot. But it couldn't cure the painful void in my chest where the Haynes family used to be.

Axel and Damian had been born Haynes, just like me and Kaylee. But they'd chosen the Fairchilds—their foster parents and foster brother Trace—as their true family and left me and Kaylee in the dust. They moved to New York City for college, even though they could have stayed back for us. And when Kaylee died from a drug overdose, my family had gone *poof.*

Evaporated. Like it never existed.

So, no, I did not want to get a casual lunch with my brother. He'd abandoned me.

I picked up my phone. Maybe the contemplative morning had been my sign from the beyond.

JORDAN: I can't today. Really busy.

AXEL: Soon, then?

JORDAN: Probably not.

AXEL: We're dying to catch up with you. Don't forget about us, okay little sis?

I swallowed the lump in my throat. *Don't call me little sis. Dying to catch up? Kaylee actually died—did you even fucking care?* All things I wouldn't say. Because not saying them was safer. Keeping them buried—along with my former self—was the only way forward. I didn't want to wade any deeper into this emotional territory than I'd already gone.

My hard-won stability depended on having these people out of my life. Continuing the status quo.

I did not need Axel, Damian, or Seven.

I didn't need anyone.

A knock on my front door startled me out of my thoughts. It had to be Seven. I peeked through the peephole—*Seven confirmed*—before pulling it open and tipping my head toward the interior.

"I'm shocked you didn't just let yourself in this time."

He stepped in, his gaze coasting down the length of my body. It felt like I was being sized up as opposed to appreciated. But when his gaze landed on my pink panties, I detected a twinge of something else. Seven was hulking, dressed to kill like always, and the scent of his cologne almost melted me on the spot. A smirk crested his lips.

"Have to keep it fresh, or else you'll know what to expect."

"Actually disappointed you didn't try scaling the exterior wall and breaking through the glass of my living room window." I pushed the door shut behind him.

"There's always next time."

I bit back a laugh. "Well, make yourself comfortable. I have no idea how I'm going to spend my luxurious day off yet, and I refuse to be hurried by a man who doesn't pay my bills, buy me dinner, or expense my clothes." I flashed him a toothy grin.

He sank into the couch, looking completely unfazed. "That's fine. Take your time. Your indecision makes my last day easier."

Oh. He thought it was his last day, huh? *Except it is—which is how you want it. Remember?* I fought the urge to correct him somehow, and I got the sensation that he *knew* I was struggling with my bratty tendencies. The satisfied smile blossoming on his perfect lips said a lot.

"Well," I went on, not wanting to make *anything* easy for him, "I kind of wanted to visit endless strings of floral shops and touch all sorts of trinkets in Chinatown that I'll never buy."

He shrugged. "Whatever."

His lack of emotion bothered me so much sometimes. He was so cut-and-dried. So *down to business.* It made me want to scream and pick at him until I broke through to something more interesting underneath.

I needed to refocus on something else. Otherwise, I was liable to get lost in that caramel gaze forever. I turned on my phone, eager for anything to distract me.

And I found a text from my boss at the strip club.

IRENE: Jordannn my sweet Sapphire, any chance you could come in last minute to cover for Opal tonight? She's sick!!

I groaned as I read it, sinking into an armchair near the front window. There went my luxurious spa day.

"This isn't about the trinkets in Chinatown plan, is it?" Seven asked.

I sighed exaggeratedly and let my head drop back on the chair. "I guess they're cancelled now. My boss wants me to cover a shift at the club tonight."

"Can you say no?"

"I could. But"—I licked my lips as I started typing out my response—"I won't."

"Why?"

"Money." I sent my text to Irene asking what time she'd need me. "Love it, need it, can't live without it. I live alone in Chinatown, remember? This shit ain't cheap."

"And it's not safe, either."

I stared at him, unamused. "Where have I heard that before?"

"You'll be hearing it plenty more times." A brow lifted. "Assuming you even look at the report."

"You've been working so hard on it, it would be rude not to glance at it."

His gaze moved toward the front windows, and I swore I caught a glimmer of a grin on his lips.

IRENE: 7-12. Doable?

JORDAN: You know you can count on me.

I sighed and set my phone down. My ankles were already not looking forward to the fourth night in a row on the stilts I called heels. I loved the job, but even I needed a break sometimes.

"You know you have two older brothers who are very eager to give you literally anything you could want or need," Seven said, as though hearing my internal dilemma.

I frowned at him. He had no fucking idea. "You can save the Fairchild sympathy. I have to work, and that's that. Now if you'll excuse me, I need to get dressed so we can get some rice noodles before we go in."

For an afternoon on a work night, I touched an extensive number of trinkets in Chinatown *and* took Seven to my favorite rice noodle joint, Yun Shin. Not because I cared about what he thought or wanted to share it with him to see what he said about my favorite restaurant. I just wanted the rice noodles. And a nice bouquet of dahlias, which were my favorite flower—especially in any shade of red.

And maybe I secretly wanted him to be sad that it was his last day trailing someone as fascinating and sparkling as me.

But the man was a brick wall. Anytime I caught a glimmer of personality, he followed it with iciness and focus on the job. When I asked him what he thought about the rice noodles, he'd just grunted and said "good" like a Neanderthal. Zero appreciation for broth. Outrageous.

I made him tag along to a few PokéStops on the way back from lunch. I caught him watching my phone curiously a time or two, but he didn't ask a damn question, and I didn't offer a damn thing. I did catch a Dragonite, though, which I shouted excitedly about. The brick wall didn't even ask what the big deal was.

Back at my apartment, I went through my usual pre-work routine while Seven lingered in the living room. Having him so close put me on edge in a strange way. I wanted to know what he really thought, and it burned me up that I wouldn't get it out of him before he was gone forever.

Once my hair was done and the base of my work makeup applied, I packed my bag and dressed in my street clothes. Seven stood as soon as he saw me approach. The way he filled my living room and seemed to tower above me made my pussy clench.

I couldn't lie—having a protector was sort of nice.

Especially one as sexy as Seven.

I refused his offer to take the private car to work, so we hoofed it through Chinatown and over to SoHo like the rest of Manhattan did on the daily. I knew this route like the back of my hand. I could probably get there sleepwalking if I had to. Once we got to the club, we parted without much fanfare, but my nerves buzzed waiting to see if I'd catch any glimpse of a reaction to my show like I had yesterday.

Seven had been transfixed, though I was sure he'd never admit it. And seeing the desire flash in his eyes felt like a small victory, even though the truth was you could truly conquer any man under purple lights with a slap-able ass and bare skin.

I tried to make the shift feel like a regular workday, but from the start, even my regulars were commenting on how nice it was to see me on a Monday. It felt odd being here—or maybe the feeling came from knowing that in a few hours, Seven would be gone forever.

Tonight's shift had me doing one main show again. I chose a black thong and fake-sapphire-encrusted bikini as my costume for the night. I pulled out all the stops, making sure to shake my ass cheeks extra hard in Seven's direction. The whole club roared and hooted as I wrapped up. And as planned, I got booked up immediately. *Per the moneymaking plan.*

Seven stayed along the back wall, surveying the room methodically as I pranced off to give some lap dances and make the rounds between champagne rooms and VIP lounges. I spotted someone familiar in the crowd toward the bar—a mess of red hair and wide shoulders. I squinted across the bar before heading into the champagne room.

Dustin.

What the fuck was he doing here?

There was no time to think about it. I was a busy lady, and I had lots of dances to give. Dustin didn't appear on my schedule, but seeing him here set off my alarms. In theory, there was no way he'd know to find me here.

But he saw the shoes....

I worked through the conundrum in the back of my mind as I entertained, popped bottles, and teased my tits for cash. Had Dustin been methodically checking out every strip club since the morning he spotted my shoes? Seemed unlikely. But there was no way he'd know how to find me. Unless he'd gotten lucky or followed me...

I tried to keep track of him, but I couldn't. By the time I came up for air after two back-to-back VIP lounges, Dustin was gone—or maybe booked with another dancer. I vowed to let it go.

Sometimes, real life people showed up in the club. That shit happened.

So why couldn't I shake it?

The end of my shift came quickly. I'd barely had time to keep tabs on Seven, either. Once I was changed into street clothes again, we stepped outside together, inhaling the humid, smog-laced night air.

"Ready?" I asked.

"Born ready. Car's on stand-by," he told me.

I tutted, shaking my head. "I knew you'd offer. But no. Besides, we need more time. It's our last day. I want to get to know you before you leave forever."

He kept pace alongside me as I started down the sidewalk, his jaw flexing. "There's nothing worth knowing."

"I beg to differ!" I laughed haughtily. "You know far too much about me. Besides, that's usually my line: *there's nothing worth knowing.* So I know it's a load of bullshit."

He said nothing as we scuffed our way down the mostly empty sidewalk.

"So, let's begin. Do you only wear button downs, or is this just your preference?"

He didn't look amused, which satisfied me.

"So I take it you've never heard of sweatpants," I pushed.

He sniffed, keeping his gaze on the sidewalk in front of us.

"There's some gray ones you should try out, especially if you go the Root Bear route. Women tip extra for shit like that. Just thought you might like that little piece of unsolicited advice."

No response.

"You're not giving me a lot of info here. Oh, here's another question I just thought of. Have you ever tried smiling?"

He bit his bottom lip, as if squashing a laugh. *Gotcha.* I poked him in the ribs.

"That was a good one, I know. Not quite as good as the Dad joke you led with, but we can't all be as skilled as you."

"Skill comes with time. With age. I wouldn't expect you to know."

I blinked back my surprise. It was gems like these I loved to unearth within him. "Are you calling me young and naïve?"

"You said it, not me."

"Let me guess what your name stands for—the decade of the year you were born."

This time, a laugh huffed out of him. I could tell he'd been fighting it.

"It's okay, I won't tell anyone that you're halfway to the coffin already. Your gym routine will probably give you a few extra years of life."

"Jesus, I'm in my thirties, Jordan, it's not like I'm not on my deathbed."

Score. I'd finagled one piece of information out of him. I should have been happy with that. But I wanted more.

"You'll probably last a little longer than average, actually, given the fact that you might be part robot."

He smirked. "What gives it away?"

"You just seem like the type of guy who wouldn't be able to identify all the bicycles in a random set of images."

"I'm very skilled at identifying bicycles," he replied, utterly unaffected by my wit.

"That's exactly what a robot would say."

We continued like this for the duration of our walk to the subway station, and then as we took the train back to Chinatown. For split seconds, we felt like friends. In other moments, I felt like this was our first date. But he always made sure to bring it back to client/hired hulk status.

When we wound our way from the subway station up onto the ground level of my neighborhood, re-entering the September night air, I slowed.

"What are you doing?" He looked over his shoulder at me, a few paces ahead.

"Can you...not follow me all the way back to my building?"

He cocked his head like he didn't understand my request. "It's two blocks away."

"I know. I just...don't like goodbyes." I shrugged. "It would be easier if you disappeared into the night."

That infuriating smirk curled at his lips. "Is that what you're used to?"

I laughed. "Brutal. And yeah. Maybe I am."

"It's after midnight and you're alone." He shook his head. "I'll come with you."

"Do you know how many times I've made this walk on my own?" I gestured at the open pavement behind me. At this hour, the pedestrians were few and far between. But I'd never had issues. Not really. "Life doesn't become more dangerous just because you show up and say it is. I've been hacking it on my own for a while now. Besides, I have pepper spray and eight-inch heels. You know I've got this."

Seven didn't agree with me. I could feel it radiating off him in thick waves. But he didn't stop me either. I took an exploratory step backward, then another.

"It's been real," I said, wanting to add more but not know what the fuck I should say. How did you sign off forever from an employee you never hired, never asked for, never wanted? This was becoming a ridiculous chapter in my life, and I was ready for it to end.

I finally turned and headed toward my apartment, walking as quickly as I could. Was it possible I'd grown to enjoy Seven's company? Maybe I was that starved for human connection. I'd convinced myself that my girl squad at the club and my coffee squad at the shop were enough. That I was experiencing the necessary closeness without actually being close at all to anyone.

It doesn't matter. It's done.

As my fingers hit the front door of my building, someone slunk out of the shadows and grabbed my wrist.

A mess of red hair; intense blue eyes. Panic hit like a sonic boom.

"Dustin," I forced out, struggling to free my hand. He wouldn't let go, just tightened his grip. "What are you doing here?"

"Hi, Jordan. You have no idea how much we have to talk about." His words came out disjointed. Everything about his energy sent me into flight mode. He brought me closer, grabbing my leather jacket with his other hand. "I watched you perform, and you were so good. You were an angel up there. I just need you to know how much this means to me. You being my friend. Being so nice to me. Being so sexy all the time."

"Dustin, *let go.*"

"It's time to get serious about what we have between us. We're the same person. We have so much in common. You're the most beautiful angel I've ever met and we need—"

"*Dustin!*" I threw my elbows, struggling to get out of his grip as he pulled me into him for a kiss. He reeked of alcohol and body odor. Eyes watering, I turned my head away just in time for his lips to graze my upper cheek.

"Let's go upstairs."

"Fuck no!"

His brows furrowed, like he didn't compute. "Why would you say that to me?"

"I want to go home and go to sleep."

"You're being a fucking bitch." His voice came out hard. He let go of my jacket long enough to pull the door open and tug me toward the threshold. "We're gonna go work this out right now."

I struggled against him as he tried to drag me inside. I knew, in the back of my mind, that I needed to scream. To cry for help. But I was paralyzed with indecision about how to get out of the situation. My pepper spray was inside my bag. My heels—my main weapon—inside my bag. And he had such an iron grip on me, I had no hope of retrieving either of them.

My fight or flight mode had abandoned me. I was just stuck in struggle and silence.

Seven was right.

CHAPTER SIX

SEVEN

I heard the scream when I was a block away.

I wasn't a fucking idiot. I didn't plan on leaving the area until I had a visual on her, safe inside the apartment. But I humored her need for the illusion of aloneness. So I waited until she was a half block away before tailing her.

My footsteps hit the pavement in marathon strides as I hauled ass to her front door. Under the streetlamps right outside her building, nothing looked amiss. But once I got closer to the shadows under that front overhang, I saw him. An unidentified assailant, gripping the front door, and Jordan resisting his attempts to push her inside.

All that registered with me about his appearance was the shock of red hair on his head. Once my hands connected with his shoulders, the cold neutrality of the job slid over me. I knew how to handle these situations. With precision. With force. I had this fucker slammed against the brick wall in less than ten seconds. He shivered like a kitten, bewilderment in his eyes.

"Hands off," I growled.

"Who the fuck are you?"

"I guess you can decide that for yourself." When he struggled to get away, I punched him across the face. There were no cameras here.

No evidence. My knuckles smarted, wanting more, as blood trickled from his nose. "A teacher? A warning? A nightmare? You pick."

He wrestled against my grip even harder, but it just egged me on. I punched him so hard both his lip and nose started gushing at the same time. A twofer.

"You have two options," I told him. "Wait until the cops show up so you can get arrested, or get the fuck out of here and never show your face anywhere near Jordan again."

"I'll go," he whispered, his front teeth bloodied.

"I don't believe you," I hissed, tightening my grip on his jacket until we were nearly touching foreheads. The man reeked, but he was a wimp. This was too easy. He wouldn't show up again. And while he would have a case against me at this point, he had no information or evidence to come after me with.

"I'll leave!" He held up his palms. "Just don't punch me again, please. I'll leave. I'll leave."

I loosened my grip slowly, watching him like a hawk to see what he'd do. He walked sideways against the brick wall, palms up. The second I stepped toward him, he broke into a sprint.

Gone.

I turned, ready for damage control. Jordan watched me with big, watery eyes, blinked once, and then bolted up the stairs. I followed her, taking the steps two at a time. She had her front door open in record time. I shut it behind me as I stepped inside, reinforcing it with the nearest chair. I didn't think that douchebag would show up again, but Jordan needed peace of mind first and foremost.

The sight of her nearly crippled me. She sat on the couch, knees pulled to her chest, face buried in her knees. Her body shook with sobs. I joined her, moving slowly. I didn't know what had happened yet, and I didn't want to make things worse. The weight of my body next to her indented the couch, causing her to fall against me slightly. I wrapped my arm around her back, wanting to comfort her—if that was what she wanted. I couldn't tell yet.

And then Jordan melted into me. She released and unfolded into my arms like an opening blossom. Even though she was at my side, I felt like I was catching her falling from some great height. She buried her face in my chest and cried. I wasn't sure what to do—pat her back, shush her like a baby, offer encouragement?—so I said nothing and held her. Until she was ready.

She must have been there for at least ten minutes. Long enough for me to get used to the weight of her against me. Her warmth. Then she sniffled hard, recoiled slightly, and said, "Oh my god. I'm so sorry."

The entire front of my shirt was damp from her tears. But it had been made damp by worse things. "For what?"

"I'm sorry." She scooted to the far end of the couch, tucking her loose hair behind her ear repeatedly. She reached for a tissue, dabbing at her eyes, and the room grew colder from her distance. "I didn't mean to...I don't know."

"You were just attacked. There's no rulebook."

Her chin trembled at that, her eyes filling up again. Her body shook with a silent sob but she seemed to force it downward before more could join. "You'd think I'd have one by now."

"I can promise you that whenever you're with me, I won't let anything happen to you."

This seemed to calm her a little.

"Do you know him?" I asked.

She nodded, folding her tissue so she could dab it at her eyes again. "His name is Dustin."

"Has he tried this before?"

"No." She drew a shaky breath.

"Are you friends with him?"

She let out a bitter laugh. "Hardly. I just know him from playing Pokémon Go. He never had any of my personal information. But he showed up at the club tonight."

She played Pokémon and was a stripper—she was a living wet dream for an untold portion of gamer guys. Not to mention the rest of the population of American men who *didn't* game. "So he...found you. Somehow."

"Yeah." She sniffed hard, examining her nails. "I thought he was harmless. A bit dense. Overbearing. But when he showed up tonight, I started to realize there might be something more to the picture."

"But you still wanted to walk home alone."

She sent me a sharp look.

"I'm not blaming. But we can't stay here. Not even for one more night."

Her throat bobbed, but after a few moments, she nodded.

"Let's pack your things. Just necessities. We'll find someplace to stay for tonight and then come back to collect the rest. You thought he was harmless, but he's proven otherwise. I don't want to bet on his next moves. I want you to be *gone*. He could show up when you're asleep and try to finish whatever the fuck it was he tried to start. We can plan your next moves from safety."

Jordan nodded gently, seeming to mull over the plan. Then she took a deep breath, straightening her back. "That makes sense."

"You pack. I'll find a place."

She headed for her bedroom while I took a few moments to collect myself. I was no stranger to crisis intervention. During my earlier years, when I was intent on doing the highest profile gigs possible, I'd experienced almost everything. I'd talked down the Princess of Monaco after an unruly crowd had gotten the best of multiple security guards. I'd arrived on site after an intruder broke into a certain A-lister's Malibu home and helped himself to countless diamonds—and on that afternoon, dried far more tears than Jordan shed tonight. The list of what I'd lived through—and put my fist through—was too long to recount. Which made my reaction tonight strange.

Jordan was different. When I held her, I wanted to continue holding her.

And that was absolutely not going to fucking happen.

It had to be the hour. I checked my watch—2:01 a.m. Yes, it was the hour, and the fact that I hadn't gotten laid in weeks. That, and I'd seen far too much of Jordan's ass that evening to be considered of sound mind. What I needed was a cold shower and a good night's sleep.

And to get laid. By someone who was not Jordan. But that would come later, once we figured out her safety.

I stared dumbly at my phone for a moment before I realized the simplest plan would be to hole up at one of her brothers' properties. They only had about a hundred houses between the three Fairchilds. She wouldn't like it—but it would be simple. Elegant, even. I pushed to my feet and went to her bedroom, rapping on the doorframe.

"You know, we could just head straight to one of Axel or Damian's propert—"

"Absolutely not."

I deflated slightly. Part of me wanted to probe into the why again, but it was neither the time nor *my place.* "I'll find a hotel."

While Jordan skittered between bedroom and bathroom packing her things, I found the best hideout hotel for a cool 5k per night.

Luxury and comfort that would provide something of a reset, which I thought she might appreciate.

I called for the car while she finished up. Legs didn't work this time of night, so the other driver, Harry, was on call. I released the chair from underneath her doorknob before we shuffled out and locked up. She didn't seem sad about leaving; instead, she remained expressionless as she slid into the waiting sedan.

I'd booked us a premier suite at the Ritz Carlton, overlooking Central Park. Plenty of space to hole up for awhile. I knew that her brothers would have insisted on getting the penthouse for their little sister, but I suspected that would just upset Jordan further. The goal was to keep her calm to figure out next steps. So hopefully this satisfied both parties.

The lobby of the Ritz was quiet at this time of night, echoing with opulence. We checked in quickly, almost wordlessly, taking the elevator to our twentieth-floor room. As we pushed our way into the suite, it was hard not to marvel over the marble countertops and gold-accented decorations. The place was spotless, neatly arranged, breathtakingly situated.

"Is there only one bed?" Jordan flicked on the bedroom lights and looked back at me, brows furrowed.

"Uh..." I reached for my phone, intending to check the reservation. "I thought I'd gotten two."

"This looks like one king. Unless there's another room I'm missing."

I scrolled through my phone until I found the reservation confirmation for *1 King Bed Suite*. Fuck. "No, this is right. I fucked it up. We'll go back down and get a different room."

She sighed, sinking into an armchair. "Do we have to? I'm ready to pass out."

I looked around the living area, jerking my chin toward the sofa. "This probably pulls out into a bed. I'll sleep here."

She tipped her head as she studied the sofa. "You think you'll fit on that thing?"

"I've slept in worse places."

"You're like, seven feet tall. Which must be how you got your name."

"Keep guessing. I'll let you know if you ever hit it on the nose."

She grinned. "You take the bed. I can sleep on the couch."

"You're not sleeping on the couch. Your brothers would kill me."

She glowered, but it was brief. "I'm not sleeping on that bed if it means you have to scrunch into a ball out here. You saved my ass tonight. The least I can do is let you stretch yours out."

I scratched at my head. She had a point. And I really didn't want to sleep on that loveseat of a couch.

"We can both sleep in the king," she finally said. "It's big enough for, like, four adult humans."

"As opposed to...a different number of adult non-humans?" I couldn't help the question, nor the fact that it came out with a smile. The grin that erupted on her face made it worth it.

"What I'm saying is...there's room. So get your ass in bed."

"Fine. Just...don't tell your brothers."

"No worries there."

"I'm going to shower," I told her, moving to the empty side of the bed. "And then we need to sleep." I untucked my shirt and reached for the Glock I kept concealed beneath my waistband in a holster. I ejected the magazine, pushed the slide back and set the empty gun on the nightstand. Jordan watched with wide eyes.

"Have you had that the whole time?"

"Every day. All day long."

"Why didn't you use it tonight?"

"I'm not trying to go to jail." I bent down and released the pistol that I kept in my ankle holster. I took that and the Glock's magazine with me as I headed to the bathroom. I trusted Jordan—but I didn't leave a loaded gun anywhere, with anyone. "These are for emergencies. I don't shoot unless absolutely necessary."

"Well it's good to know we have *options*," Jordan said as I walked into the bathroom.

"None that involve gunfire." I shut the door behind me, setting the magazine and the pistol on the bathroom countertop.

The silence that settled around me wasn't the kind I was used to at the end of a day. I wasn't sure I'd be able to settle down long enough to sleep with Jordan at my side. My days as a Marine had taught me how to handle sleepless nights on duty. I wasn't afraid of that.

No, I was afraid of something much simpler. Much softer. Much more alluring.

Something I forbade from entering my life ever again.

Tragedy shaped a life, forced it into unknown, contorted forms. Mine had created the man that Jordan saw. I knew a little about the tragedy that shaped Jordan's and her brothers' lives. But they didn't know about the one that shaped mine—the tragedy that had stalked into my fiancée's bedroom one night while I was on patrol in the California desert and ruined the future we'd planned together. Reshaped my future into a barren husk, leaving me too heartbroken to ever consider opening myself up to that pain again.

They never found the gunman. It was an unidentified serial killer, the police had concluded, ultimately linking it to two other homicides in the area around that time. A random act of violence that crushed my heart.

One I could have prevented, if I'd been home.

One that refused to make sense, no matter how many years I spent mulling over the events.

After a certain amount of time, tragedy needed to be dealt with. Somehow. I could never properly seek revenge for my fiancée's murder. All that was left was to bury it. Become the unfeeling monster.

I had no elasticity left in me to be reshaped by any force other than focus.

Love, and all things soft and alluring, just didn't fit alongside the coffin of my buried tragedy.

CHAPTER SEVEN

JORDAN

I awoke to a darkened room. Unfamiliar shadows. My limbs went rigid as I struggled to piece together what I was seeing and where the fuck I was. The luxuriously soft sheets beneath me were the first clue. The rhythmic breath of someone beside me.

I propped myself on my elbow, rubbing the sleep out of my eyes. *Ritz Carlton.* I squinted through the darkness, groping for my phone. I peeked at the screen: 7:01 a.m.

Great. Seven a.m., and Seven at my side.

Again.

I settled back into bed, now that I was sure everything was fine. I'd barely slept four hours. Surely I could fall back asleep in this dark haven of comfort. But within a few moments my mind began wandering.

The way Seven had peeled Dustin off of me like a rag doll.

The way he didn't even flinch when he turned Dustin's face into a bloody mess.

How safe I'd felt cradled in his arms, crying like a baby. A safety I hadn't felt in...*fuck.* Too long to remember. The sad part was I didn't think I'd ever felt that safe.

I'd never watched someone beat back my tormentors or bullies. Not successfully, anyway. Kaylee had tried, when the foster home assignment was too rough. But it usually just ended up with her getting dragged under, too.

My throat tightened and I rolled onto my side. In the shadows of the room, my gaze landed on the outline of Seven in bed next to me. He was practically an arm's length away, yet I could feel the heat of him as if we were touching.

Sleep would be impossible. Or maybe I just had to pee?

Definitely needed to try peeing.

I slipped out of bed as quietly as I could, tiptoeing toward the bathroom. I tried to shut the door as quietly as humanly possible—so slowly and carefully that it seemed to take ten minutes to actually accomplish. I turned on one of the backsplash lights, hesitant to jostle myself into daytime mode with too much light and activity. I needed more sleep, dammit. Even if sharing a bed with Seven made that impossible.

I sat on the toilet for a while, trying to pee and failing. I looked at my nails. I rearranged the part of my hair. I inspected my thighs for cellulite. When either ten minutes or an hour had gone by, I gave up and began my silent trek back to bed.

When the door latched, it made a click that reverberated so loudly through the quiet bedroom that I winced.

And then I heard another *click*.

Seven's hand was on the Glock and he was rising from the bed.

"Don't shoot!" I lifted my palms. "I just had to pee."

Seven dragged his bleary gaze my way, and then dropped the gun. He collapsed back into bed, the dim outline of his bare chest erasing whatever brief panic I'd felt as a mistaken intruder. I couldn't pry my eyes off him as I made my way around the bed and back to my side. Why didn't this room have more nightlights? I was desperate for a good look at the man. He was all hard lines—slept with a literal *gun* in his hand—but he was somehow the safest, softest spot I'd come to know.

And I didn't even know this guy. Not fully.

I resumed my previous position in bed, my back to Seven, snuggled into endless pillows. But sleep didn't come. Daylight sure did, though. It crept through the one room-darkening curtain I'd failed to close entirely, giving the room enough of a glow to ensure I didn't fall back asleep. I sighed, flipping onto my back.

And then I turned onto my other side, facing the wide expanse of Seven's back.

Goooood morning.

I gobbled up the sight as if it were my first drink of water after a full night's shift at the club. Cut lines, defined traps, a wonderland of muscle and olive skin. Scars crisscrossed his left shoulder. I admired the precise lines of his fade for what felt like a half hour. When he turned onto his back and slung an arm over the top of his face, I relished the opportunity to see his body from a new angle.

Wiry, dark armpit hair. Finally, *blessedly,* I saw the biceps that made his button-ups strain at the seams. I squeezed my legs together, my gaze drifting lower. The sheet was pulled over his stomach. But the man had to have perfect abs. With arms like this, it would be illegal not to.

For God's sake, does this man have abs?

Seven sighed, moving his arm from over his face. He turned his head toward me, peering through one slit eye. "Do you always stare at people while they sleep?"

I was so dumbfounded by the fact that he'd noticed me staring that my mouth flopped open like a fish's.

"You're making it impossible to actually stay asleep," he added.

My brain kicked into gear. "Just trying to figure out where you store all your warmth and good humor."

A smirk curled at the edge of his mouth as his eyes drifted shut. "You'll never know."

I sniffed, turning away from him. "I'm beginning to think you don't have any at all."

"Close protection officers aren't required to have any." The early morning grit of his voice made my pussy clench. I squeezed my eyes shut. Why was this man so unbearably attractive?

"Then I can call off my search." I fluffed up the pillow beneath my head, already wanting one more glimpse of his sexy face. All I could think about was how he might feel against my bare skin. Wrapped up in him, beneath the sheets. We were so close, but a world away.

The sheets rustled from his side of the bed. The bathroom door clicked shut a moment later. I looked at his abandoned spot in the bed—searching, but for what, I didn't know. Part of me wanted to sniff his pillow, but that was fucking weird—too weird even for me. I huffed, throwing back the covers. Might as well get up and start figuring out what came next. I tore open the curtains, letting in the blinding and beautiful morning. I actually gasped at the view of Central Park through the windows.

I'd never seen the park from this angle, in all my years living in the city. While I knew that Central Park was technically large, seeing it from this high made it seem like a sprawling jungle. The canopy of trees ranged from dark green to vibrant yellow, orange and rusty brown in various shades of autumnal glory.

The bathroom door opened and I turned to face Seven. I don't know what I was expecting. Fully clothed, gun in holster, regularly scheduled programming? I wasn't prepared for what I saw.

Tousled, black hair. The square jawline that framed those perfect, plump lips. His chocolate puppy dog eyes sweeping over my body, leaving tiny explosions in their wake. And his body—gloriously uncovered, available for viewing. His silky black boxer briefs had an unnaturally large bulge between his legs. I blinked a couple of times, wondering if this was an optical illusion. *His dick can't be that big when it's soft, right?* I tried desperately not to stare, moving my gaze instead to his sculpted thighs. Dark leg hair. And the abs—oh, fuck me, the *abs.*

My brows furrowed as I beheld him. The longer I looked at him, the angrier I got.

He paused in the doorway, squinting at me like this encounter could go sideways. "Why do you look so angry?"

"You're just...wearing underwear."

He blinked a few times. His confusion helped me realize that I hadn't made any sense at all. But there was no way I could explain. Not without outing myself.

"So are you," he said.

"Right, but I'm like..." I gestured at my simple tee and undies, which were mostly hidden by the shirt. "You've seen me in way less."

"Should I put pants on or...?"

"No. It's fine. I mean, unless you were planning on it. I don't want to plan your clothes out. I'm not your mom." I breezed out of the room, trying to act confident. But internally, I was melting down. Not a word I'd said made sense.

I just needed to get away from those man thighs. And the possible monster dick.

After opening all the curtains in the living room and watching the treetops of Central Park for a few minutes, I decided my fascination with Seven's body could be done now. I'd seen plenty of good-looking guys in my time. His abs were nothing new, even though I could have absolutely cleaned a pair of socks on them if necessary. That bulge in his underwear? Probably stuffed with toilet paper to look more impressive. And now that I thought about it, the narrow, slightly crooked nose of his wasn't all that uncommon. I'd seen more bronzed skin, more precise hairstyles.

"So I take it you're ready to start the day?" His gravelly voice in the living room startled me out of my thoughts. I spun around to respond, but my voice withered and disappeared entirely. He wore the same black, pressed pants with a belt....and nothing else. The sight of his trim torso cutting away to the dress clothes nearly undid me on the spot. He watched me with a curious look as he sat in an armchair facing me. The crinkle of his belly started a whole new wave of flutters through my pussy.

"What's wrong now?" he asked. "I put pants on."

I sighed and turned back to the window. "I really wanted to sleep more. But it's too bright now. I just can't."

"Starting the day early isn't a bad thing. We have a lot to get done."

I crossed my arms, getting lost in the trees of Central Park again. "I guess I do need to pack up my apartment."

"We'll send someone to do that for you. You don't need to go back there—in fact, you shouldn't. What I'm talking about is the elephant in the room."

I bit my lip. I must have been so transparent. Did he know how badly I wanted to have sex with him? "And that is...?"

"Getting on the same page with your brothers."

My shoulders sank. "Oh."

"After what happened last night, we need to go talk to them. I haven't told them a single word about Dustin, but I'm going to. You should be there to give your input."

"Can I submit a written statement instead?"

Seven sighed, the first bit of honest exasperation I'd heard from him. I turned to watch him as he buried his face in his hands. "How can you possibly be this resistant to your brothers trying to help you?"

The question floored me. Mostly because he'd asked it so honestly.

I didn't know how to answer without revealing the gaping caverns of my heart.

"They've never been there for me," I finally said. "Why are they starting now? It's too convenient."

"They didn't even know you were alive," he said succinctly. "How could they have been there for you when they thought you were six feet under?"

"It would be easier for all parties involved if they continued thinking I was dead," I retorted. "Then we wouldn't have to go through these stupid charades."

"And you'd have been raped in your hallway last night."

Silence thudded between us. My gaze dropped to the floor because I couldn't handle Seven's intensity right now.

"Sounds like they *are* looking out for you," he said a few moments later. "Now that they know you're alive."

"Well that's what you think," I muttered, feeling a lot like a petulant teen.

"Knock off the immature bullshit."

"Being abused for years in the foster care system isn't immature bullshit," I spat out, leaning forward. "Watching my sister be sold into sex trafficking isn't immature bullshit."

Seven rubbed at his face again. "That's not what I'm saying."

"Everyone's Team Fairchild, but not a single person has stuck around to be Team Haynes. And that's been true since they changed their name. Remember that when we visit your *precious employers*." I stormed past him and into the bedroom, eager to end the conversation. Emotion clamped at my throat and I didn't want to cry in front of him. Not again. Not twice in twelve hours, please God.

I beelined into the bathroom to start my morning routine. He wanted to visit them—fine. I'd go. But it would be quick. And only this once.

Kaylee would have to understand, wherever she was in the Great Beyond. Kaylee had railed harder and harder against Axel and Damian the older we got. They left us. Abandoned us. Turned their backs on us. They were the lucky sons of bitches who got the good family and never once tried to bring us along.

Kaylee was three years older than me, so she was thirteen and I was ten by the time we hit our final foster family. The one from hell. Kaylee had already had sex by then. Obsessed with boyfriends, fitting in, looking cool. She put makeup on in the bathroom at school after we got off the bus and some nights never even came home. Our foster mom Tyla never cared. We were living checks to her, an excuse to get paid. There were five other foster kids in that house, ages ranging from seven to seventeen. A few of them liked to gang up on me and the youngest one however they could. Kaylee stopped it when she was home, but when she wasn't, I got locked in closets or garages for hours, starving and cold and desperate for dinner.

It got worse as we got older. Shit I didn't like to think about. We tried to hide the bruises with long sleeves and makeup. When Tyla started demanding we help pay for rent, she already had a "job" for

Kaylee, since she was older. She could meet with one of Tyla's guy friends and talk to him for a little bit. Just talking. That was it.

I never saw what happened when Kaylee disappeared into the vehicles of the "guy friends," but she always came back silent and brimming with tension. Sometimes she'd disappear for days at a time, then come back with a fat wad of cash, looking jittery and strange.

That's when I found out how drugs changed a person. Firsthand. Kaylee was fourteen when she told me she was addicted. I was eleven. I had no fucking idea what that meant. But she wore it as a badge of honor, and I didn't know enough to help her.

By the time Kaylee was at her worst, our brothers were seniors in high school. Kaylee wanted nothing to do with them; she didn't want anything to do with me, either. I barely recognized her by then and was afraid to be around her.

She died months after turning seventeen. And I realized my sister had been right about our brothers.

After they graduated, they could have come to get us. They could have taken us. They could have been our adults. But they went to New York City instead. And then we never heard from them again.

Protecting me from getting raped in my hallway barely scratched the surface of making up for all the other things I hadn't been protected from during my childhood.

I didn't know how to tell Seven that the sudden *care and attention* from my brothers meant nothing.

A knock sounded on the bathroom door, startling me out of my thoughts.

"What?" I called out, patting foundation on my face.

"You decent?"

"I'm never decent. What do you want?"

"I'm going to let your brothers know we'll be there in an hour. Sound good?"

"Whatever you say, Overlord." Getting under Seven's skin was my new goal in life, especially since last night's events had removed the end date from our arrangement. I put on a minimal face of makeup, added lip gloss, then went back to the bedroom to change into leggings and a top. As always, I paired them with my boots and leather jacket—my go-to outfit in my off time. By the time I was ready to go, it was just before nine a.m.

When I rejoined Seven in the living room, a spread of food awaited me. He tipped his head toward the surprise breakfast—omelets, hashbrowns, tiny waffles, an entire fruit platter.

"Complements of Team Fairchild," he said, that self-assured smirk returning.

"Very cute." I side-eyed him as I popped a grape into my mouth. "Glad to see you've finally fully dressed."

"I was just about to say the same to you."

I snorted, reaching for a small plate and loading up on the hashbrowns. "Did you eat?"

"I don't eat this early."

"Oh." I looked over my shoulder at him, feeling the quip burbling up inside me until it was too loud to keep inside. "Must be because you're getting older, huh? Hurts your digestion to eat outside your regular routine?"

Amusement shone in his eyes though he didn't grace me with a smile. "Doctor's orders."

"You probably visit him a *lot*."

"Will you eat so we can leave?"

"Sure." I grinned as I added a tiny waffle to my plate. "But now that you said that, a lot more slowly than I'd planned on."

About an hour later, Seven and I rolled up to a towering building on Wall Street. I never made it to this part of Manhattan, so the whole neighborhood was new to me. I craned my neck to look up.

"Which floor are they on?" I asked.

"Penthouse."

Curiosity prickled through me, though I didn't want to admit it. Seven hopped out of the backseat of the SUV and waited for me to follow. He led the way into the building, clearing security with the flash of a badge before veering off toward a private elevator tucked into the back corner of the lobby.

"This place is pretty swanky," I murmured as we waited at the elevator.

Seven's dark gaze skated around the lobby. "This is where their primary residence is, as well as their business headquarters. The business currently under investigation."

The doors opened, revealing a mirrored, gleaming box. We stepped inside, and I leaned against the railing as he hit the P button and swiped a keycard.

"I remember hearing something about an investigation."

"You haven't kept up with the news about them?" he asked.

"I try not to. But sometimes they make it impossible."

He found my gaze in the reflection on the elevator wall. "The SEC has filed charges accusing them of financial fraud."

I squinted, trying to remember what that stood for. "SEC..."

"Securities and Exchange Commission."

"Sounds very formal."

"It's the governmental agency that makes sure people aren't committing financial crimes and manipulating the market," Seven said.

"Wow. So if the SEC is involved, they clearly must have been in some deep shit. They don't sound like the stand-up guys you made them out to be. I thought you said you'd do anything for them?"

He narrowed his eyes at me. "I did say that. Because it's true. The case is outrageous. Their business didn't have any complaints against them until this came up, apparently out of thin air."

"So what does it mean for them?"

Seven shrugged, finally looking away from me. "They're in the process of figuring that out. There's a trial happening this fall, to determine the consequences. They're pretty sure there will be a hefty fine either way. But right now, the main recommendation is prison. Up to ten years."

"Wow. My brothers the felons," I muttered.

"The world would be worse off without their contributions and support," he confirmed. "The amount of money they donate to help foster children alone each year would take your breath away. And that doesn't include the multiple other areas they support."

I cleared my throat. I supposed I couldn't be too loudly opposed to the Fairchild Propaganda, considering I was hurtling closer to their home with every passing second. This came with the territory. "I'm sure there are many appreciative children."

The elevator slowed. We were almost there.

"It's helpful for you to have a more complete picture," Seven said, this time looking over his shoulder at me. "Before you say something stupid."

I ran my tongue along the inside of my cheek. I had thirty-five responses at the ready for that little comment, but none made the leap past my lips before the elevator doors slid open.

We had arrived at the penthouse.

The sizzle and pop of cooking eggs reached me first. Seven led me through what looked like a laundry room and storage area before we emerged into an enormous kitchen.

"Oh my God, you really still don't know how to crack an egg, do you?" Axel's voice drifted toward us as Seven guided me through the kitchen.

Damian and Axel stood in front of the range—large enough to be used in a restaurant, surely—beneath an expansive hood, wearing what looked like lounge clothes. They were both tall, had similar muscular builds, and dark blonde hair...like mine. I was sure it wasn't a stretch to guess who the blood related ones in the room were. As we approached, a stocky dog with a dark, glossy coat rose to his feet, watching us intently with his ears perked up.

Damian slapped Axel's back just as we walked up. "I've cracked more eggs than you've ever seen."

"Fake news," Axel retorted.

"I fucking worked at Mr. Grady's chicken coops all of sophomore year," Damian said, laughter mingling with incredulousness. His hair was longer, possibly in a state of growing out, as he continually tried to tuck it behind his ear while it continually slipped right back out. "He had us crack eggs on our foreheads the first day just because. How could you even—"

"Good morning," Seven said coolly.

Damian and Axel swiveled to look at us, bright smiles hitting their faces as their gazes landed on me. Looking into their faces was like looking into a carnival mirror. Vaguely familiar in an unsettling way. Axel's ice-blue eyes looked closest to mine and Kaylee's. I wasn't sure where to focus my attention first. Their kitchen was larger than my entire apartment; they had *three* islands, all marble waterfall counters.

And not only was I surrounded by opulence...my *brothers* owned all of it.

"Jordan! Seven! I'm so glad you guys are here," Damian said.

"Stir the eggs," Axel hissed, glancing back at the sauté pan. "Jordan, are we at hugging status yet, or no?"

I opened my mouth to respond but wasn't sure how to tell them *fuck no* without the *fuck* part.

"I think that's a no," Damian said.

"Yeah, that's a no," Axel said softly. "That's okay. We have time. We'll get there."

I didn't necessarily agree. But the plan was to get out of here as quickly as possible. So I kept my mouth shut.

"How about we do some introductions? Jordan, meet Zero, my Rottie mix." He ruffled the dog's ears. "Zero, meet your Auntie Jordan."

I wiggled my fingers in Zero's direction, who snorted and sat on Axel's foot.

"So, tell me—how have things been going with this guy?" Axel tipped his head in Seven's direction. "He looks tough but he's made of butter on the inside."

"Hey now," Seven warned.

"Very firm, immobile butter," Axel clarified.

"Steel butter," Damian offered.

"He's all right." I crossed my arms, leaning against a slate gray cabinet that extended so high, it could only be hiding something big, like a fridge. I'd never seen a luxury kitchen like this up close, only on reality TV. "He saved my ass yesterday."

Both my brothers leaned closer. "He did?"

"Yeah." I figured I'd get this show on the road. Tell them the news, then GTFO. "I got attacked."

Damian stepped toward me, concern etched across his face. "Oh my God, are you serious?"

"Jordan, this is—" Axel let out a burst of air. "Do you know who it was? Can we track him down?"

"Are you okay?" Damian asked.

"I'm fine," I said, just as Zero approached me, sniffing curiously. I held out my hand to him as I continued. "I mean, I'm as fine as I'll be. Seven was in the right place at the right time. I owe him...a lot."

Both of my brothers visibly relaxed.

"See," Axel turned toward Damian, "This is why you hire the best. You fucking start at the top."

"You're right, you're right," Damian said, then swore loudly. "*The eggs.*"

I bit back a laugh as Damian scraped at the pan, trying to salvage the breakfast. Zero nudged my hand with his snout so I offered him a little head stroke.

"You know, we have people that can do this for us," Axel said. "They're called chefs, and they excel at things like eggs. They also didn't grow up cracking eggs on their foreheads like sociopaths. Maybe you've heard of them?"

"I am going to chef you in the ass if you don't shut up," Damian said as he snapped off the burner.

"Just trying to help." Axel clapped him on the shoulder. To me, he said, "Let's get back to the important issues. You were saved by Seven—bless this man. Perpetrator is pending payback, right?"

"Working on it," Seven said.

"Good. Where do we go from here?"

"My advice is to abandon the apartment entirely." The grit of Seven's bass voice scraped through me. "It's failed every security check presented so far. It's a shithole."

"But it's *my* shithole," I said, now fully petting Zero's glossy head. He plopped his big butt next to me and his tongue hung out as I stroked his fur.

Damian smiled sadly, his mossy green gaze growing nostalgic. "I've felt that way about a place in Chinatown a time or two."

"She needs new housing immediately." Seven's tone left no room for argument.

"Okay. So, let's tackle new housing." Axel clapped his hands, brows scrunching together in thought. "Where do you want to live, Jordan? You pick. We'll pay."

I cleared my throat. Maybe I was approaching this all wrong—who wouldn't love the blank check scenario after a lifetime of foster care and barely scraping by? But even though Axel and Damian had all the Warbucks vibes, I was no Annie. Not at this point in my life.

"I can't accept that," I told them, dropping down to be on Zero's level. I stroked the fur of his back, all the way down to his stubby, wagging tail. I had a soft spot in my heart for pets—I'd always wanted one, but never had any growing up. "I need to support myself."

Damian dropped his chin, giving me a *come on* look. "We can pay."

"I would feel more comfortable staying within a budget I know I can continue without help," I said. Zero let out a soft bark, which I took as his agreement.

Axel frowned. "You don't think we'll be able to pay for it indefinitely? The SEC case....it hasn't been finalized. But even if we go to prison—"

"Can we not say that word?" Damian interjected softly, his eyes pinching shut.

"—We're preparing for what comes next," Axel went on. "And that would include continuing things like an apartment for you."

Damian had been right on the phone earlier that week. The tension that had descended over the kitchen proved there *was* a lot I didn't know. But Axel wasn't even remotely right about my reservations. This was a matter of pride.

"I've worked hard to build my life. It would be a cop out to just let you guys take over. It wouldn't be...*mine*.

Axel nodded. "I get that. But what if we pay, like, half?"

"Like a farm subsidy," Damian added.

"Like the subsidies Mr. Grady probably received only to have you crack eggs on your forehead," Axel said to Damian.

Damn, they were comical. I didn't remember them like this from my childhood. But then again, we'd never met in relaxed circumstances, ever. It was always a stiff visit arranged by care workers, a stolen moment before or after school, a random meeting in a public space, like the mall.

"I've lived my entire life without help from you." I focused on the dark brown hair of Zero's coat as I dragged my fingers through it. "I don't plan on changing that now."

"What if you moved in here?" Damian asked. "We're not here all the time. And there's plenty of room for you. You could have a whole floor if you wanted."

"I'd rather not live with strange men."

Axel winced. "Ouch."

"Is there a getting-to-know-each-other phase that we can formally begin?" Damian asked. "Because I feel like I've been trying to change that *strange* part…"

"Oh, there's that *no* face again," Axel said. "I heard Seven booked you a room at the Ritz. We can upgrade you to the penthouse."

Seven coughed lightly from my side.

"I don't want to live out of a hotel," I told them. I wasn't trying to be difficult. Ritz or not, I had negative associations with hotel life. I didn't know how else to put it—I wanted my own space, paid for by my own money. And I'd accept nothing less. Or more.

Damian didn't look amused. He sighed testily, crossing his arms as he leaned against the counter near the stove. "Fine. Then why don't you move in with Seven?"

I blinked. This idea hadn't even occurred to me as a possibility. I wasn't sure I'd even realized that he had a home. He was simply Seven, the impossibly hot man who followed me. "Uh…"

"You're already familiar with him. He's proven himself a valuable asset in an emergency." Damian gestured toward Seven, as though I needed any reminder. "You wouldn't mind, right, Seven? It might even make things easier until she finds a permanent spot."

I turned just in time to catch a barely masked look of panic on Seven's face. "There's not exactly a bed ready…"

"We can fix that, and provide anything that's needed, obviously," Axel interjected. "Your apartment is huge though. It should work fine as an interim solution."

Seven cleared his throat, and the taste of his discomfort was a nectar I was desperate for more of. Though I usually loathed the idea of living with someone, I could make an exception for the Hottie Roboto. Something told me living with him would be easy for me and annoying for him, which made it the perfect plan.

"I love this idea," I gushed. Zero licked my hand, which had stopped petting him momentarily.

"She loves the idea." Damian looked genuinely proud.

Axel nodded, smiling between me and Seven and Zero. "If my little sister loves it, I want to give it to her. What do you think Seven?"

His jaw ticked. "That should work for the interim."

Axel's smile faded. "Only problem is, I don't like the idea of my little sister moving in with a bachelor of any sort..."

"Any funny business would be the absolute end of your contract," Damian told Seven with an extra edge in his voice.

I snorted. "You guys don't have to worry about anything like that. Seven is only recently learning about human emotions in his transition from a robot."

Damian looked like he was fighting a laugh. Seven, on the other hand, only looked annoyed.

"I've never engaged in inappropriate contact with any of my clients or their siblings, and I don't intend to start now," he said tersely. "My professional conduct is top-notch, and that's something I take very seriously. Besides," he sniffed, glancing my way, "she's a brat. No offense."

I tried to look offended, but I could only laugh.

"Well I think we can mark this item off the to-do list," Axel said. "Now, it's time for subpar eggs."

Seven's face returned to that neutral mask I was used to. But it was fine—I knew he disliked the idea of me moving in. That's all I needed from him.

I, on the other hand, had not been exaggerating.

I fucking loved this idea.

And I planned on milking it for every drop of fun I could.

CHAPTER EIGHT

"One thousand square feet of bachelor paradise," Jordan murmured the words her brother had used to describe my apartment during our marathon meeting over subpar eggs. She paused in the middle of the great room—exposed brick, freshly updated wood floors, industrial style lighting that could be toned up or down a million ways depending on the mood. She nodded as her gaze skipped around the room then finally settled on me.

She looked too fucking pleased with this situation.

"What's with the messy floors?" She jerked her chin toward the wood shavings scattered near the trash can. *Oops.* I'd cleaned up before I rushed out the door to meet Jordan the day before, but had apparently missed the mark when I tossed the remnants from my latest project.

"Can't a guy forget to sweep once in awhile?" It was easier than telling her the full truth. It seemed wise to keep her at arm's length, even though now we'd be living a breath away. "I'll show you where you'll sleep." I led her to the faux bedroom set up at the back of the apartment. "It's not as luxurious as the Ritz, but I think you'll survive."

I opened the door to a minimalistic spare room, an add-on by the previous tenant.

"Couldn't even finish the walls, huh?" Jordan teased.

The walls didn't fully touch the ceiling, a common tactic to get around the strict Manhattan renovation codes, according to the agent who showed me the apartment. I hadn't gotten around to setting it up as a true guest room since arriving in the city.

Well now I had a guest. The most unexpected one imaginable. And the brothers had already ordered her a brand-new king bed, which was en route to my apartment.

"I didn't think I'd have a house guest," I told her.

"How am I supposed to use my vibrator in peace?" she countered. "You'll hear every second of it."

I clenched my teeth. Not the mental image I wanted to start our cohabitation with. I was already tortured enough by seeing her on a near nightly basis under purple lights, writhing against a steel pole in little more than a strip of spandex and a few pieces of glitter.

"Would it trouble you to believe that you can do whatever you want in these four walls without me giving a damn?" I turned toward the kitchen. The Fairchilds gave me a blank check to outfit this place as I wanted, including hiring an interior designer to completely make over the space. The result really *was* the bachelor pad of my dreams—minimalistic, tasteful, and modern. All new appliances. Gorgeous black marble countertops. An entire set of weights and resistance bands next to a flat-screen so large I could climb inside if I wanted.

It was my oasis from the outside world—the chaotic NYC I was still getting used to but already loved.

And though part of me was eager to latch on to the idea that Jordan was invading my oasis, a larger part of me was curious to see what happened.

"So where's your room?"

I tipped my head toward the tiny hallway tucked behind the kitchen. "That way. Bathroom too."

She watched me expectantly.

"You need to see it all, huh?"

"I've seen you in your underwear; now I need to see what color sheets you have."

It amused me that she was interested enough to mention it, but I made sure to school my reaction to zero. I led her to my bedroom door, opened it, and let her peek inside. The bed was still made from the morning before, light-blocking shades drawn over the windows that overlooked the busy street ten floors below.

"Gray comforter..." she began.

"Gray sheets," I finished for her.

She nodded to herself, as if this confirmed something. "Just a bed and a rug. Not even a dresser."

"I have nightstands," I corrected her. "And my clothes go in the closet." I couldn't believe I was rationalizing my bedroom to her, so I clamped my mouth shut.

"I'm surprised you even have a bed in there, since I was sure you just roll into the closet at night to plug in." She sniffed, heading down the hallway for the bathroom, pushing the door open. "Nice. Roomy enough for my skin care routine. Yeah, I think I can stay awhile."

"Temporarily."

"Right." She smiled brightly at me, blinking a couple of times. "So do you have sweatpants inside your closet or do you just have thirteen sets of this exact outfit?"

I brushed past her, heading to the kitchen. It was time for a protein shake. "You'll never know."

"Well now we're roommates. I can snoop. I'll find out if you're secretly a robot."

"You don't want to start that game," I warned her, pulling open the fridge. "There will be consequences."

"Now that I know you sleep with guns, I don't doubt that. Can I at least borrow a comfy T-shirt?"

I gritted my teeth, studying the contents of my fridge without having any idea what I was looking at. "All your things are being packed up for you. They'll be delivered later." Besides, seeing her in one of my T-shirts would be the final straw. I was hanging on by a thread as it was.

"But yours would be better."

I finally remembered I was looking for a protein shake and snagged the bottle from the shelf. In lieu of a response, I twisted the lid and chugged. When the bottle was half drained, I sent her a stern look. "What are your plans for today? Because I have some things to take care of."

"Oh. By all means." She gestured at the thin air between us. "Take care of your things. I'm off today, so I'll just be spending the day getting settled into my new home."

"Interim solution."

She sent me a pretty smile and batted her eyelashes. "Right."

I'd been stationed in Afghanistan. I'd been put through the wringer as a Marine. I'd dealt with more loss than I wanted to think about.

But Jordan tested me. There was only so much near-naked writhing I could absorb from her tightly packed frame before I busted a nut in public.

Which meant I needed to take matters into my own hands. Literally.

By day three of co-habitation, I was at my fucking limit. Sure, she paraded around nearly nude at least three times a week at the club, but that was no match for how many times I'd glimpsed her *fully exposed* in my fucking apartment.

I should have demanded a signed contract before allowing her bed to be delivered. Something like *I do solemnly swear to always wear clothes in the common rooms and never drop my towel accidentally when I leave the bathroom door open for the fifteenth time, thus allowing Seven to enter the bathroom when he thought it was empty.*

The number of times I'd seen her athletic ass cheeks and the immaculately trimmed hair between her legs made it hard to do anything but stay locked in my bedroom and beat off. And when I finally got the bathroom to myself—properly locked, of course—there was no way to stop what came next. Specifically, my cock. All over the side of the shower wall.

That's where I found myself yet again that Friday morning after my early workout. The water rushed over my shoulders in a warm stream, and my cock strained as I pumped my fist along my length, balls to tip. She had a night shift at the club later, so I needed to be fully drained. I needed to be so non-horny that I wouldn't spend the entire shift thinking about the heat I might find between her legs or how tight and silky she'd feel if I were to slip myself inside. She was five foot nothing; I was a beast in comparison. I'd need to spend a few hours stretching her with my fingers first, which only sent my balls tightening.

I grunted. My fist slid faster over my cock, thoughts homing in on my favorite outfit of hers so far at the club, a one-piece white fishnet bodysuit, crisscrossed with strings down the center, as good as see-through. I wanted to tear it off her body with my teeth. I'd buy a hundred versions of it and destroy them all.

My thighs tensed and I squeezed my eyes shut. I wasn't supposed to be thinking about Jordan like this. I wasn't supposed to be thinking about *any* client like this. But fuck if I could help it. She was all I could see—in my life and in my head. I was fucking drowning in this woman, and the scariest part was that I wanted so much more of her.

Absolutely, unequivocally not allowed.

I teased myself with thoughts of Jordan on her knees in front of me, wrapping those pretty lips around my cock and swallowing me whole. That did it. I swallowed a groan as my cock pulsed in my hand, shooting out round after round of milky cum that disappeared down the drain with the water.

Done and dusted.

Now my fucking day could begin. I finished washing up, snapped off the water, and dried my body, eyes on the door in case Jordan somehow picked the lock and pretended it was an accident. She was a brat, so I wouldn't put anything past her. Part of me wondered if she wanted me even half as badly as I wanted her.

But it doesn't matter. Because it'll never happen. She'll move out soon, and you won't be her CPO for much longer. Then this inconvenient attraction will be easier to deal with, by ignoring it completely.

That was the kernel I needed to hang on to. My close protection company was one step closer to being a reality, since I'd filed the paperwork earlier that week. The Fairchilds knew of my plan and fully supported it; in fact, they planned on becoming my primary clients. While I was happy to gain a fuller understanding of Jordan's needs and risks while getting her protection plan off the ground, they knew that I'd eventually hand her protection over to someone I considered equally qualified.

That was the plan.

And I'd arrive at my destination much more quickly if I had more time to begin the hiring process. But Jordan's work schedule was nonstop. And almost all downtime was now devoted to counseling myself through this intrusive attraction to her.

I stepped out of the bathroom with my towel knotted around my waist. Just as I did, a knock sounded on the door. Jordan met my gaze from the living room, where she was stretched out on a yoga mat.

"Expecting anyone?" she asked.

"No." I headed for the door, running a hand through my damp tresses before peeking through the peephole. Axel and Damian stood on the other side. "Looks like it's for you."

Jordan's brows knitted together in confusion as I tugged open the door. Axel waved at me, holding a bag of takeout food in the other hand. "Morning."

"Hey." I stepped aside so the brothers could enter. Both wore standard business casual attire, dark slacks and button-ups, as if they'd come straight from the office. "Come on in."

Jordan remained silent, burying her face in her mat in a deep stretch.

"Hey, Jordan," Damian called out hopefully.

"Morning, little sis," Axel added.

She mumbled something unrecognizable and kept her face buried in her mat.

"I think that was hello," I offered.

"We brought breakfast," Axel said, lifting the bags slightly. "Since it's been, you know, hard to get this one on our schedule." He cocked a thumb toward Jordan.

"Are you hungry?" Damian called out, dropping his bags on the counter before running a hand through his longish dark blond hair.

Another unintelligible mumble.

"I guess she's doing her workout," I said.

Axel hummed to himself as he arranged the bags on the island, tattoos peeking out from behind the cuffs and the collar of his shirt. His gaze swept my way, clearly sizing me up. "Damn, Seven. What's your gym routine? I need abs like that."

"It involves a lot of push-ups."

Axel leaned closer, pointing. "I've never been able to get these divots. Do you think they help your skills as a bodyguard, or are they just to inspire confidence?"

I wasn't afraid of laughing with the brothers. They didn't threaten to unravel me and my very foundation if we became close. I cracked a smile. "I can't answer that with a client in the room."

"Fair enough." He turned toward Jordan. "Okay, little sis, we're gonna lay out the spread now."

Damian got to work unloading the bags and filling up my kitchen island with boxes of food. The scent of eggs and pancakes hit me, making my stomach rumble. "I'm gonna go get dressed. Give you some, you know...time together."

Damian sent me an appreciative look and I headed to my bedroom. Inside the quiet, dark haven, I let my towel crumple to the floor and heaved a deep sigh.

Living with Jordan wasn't all bad. For how much of a brat she was, she kept to herself when she wasn't flaunting her body and forgetting how doors worked. It made me wonder what the hell she was getting up to in her bedroom when she disappeared for hours at a time. But there was no way in hell I'd ever ask, because it would only take one more mention of her vibrator to break me entirely.

Even though I'd nutted in the shower that morning, it didn't mean I was fully prepared for tonight's shift. Jordan had a later shift at the coffee shop, eleven a.m. to close, and then the evening would be spent under the purple lights, watching her hump steel and shake her ass cheeks. Fuck, I was getting hard just imagining it. The more worrisome part of this arrangement was that now, when she sauntered onto other men's laps and let them put their hands on her hips, heat prickled up my spine and across my shoulder blades. My hands formed fists without wanting to.

I needed to get my head straight—I needed time *away* from her, where I knew she wasn't holed up inside my guest room. I just wasn't sure how to get it.

In my closet, my gaze fell to the mess of woodworking tools I'd thrown inside hastily from my last carving session. I couldn't stand leaving everything out, especially with how much dust and wood shavings it created. But I carved as frequently as I could. It was the one surefire way to get my mind calm and on track. I needed it more and more lately, it seemed. One of my base blocks tumbled out—balsa wood—and I stacked it back up for whenever I had a chance to work next.

I pulled out my standard attire—black button-up, black slacks, a belt. Contrary to Jordan's beliefs, I didn't have thirteen version of the same outfit in my closet. I had seven. It was a good number.

Besides, there were minute differences in the clothing—different brands, different quality fabrics. Not that she'd know that.

I took my time getting ready. Maybe she'd open up a bit with her brothers. Her petulance around them irked me less since she'd snapped at me at the Ritz Carlton. Jordan had her reasons—and even though I didn't understand them fully, I respected them. She was entitled to her own secrets. We all had them, were driven by them. But if they had a shot at reconciling and really connecting, this was it.

Once she flew the coop into her own place after this "interim stay," I doubted she'd send check-in texts or make lunch dates with the brothers. Hell, once she fully recovered from the shock of the recent assault, I wasn't even sure she'd keep me on as a full-time protection officer. I was prepared for her to call her brothers out of nowhere one day and ask to end my assignment.

I just couldn't figure out if that would be a relief, or a disappointment.

I dressed slowly then brought out my laptop to check email and do what little work I could on my fledgling business. The most important part was the hiring process, so I created a decent *help wanted* ad and saved it. But that was all I had time for. Jordan would need to leave for work soon, and the day would melt away from there.

Out in the living room, Damian and Axel sat on the couches. Jordan was still on her mat, cross-legged, holding a plate of food as she shoveled a bite into her mouth.

"Everyone behaving out here?" I asked in my best bouncer voice.

Axel twisted to smirk at me. "You know, with those abs and that voice..."

Damian sent him a withering look. "Axel. Can you please stop objectifying Seven?"'

"I'm just asking for it, aren't I?" I teased, heading for the open end of the couch. "I've heard that line before."

"Are you hungry?" Axel tipped his head toward the kitchen. "We brought enough for everyone and their bodyguard."

Jordan's gaze sizzled on me. But when I flicked my gaze her way, she jerked her eyes to the plate in her hands.

"I'll grab something on the way out," I told him.

"He's very particular about what he eats," Jordan said, suddenly popping to her feet. "He has indigestion. Or maybe it's IBS. Possibly various food allergies. Very dangerous to eat outside of his prescribed routine."

Axel and Damian laughed under their breath as Jordan strode to the kitchen to drop off her plate.

"Do you need a doctor recommendation?" Damian asked.

"I'm fine," I reassured them. "She's just..."

"Watch your words," Jordan warned from the kitchen.

"Sassy," I finished. "She thinks I'm geriatric because I'm in my thirties."

"Hey, we're in our thirties." Damian tipped his head back to look toward Jordan.

"You're all extremely old and brittle," she informed us. "At death's door. No amount of exercise will save you." She flashed a plastic smile as she headed toward her bedroom.

"At your age, your brain isn't even fully developed yet," Axel shot back.

She stopped just as her hand hit the doorknob. "My brain is fully functional, thank you very much. And it can recognize an old man when it sees one. Time to get ready for the coffee shop, boys."

"I'm not old, I'm distinguished," Axel called out as her door swung shut behind her. Then he laughed. "It's nice to be harassed by my little sister."

"How did it...go?" I kept my voice low, looking between them.

Damian tipped his head back and forth, and Axel lobbed a sigh. "We'll talk another time." He clapped my back before coming to his feet. "We're gonna head out, since the workday is starting."

"Thanks for the food. Stop by anytime." I stood too, trailing them to the front door. They were both over six feet tall, but I towered over them.

"We plan on coming by as often as we can," Axel said in a low voice, his gaze drifting toward Jordan's door. "With breakfast or lunch, just to see if we can... you know." He shrugged. "Baby steps."

"Appreciate you, Seven," Damian said, giving me a meaningful look as he opened the door. "Oh, and we'll let you know when the uh—"

"Fuck, we didn't tell him," Axel interjected.

Damian grimaced, looking over at me. "Shit, that's right. You were in the bedroom."

I blinked. "What did I miss?"

"We asked Jordan what she wanted for the apartment here," Damian said. "If there was anything we could send or provide. And she said she wants a pole, for practice."

"You're cool with that, right?" Axel asked.

Every last organ inside my body was groaning at the news. But I *had* to be cool with it. This place was on their dime. I had no right to refuse something they wanted to gift their little sister.

"I'm sure she'll love it," I said, unable to make my lips curl upward, so I resorted to making my eyes smile. Or at least trying.

"Awesome. We'll handle the details. You just let the guys in when they come to install it," Axel said, squeezing my shoulder. "See ya later, Seven."

When the door shut behind them, I pinched the bridge of my nose. *Fuck.* Just what I needed. Private exotic dancer performances in my own fucking home. As if seeing her on the stage several nights a week wasn't tantalizing enough. Now I had to potentially start my day watching her toned and limber body slide down a pole?

I wouldn't last a week. But I tried to swallow the panic. To focus on something else. I spotted the leftovers of their breakfast spread. Food was a good idea. Feed the beast of hunger, so that the beast of sexual desire might shut the fuck up for a second.

I grabbed a sausage link, checking my watch. We needed to be out of here in three minutes to make Jordan's shift on time if she planned to use public transportation. I was her bodyguard, but I wasn't her mom, so I didn't plan on reminding her. I snagged my laptop from my bedroom, shoved it into its case, and loaded it into a satchel I slung across my chest. Today's goal was to make more progress on the hiring front. Handing off Jordan's care to a trusted new hire was the only way I'd stand a chance of making it through this assignment without doing something I deeply regretted.

Once I reentered the kitchen, the door to her bedroom opened and she breezed out. She had winged eyeliner on, a simple lip gloss, and the Black & Brewtiful ballcap covering her dark blonde ponytail.

"Ready?" she asked.

I swallowed the rest of my sausage link. "Born ready."

"I bet you just tremble in anticipation waiting to use that phrase, don't you?"

"Born to use it."

She rolled her eyes, then snapped the black strap of my cross-body bag. "What's this?"

"A strap."

She cocked a hip, narrowing her eyes. "No shit. What's in the bag?"

"Why do you care?"

Her nostrils flared. It was too easy to poke her—and be poked by her. It made me want to spend the whole day just diving into this dynamic that had been growing between us. Even though that was the absolute last thing I should be doing.

"You hide all your weapons in your pants. Why can't you just put whatever's in here in your pants too?"

I laughed—on accident. It just slipped out. She looked delighted.

"I only have so much room in there," I told her, grabbing another sausage link.

"I thought it was like the closet to Narnia or something." Her eyes were on me as I wolfed the sausage link and went for another.

I swallowed the rest of my food. "I'm not that magical. Still just a man at the end of the day. Can we leave?"

She sighed, but I could tell it was just for dramatics. She tugged her ballcap lower on her head. "Could have fooled me. I swear you need to plug into the wall at night to recharge."

"I'm not a Tesla."

"But you do admit that you're part electric?" she challenged.

I made sure to not even twitch with amusement. "No comment."

"Fine. Let's go, Mr. Roboto." With her black jeans, ballcap, and leather jacket, she looked every inch an undercover celebrity. The secretive aura she pulled tight around herself only contributed to her mystique.

Once the door opened, she sprinted down the steps, and I was compelled to chase her. Something about Jordan activated my beast mode. I wanted to protect her at any cost. But I always wanted to consume her; make her mine; fill her and fuck her. Chasing her sated at least part of this forbidden desire.

Five floors down I managed to elbow past her, but she shrieked with laughter and grappled at my arm and yanked me back. I let her slip past me again and she tore down the steps, our footfalls making a thunderous noise in the stairwell. By the time we reached the ground floor, we were both breathing heavily.

"I won." She launched a fist into the air.

I pulled open the door for her to pass through to the lobby. "I let you win."

"Now, now, now. Don't be a sad sack thirty-something." She strutted through the lobby, impossibly cocky, her persona cracking only momentarily to wave at Arthur the doorman. "We just need to work on your fitness level."

I fought the grin. "Oh, are you a personal trainer now too?"

"I can walk in eight-inch heels for eight hours and launch my body weight up a steel pole. I think I'm qualified."

She had no argument from me. I saw the way her muscles worked under those lights. I was, among other things, an admirer of her fitness. Not that I'd ever share that with her.

"You might benefit from starting a pole routine," she said over her shoulder as she pushed through the main doors and onto the streets of Tribeca. "Once it's installed, I'll work on getting you into shape."

"I don't think that's going to happen," I said, falling into step beside her as we strode toward the subway station. I didn't plan on informing her that I was *already* in shape.

"Oh, it will. Unless what you're saying is that…you're too insecure in your masculinity to try the pole?" The way she looked at me, her eyes alive with mischief, told me she relished pushing my buttons just as much as I suspected.

"It has nothing to do with manliness," I said.

"A real man would try."

"Listen, I get that you want to see me work the pole. But Root Bear isn't coming out to play."

"So you're saying he's in there somewhere." Her brows lifted and she nodded. "Okay. I can work with that."

"You'll be working with nothing," I reminded her.

"That's what you think."

We spent the rest of the walk bickering like siblings—about pole dancing, about fitness, about nothing at all. It was equal parts amusing and cathartic to just shoot the shit like this with someone. To poke endlessly, to tease, to challenge.

By the time we'd made it to East Eighth, I was grateful for the chance to get some alone time. I needed to focus on my business. Not on my out-of-check-and-only-growing attraction for my client's sister. I pulled her aside before we entered the warm haven of espresso and muffins.

"You're off at two, right?"

"Yeah," she said, "but we won't be going straight to club after this. I need to make a stop in Chinatown after my shift."

I narrowed my eyes. "Why?"

"I need to swing by my old apartment."

"We already got your things," I reminded her. "There's no reason for you to go back there."

She nibbled on the inside of her lip for a moment, glancing away. "There is, actually."

"What is it?"

Her brows drew together for a moment and she tugged at her black ballcap. "There's a cat who lived in the neighborhood..."

"And...?"

"He was sort of mine," she finally said, crossing her arms. "I need to check on him. It's been too long."

I let this information sink in before I continued. "A cat."

"Yeah. Have you ever heard of a thing called a pet? Humans have them as companions—"

I lifted a palm to silence her. "I know what a pet is, thanks. But you didn't mention a cat before. Why is this just coming up now?"

"Because he's a street cat," she hurried to explain, "but he's *my* cat. He didn't live inside with me. At least not all the time. I just need to make sure Ranger is safe. I saved him once, and I can't go abandoning him like everyone else has in his life."

"Fine. We'll go check on Ranger. Until then, I'll be in the corner working." Pedestrians filed past us on the sidewalk. "Just let me know before you leave for a break or anything."

"Should I tell you when I have to tinkle?" she asked.

"You can keep that to yourself."

"Okay. Just be sure to order an Earl Grey or something. I don't want them thinking you're my boyfriend or stalker."

I blinked. "You haven't told them about the arrangement?"

She scoffed. "Of course not. I'm not trying to look like a freak."

"You haven't told *anyone* about what's going on, have you?"

Her brows furrowed, and there was real frustration burbling in the background. "No. Why would I? I need to go—I'll be late." She pulled open the tinted front doors of the coffeeshop and headed inside, leaving me with my growing suspicions.

Jordan didn't share shit with anyone. Not even her supposed friends. There wasn't a single person in her life—that I knew of, at least—who knew she was linked to the Fairchilds and had twenty-four seven protection. And I had a feeling it wasn't because of who the Fairchilds were.

Jordan was a lone wolf and wanted to stay that way.

You know someone just like that.

I pushed the thought away. I didn't like drawing parallels between Jordan and myself. Not only did it leave the door open to an emotional connection between myself and a client, it would almost certainly lead to me digging deeper. Getting to know her even more because I was so damn curious. I was already at risk of knowing too much, simply from living with her. I was an expert at keeping up walls, but this was getting to be too much.

How could I keep up the walls without shutting her out completely? I still needed to fucking protect her.

A flash of red hair further down the sidewalk caught my eye. Jordan had confided in me that redheads made her anxious now, until she could verify they weren't Dustin. I'd been on high alert as well.

Every instance had been a false alarm.

Except for this one.

Dustin locked eyes with me from about a half-block away, looking spooked. Then he turned on his heels and walked the other way. Electricity sizzled through my forearms, sending me into high alert. I was prepared to chase him down and shove his face into the cement. But I took a deep breath and held my ground.

So Dustin *did* have the balls to show up again after what I'd done to him.

I couldn't be sure whether his appearance on *this* street was co-incidence or not. But it was too close to Jordan's orbit for comfort. I'd have to inform Jordan, even though it would spook her. And I'd have to let her brothers know.

I called Damian to give him the news. He was dismayed, of course, and wanted to continue with our current around-the-clock protec-tion plan. And I couldn't disagree with him. Dustin seemed like a wimp—but I knew better than to underestimate him. Who knew his connections? His secret interests? His dark fantasies? There were a thousand ways one encounter could unfold with someone who was mentally disturbed and unnaturally obsessed. I wouldn't put Jordan at risk like that while her protection was in my hands.

Lingering outside on the sidewalk for awhile seemed best. I could monitor the flow of pedestrians, stake out the area from a few differ-ent locations. After about a half hour passed with no sight of Dustin, my mind resumed its former cartwheels about my inconvenient feelings for Jordan.

I reached for my phone. I needed reinforcements. I needed the insight that only my best friend in the entire world could offer.

Trojan. My brother in arms. My confidante. The one who kept me sane and stable.

It was almost noon. He was stationed out in California on assign-ment, so I knew he'd likely pick up. When one of us called, we always picked up. Even if we were in the middle of a warzone.

Trojan's familiar bass rumbled in my ear after two rings. "Seven-nnn."

"What's up, man?" I smiled in spite of my internal confusion, watching without registering the people flowing past me. "You busy?"

"Nah, I'm off today. You caught me at a good time. Everything okay?"

He was, like me, someone who floated in the wind. Letting his jobs take him wherever they may. A bachelor, untethered, hard drinker with a fitness routine, no plans for slowing down or putting down roots. We shared the same outlook. The same goals. The same past.

We were practically the same person in different forms. Which meant he knew me better than literally anyone else on the planet.

"How'd you guess I need some Trojan advice?"

"I can smell the desperation from San Diego," he said with a laugh.

I heaved a sigh, my gaze landing on the stopped traffic on the street. "I got a new assignment. And I'm not sure how it's gonna work out."

"I thought you were set to open the business."

"I was. But the brothers found out a few weeks back that their lost sibling was..." I paused, assessing my surroundings.

"Not lost?"

"Nailed it. I'm on close protection detail until further notice. And Trojan..." I sighed again, checking to make sure Jordan hadn't suddenly materialized on the sidewalk beside me to give me more shit about learning a pole routine. I lowered my voice, just in case she developed bat hearing for this particular admission. "She's twenty-five, she's a stripper, and she's hot as fucking sin. I need to get the fuck off this assignment but she's high risk right now. She's moved into my apartment temporarily until we can situate her into more stable housing."

Trojan let out a disbelieving laugh. "All right. That sounds...tense."

"Yeah, tense is one word you could use." I expelled a burst of air, but it didn't relieve enough of my pent-up frustration. "Plus, I swear to God this girl does not know how to cover herself up after a shower."

Trojan groaned. "You're living with an exhibitionist?"

"Feels like it."

"My man, you know what to do."

"Fuck her brains out?" I pinched the bridge of my nose.

His sarcastic cackle told me that this was not the right answer. "Not unless you want to lose the assignment. But you *do* need to get laid. When was the last time you got some action?"

I groaned. "Nothing since coming to New York."

"Well, start there. You just need to let off some steam. That's all. Once you get your clarity back, you'll be able to handle the day-to-day a lot better. No matter how glorious her tits are or whatever this stripper has that's got you in a chokehold."

"She's smart as hell. She's *funny*. She's incredibly fit—you have no idea."

"Stop right there. She's your assignment. I don't want to hear how you two are meant for each other."

I smirked as I glanced back at the doors of Black & Brewtiful. "I never said that."

"Well you were heading there. Just go get laid, okay? Or I'm gonna have to come there myself and make sure you find a girl to take your mind off the assignment."

"Aww, you would do that for me?"

"I've got some PTO coming up, and Manhattan seems like as good a place as any to visit. Besides, I miss my Sevvy."

I laughed at the ridiculous nickname. "Don't fucking start. I'll punch you as soon as you get off the plane if you call me that again."

"See you soon, Sevvy."

The line went dead, and I pocketed my phone, laughing to myself. I loved that fucker—he knew how to help whenever I was feeling lost. And if he was serious about the visit, it couldn't have come at a better time.

Just go get laid.

It seemed easy enough. There were a million apps for this sort of thing. I could have a hot blonde in my lap by the end of the day.

So why was I only able to think about the blonde inside the coffee shop?

CHAPTER NINE

JORDAN

I woke up humping my pillow again the next morning.

I wasn't proud of it. I sure as fuck didn't do it on purpose. But my subconscious had a funny way of reminding me I was hung up on Seven.

Every morning, I woke up horny as hell. My pussy dripping. Clit throbbing. Humping a spare pillow like some sort of hormone-flooded teenager. This morning in my dreams, he had me cornered in a VIP room at work, his fingers dancing beneath the wet strip of fabric that covered my pussy. He had me backed up against a wall as he rubbed and teased and nipped at my clit. I'd been seconds away from coming before I woke up—only to find myself stuck in reality, which included a total lack of being fingered by Seven.

This job needed finished, and fast. I rolled onto my side and rummaged in the nightstand drawer. Of course, it was filled with my vibrator collection. I was an expert in self-pleasure, because so few men were granted access to my peace, my space, or my body. A small, quiet vibe would do the trick, since I was so close to the edge. I turned it on and slipped it into my panties. My hips bucked instantly, and I buried my face in my pillow before the groan escaped.

The orgasm hit like a tornado. It swept through me from head to toe, making every inch of my body quiver. When my leg stopped jerking, I turned off the vibe and took a few moments to recover, breathing heavily into my pillow.

Fuck. I needed this man. But he was immune to sexual advances.

Maybe you just need to lay it out more clearly for him.

I'd done my best so far. I'd played dumb in the bathroom more times than a functional adult human should. Other than a few glares, I got nothing from him.

Seven was either actually a robot, or he had no interest in me.

And I couldn't bear the second conclusion. In fact, it would be far preferable to find out that Seven really was part AI and wore a human suit over his mechanical skeleton.

What does it matter if he's interested in you? He's your bodyguard. You'll be moving out soon. You don't even want to get close to anyone.

Even I didn't know what I was after. A good dicking down? It'd been so long since I had sex and enjoyed it that the concept seemed like something out of a fantasy novel. I could count on zero hands how many times I'd climaxed during sex. I'd need both my hands and the hands of several strangers to count how many times I'd had sex and detested it.

My chest tightened at the onslaught of faceless yet painful memories. My adolescence and young adulthood felt like one huge block of heaviness whenever I recalled them. It could choke the life out of me on a bad day, send me into a spiral and panic attack. But still, I held out hope that someone, somewhere, might actually make sex feel like romance novels said it could be. So far, it had been something I begrudgingly tolerated, or, in the worst moments, fought against.

Which made my swirling, desperate desire for Seven all the stranger.

He probably wouldn't even know what to do with a pussy. He's too pretty to need to learn how to satisfy a woman.

I heard the voice of Roxie in my head. Those had been her comments about Seven the night I ran into him at the bar. I explained him away as a former interest that just hadn't worked out—Roxie sensed a need to console me, so she offered those wise words. And she was probably right.

I just wished any of these very logical rationalizations would reach my aching core.

I stuffed my vibe back into the bedside drawer and pushed myself out of bed. Time to start the day. And after my tormented post-orgasm thoughts, it seemed wise to start the apartment hunt. I grabbed my iPad and pulled up a basic search, limiting the results to a specific price range. A few dozen results popped up—I'd definitely need coffee to sort through these. Since Seven had given me his official report – six pages of findings, feedback and recommendations—I knew what to look for now to satisfy his safety stipulations.

I slipped out of my bedroom, scanning the common areas for Seven. No sign. I set my iPad down on the kitchen island then slipped into the bathroom, shutting the door quietly behind me. My movements echoed in the cool, tiled bathroom as I completed my morning routine. Once I was feeling refreshed and ready for the day, I went back into the kitchen.

Seven stood in front of the open fridge peering at the contents. He wore a baggy tank top with exercise shorts, with bare feet and his big biceps on display. I tried to take it all in without feeling like one of those cartoon animals with the bulging eyes and the *awooga* noise in the background. Stripped down like this, without the perfect clothes and the hidden guns, his masculinity hit in a different way. He didn't look at me as I took my seat at the island.

"You feel like bacon?" he asked.

"Good morning to you, too."

He glanced back at me, then made a big display of looking at the clock on the wall. "It's after noon."

"By like, two minutes." I pursed my lips at him. His hands were coated with a fine dust, which made no sense. Had he been boxing? Was that chalk for his hands or sawdust?

"What's on your hands?"

He turned to the sink next, washing off the mystery dust. "Nothing." We were facing each other across the island, which offered me a perfect view to watch him perform the most mundane tasks. He took some ingredients out of the fridge and laid them out on the island. I got lost in the measured movements of his hands as he unwrapped various blocks of cheese, brought out an onion, laid a knife next to the cutting board.

"You want coffee?" he finally asked.

"I'd take a cup." I swallowed, looking at his thick knuckles. Did those hands know how to handle a pussy? They certainly knew how to handle a gun. He turned toward the back of the kitchen, prepping the coffee maker. My heart fluttered. He was making coffee for me. Somehow, this was sexier than the dream had been. This reeked of domesticity. Of stability. Of...partnership.

"You looking for apartments?"

His question startled me back to reality. I looked at my iPad, which still showed my search results for the lower Manhattan area. "Yeah, uh...I figured I better get a jump on it."

"Anything good coming up?"

I cleared my throat, zooming in on the map of Manhattan. "There's this really nice place in Chinatown here...it says it comes with zero security and a super who can be wooed by a strange man with flowers."

Seven snorted, his knife clacking loudly against the cutting board as he diced the onion. "I vote no on that one."

"Well, I'm still looking. Though I'm not sure anything I find will pass the Seven Pillars of Security that you outlined in your report." Those were my words, not his.

"You'll find out as soon as I review it."

"My next place needs to be cat friendly too." My gaze drifted back to him. His muscles flexed even while dicing onions. This seemed inappropriate somehow. Why was he so sexy in every task? I gnawed on the inside of my lip, trying not to let my thoughts sizzle on my sexy dream for that morning. Sure, I'd orgasmed less than a half hour ago, but my body needed more, specifically from Seven.

"Why do you have that angry look on your face?"

I frowned, directing my attention back to my iPad. "Just thinking about all those cuts I found on Ranger yesterday. He's too far away from me and I don't like it."

A moment of silence settled over us, broken only by the sounds of his food preparation. I didn't know what he was making, but I was curious. And growing hungrier. The coffeemaker dinged, and Seven turned to face it.

"You take one spoonful of raw sugar, right?"

The way his shirt hung off his meaty shoulders made something deep inside me coil like a loaded spring. "Yeah. I didn't realize you'd noticed."

"I've seen you make your coffee before."

My mouth flopped open as I struggled to respond. I'd lived with people for years that never knew how I took a drink or what my food preferences were. Seven turned around with a coffee mug in his hand, and I straightened.

"Let me know if I did it right."

The coffee steamed lightly. He'd chosen one of the mugs I'd unpacked from my apartment: POKÉ-SLUT.

I rolled my lips inward, trying to stem the sudden urge to cry. "Thank you," I forced out.

He turned back around. Mugs clanked again, then he held his own steaming cup, a tea bag sticking out. His mug read FUCKBOI.

"Cheers." He lifted his mug.

I dissolved into laughter, my body shaking helplessly as I clinked my mug against his. "Excellent selection on the coffee mugs today."

"You have quite the collection."

"You could call it a passion of mine."

He blew on his tea for a moment, then set it down untasted and went back to food prep—grating cheese into a bowl. I took an exploratory sip of my coffee—way too hot, which I knew it would be—and resumed my search on the tablet. After a few underwhelming search results that featured crumbling infrastructure and a definite lack of security cameras listed in amenities, I heaved a sigh.

Seven's gaze flicked up to me for a moment. "So why don't you accept your brothers' offer to buy you a place again?"

Some of my vehemence about this topic had dissipated over the past week. Maybe their little brunch with me the day before worked its black magic on me. I hadn't exactly been friendly with them, but it had also been...nice. To see them. To talk to them. To just be around them.

Even though I was still pissed about a lot of things, it felt surreal to be with blood family again. I just hoped Kaylee could appreciate that from the afterlife.

"It's important to me to make it on my own," I said. "I'm all I've got. I'm all I'll ever have."

"But you let them give you a bodyguard," he said with a smirk.

I swallowed hard. "Well, it turns out, you're pretty handy to have around." The news that Dustin had been spotted coming toward Black & Brewtiful yesterday was an unexpected wrench in my return-to-independence plans. I'd thought Seven had scared him off for good, but part of me wondered if Dustin's appearance was just a fluke. Maybe he'd been going somewhere else.

Would I have to worry about Dustin forever? My brothers were just as spooked by his appearance as I was, and I hesitated to imagine how any of these recent events would have gone down *without* Seven in my life.

"You're still against roommates?" he went on.

"Forevermore. Unless it's Ranger. I've earned my solitude and my stability." Tender and painful memories thrashed around inside my heart, desperate to escape. I never opened up to anyone about my past. But something about Seven told me he'd be gentle with my hard truths. Maybe it was the fact that I'd already cried into his chest once. Or maybe this was simply a consequence of my outrageous attraction to him. Whatever it was, I kept talking.

"I spent my entire life sharing rooms and houses with people that didn't give a fuck about me." I dragged my fingertip along the perimeter of the tablet as I spoke. "Supposed caretakers that made fun of me, locked me in closets, hid food from me. Then later on, roommates that gaslit me, used me for sex, stole my money." I looked up at him, finding his warm gaze focused only on me. "I don't want another living soul in my space or in my heart. And that's not going to change. Even if it makes financial sense to find a roommate, I won't have one."

His gaze dropped, and he continued working on the meal. My words pounded in the air between us. I didn't even mention that while I'd been starved and beaten up, Kaylee had been forced into sex trafficking and eventually died from her addiction. And that was *because of* the people paid to look after us.

Despite how true my words were, there was an important addendum.

Even just four days in with Seven, I knew I could probably live with him for the rest of my life without a single issue.

I'd never experienced that. His mere presence calmed my nervous system. And as much I pushed and poked him, the fact that he didn't use it as an opportunity to further his own agenda was like an Earth-sized sigh of relief.

Seven was safe.

I'd been looking for safety my whole life.

I nibbled on my lip, the tears threatening again. Why the fuck was I so emotional this morning? I really needed to get my sass and glitter back in place.

"You're going to need to pull in some more money," he finally said.

I swallowed hard, nodding. "Yeah. I'll figure something out. I might try picking up an extra shift per week."

Seven headed back to the fridge, returning with a package of mushrooms and a fistful of scallions. "You already work damn near seven days a week."

"Well, I'm young. Now's the time."

He looked doubtful. "Just don't overexert yourself. If you push yourself too hard, there are other consequences."

My gaze drifted back to him, taking in all the small details of his face. The barely-there laugh lines around his eyes—because the man did laugh, just never for me. The slightly crooked nose, the black stubble casting a shadow across his jawline and above his lip. The scar on his cheek, only visible when the light hit it right.

He must have sensed me staring at him because he looked up sharply, catching me off guard. "I had some shitty stepfathers growing up."

I softened, leaning toward him so I wouldn't miss a word. Seven hadn't volunteered a single piece of information the entire time I'd known him. The most I'd gotten out of him was his accidental admission of his age. This felt like a real treat. "Yeah?"

"My mom bounced around between husbands like it was a sport." He got a distracted look on his face as he assessed the mushrooms and rinsed the dirt off them. "She always went for the bullies. The ones who beat up on her."

"I'm so sorry," I whispered. "That must have been hard to see."

"After a certain age, I started inserting myself into their fights. Trying to protect her. Stop the abuse. Sometimes it worked. But a lot of times it didn't." He hefted with a humorless laugh. "I just couldn't understand why she wouldn't leave them behind and let us go start a life by ourselves. Without any of these idiots to ruin everything. When I left for the Marines, she had just moved in with a new guy. And I wasn't around to protect her anymore."

"Was she okay?" I was scared to even ask the question.

"He wasn't as bad as some of the ones who came before him. I think she was just scared to be alone. Terrified, really. Your attitude is what I always wanted her to find somewhere deep inside her. That strength to leave it behind instead of seeking it out."

I blinked rapidly, another wave of emotion overcoming me. I hadn't expected that subtle compliment. I almost didn't know what to do with it.

"Is she...still around?" The words barely made it past my lips.

He nodded. "In a nursing home in Nebraska."

"Oh, are you from...Nebraska?"

He smirked, opening the carton of eggs. "Maybe." One by one, he cracked six of them into a bowl.

"Wow. Didn't peg you as a Nebraska boy."

"Didn't peg you as a Pokémon slut."

Laughter rocketed out of me. I caught a small smile on his lips as he started beating the eggs.

"You win that round," I told him. "Speaking of which, can we leave for the club a little early today? I want to do some hunting in the park."

"Whatever you say goes."

I felt a wicked smile begin to spread. He must have noticed because he quickly added, "With regards to your schedule."

Seven greased up a pan and cooked the vegetables with a shiny wooden spoon. I watched him for a moment. Why was I so attracted to his wooden cooking spoon? It didn't make sense, other than I was attracted to everything about him, including inanimate objects he touched. I decided to return to my apartment hunt. A few moments later, eggs began sizzling. It wasn't long before Seven was plating two perfect veggie omelets. He grabbed for my chipotle cashew sauce and added a healthy drizzle to the top of both omelets.

He pushed a plate my way. "Ready."

I bit my lip, looking up at him. "Is this really for me?"

"Of course. You live with me. You think I'm going to stand here and cook in front of you for a half hour and not share the end result?" He shook his head, forking off a bite of omelet. "Let me know what you think."

I picked up the fork and dug into the omelet, making sure to mix in the cashew sauce. The flavors exploded in my mouth—mushroom, bell pepper, onion, a delicious cheese blend I couldn't identify beyond the Havarti I'd watched him shred. Perfectly salted and seasoned.

I moaned without meaning to, my eyes drifting shut. Once I swallowed, I nodded. "What I think is *yes*. Absolutely yes."

When I looked up, he watched me with a cocky smile, eyes sparkling. This moment, more than anything, told me I was seeing a different side of Seven. *Finally.*

"Gotta get you nourished before your big day." The way the air tightened between us, I could tell he was about to deliver some snark. "A staircase race you're gonna lose, some poké-hunting in the park, and then a full night of dancing."

I jabbed my fork in his direction. "There were two truths and one lie in what you just said."

"Zero lies, three truths." He forked another bite into his mouth.

"Don't bring that Nebraska sass right now," I warned him. "This will only come back to haunt you when that pole gets installed in the living room."

His shoulders shook with repressed laughter and my heart swelled. I eyed him as I ate, relishing this unexpected afternoon of vulnerability and connection. My whole body grew warm and buzzy. But by the time our plates were empty, my heart was constricting again. Telling me this was unsafe, destined to bottom out, a waste of time.

I offered to wash the dishes and then retreated to my bedroom to collect my thoughts. I felt tapped out, and the day had barely begun. That wasn't a good sign. So once my food digested, I focused on stretching and listening to music. Eventually, the playlist transitioned to upbeat electronica, which meant my workday prep had begun.

Straighten hair. Apply base makeup. Put on street clothes. Pack outfits for the shift. Get myself jazzed for an inordinate amount of extroversion. The standard workday checklist. By the time I stepped out of the bedroom, backpack slung over my shoulder, Seven was dressed to kill and waiting for me in the kitchen.

"You ready, Seven?" *Please say 'born ready' so I can give you shit about it.*

"I was birthed prepared."

Laughter cascaded out of me. "That's one way to get around saying 'born ready.'"

"Gotta keep you on your toes." He grabbed his apartment keys as he followed me out. The same warmth from earlier returned—seeping down to my bones, prompting the smile to linger on my face. We launched another staircase race—Seven fucking won, dammit—and then had a quick prework detour to City Hall Park to hunt for Pokémon—none found, unfortunately. But as for keeping me on my toes, Seven did exactly that again when he revealed he'd downloaded the gaming app and played right alongside me.

After I said my goodbye to Seven near the front of Gemstones, a strange chill whooshed through me. I liked having him at my side. A lot. More than I wanted to admit. I stewed over this fact and a lot of other confusing things while I got ready at the back of the house. I was still occasionally jittery whenever a redhead walked into the club; but I knew Seven's presence would more than take care of Dustin if he dared show up again. I tried to tell myself that I was merely turned on by the solidness and security that Seven offered. But I knew deep down it was so much more than that.

I took my time, chatting with Roxie and some of the other girls, catching up on the new drama since I'd last been there twenty-four hours before. Apparently one of the newer dancers tried to make off last night without paying her cut to the house mom, which was a mortal sin at any club. Everyone tipped out Clara, our house mom. She kept us fueled and running, stocking up on protein bars, snacks, hydration drinks, and so much more so we didn't wilt and die while we worked our asses off.

When it came time for me to go on stage, I gave myself a final once over in the full-length mirror. I'd chosen my standard transparent eight-inch heels—my favorite work shoes—and paired a shimmery black tutu with a bedazzled bikini top. A black thong to match, and plenty of skin in between. My makeup was dark and smoky, and my hair was pulled into a high, slick ponytail, stick straight. I loved that every night I looked completely different. A new character, a unique vibe. It satisfied my need to keep things fresh and interesting.

But as the music thumped and my performance unfolded, I knew tonight was different. I had a lot of pent-up energy. All that sexual frustration from living with Seven was coming to the surface. I danced more passionately, more intensely. I was sweating within minutes, and that wasn't normal. I tried new things in my routine that I didn't normally include.

The clapping and hollering for "Sapphire!" boomed through the club as I performed, louder than usual. I tried to keep an eye on Seven, but it was hard under the lights while he was bathed in darkness. I couldn't see him, but I could feel him. The energy seemed to crackle through the air between us. Could he feel that connection too?

I ended my performance on my knees in a sweaty puddle. My chest heaved as I struggled to gather the floating cash and receive the adulation being hurled my way. Once I tottered off the stage, I was swarmed by men wanting to book me. The owner, Eddie, stepped in to help organize the requests. I watched over his shoulder as he filled out the tablet that held our VIP room reservations.

The docket filled up. Almost my entire shift was already spoken for. The thought of not being able to connect with Seven the whole night, not even for a little banter, struck cold fear into me. The night seemed interminable, and I was already aching for more Seven. Before Eddie could finalize the list, I touched his arm gently.

"Hey, I need you to put someone in the VIP room for me," I told him. "My friend, Seven."

Eddie nodded. He knew that Seven was something of a security detail for me. I'd worked it out that Seven didn't have to pay each night, and he wasn't on the hook for purchasing drinks or packages with the girls. It had been the only way to make this arrangement work. When Eddie asked why I had the babysitter, I explained that a recent attack had changed things. He didn't press for more details, and I didn't provide them.

"Who's covering?" he asked as his fingers swiped across the screen, entering Seven into the VIP lounge slot.

"I will. It's a gift."

He hefted with a laugh. "Nice gift. I got him in. Go get 'em, girlie."

I took a deep breath, readying myself for the first VIP room booking of the night. Only a few Random Johns to make it through before Seven and I could get some time to ourselves.

I knew it was a bad idea, or possibly just a stupid idea. But I had to try.

Under the purple lights, freedom swirled, lifting me into my most powerful form. Like I could do anything—even seduce the one man who seemed immune to seduction.

This was my chance to push the envelope, and I had to take it.

CHAPTER TEN

SEVEN

Three hours of playing guard dog outside this damn VIP room.

I'd spent many more hours in worse places, but damn, this shit was boring. I didn't let it distract me from the task, though. Vigilance was always the priority. Any flash of red hair, any gaze that lingered too long on Jordan, anyone who seemed even remotely inclined to consume too much of her attention: I was ready to intervene.

Jordan's performance that night had been...I didn't even know how to describe it. I could have nutted in place, but the sheer embarrassment of being a wallflower in a strip club, coming in his pants, prevented me. It was breathtaking. It was compelling. It was too good—and now her VIP bookings list was a mile long, and I was the one who got to watch countless men wander off looking dazed and satisfied.

I checked my watch. Three more hours of this: standing around, wondering just what Jordan was doing in there, trying not to imagine what her bare breasts would feel like in each of my hands. I squeezed my eyes shut, pinching the bridge of my nose. The damn strip club hormones were getting to me again.

The VIP room door swung open and I straightened, eyeing the latest release. A very tall, very thin man stumbled out, smoothing the front of his polo shirt. He eyed me briefly before wandering away.

Jordan poked her head out a moment later, smiling coyly.

"All right, Seven." She tipped her head toward the interior of the VIP room. "It's your turn."

My brows drew together. "What?"

"Come on in."

The confusion didn't leave me, but I did as she said. She shut the door, drowning out the thumping music from the main stage.

"Aren't you done in here?"

"Actually, the next block is yours, if you want it." She smiled sweetly, sauntering toward the pole in the center of the room. Her calves flexed sexily under the low lighting. "The guy who booked this spot originally didn't show up. So we'll just pretend it's taken until the next one."

Some of my confusion dissipated and I glanced down at the couch behind me. Sitting down did sound nice. "Does this need to be sprayed down? You had a lot of admirers in here tonight."

She laughed, hanging onto the pole with one hand as she started a lazy circle. "There's no bodily fluids, come on. Everyone behaves themselves."

"Just checking." I smoothed my tie against my shirt before I sat down. She circled the pole. "I'm surprised you don't need a break by now. You've been going nonstop tonight."

She heaved a sigh, then shook her head. "If I sit down for too long, I won't get back up again." Her gaze drifted my way, locking on to me in a way that made my balls tighten. "It's best to just keep my momentum up."

I relaxed into the couch, propping an arm behind my head. Her gaze didn't leave me. And I couldn't stop looking at her.

Something unspoken throbbed between us. I had a feeling it had started building earlier that day. We'd cracked something open in my kitchen—at least I had. I never told anyone about my mom and her shitty ex-husbands. But there was something about Jordan that begged me to try new things. Be vulnerable. Open up.

And when she focused that blue-gray gaze on me, I was helpless.

"Do you want anything to drink?" she asked me.

I shook my head. "You know the rules."

"Not even water?"

"I'm hydrated enough. What about you?"

She shook her head. "I'm fine." She leaned her back against the pole, facing me directly. Wheels were turning inside her head, but I couldn't tell what she was mulling over. A few moments of silence passed, broken only by the muted undertones of the music outside.

"I have a weird question to ask."

"Go for it."

"Well, I've been thinking about what you said, needing to bring in more money..." She bit her bottom lip, gaze drifting to the floor. She was a living, breathing pin-up girl. Sometimes when I looked at her, I couldn't believe what I was seeing.

I rubbed my chin, trying to focus. "Right."

"I was trying to come up with a new routine. I was wondering if I could...try it out on you."

I didn't want to misunderstand this. Or read too much into it. "Like..."

"Like I'll pretend you're a regular customer in the VIP lounge," she finished for me. "You don't think it'll be too weird, right?"

I cleared my throat, tapping my fist against my mouth. "No. This is your job. Why would it be weird?"

She nodded, looking relieved. But she was brimming with nervousness, which I didn't understand. Unless she was planning on introducing a trapeze act into her routine, what could possibly be so new and different for her?

Jordan stepped off the mini stage in the center of the room and strutted my way. She fingered a long, slender cylinder that hung around a chain between her breasts. She stopped between my legs, and placed a hand on my shoulder.

"So. First things first." She held out the necklace, looking down at it. "This is a vibrator."

I straightened, rolling my neck in slow circle. "Okay."

"And I thought we could have some fun with it."

Her words slammed through me. My cock twitched in my pants as she reached behind her and yanked at the bikini strings. The fabric of her top went slack a moment later, and then it dropped away entirely. Her perfect tits were just above my eye-level.

My mouth parted, fingers curled.

She toyed with the vibrator again, looking at me coyly. "Where should we start?"

I tried to laugh, but it came out a stutter. *She's your client's sister. Off limits.* But the warning bells inside my head were hard to hear over the roar of attraction. And that roar was only growing louder. My cock had gone from twitching to fully hard in about three seconds flat. There was no hiding the bulge, but with how close she was, maybe she wouldn't notice.

Jordan slid both her hands along my shoulders, massaging as she went. My head dropped to the back of the couch and I drew a deep breath.

"Just relax. You don't have to be my bodyguard right now." She floated closer, her nipples two tight, rosy points hovering within tongue's reach. "Right now, you're just a man. Do you like what you see?"

I squeezed my eyes shut, starting a slow count in my head. I could not lose control. Not here. Not now.

Even though it was all I wanted to do.

"Jordan, why are you doing this?" I dared myself to open my eyes and meet her gaze.

"I told you." She had a little pout as she spoke, leaning closer. Her breasts almost brushed my chin. "I'm trying something new."

I balled my fists at my side. All I wanted to do was cup those perfect, perky tits in my hands. Squeeze them. Lavish them in kisses. Slide my hands up the backs of her sexy thighs.

"What happens in here...nobody has to know." Her voice had dropped to a whisper as she leaned down, closer to my ear. My cock was absolutely throbbing.

"But I'll know," I bit out. "And you'll know. And we both know we shouldn't."

Her lips grazed my earlobe. My fingers curled against the cushion as she murmured, "Just tell me. Do you like what you see?"

Do not say yes. Even though you fucking love what you're seeing.

"Or maybe I should stop," she went on.

Her words jarred a cold fear into me, and I reached for her legs to stop her from leaving. I didn't want to continue, but I sure as fuck didn't want her to stop. It was a catch-22. There were no good outcomes anymore.

You're fucked.

So you should just fuck.

"Don't," I whispered.

"Don't keep going?" She swayed slightly in front of me as my fingers trailed up the sides of her legs. Soon, I'd found my way beneath her useless tutu, learning the silky contours of her ass cheeks.

I was a strong man. But I wasn't strong enough to resist Jordan. Not when she was literally in the palms of my hands.

I squeezed her ass cheeks and she tipped her head back, moaning low.

"So I think I *should* keep going." She wore a lazy smile as she sank to her knees on the couch, straddling me. She didn't sink all the way down onto my lap, so she still didn't know that I had a hard-on that could double as a weapon—one that was painfully trapped behind my *actual* weapon, in its secret holster. She knew what she was doing, how to maintain minimal contact while teasing at every turn. I dropped my head to the back of the couch, but her hands smoothed their way to the back of my neck, bringing my head back up so I had no choice but to look at her.

"Is this what you call behaving in here?" My voice came out like sandpaper.

"We're not doing anything wrong."

"Yet," I corrected her.

"Do you want to?" she asked.

I laughed, but it was humorless. "That's irrelevant. I know you don't go past a certain point in here. I'm shocked you even let me grab your ass."

"This is for a new routine, remember?"

I ground my teeth, conjuring every last ounce of willpower that remained. This was the final frontier. Her bare tits brushed against the fabric of my shirt and I was a half-second away from demolishing all the rules.

"It'd get you fired," I bit out.

"New service I plan to offer on the side," she said into my ear. Then she bit my earlobe. I squeezed my eyes shut, steeling myself against the heat sizzling through my veins. I would not fall victim to Jordan's sexiness. *Could not.*

"That's what I need to test out," she went on when I didn't say anything. "You're not a paying customer in here, so this doesn't break any rules."

"I didn't peg you for wanting to get down and dirty with strange men outside of the club," I forced out. My rational brain was floating away. I couldn't believe I still knew how to form sentences.

She paused, like maybe this was a record skip in the rationale. "I plan to be *very* picky about who I do this for."

Then she dipped her head down, though for what, I had no idea. Maybe she wanted to say something or whisper another sweet nothing. But my primal brain kicked in. I needed her. I'd reached the end of my rope when it came to resisting her. She was a gorgeous, writhing bombshell on top of me, and I wanted to dive headfirst. I wanted it more than air.

I caught her lips before she could utter a word. She didn't miss a beat—when my mouth found her silky lips there was no hesitation, only hunger. Jordan clutched my face as we kissed hungrily, intensely, our tongues meeting forcefully in the middle. She fell against me as we kissed, making small noises that nearly undid me. I gripped the fleshiness of her ass, desperate to grind against her, but she was still on her knees above me.

When we broke for air, her chest heaved. She watched me with an accusatory look.

"Jesus Christ, Seven."

I pushed my fingers beneath the sides of her thong, desperate to learn every curve of her body. "What?"

"I didn't think you'd kiss like *that.*"

I blinked, still lost in the bliss of that make out session. She clambered off me unsteadily. I needed her back on top of me. I needed to be on top of her. I needed to tear off the remaining shreds of clothing separating our bodies and sink so deep into her she couldn't work for a week.

Every ounce of logic and rationality had left the building.

"Maybe it was a fluke," I admitted. "We should try again and see."

She pressed a hand to her forehead. "I can't think straight now."

"You should sit down," I told her. "Right back where you were."

She laughed, but instead of doing as I suggested, she sank to her knees in front of me. My heart rate picked up.

"It's time for my new move," she said, trailing her hands up the sides of my legs.

My entire body prickled with anticipation, and somehow my cock found an extra quarter inch of length at her words. My Glock dug into my dick at an awkward angle, but I was too turned on to notice the pain.

"But first"—she slid her palms up my thighs, heading for my crotch—"I need to pull your pants down."

I tipped my head. According to Jordan, the golden rule of Gemstones was that nothing ever happened in these VIP rooms that involved bodily fluids. But if my dick came out to play, there would absolutely be bodily fluids after I left.

"Why?"

She hooked her fingers along my belt and tugged gently. "Because I don't want to ruin your nice pants."

"Ruin them?" Maybe my brain was too hazy to understand what she was getting at. That kiss had knocked a few wires loose on my end, too.

She laughed softly as she undid my buckle. "Seven. There will absolutely be a mess if I sit on top of you. I can't let you go back out there looking ridiculous."

The meaning refused to click. "What mess?"

"Do you want to feel for yourself?" She surged to standing, reaching for one of my hands. She guided it beneath her tutu and between her legs, allowing me the briefest brush against the soaked crotch of her thong. The heat there threatened to unlock my beast mode. My fingers were glistening when she released my hand and sank back to her knees between my legs.

I groaned, my cock growing even harder. *Not fair.* "Oh my fucking God."

She had a satisfied smile as she tugged down my pants, revealing the secret holster, my Glock, and my absolutely enormous hard-on. She gasped, looking up at me.

"Seven. I had no idea you were enjoying this so much." She pulled my pants clear down to my knees and I removed the Glock from its holster, setting it aside. Her hands grazed the thick ridge of my hard-on, dancing over it so lightly my hips bucked automatically, seeking more.

"Don't play stupid."

"What?" She was trying her best to sound genuine, I could tell. But this was all a fucking act. It had to be. She dragged her thumb up the length of my briefs-covered cock, right over the damp patch of precum. She tipped her head as she watched my face for a reaction. I was trying my best to play it cool, even though I was seconds away from flipping her onto the velvet couch and fucking her brains out. This was her show—I was just a willing victim.

"You know exactly what you're doing," I bit out, my voice gritty from restraint.

"I'm working on new ways to make money," she said, so sweetly that it couldn't be genuine. And then she climbed up to straddle me again. Except this time, she plunked her ass down right on top of my cock and settled in. A low moan escaped her, her nipples tight rosebuds in front of me.

I was losing control faster than my blood was pumping to my cock. I cupped those perfect tits in my hands and leaned forward, covering one pink nipple with my mouth, then the other. Jordan gasped, arching toward me.

"You're being a brat," I said between lavishing attention on each nipple. "And you fucking know it."

She bit at her lower lip, trying to hide a grin. "I'm not being a brat."

I pushed my palms across the small of her back, and up the bumpy ridge of her spine. Then I tightened my arms around her so there wasn't even a breath of space between us. Her tits smashed against my chest, her breath coming out in puffs against my chin. Her legs straddled me, her pussy right where it needed to be.

This could be fucking heaven.

"I just need to try out my new move," she finally said.

I had to laugh at that. "Oh, you still haven't shown me? After all that?"

"It involves the vibrator."

I dove in for another kiss, capturing her lips and taking another juicy helping of her mouth. She melted against me, offering up her tongue and so much passion it nearly choked me. She clutched the sides of my face again as we kissed, growing needier and hungrier every moment.

"Oh, Seven," she moaned when we broke for air and my kisses drifted down the side of her neck. I was a goner. Goodbye, any chance of escaping this room without fucking her. Goodbye, career. Goodbye, morals.

"More." My voice was hoarse. I tugged on the end of her ponytail, exposing more of her neck as her head tipped backward. I latched on, trailing kisses along her neck. She started grinding on top of me, rhythmic and desperate. She whimpered, like she was already close. With how wet she'd been, I didn't doubt she had a big need to satisfy. Just as big as my own.

"What's your end game?" my voice came out almost a growl as I matched her movements. "You want me to fuck you in here?"

She moaned, digging her fingernails into the ridge of my shoulders.

"You brought me back here so I'd fuck you," I confirmed. "You just want me to stick my huge cock in this little pussy, huh?" I wet my bottom lip as I pushed a hand beneath the tutu, desperate to feel that wetness against my fingertips again. To get a taste for myself. "Rub my cock over your clit. Push it in and out of that tight pussy until your whole body goes hot and you can't see anything."

She whimpered again, squeezing her eyes shut. "Maybe I do. And maybe you want that, too."

I wanted nothing more. I'd sacrifice my career and my reputation for a chance to fuck Jordan. She'd blown the lid off, and there was no stopping me.

I slid my hand up her neck, framing her jaw with my thumb and finger. She was so beautiful. Even my wet dreams hadn't been this hot. My other hand made contact with the slipperiness on her inner thigh. She rocked against me, moaning loudly.

"Please, Seven," she begged.

Thump thump thump.

I fisted the tulle of her tutu, turning to look at the door.

Thump thump.

"Fuck." She made no move, but a sigh escaped her. Clarity zipped through me—moments too late for my liking.

I pushed at her hips, eager to get my holster back in place and my pants on. Disappointment lapped at the edges of my awareness, claiming its throne in my subconscious.

What the fuck did you get yourself into, Seven?

Jumbled shouts on the other side of the VIP room door told me it was time to get back on track. Stat.

"Who is that?" My voice came out sharp.

"I have no idea." She stood and stumbled away, reaching for her strewn bikini and quickly retying it. I had my holster in place, pants zipped, and belt buckled just as the door flew open. I surged to my feet, my heart hammering for a different reason altogether now.

"It's my turn!" A squat, pear-shaped man burst into the room. Hands grabbed at him, trying to pull him back outside. My hand hovered over my hidden gun.

"I said it's not your turn!" A feminine voice shouted. The hands holding him slipped, and he burst back into the room.

"My slot started five minutes ago! I get Sapphire now, what the fuck is the problem?"

I stepped toward the guy, placing myself between him and Jordan in case he decided to lash out. But my read on the situation was that he was horny and impatient. *I can identify with that.*

"You need to back off," I warned him, approaching slowly. I could have him on the ground in two seconds. But I didn't want to escalate the situation unless absolutely necessary.

"Sir, you cannot act like this!" Jordan's friend Roxie—gemstone name Amethyst if I remembered correctly—grabbed at him again, and the owner approached from behind.

"Please step outside of the VIP room." The owner's stern voice made the belligerent customer turn.

"Why the fuck do you have us sign up for these slots if some shmuck is gonna take up his own slot and then all of mine?"

He was referencing me. I was the shmuck.

Maybe Jordan and I had lost track of time. I'd have kept her in there for another three hours if I could.

The owner and Roxie argued with the man just outside the VIP room. When I did a final sweep of the room to make sure Jordan and I hadn't left anything behind—like a thong or my better judgement—I realized Jordan was gone.

She'd slipped out of the room.

I excused myself as well, leaving the heated tones of the customer dispute behind me. In the bathroom, I took a few moments for myself at the sink, splashing cold water on my face and trying to wrap my head around what just happened.

You gave in to your base desires, almost fucked your ward, and ruined any bit of moral standing you might have accumulated in your stupid life.

Disappointment shuddered through me again, alongside lightning bolts of excitement as flashes of the VIP room came back to me.

It had been the hottest moment of my life. Didn't make it right or something I could do a second time.

That had to be that.

I left the brightly lit bathroom and returned to the sultry, thumping strip club. Outside the VIP room, I felt back in one piece, sewn together with regret. I swept the club, scanning for Jordan. I spotted her coming out of the staff area a moment later, deep in conversation with Roxie. Their return to the VIP room marked my return to guard dog status.

Jordan appeared unaffected as she breezed past me to confer with the owner once more. The belligerent customer had been kicked out, which meant her next booking would begin early. She disappeared into the room with two very eager looking men who were probably not even thirty years old, and the door shut.

I leaned against the wall, resuming my bored scan of the area while Jordan entertained the next clients.

But no matter how bored I seemed, my insides didn't match.

My head and my heart roiled. Fingers curled at the thought that she might be doing the same exact moves with the two that just walked in there. Desperation clawed at me, urging me to kick them out and continue where she and I left off. I knew, deep in my bones, that we could *never* continue what happened in the VIP room if I wanted to keep her on my client roster and maintain a working relationship with her brothers.

I considered all possible scenarios while she worked.

Scenario one: She'd lured me in there to get me fired, so she could get out from underneath my and her brothers' thumbs.

Scenario two: She really just wanted to practice a new move on someone safe and the chemistry between us had popped off unexpectedly. She never meant to kiss me or have me respond like I did.

Or scenario three: She'd been trying to tease me at my apartment all along and took her chance to take it further after someone cancelled their reservation...because she felt the same flutters of something inconvenient darting through her chest that I did.

I didn't know which one was the most likely. My head spun by the time the door opened and the two guys wandered off. Her shift was over. I wasn't convinced that meant I'd get any clarity, though.

I didn't know what awaited us back at the apartment. Crippling awkwardness seemed likely.

"Hey," she said, glancing at me quickly before scanning the room as if she was looking for someone. "I'm gonna head to Roxie's after work."

"Excuse me?"

"I need a girls night." She crossed her arms, sending me an annoyed look. "Can't a girl spend some time with her friend once in a while? I'll take a taxi to your apartment afterward. Can you allow that, My Overseer?"

"No. Girls night is fine, but you're not taking a taxi from here, or from anywhere else. Fairchild vehicle only."

She heaved a sigh, but she didn't protest.

"And you sleep at my apartment, too. Not at Roxie's. Or else I'll show up myself and make it coed night."

She didn't meet my gaze, just looked out at the club and shook her head. "Fine. Whatever you say, boss."

"The car will be waiting for you and Roxie when you're done changing," I told her.

She huffed but nodded. I figured she disliked the plan because it would involve her needing to share more details about her situation with Roxie—like why she had access to a private car—but I didn't care. Her safety was priority. Nothing else. Least of all my dick. I opened my mouth to say more, to acknowledge the heart-stoppingly hot session we'd shared in the VIP room, but nothing came out. What else could I possibly say? We'd both been there. And now we weren't. It had to have been a one-off.

"I'm gonna change," she finally said, averting her gaze. She glided toward the other end of the club, beelining for the staff area.

I drew a deep breath, pulling my phone out of my pocket. I'd get the Fairchild drivers caught up on the plan for tonight. I recognized her sudden girls night for what it was.

An opportunity for a reset.

I needed to remember what life was like without Jordan breathing down my neck every day. What life *alone* felt like.

I knew better than to get comfortable, to get lured by false promises of happiness or whatever the fuck it was I felt when my heart got tight and the butterflies showed up.

I'd survived the infamous twins heartbreak and tragedy once. I didn't need to welcome them to my doorstep again.

And wherever the fuck Jordan had tried to take me tonight would only lead to those two unwelcome visitors showing up in my life once more.

CHAPTER ELEVEN

JORDAN

I sat perched on my bed the next morning like a statue, afraid to breathe.

Was Seven outside? Could I run to the bathroom without seeing him? Would I have to confront him in full mortification and morning breath?

It was eerily silent, but every so often I thought I heard a strange *whuff* noise. My bladder was bursting. I listened harder, unsure of anything outside the door. All I could hear was the beat of my own heart, reminding me of last night: *What. The. Hell. What. The. Hell.*

Fuck it. I couldn't wait. I slipped out of bed, opened the door as quietly as I could, and darted like a mouse through the apartment. I spotted Seven in the living room, mid-pushup. So *that* was the whuffing: the sound of his impeccable fitness. I rounded the corner silently.

Like a ghost.

I exhaled with relief as I shut the bathroom door behind me. After what was arguably the best pee of my life, I opted for the full morning routine. Why not? I wanted to avoid Seven for as long as possible, so it seemed only natural to hog the bathroom for an hour or so.

My head throbbed distantly, but I wasn't sure if it was due to my residual mortification or the fact that I was tipping back tequila last night at Roxie's like it was my job. I suspected it was a combination of both.

In the light of day, surrounded by clean, white tiles and my skincare routine, I could not figure out what the fuck I'd been angling for last night.

The girl that invited Seven into the VIP room felt like a stranger to me now. Awash with regret and queasiness, I struggled to figure out the new equilibrium. The one that would let me conduct myself with confidence around Seven. The new normal that allowed me to speak to him without thinking about the intensity I'd discovered on his lips, in his fingertips, pouring out of his body.

A shiver raced through me. As I waited for the shower to warm up, I let my head fall into my hands.

Bad move, Jordan. Now shit's gonna be weird, and you're only going to want him more.

I was a fly caught in a spiderweb. Except I was also the spider who built the web.

Once the water was warm enough, I stepped in and rinsed off. Some of my tension dissolved, but anytime my mind drifted, it went straight to the VIP room.

The sexy grit of Seven's voice as he asked me if I wanted him to fuck me right there echoed in my ears.

I squeezed my eyes shut, letting my head tip to the side as my thoughts wandered.

You just want me to stick my huge cock in this little pussy.

Another shiver up my spine. My nipples stiffened and I cupped one of my breasts in my hand. It elicited nothing—nothing like what Seven's scorching grip had accomplished. I tweaked my own nipple.

The tiny jolt was nice, but I wanted Seven's hands on me again. And I didn't want them anywhere near me.

That conflict was exactly the problem.

I wanted so much intimacy from Seven, but I was so conditioned to run from it. To fear it. To reject it, because it led to bad things.

I'd never been turned on like this before—and that brief stint in the VIP room told me Seven had some surprises in store.

I huffed. It was okay to give in to my desires here. I was safe in the shower by myself. This didn't have to mean anything. My hand wandered between my legs and my mind locked in on the most delicious memories of last night. Discovering the thick bulge in his boxer briefs, the absolute steel caused by his attraction. The heated brush of his fingertips against my pussy. The way he'd begged for more kisses, more *me*.

My fingers danced over my swollen clit. It didn't take long; I'd been primed since the night before. The pleasure coiled tight inside me and then popped like a confetti gun. Sparkly bits coursed through my veins, but as soon as my breathing regulated, I knew it wasn't enough. Nowhere close.

I needed Seven.

I vowed not to think about it or him for now. I washed my hair and body and resumed my morning routine at the mirror. Once I was moisturized and glowing, I headed back to my bedroom with my towel wrapped tightly around me.

Seven was still in the main room, sitting on his workout bench while he did bicep curls shirtless. I wilted, staring for longer than was healthy. Sweat glistened between his shoulder blades as he did his reps. I definitely needed a session with my vibrator now, even though I'd *just* masturbated in the shower.

Thunk.

My shoulder smarted, and it took me a moment to realize what happened. I'd walked right into the doorframe of my bedroom. I was so consumed with Seven, I hadn't even noticed.

My cheeks caught fire. *Fuck.* I scurried inside the room and locked the door behind me. Not that I worried Seven would come in. It was mostly to keep my humiliation from following behind too closely. I sank onto my bed, rubbing my head.

I was losing my fucking mind. Plain and simple.

Something needed to change. And it started with moving out of here. If only an apartment in my price range and any desirable neighborhood would stay available for more than thirty seconds, I might have a shot at moving out of Seven's apartment.

I took my time dressing, opting for loose lounge pants and a baggy shirt since I was off from both jobs today. Normally I was grateful for a fully off Sunday like this, but with the way my morning was going, I worried what embarrassment awaited me.

When I finally emerged from the bedroom, the first thing I saw was Seven in the kitchen. He now wore a sleeveless workout shirt, which was both better than being shirtless and worse, because it directed my gaze to his biceps.

Lose-lose with this guy.

I approached the kitchen island sheepishly. He turned around from the stove just as I sat on the stool facing him.

He blinked. "Oh, hey."

"Morning." I cleared my throat, glancing at the clock. "I mean, afternoon."

He nodded like he approved of my correction, and then turned away from me again. "You want some of this toast?"

"Uh...yeah." I swallowed hard as silence descended between us, save the sizzle from the pan. Based on the ingredients he had out—thick whole grain bread, shallots, and eggs cooking over medium in the pan—I guessed he was making some sort of stacked toast. I clenched and relaxed my fists in my lap, over and over again, trying to figure out if this was going to be normal between us.

Silence dragged on. I ran a hand through my wet hair.

"I'm gonna make some coffee."

Seven nodded, one of his ridiculously attractive wooden spoons in his hand. Tension brimmed between us. I came around the island and stood in front of the coffee maker. Freshly ground coffee waited for me in the filter, ready to go.

"Did you get this ready for me?" I asked, hoping we'd strike a good-natured chord somewhere along the way.

He nodded. "Yep. But I wasn't sure when you'd be coming out."

His thoughtfulness warmed me. Maybe things would be normal after all. I turned the machine on, selected my mug du jour—a punk Care Bear mug I'd found in a free bin at a flea market—and leaned against the countertop as it brewed. Seven hulked at my side, tending the eggs effortlessly.

Silence descended again. This was brutal. Or was it normal? I couldn't tell. And it was driving me fucking nuts.

He snapped off the stove just as the coffee began filling the pot. I watched the trickle of liquid as if my life depended on it. Dishes clanked, then a moment later, Seven had whipped up some sort of spread with the shallots. He smeared it on the toast, then topped it with eggs and a sprinkle of thyme and parsley.

He rustled in the silverware drawer. I couldn't look at him.

"Can we talk about last night?"

His question made my stomach plunge to the center of the Earth. I would have crumpled to the floor if it weren't for the counter holding me up.

"What's there to talk about?" I tried to make my voice sound bright, but it came out unnaturally so. I still couldn't look at him.

He laughed, but it was humorless. "Uh...there's a few things."

I cleared my throat, waving off his words. "I thought I told you already. I was trying out a new routine." My entire body vibrated with nerves. *Do you believe me yet, Seven?*

The hollowness of my voice startled even me. I barely recognized the words coming out of my mouth. I filled my mug to the brim, not even leaving room to stir in my sugar. I had no idea what I was doing. How to behave. I wasn't even sure I'd know how to eat the toast. I carefully moved the mug over to the island without spilling and came around to the other side to sit down. Seven stood near the sink, already one bite into his food.

"Okay."

That was it. *Okay.*

Both perfectly fine and somehow the worst response of all time.

I focused on my plate. Could he hear the hammer of my heart? I took a few bites before I realized I had no idea what I was eating.

"This is great," I said. "Thanks for feeding me. Again." I laughed, but it came out nervous. Psychotic, even.

Seven dragged his dark gaze my way. "You're welcome."

I shoved as much food into my mouth as I could. I couldn't spend another second around this man or his sexy wooden spoons. I needed to fester in shame and regret until I molted into a new version of myself. Regular Jordan. The one who didn't pull stunts like that or get close to anyone.

Once I cleaned my plate and put away what I could in the kitchen, I headed back toward my bedroom.

"Hey, there's something happening tonight that you should know about."

I froze mid-stride back toward my bedroom. Ice coated my veins. He was kicking me out. Retiring from close protection. Installing a steel trap chastity belt around my pelvis. "What is it?"

"A dinner party. Sort of." He lifted a shoulder as he rinsed off a dishrag. "Kind of a work thing, too. Your brothers and I do it once a quarter."

"Oh." My tongue stuck to the roof of my mouth. I didn't know what I'd been expecting, but it wasn't *that*. "That sounds great."

Even Seven looked suspicious of that response. Did he realize yet that my brain had disconnected from my mouth entirely?

"Yeah. They'll be over around six. Just wanted you to know." He sent me something like a grimace smile, and then started wiping down the island. The sight of him performing a domestic task with those biceps was too much. My useless, non-functioning brain started short-circuiting again so I dipped into my bedroom.

Fuuuuuuuck.

I threw myself face down on my bed and stayed there, stewing in my indecision and fucked-upness.

I didn't want Seven to know how much I wanted him. I didn't even want *myself* to know how much I wanted him. So that slipup in the VIP room needed to stay exactly what it was. A one-time mistake.

But how are you supposed to continue living knowing how well that man can kiss?

It was a question with no real answer. My only answers were a lobotomy or steel willpower. And neither seemed possible.

I sighed into my pillow, remembering the way he'd tonguefucked me. How he'd gripped my jaw, pressed his fingers into the side of my face, as if claiming me as his.

More shivers. I squeezed my thighs together.

Fuck, I was in so much trouble.

Time melted away in typical Sunday blur fashion: laziness, coffee, and lounging in the restorative cocoon of my bedroom. Even though this was my temporary spot, I'd made it mine as much as possible: big, earth-toned tapestries on the bare walls, small lamps that offered mood lighting, my full collection of weird anime statues and Pokémon characters laid out on the one lone shelf. I needed a day of rest, after the brutal beatdown of long-haul back-to-back shifts at the club. I felt like Taylor Swift, who needed a full day to recuperate after a weekend of shows because of how intense her concerts were.

I laughed to myself, snuggling deeper into bed. The lazy Sunday could have been improved only by adding someone into this bed with me. Someone roughly 6'4", with almost-black hair in an immaculate fade, a strong jawline, and abs sent from Heaven.

A knock at the front door startled me out of my sexy reverie. I checked my phone. It was only four. Who the hell was here? Thanks to the Manhattan renovation code workarounds of my room, I could hear everything as Seven approached the door and pulled it open.

"Hey, we're here for the install." A Brooklyn accent. Male. Nobody I recognized.

"Great. Come on in." Seven at least seemed to understand what was happening, so I relaxed into my bed, eavesdropping on every word. Footsteps clunked across the floor.

"We're Bobby and Rick. Should be a quick job." Another voice. "Where you want it?"

Seven cleared his throat. Then he shouted gruffly, "Jordan!"

Butterflies and pinpricks flooded my body. I scrambled from the bed, nearly tumbling headfirst to the floor, and joined Seven in the living room. Two fit men unpacked a long box in the living room.

From the size of the packages they pulled out of the cardboard, I understood immediately.

My stripper pole had arrived.

"They want to know where to put the pole," Seven said, crossing his arms. He'd barely looked at me today, which only made the humiliation lash harder through me. I should never have dared open myself up to someone—and why did I pick the man who hadn't shown me an ounce of interest? *Of course* he got turned on after I trapped him in the VIP room and took off my top. I'd imagined this connection between us. The intimacy we shared in the kitchen the other day, about our histories...it had been platonic.

I was an idiot.

"Jordan?" Seven asked.

It took me a moment to remember what I was supposed to be doing. Maybe he thought I was pondering the placement instead of rehashing my regrets from the night before. "I think this empty end of the room? So it's not in anybody's way."

Seven nodded, heading for the workers. I sank into the couch to watch them work as Seven instructed them where to set it up. The two men tested the ceiling, tested the floor, brought out tools, hammered different spots. Seven stayed close, occasionally lobbing a question their way. They were happy to answer, opening up about some of the difficulties of installing fitness poles.

"So which one of you is planning on using this?" Bobby—or possibly Rick—sent a good-natured smile toward the two of us as they brought out the pole.

"It's for him," I spoke up before Seven could respond. "He's been dying to learn."

"It's a hell of a workout," Rick conceded.

Seven looked back at me and dropped his chin, his mouth a thin line.

"He's just been so incessant about starting a pole routine, I said, *fine, I'll get you a stripper pole.*" I smiled sweetly toward Seven as his look morphed into a glower. "You know how men can be when they set their mind on something."

Bobby and Rick chuckled politely, while I relished Seven's annoyance. Things felt back to normal like this—with strangers acting as a buffer and a safe distance between me and those lips of his.

"I just made him promise to show me one new routine by the end of the month," I went on. "That was our deal. And he agreed. So here we are."

Seven cleared his throat, crossing his arms. "Are you done?"

"He's got a good body for pole dancing, don't you guys think?" I hopped up from the couch, sauntering past him with an evil grin on my face. He rolled his eyes, and just before I was out of earshot, I heard him add something that sent my heart pounding:

"Brat."

I was ready to respond, but an unexpected sound caught me off guard.

Meowing.

My eyes widened and I looked back at Seven. "What was that?"

A strange smile spread across his face. "What was what?"

"The meowing. Like a cat."

"Probably a cat meowing, then."

I narrowed my eyes at him. "Have you had a cat this entire time?"

His smile went from mysterious to shit-eating. "No. But I heard you did."

I perked up. "What?"

He came closer, the familiar dynamic surging between us, reminding me of how fucking *good* it felt when things flowed between us. "You take long cat naps. So I catnapped Ranger."

I gasped. "You did? How? When?"

"Before you got up. I knew you'd sleep in, but I left a note for you in the kitchen in case you came out while I was gone."

"Where is he?"

"I didn't want him to get spooked by the installation; he's in the bathroom for now."

My mouth parted as I beheld him; holy light practically radiated from his body. Not only was he gorgeous and safe and protective and funny; he had rescued my cat. My sweet rescue cat.

Roxie was wrong. Those hands *did* know how to handle a pussy. More than one kind, it seemed.

Seven, you're perfect.

I was too preoccupied with denying my intense feelings for Seven and helping Ranger acclimate to the apartment to even worry about the fact that my brothers were going to spend the entire evening in my breathing space.

And maybe, at this point, it didn't bother me as much as it used to. I figured Kaylee would have to understand. They brought me breakfast sometimes; they always texted and checked in, even when it annoyed me. Hell, they'd hired this *bodyguard*.

I mostly wanted it all to go away still. Maybe. And until it did…it didn't seem wrong to enjoy it a little. I was still looking for apartments, after all. Though nothing was coming up in my price range, I knew it was a matter of time until the right place popped up.

At five o'clock, a gourmet chef showed up and got to work arranging bowls of pre-prepped food on Seven's island. I tried not to act too curious about the unfamiliar scents wafting from the kitchen as he silently prepared Willy Wonka-esque frothed whatnots and whipped whatsits. Or maybe I was just uncultured.

Once I'd gotten Ranger's litterbox set up and some new toys—courtesy of a mystery delivery that showed up at the door—scattered around the apartment, I decided to break in the new pole. I climbed to the very top—thank God for Seven's ten-foot ceilings in this converted-warehouse apartment—and perched up there, watching what the chef did. Occasionally he glanced up at me, maybe unnerved by or maybe just curious about the weird girl at the top of the stripper pole, watching him like a bat while he cooked. Well that made two of us. Seven came out of his bedroom, spotted me at the top of the pole, and immediately went back where he'd come from.

A little after six the knock came. I knew it had to be my *family*. The word felt weird floating around inside me. I had seen Trace here and there throughout the years growing up, whenever I would catch a glimpse of Damian and Axel during the foster family shuffle. But I didn't know him and didn't consider *him* family. I didn't know any of their significant others, either.

As much as the thought of treating these strangers like a family unnerved me, it was also oddly exciting.

This is what you've wanted your whole life. The big family. People to look out for you. That closeness you could count on.

Except part of my family had abandoned me, and one of them was dead. Why did I have to remind myself that these brothers of mine weren't the family my heart craved?

I frowned, hauling myself up to the top of the pole. I swung my legs above my head, wrapping my thighs around the pole.

More knocks. "Seven!" I hollered.

His bedroom door slammed a moment later and he came out in a new outfit. Distressed jeans hugged his ass perfectly, and his simple white graphic tee couldn't fight the swell of his biceps. I almost gasped. *He has different clothes and he didn't inform me.*

"I've got it," he called out, though I wasn't sure if it was directed at me or the chef.

I watched him from my upside-down perch. Despite all the blood rushing to my head, there was a lot rushing to a different part of my body as well.

The door opened, and loud conversation jolted through the apartment. Booming greetings, lots of hugs and back slapping. Girlish laughs. Anxiety slithered through me as I saw these beautiful people file in. The boys were dressed down, similar to Seven, in relaxed but likely designer duds. I spotted Mercedes—my favorite coffeehouse customer who proved to be the unwitting link to my family—*what were the odds?* Then there was a redhead and a glossy, dark-haired beauty who looked so familiar.

That was Cora, the real estate heiress I'd seen on the news, in tabloids, on the insides of magazines touting luxurious investments I'd never dream of going near.

"Oh my *goodness.*" The redhead drifted my way, her hand pressed to her chest. She was voluptuous, bright eyed, stunningly beautiful, and genuine. I could tell this after three words and from looking at her upside down. Reading people's energy was a skill I'd been forced to learn after too many bad actors in my past. "Look at you! You are just...flying."

I grinned down at her, watching as Cora and Mercedes came over next, both wide-eyed and smiling. The brothers smiled over at me from near the door, where they were slipping off their shoes.

"I'm Jessa," the redhead said, eyeing me with wonder as I completed a slow drop, upside down, ankles wrapped around the pole. She pressed her hands to her chest. "Your new biggest fan."

I released my legs and performed a backbend off the pole, landing on my feet on the wood floor. Jessa gasped, clapping wildly.

"Nice to meet you, Jessa," I said, as the blood redistributed itself through my body. The wooziness only lasted a second.

Cora surged forward next, her soft green eyes looking misty. She stuck out a hand. "Jordan. I'm Cora Margulis. I am so honored to meet you."

I swallowed hard, gently taking her small, cool hand. Cora, the real estate heiress, was honored to meet *me*? Her last name was on the side of a skyscraper in Midtown. This had to be a dream. Was I still asleep in my room while the pole installers worked?

"I...It's nice to meet you," I forced out.

"I never thought this day would come." Cora clasped her other hand around mine. The sincerity poured out of her; it almost choked me. Why was this woman almost crying? Emotion swelled inside me too, prompting more questions. "I would love to get to know you better. I just want you to know that."

If I'd read something in Jessa just from looking at her, I knew a book of things about Cora after that exchange. When she let go of me, I was almost in tears. I nodded, surprised as the words poured out of me. "I would love that."

"I'd introduce myself too but I know I don't have to. Even if she forgot my name, she'd know my drink order," Mercedes piped up, smiling cheekily.

That sweet blondie pushed me to my breaking point. I threw my arms out, looking for a hug. *What the fuck is wrong with you?* I never hugged people unless drunk or, in Seven's case, recently assaulted. But something about these three had me swimming in feels. Mercedes and I shared a short, warm hug that left me smiling so hard my cheeks hurt.

"I want you to meet Willow," Mercedes said. "Trace's niece that we're in the process of adopting. But she gets spooked by lots of people, so we left her with the nanny tonight."

"I can't wait to meet her another time," I told her.

My brothers and Trace strutted over, smiling in a way that made my chest feel tight. I had to look away.

"Hey, little sis," Damian said. He smiled so warmly at me, I almost crumpled to the floor.

"That was a strong introduction for welcoming company," Axel added, glancing toward the pole.

Trace nodded my way, a genuine smile stretching across his lightly stubbled face. His nearly black hair betrayed the fact that he wasn't biologically related to Axel and Damian. "Jordan. It's amazing to see you again."

"Hi, guys." I took a deep breath. All their eyes on me only solidified this bizarre sensation that I meant something to them all. Which I didn't believe could be true. Kaylee and I spent our adolescence believing the opposite, but their intense interest and affection had me second-guessing things. "I didn't mean to be the weird bat dangling in the corner when you showed up. But that's how I decompress."

"We all have our ways," Damian said. "I wouldn't mind trying that, to be honest. I've used some questionable methods in the past."

"I'll teach you," I offered, before I could think better of it.

"If Damian learns, I need to learn," Jessa said.

"If Jessa learns, I need to learn," Cora spoke up.

I laughed, looking at everyone. "Well, I could teach *all* of you. Get some lessons going. Have a little friendly showcase sometime."

"Deal." Axel mimicked slamming a gavel.

"I love teaching the pole. And just *being* on the pole. I might have weirded out the chef," I admitted.

"He's used to it by now," Trace said.

"What's Seven's favorite way to decompress?" Axel asked, giving Seven's shoulder a friendly squeeze.

"I'll have to let you know once I finally see him decompress," I said. "He's so uptight."

Seven's eyes narrowed to slits.

"Seven, you deserve to decompress," Mercedes said, patting his arm as she flitted by him, heading for the kitchen. "We all do."

"I decompress," Seven shoved his hands into his jeans, "the best way I know how."

The men erupted into laughter. Cora sighed while Jessa rolled her eyes.

"Typical men."

"Jordan, let's go over *here*," Cora said, ushering me to the low sectional nearby. "Away from the men and their crudeness."

She and Jessa laughed as we settled into the couches. I bit at my lip, glancing over at Seven and *the Fairchilds* standing just beyond the couch.

"Do we need wine?" Mercedes called from the kitchen.

"Dry white to start," Cora called out.

"She really knows her wine," Jessa said in a stage whisper.

"It's all about staging the right flavors in the right order," Cora explained. "The end result is magical, especially if you find the right cheese."

"I...don't know much about wine," I admitted, feeling suddenly small surrounded by these women. Older than me. Established. *Gorgeous* in a way I didn't think I could ever truly feel. Probably rolling in dough, not even needing a dumb bodyguard, who wasn't even dumb to begin with. "I pretty much drink whiskey and rum."

"Not surprised. She's a Haynes tomboy," Axel clarified, leaning against the back of the couch. Seven and Trace retreated to the kitchen for who knows what, while Damian came around to the other end of the sectional and sat down. "It was obvious even when she was a toddler. Constantly found her eating dirt in the backyard. Damian and I would crack up laughing at the things we stopped her from eating."

"One time, she almost ate an entire worm," Damian said, grinning.

I gasped. "Really? Was it alive?"

"Absolutely. But the louder we shouted about it, the more you wanted to eat it."

I snorted. "Sounds about right." I glanced over at Seven, but his back was to me, too far away to know what we were talking about. I was almost sad he'd missed his chance to opine.

"One time you ate the paper menu at a restaurant," Damian added, bursting into laughter.

Axel stroked his chin. "Classic Jordan."

Seven and Trace joined us a moment later, settling into an open space on the big sectional. "Everyone's laughing. What did we miss?"

"Just reliving the ridiculous things Jordan used to eat when she was a toddler," Axel said.

I tucked my legs under me, trying to imagine what it must have been like when we were a complete family, when all my loved ones were around me, looking out for me, keeping me from eating worms.

"Maybe that's why she eats like she does now," Seven piped up.

His addition to the conversation sent prickles along my forearms. I tried not to look too interested in what he had to say next.

"Oh yeah? Still begging to eat worms?" Damian teased.

"Next best thing." Seven paused as Mercedes arrived with glasses of wine in her hand. She handed two to Trace and Seven first then flitted back to the kitchen. "Jordan has an obsession with rice noodles."

I stifled a laugh. Axel looked delighted. "It was a premonition."

"Rice noodles hardly mean I crave live worms," I said, meeting Seven's gaze for an electric second. Mercedes continued bringing wine glasses to the rest of us in rounds until we each held a glass of dry white wine. "It just means I crave the blatant superiority of rice noodles over any other form of food."

Axel and Damian whooped, a lively debate erupting. We sipped wine, interjecting and pleading our cases as we compared cuisines, methods, salt content, and more. Time melted away as the eight of us discussed, chatted, and laughed. Before long, we were called to dinner. Eight place settings had been carefully laid out, filling the enormous dining room table. I sank into my seat directly across from Seven. Our gazes met briefly and the same electricity zapped through me, leaving me wobbly.

The chef—named Gaston, which was the most *French Chef* thing I'd ever heard—brought out various courses, waiting dutifully until we completed each one before delighting us with the next round. We ooh-ed and aah-ed our way through French onion soup, a wild mushroom ravioli with shaved Parmesan on top, and beef short ribs with creamy polenta. Each course was a brand new flavor explosion that had never hit my palate before.

By the end, drunk more on the perfection of that polenta than on the wine, I was the one leading the applause for Gaston.

"You cooked this well because I stared at you upside down the whole time, isn't that right?" I asked him as he came by to collect my plate.

He smirked but said nothing.

"He doesn't speak much English," Axel explained.

"I will learn his language to ask that exact question," I told him.

"I can't tell if that's a promise or a threat," Damian quipped.

"I think that depends on how responsive he is to her hanging like a bat in the corner again," Seven added.

The rest of the table erupted into laughter, and I fought to hide a cheek-splitting smile. My chest split open, allowing that old, gaping hole to be filled anew with the genuine laughter, the delicious food, the way that people at this table, in some way, *knew me*. Not just my name, but my preferences. My habits. My quirks.

It was so heart-warming that it bordered on fire. And that type of warmth...I wasn't used to. I craved it, but the cold was what I was familiar with. Comfortable with.

The warm chasm cooled as my logical mind fought to heal what it perceived as a sudden wound. Any opening in my heart space was an invitation for pain, infection, and hurt.

My tablemates continued talking, unaware of the emergency medical procedure I'd completed on the interior of my chest as the conversation turned to other things, like trips to the French countryside, learning new languages, and whether anyone had actually seen bobsledding in real life.

I participated as much as I could without allowing the warmth to take over the vulnerable inner parts. I needed to stay in a safe zone—I'd become so used to hacking it on my own, it felt wrong to be seduced by the allure of this so-called family.

We were connected, for better or for worse. But the only safe way forward was alone. Undisturbed. Distanced. In control. I'd learned this lesson enough times already.

I was ready to slip away on my own. The wine threatened to loosen me up again, and despite how much I reminded myself that distance was smart, my heart craved the closeness. Even if it was a ruse.

"Jordan." Amid clinking glasses and dinner plates, Damian sat in the empty chair next to me and pulled out his wallet. "I almost forgot. I brought something for you."

He fished out a small photo between thumb and forefinger. It looked old, like something from a real film camera. He offered it to me and I plucked it reluctantly from his fingers.

"I want you to have this," he said quietly.

My gaze swept over the faded image. I recognized Damian's young face first, tucked between the shoulders of two adults—our parents. Axel was at our father's side, then Kaylee beside our mother, a bright-eyed four-year-old. I was a toddler in my mother's arms.

A picture-perfect family.

A spear to my heart.

"It's one of the last photos taken before the accident. Before...everything changed." His gaze dropped to the floor, and he looked like he wasn't sure what to say next. His jaw flexed for a moment. "I wasn't sure if you had anything from them."

"No, I don't." My voice was hoarse as my gaze swept over the photo. When our parents had passed away from the Christmas Eve car crash, we'd only had one living grandma at the time. She was too feeble to take us in—destined for a nursing home herself—so all four of us were kicked to the foster system. I didn't even have a memory of what my parents looked like. I had no baby pictures. Nothing but sadness that covered my mind like a thick quilt, and a longing for so much more than I'd received.

"You should definitely have this then."

"But won't you miss it?" I couldn't rip my eyes from the picture.

"I've made a high-res copy. Besides, if I ever want to see it, I can just ask you." He offered a smile and squeezed my wrist. The small gesture made my throat clamp. I had to get out of there. Immediately.

"Thank you," I forced out past dry lips. I tried to smile, to say more, but I couldn't. The tears were coming now, which meant I had to leave. I shot to my feet and silently retreated to my room.

Only in the dim light of the bedroom did I let the sob bubble up and out of my chest. I knew how to tamp it down—I'd been practicing the art of silent crying my entire life. I sank to the floor at the foot of the door and clutched the picture to my chest, tears streaming down my cheeks.

I'd been part of a family once. I'd been born into and raised with love—until it all changed.

Seeing the evidence of this truth felt unbearable. Heart-wrenching in a way that could only be expressed with jaw-breaking sobs.

And while Damian's gift was a sweet gesture, it was also a warning bell.

You need to act fast. The longer you stick around, the harder it will be when you have to leave.

But at this point, I wasn't even sure I wanted to leave.

CHAPTER TWELVE

The days dragged on, the awkwardness between Jordan and me fermenting into something new, something sour, like the most disgusting kombucha.

Every second she was unoccupied and safe at the apartment, I busied myself in my work. I had plenty to do. I'd gotten a few leads from the ad I'd posted last week, and I'd already met with three potential new hires, each with their own strong, unique background.

I couldn't keep this shit up much longer, though. I needed Jordan out of my sight, at least for the majority of the day. Being around her only reminded me of all the things I liked about her. Of the things I wanted to do to her. The banter between us—when we allowed it—was too gratifying. The easy way we could co-exist—when we weren't stewing in our awkward-as-fuck juices—was the type of thing that reminded me of the old days, back when I'd been engaged to Olivia. The glimpse at the sexual connection between us—I couldn't even fucking think about it. *Dangerously* gratifying. Everything about Jordan promised to be a minefield of pleasure. I needed her under someone else's care as of last week.

My phone vibrated on my bed next to me as I responded to the latest email with a job applicant in his late twenties named Chico. That wasn't his nickname either. He'd won the hiring race—motivated, punctual, with a military background and complete flexibility. I extended the job offer, and now we were wrapping up the final contractual details. My head spun. My biggest dream was officially off the ground—my own bodyguard business. I was almost *the boss*. Only a few steps remained between me and my goal of CEO.

It took me a few minutes to remember my phone had buzzed. When I checked it, a text from Trojan waited. *"You ready for this jelly?"*

I smiled as I wrote back. *"Must mean you've arrived in NYC."*

"Knife at the ready. And yes, that's a fucking metaphor."

I laughed, excitement replacing some of my existential dread. Trojan's trip to Manhattan had worked out—and not a second too soon. I needed my best buddy to get my head straight. To replace it entirely with a brain that functioned on logic and reason again.

"Metaphor for your dick, right?"

"No, meatwad. A butter knife. To spread your sweet jelly."

I laughed and sent him the address of the hotel I booked him. We were buddies, but we weren't share-the-same-bed level of buddies. I booked him a stay at the Hyatt, because I was fucking nice and I missed him. Plus, I had a big favor to ask of him.

There had been one thought knocking around in my brain since Jordan's surprise performance in the VIP room: *she wanted more, just as much as I did*. But my logical side accepted Jordan's explanation. It was easy to tell myself I was the one who made things weird. That the sparks and feelings between us were one-sided. I couldn't get past this until I knew, without a doubt, that Jordan had fucking lied to me about that "new routine."

I needed to know that what happened between us wasn't going to be happening for a few lucky guys on the side, like she'd claimed.

And the only person who could test this theory was my good buddy Trojan.

This was a big ask—go into a VIP lounge, provoke a stripper, swear to not touch her lest she take things further, and then give me every sordid detail afterward, no matter how tight my fists got.

I needed to get him nice and buttered up.

Jordan's shift at the club started at seven that evening. I knew the drill. At five, I set my work aside and went to the kitchen for a protein shake. She was already there, packing her backpack. Without looking at me, she asked, "Feel like some rice noodles?"

The least surprising thing she'd ever asked me. I got this question at least three times a week. "If you insist."

She shoved her heels in her bag, followed by a scrap of fabric I assumed she'd be putting on her body in mere hours. I gritted my teeth, trying not to imagine too much of what I'd be seeing that night. Every ounce of my energy was dedicated to keeping my thoughts off Jordan's body, the way she felt in my arms, and the memory of her damp inner thighs against my fingertips. Those thoughts were forbidden.

Until I was alone in the shower each morning, when those thoughts slunk out of the shadows.

She still insisted on taking the subway every day, despite the fact that she had a fleet of private cars at her disposal. But who was I to complain? This was her show, and I was just a transfixed member of her audience. We headed for the door, turning off lights as I went. Our footsteps fell quietly in the hallway as we speedwalked to the stairwell. I knew what lay ahead. It was more than routine by this point; it was something I almost needed for my day to feel complete.

Once the door swung open, the race began. Our feet clattered down the metal steps and a delighted sound squeaked out of her. She elbowed me. I pulled ahead.

"Fuck you!" Her voice echoed in the stairwell as I bolted down the next few flights a few steps at a time.

I won with seconds to spare. I held the door open for her, my chest heaving.

"Sucks to lose," I said as she walked past. I made sure to keep my win-loss ratio at about fifty-fifty. Couldn't have her thinking she was hot shit. Even though plenty of those times, she'd beaten me fair and square.

The clamor of the street distracted us from needing to talk too much. The less interaction, the better. That's what my logical mind knew, even though it felt disjointed and wrong. We walked a few blocks to her newest favorite rice noodle spot in my neighborhood, cramming into the bustling little storefront and joining the winding line to order. I knew what she was getting without needing to hear—beef slice rice noodle—while I got my own personal favorite...beef slice rice noodle.

I wasn't trying to copy; the woman knew what tasted good.

Once we got our steaming bowls, we retired to a bar-height table with two stools. We slid into place, her eyes practically shooting stars as we laid out our silverware.

"I've been waiting for this moment," she whispered.

"Since two days ago, when we were here last?"

She narrowed her eyes at me. "Don't sass me. I don't want your sass ruining my rice noodles."

"That wasn't sass, it was fact."

I could see her trying to fight a smile. "Zip your lips." She shifted in her seat, our knees knocking beneath the table. I fought to ignore the warmth that shot through me. She didn't even seem to notice as she dug into her food; so I did the same, ignoring the way her knee settled against mine and stayed there.

It was like the buzzing of an electric fence. A dangerous, fatal current below the surface. Everything would be fine if we just left it alone. Obeyed the safety procedures. Followed protocol.

I hated how much I had to remind myself of this.

We inhaled our food in record time. When she got up to dump her empty bowl, an icy breeze whooshed past where our legs had been touching. I tried not to notice. She offered to take my empty bowl, and I nodded, yanking my gaze off her receding frame and to my phone.

Trojan had been texting during our dinner. He was at the Hyatt and ready for the next move.

I typed out a quick response.

SEVEN: I'll call you in an hour and explain the agenda.

TROJAN: Sounds like you've got something saucy in store.

SEVEN: Hope you brought a ladle for that sauce in addition to the butter knife.

The trip to Gemstones passed quickly, thanks to the pitstops along the way and at the park nearby to hunt Pokémon, followed by an overstuffed train and the fact that there was a man in a full Easter Bunny suit—despite it being early October—taking nips from a flask and shouting out bad advice whenever someone dared give him a side-eye.

Once Jordan was safely inside the club, I slipped into the quiet alcove near the bathrooms and called Trojan.

He picked up immediately, his coarse voice prompting a smile before I'd even digested his words. "Is this the call where you finally explain why you put me up in a swank ass hotel like I'm your secret lover?"

"Some things don't need to be explained by anything other than you're my friend. And you deserve the best."

He snorted. "Bullshit. The last time you footed the bill for our hotel it was a Super Eight."

"Times are different. I'm a businessman now." I could feel the grin blooming across my face. Trojan likely earned at the same level as me. He'd had just as many high-profile protection jobs and had been employed by a Fairchild or two in his life. People like them weren't afraid to pay a premium for the best.

"I guess that means drinks are on you tonight, huh?"

"Of course. Whatever you want, Trojie."

"Don't start with the stupid fucking nicknames," he warned. "Unless you really plan to take me as your secret lover."

"Not a chance in hell."

"That's right, because you've got a hard-on for your client."

I cleared my throat, wishing he was in front of me so I could punch him in the gut for that comment. "Listen, I'm going to send you an address—"

"Oh, I love it when you get all CIA operative on me."

"—and I need you to show up and act like you don't know me."

His cackle prompted a laugh on my end, too. "Fine. Go on."

"Start a tab if you want. I'll pay it. I'm also going to pay for a special...visit, while you're here."

Trojan groaned. "Seven, promise me what we're getting into tonight is *legal*."

"Of course it is," I assured him, stepping aside as a man entered the bathroom. "I would never lead you astray."

"I'll determine that when I see where your mystery address takes me."

"You'll love it. I promise. But I need something in return: a full report of what happens during your special visit." My heart hammered, not that Trojan would know. I was desperate to be proven right that Jordan disguised the same feelings I had via that flimsy excuse about "trying out a new routine." It shouldn't have even fucking mattered, but I was dying to know if I was the only one feeling the burn of this attraction. I had to know. For science.

He cleared his throat. "Listen, is your fucking phone tapped or are you just being cryptic to piss me off?"

This time, I was the one who cackled. "Maybe a little of both. Truthfully, I just don't want to be able to hear you judging me once you realize what I have planned for you."

"Son of a bitch."

"I'll see you here, okay?"

Trojan heaved a dramatic sigh, and I hung up on him then sent him the address. He'd give me shit about what I planned for him, but the sheer amount of buttcheeks and tits in this place would quiet him down. There wasn't much that a neat whiskey and a lap dance couldn't solve for most men. As long as they weren't head over heels for a stripper ten years their junior that happened to also be their *client's little sister*. Even a lap dance couldn't help that.

By the time I returned to the main area, Jordan's show was just beginning. She stepped onto the stage accompanied by a thumping beat, her eyeliner winged, her pouty lips painted a deep burgundy. As expected, the scrap of fabric I'd seen her stuff into her backpack was now stretched across those perfect palm-sized breasts and down over her toned and tiny waist. She wore a black thong bodysuit that looked more like a one-piece bathing suit had lost a fight with a paper shredder. Strips of tasseled fabric splayed out across her muscular ass as she strutted the stage. Once again—as always—I was rooted. Along with every other human with a set of eyes in the building.

I tried to keep to the back wall and scan my surroundings instead of watching the show. After all, I needed to be on the lookout for Trojan. But I couldn't keep my eyes off her. Not when she was sharing the same airspace as me.

Trojan knew it. I knew it. And I prayed to God Jordan didn't know it.

I *did* have a hard-on for this woman. And it wasn't because she wore outfits that looked like they came pre-shredded or she specialized in wearing floss between her ass cheeks. Those were the last things about her that mattered.

I didn't want to think about this anymore. I tried to distract myself with thoughts about my business and what came next now that I'd sent the contract to Chico. Once he sent me back the signed contract, we'd start immediately with the first assignment. Something safe—a "babysitting" session in my apartment or similar.

Until I could determine when it was safe to fully hand over her protection to someone else, I'd remain on the job. Dustin hadn't dared show up recently, but it didn't mean he wouldn't. And Jordan's brothers still wanted full-time protection for at least an additional month once she found her own place, until the threat could be reassessed from her new apartment.

Jordan whipped herself around the pole, and the dollar bills rained down. Every time my gaze slid back to her routine and settled there, I forced myself to check my phone or focus on something else.

Trojan showed up just after she cleared the stage. He and I were the same height—six four—but he looked like the burly woodsman to my clean-cut vibe. Since leaving the military, he'd rocked a beard in various stages of growth and even had a whole flannel collection. Tonight, he wore dark jeans and a gray button-up, striking the balance between off-duty bodyguard and out-of-place lumberjack in the city with his full, dark beard.

Our gazes met across the room, and he shook his head at me with narrowed eyes. I fought back my smile. He headed to the bar immediately, and as he leaned against it, I got a text message from him.

TROJAN: A fucking strip club.

SEVEN: I told you I didn't want you judging me.

TROJAN: Because you're about to send me on some wild-goose chase for your stripper girlfriend, aren't you?

SEVEN: She's not my girlfriend.

TROJAN: So that sounds a lot like a yes to what my mission is. I'm getting a double and tipping 200%. Enjoy the tab later.

Jordan lingered near the front of the stage, playing coy with a few different men. I needed to get Trojan on her schedule before it filled up. I spotted the owner, Eddie, heading to the main lounge area in front of the stage with the tablet in his hand. I flagged him down before he got lost in the crowd.

"Hey, man. Any chance I could book a VIP slot on Sapphire's schedule?" I almost let it slip that it was for my friend but thought better of it. I didn't want Jordan to find out I'd sent someone to test her. I wasn't even supposed to care, much less crave her the way I did.

"Yeah, you get first pick. When you want in?"

"Just put it under Troy," I said, giving Trojan's legal name. "Next available is fine."

Eddie filled in the slot on the tablet, then I slipped him the bills needed to finalize the reservation.

"Don't mention it to Sapphire, if you can help it," I added. Her finding out I'd sent a friend would be the worst-case scenario; but her finding out I'd snagged a slot in the first place would raise too many question marks. "It's kind of a surprise."

"No problem. Happy to do business with you." He clapped me on the back, then strode into the lounge area where the men prowled like sharks, though he probably only saw them as dollar signs. I brought my phone out again, sending the next batch of instructions to Trojan.

SEVEN: You've got a special appointment in ten minutes. Head to the VIP room, you get a half hour with Jordan. In here, she's called Sapphire.

Trojan turned around to stare at me with one squinted eye from across the room.

TROJAN: If you guys are into threesomes, I hate to tell you, but that's not my style.

SEVEN: I'll be outside, standing guard

TROJAN: Even creepier. What the fuck?

How to explain myself as much as possible without giving away the truth? I couldn't admit that I was desperate for Jordan. Almost as desperate as I was to be rid of these feelings.

SEVEN: I just need you to see what happens in there. Ask for her special move. See if there's anything new or exciting she can show you. Push as much as you can. Offer extra money. But do not even think about touching her. I need to know something and you're going to find out for me.

I scanned the room between texts. Jordan dragged her finger along the bottom of an old man's chin, saying something I couldn't make out.

TROJAN: This is weird dude.

SEVEN: You're getting a half hour with Manhattan's best stripper. I think you'll survive.

TROJAN: You promise you won't hurt me when I come out of there?

SEVEN: Promise. Because we both know you won't enjoy it when I'm waiting out here to break your jaw if you so much as touch her.

TROJAN: So let's recap. Get lured to a strip club by my best friend, forced into a VIP room with the best stripper on the planet with the strict instructions to not enjoy it or touch her, then come out and tattle about what happened. Is that right?

SEVEN: Spot on.

TROJAN: Jesus fucking Christ, you've got it bad for this one.

I pocketed my phone without answering. I was almost entirely sure that Jordan had made up the story about trying out a new routine, even if she purportedly planned to use it only with *exclusive* customers. But for now, I just needed to test the theory and prove myself right, or I would internally combust.

His head tipped back as he downed his shot. Then he headed my way, shouldering into me on his way past.

"Oh, I'm so sorry, kind stranger, I didn't see you there."

I stifled a grin. "Move along. If you're looking for the VIP rooms, they're right over there." I tipped my head in the direction he needed to go. "The first one. Your time slot starts in two minutes."

"So gracious." The sarcasm leaked out of his words. Jordan was headed this way, which meant I didn't give him the shove he de-served. She clomped over in her sky-high heels, adjusting the strap of her bodysuit along the way. She glanced at me briefly, lifting her brows before heading for the VIP room. She greeted Trojan, then took him by the hand and led him inside.

Now all I could do was stand beside the door and watch the clock.

Time moved at a glacial pace. My stomach twisted into knots. I tried to imagine what I'd do if Trojan came out of there and told me she offered to use the vibrator with him, like she told me. *Seriously, what the fuck did you just do? Tell him to ask for the special move, but then he can't touch her if she goes there. But if she does the special move and grinds on his cock like she did with you, it doesn't matter if he gives in, because you can't move forward with her. Even though there's no* forward *to be had with Jordan. So none of this matters. This is pointless. Just give it up.*

My thoughts were folded up into origami. None of this made any fucking sense.

I tortured myself with thoughts like these until Trojan's time was up. The door swung open. Jordan's giggles reached me first, then Trojan stumbled out a moment later.

"Had a blast, thank yooou," Jordan cooed.

Her next booking had been lurking outside the VIP room for the last ten minutes at least. When Trojan cleared out, Jordan welcomed in the next guy, wiggling her fingers at him. After the door shut behind them, I whistled to snag Trojan's wandering attention and tipped my head toward the back hallway.

"Holy shit," was the first thing he said once we were stationed in front of the men's room.

"I need to know what happened."

He blinked a few times, still dazed. "Have you seen her dance before?"

"Of course."

"Holy shit. She's like...*good*." His mind was blown. "The shit she does on that pole? Dude, you could have warned me."

"I told you she's the best stripper there is. So did she rub on you?"

The question seemed to confuse him. "Wh—"

"Did you ask for the special move?"

"I did."

"So did she grind on your lap? Take your pants off? Bring out a vibrator?"

Trojan lifted his palms, laughing a little. "Whoa, man. Are you telling me all of that was supposed to be part of the package?"

I raked a hand through my hair. "It's what happened when she invited me in there last week. She claimed it was a new routine for exclusive clients, but I think it's bullshit. That's why I needed you to go test it."

"I asked for the special move like you asked. I pushed it a few times—she just kept brushing it off, saying I'd be perfectly happy with her regular routine, because it was *all* special. When I offered her extra money for a little something extra *physical*, she just laughed. She didn't even touch me."

I crossed my arms, stewing over this information. All of my vital organs unclenched. I could breathe easily now. Yet somehow, this was all so much more complicated now.

Because Jordan had lied about testing out a new move.

"To be honest, I could have gotten off without her even touching me," Trojan continued.

I pressed my forearm against his chest, backing him up against the wall. "That's enough."

A shit-eating grin spread across his face. He lifted his palms in submission. "Just doing my job, buddy. The one you sent me in there to do. *Remember?*"

I grunted, standing down. He straightened his shirt, adding, "So is this the proof you needed? You're officially in love with her. And it sounds like she's in love with you too. Great. They have another term for this, and it's *career suicide*."

I sighed, pinching the bridge of my nose. I didn't have it in me to correct him about his use of the L-word. I didn't even know what I'd say to defend myself at this point. Jordan had already consumed me; now I was roping in my friends to prove something I didn't fully want to acknowledge.

"I told you to get laid," Trojan said. "You clearly did not listen to instructions."

"I haven't had time."

"Well, I'm in town now. You'll *make* time."

I wanted to fuck someone's brains out, that much was true. But it wasn't a random girl.

"I'll be here with Jordan until at least one in the morning," I told him. "You're welcome to stay. Like I said, drinks are on me. I appreciate you doing my dirty work."

He clapped me on the shoulder. "Any time, brother."

"I'll hit you up tomorrow," I told him. "We can figure out the plan."

"I already know the plan. Rib eyes and a fuck-ton of alcohol. And then I'm getting you under some sweet little thang. I'll start crawling the dating apps now."

"Do *not* catfish some poor girl in the name of my dick," I pleaded.

"It won't be catfishing," he assured me. "I have your pretty mug on my camera roll, and I know you well enough to pose as you. I could fool your own mother."

"Not fair. She's got dementia and lives in a nursing home."

"You know what I mean."

I gave him the shove I'd been holding back, sending him on his way, then I headed back to my post outside the VIP room.

Trojan was certain that my fucking a random girl would be the solution to my problems. But I knew the truth. The only possible solutions were either getting Jordan out of my sight or getting her back into my arms, where she fucking belonged.

I knew how to fall in line, to follow commands, but when it came to Jordan, I wasn't sure how much longer I could convince both my heart and my cock to stick to the rules.

CHAPTER THIRTEEN

JORDAN

Last night's late shift transitioned into an extremely early pick-up shift at the coffee house. Both Seven and I were bleary eyed as we raced down the stairwell that morning—it was a tie. I needed extra espresso at work and even comped Seven's Earl Grey. I caught his eye too many times across the coffee shop as he worked on his laptop, curiosity burning through me.

"Admit it," Mitchell hissed in my ears as he caught me lingering by the sugar and creamer station. "You and Mr. Bodyguard are dating."

I turned, startled. Mitchell wore a haughty smirk as he dropped off a sani-bucket full of cleaning liquid.

"Don't be ridiculous." I'd been careful to dance around the topic of my having a bodyguard at the coffee shop. At Gemstones, they knew Seven as a protector type, but not here. Seven just had the vibe.

"You two show up together, leave together. You probably *live* together."

My cheeks heated up. With the rotating shifts at the coffee shop, not every coworker noticed that Seven was always lurking during my shifts. But Mitchell had been eying Seven from day one. I sure as hell wouldn't tell him—or *anyone*—what was happening under the surface. Admitting I lived with Seven now would just raise a billion follow-up questions: *He's paid to protect you? Who's paying for that? What kind of family needs to protect you from something? Protect you from what? What family did you say you're part of again?*

How could I answer? Even I didn't know what the hell was going on. I'd just had a heartwarming family dinner with my brothers a few nights ago. Seven felt like both hired protector *and* impossibly sexy best friend. Nothing made sense.

"We've been...talking." That was at least easier to admit than the tangled truth.

Mitchell gasped, his hand shooting out to grab my arm. "Shut *up!*"

"It's new," I said. "Kinda hush-hush."

"Oh my god, I won't say a *word*." He mimed zipping his lips shut and throwing away the key. "But tell me, how is the sex?"

I laughed, my cheeks flaming now. I could see Seven across the room, and his gaze—electric hot and tender—met mine. It was as if he knew what we were talking about.

"I need to get back to work," I said, suddenly feeling dizzy.

"I want *details*, missy," Mitchell said over his shoulder as he sauntered back behind the counter. "When you're ready."

I'd never be ready. Getting vulnerable with people was about the hardest thing in the world for me to do. Once my brothers fucked off to New York and then Kaylee died, I shut down more than ever. There had been too much grief and confusion for me to process back then, but the inability to open up became a habit as a result. A familiar tool—or weapon—when things got too hard.

Other girls my age, with my history, might have shared their story with anyone who would listen. They might have sought boyfriend after boyfriend to fill the void in their hearts and between their legs.

Kaylee had been that way. But my pain pushed me in the opposite direction.

I'd been chronically single since the pivotal moments in my early adulthood taught me that I was better off alone. I'd had a fucked-up childhood, but even I knew that boyfriends weren't supposed to push themselves on you or into you when you said no.

My stomach took a nosedive as familiar feelings crowded my body. Prickling forearms. Sweaty palms. A deep and insistent urge to disappear entirely. And all of this because I merely considered the idea of admitting the truth to Mitchell.

I found Seven's gaze across the coffee shop again, and this time he looked concerned. He pushed up out of his seat and crossed the room in a few powerful strides. He was at my side a moment later, neck bent to seek out my gaze.

"Are you okay?"

I tried to soothe the warring sensations inside me. Insinuating to Mitchell that I was dating had catalyzed this chain reaction. Even lying about having a boyfriend was too much for me.

But Seven's presence at my side was the balm to soothe the turmoil.

"You looked like you were going to fall over," Seven said.

"I'm fine," I forced out, my lips dry. "I, uh..." I brought a hand to my forehead, rubbing my fingertips back and forth.

"Did he say something to you?"

I swallowed hard, opening my mouth but no sound coming out.

"Do I need to go have a talk with him?" His voice held an edge that suggested exactly what "a talk" might mean.

I laughed weakly. "No. He's fine. It was innocent. It just...sparked something in me that I...struggle with."

The words clattered inside my head. Why didn't I write it off as something else? Being too tired? Working too late the night before? I looked up and found Seven's gaze. The tenderness there nearly cracked me in two.

"You need anything?" He squeezed my arm gently, heat spreading through me. It might as well have been a hug for how intimate it felt.

"I'm fine." Emotion swelled inside me like a tidal wave, and my chin trembled as I tried to shove all the feelings back down. Seven must have seen right through it because he gripped my chin between his thumb and forefinger.

"You need to go have a good cry in the corner?"

The suggestion prompted a big burst of laughter, which helped my insides stabilize a little. The corner of his mouth turned up.

"I'll be fine. I promise." I took a deep breath, turning to the sani-bucket. "They should call you Mother Hen instead of Seven."

"Who are 'they'?" he asked, a genuine smile covering his face. It stunned me in the way sudden sunlight during a thunderstorm can stop someone in their tracks. My heart plummeted to my feet, tingles swarming my limbs.

"You know, anyone who has to refer to you," I teased.

"Be sure to put out a memo." He laughed as he said it. I tried not to sigh and stare dreamily as he retreated. Mitchell leaned across the counter near the registers, sending me a dramatically loud *Psst*.

"Just talking, am I right?" He sent me a stage wink.

If me humping Seven in the VIP room made things murky and strange, then his offer to let me cry with him in a corner was something of a balance.

I didn't want to fuck things up again, but the more emotionally open I was with him, the more desperate I was to see his cock. There was a distinct correlation. Who was I to challenge it?

When we returned to his apartment after my coffee shop shift that afternoon, we each went our separate ways. I took a quick nap in my room, and when I emerged just before dinnertime, Seven rushed around the kitchen like he was in a hurry.

I had to blink a few times, unsure if I was really seeing things correctly.

He wasn't in his standard attire. He wore charcoal gray slacks, which fit in such a way that looked like he planned to attend a men's fashion show, paired with a white, short sleeve polo that hugged his pecs and strained to encompass his biceps. I could only stare as he pulled out a pre-mixed protein shake and took a quick chug.

"What are you doing?" I asked, without even realizing.

He turned to look at me, wiping his mouth with the back of his hand. He placed the shake back in the fridge and then cleared his throat. "Just getting ready."

"*Getting* ready?" I challenged. "I thought you'd been brought into the world that way."

He didn't take the bait, another sign something was off.

"I mean…this." I gestured to his outfit as I drifted toward the kitchen island. He was wearing different clothes for God's sake. When I got closer, I caught a faint whiff of his manly cologne. All I wanted to do was wrap my arms around his chest and settle into the warmth there. My knees nearly buckled.

"My clothes?" His brow arched. "I have plans tonight."

My brows drew together and confusion settled on top of me like a storm cloud descends before a tornado. "What?"

"Yeah. I do things on occasion, Jordan. It may surprise you, but I do have a life." He flashed a humorless smile. "I have a different protection officer coming over to fill in for tonight. He'll be here shortly so you can get to know him a little before I leave."

Everything that he'd just said felt like steel wool against my skin. Different officer? Plans tonight? No and no.

"Were you planning on informing me of any of this?" I spat out. The way my heart thudded against my ribcage told me my reaction was on the dramatic side.

"I'm informing you now," he said coolly.

I tried to think of some good reason why his plan didn't—couldn't—work, but I came up with nothing. He was allowed to do things away from me. I just hated that it bothered me so much. *Why does this bother you? Aren't you supposed to be moving out and moving on from Seven and your brothers? This is what you want!*

Except it wasn't what I wanted. Because as a knock sounded on the door and Seven said, "There he is now," I realized what was *actually* bothering me.

Seven was going on a date.

He was going out to meet a woman, and I couldn't fucking stand the idea.

My brain whirred so loudly I barely noticed when Seven opened the door and warmly greeted the *replacement*. I missed his name entirely, finally remembering to yank myself back to the present when a tall, youngish-looking guy was suddenly in front of me, offering me his hand.

"I'm Chico. Nice to meet you, Jordan."

I blinked at his hand, and then took it quickly. With almost jet back hair, longish and parted on the side, he looked like Seven's younger, unrefined brother. Hardly the type to yank someone like Dustin off me during an attack at three a.m.

"So you're the replacement?" I asked.

Chico laughed softly, shoving his hands into his pockets. "I am. I'm looking forward to working with you."

"What are your qualifications?" I snapped.

"He's been vetted," Seven interjected, stepping forward. Next to Chico, Seven loomed. Chico was probably six feet tall or close, but next to Seven's bulky girth and massive biceps, he looked like a teenager.

"Four years active duty, army," Chico said, undeterred. "Two years reserve, four years working in the personal protection business in the Maryland area. I can provide a list of former clients if interested."

"Do you have a gun on you?" I crossed my arms.

"No, ma'am," Chico replied.

"I asked him not to pack," Seven offered. "Here in the apartment, for my quick night out, you two will be fine. Besides, he'll be briefed on the necessary information, in the event that an emergency response is required."

I had no more hard-hitting questions to ask Chico that wouldn't reveal the jealous rift in my heart growing larger by the second. So instead, I turned my attention to Seven. "Where are you going?"

"Out."

I sniffed. "What does that mean?"

"It means I'm going out, Jordan. I'm having dinner with someone." He sent me a warning look, then shifted his gaze to Chico, tipping his head to the side. "Chico, come with me. I'll show you around."

Someone. Code for *another woman,* no doubt. I glared at Seven's back as he led Chico toward the hallway. Seven was perfectly within his rights to take a night off or go do something away from me. But with another woman? I swallowed the bitter tang of jealousy. I needed a game plan—I just didn't know what it would be.

I made myself a quick sandwich while Chico and Seven had their little talk in the back.

When they emerged, Seven was peering at his watch. "All right, I better head out." My stomach twisted. "You two take it easy. Order in if you want. Usually this is a rest day for her anyway after the club shifts all weekend."

I frowned. Him explaining my schedule to this man-child—who was probably close to my own age but still, I refused to see Chico as anything other than a boy right now—grated on me.

"Sounds good. I think we can take it from here," Chico said confidently.

"Awesome. I'll see you guys later." Seven sent a quick smile toward Chico and reached for a khaki sport coat that he'd draped over the back of the armchair. He slipped it on as he strode to the door, pausing on his way to lean toward me and say, "I need you to behave."

I whipped around to stare him in the eye. "What could that possibly mean?"

"Just be nice," he said in a low voice. "Don't scare the talent away."

He bridged the remaining distance to the door, and I followed him. "*The talent*? I don't understand what you're talking about. Are you starting a business or something?"

He sent me a stern look and pulled open the door, walking through without answering my damn question. "Be good." When the door thudded shut behind him, I expelled a sigh. This felt wrong, and I hated that I couldn't fully explain *why*.

All I knew was that it violated the strange code of conduct Seven and I had established.

"So he's your boss, huh?" I asked Chico, resuming my previous task in the kitchen: eating my damn sandwich. Except now it was flavorless and dull. I wanted to be anywhere other than here right now.

"Sure is." He came to the island, an easygoing grin on his face. "I'm still in the trial period with him, but I hope to be full-time by the end of it."

Full-time? Doing what? I bit angrily into my sandwich, trying to piece together what was unfolding in front of me without looking like the ignoramus left in the dark. Because that's what I clearly was—left behind. Out of the loop. The only one who didn't fucking know what was going on.

"How long does the trial period last?" I asked as casually as I could muster.

"Until it's clear if I'm a good fit to work with him."

There was even more I didn't know. This wasn't a one-off replacement guard who I'd meet once and never see again. This was a whole organized *effort*. How could Seven keep this from me?

Not only was I jealous that he was going out on a date with some unknown woman who was probably desperate to spread her legs for him—because who wouldn't be?—now I was also hurt because Seven had been keeping his whole entire life from me—including some mysterious expansion that he needed a second guard for.

And here I was, the idiot opening up to him. Sharing my heart with him, wanting to get closer. The hurt lashed so deeply that I almost couldn't see straight. I focused on eating my sandwich for a few moments, trying to calm the inner storm.

"So do you know where Seven's heading tonight?" I tried to sound relaxed, but I suspected even the new guy could hear the strain in my voice.

"He didn't say exactly where," Chico said diplomatically. "But if we need him for anything, I'm sure we'll be able to get ahold of him."

"Hm." I took another bite, my mind working overtime. It was Sunday—not exactly prime date night, but in a city that never slept, any day was as good as another for dating.

My mind raced as I pieced together a plan. Seven wouldn't tell me his whereabouts, and neither would Chico. But I bet someone else would.

And once I found out where that place was, well, it seemed like the perfect night for a date of my own.

"It's kind of silly for someone with such extensive training as yourself to be stuck *babysitting*, don't you think?" I glanced up at Chico, drawing invisible patterns over the countertop with my finger. "I mean, that's pretty much what this is. You're just being my babysitter tonight."

"Well, I'd call it more than babysitting." He offered a warm smile. "You're an important person who needs protected."

"Sure." I gnawed on the inside of my lip as I weighed my next words. "But what if we...I don't know...did something?"

Chico's brows drew together. "Like what?"

"Well, it's my off night, and I usually don't do much, but after the nap I had, I'm going stir-crazy." My heart thumped as I wondered if he'd see through my plan.

He shrugged. "Whatever you want. I'm here to make sure you're safe, whatever it is that you need to do."

I flashed him a pretty smile. "Love to hear it, Chico. You're rapidly becoming my favorite guy around here. And so cute, too. Let me go get ready and we can head out, 'kay?"

I could have sworn a little blush stained his cheeks as I winked at him. I knew how to work the crowd so he wouldn't suspect what this was *really* about.

I drifted off to my bedroom, ready to enact the next pieces of my plan. I started with a quick text to Roxie: *Girl are you up for an impromptu girls night? I have a plan and I need help...*

Then, I tapped the resource I knew would be most willing to help me: my brothers.

I was aware of how underhanded this seemed. I didn't want to play the *I'm you're wittle sister* card, but I needed this intel about Seven more than I needed air. If anybody could squeeze the needed info out of Seven, it was his fucking employers.

I shot off a quick text to Damian:

JORDAN: Hey, random Q, but...is there any way you could reach out to Seven and ask him where he's at tonight? He's on a much-deserved night off and I want to send him a little surprise as a thank you. But he can't know I'm asking!!! I just need the address. Can you help me??

Damian didn't know my surprise would be me, in a skintight little black dress, ready to crash whatever date Seven thought he was going on.

Damian's response was lightning fast: *On it, little sis. Hang tight.*

Roxie's response came next: *Girl I was just wanting to text you about going out but thought better of it because it's Sunday LOL. Where we going and what's the scoop?*

Everything was falling into place.

Everything except the biggest piece of the puzzle: the irrepressible truth of my attraction to Seven.

CHAPTER FOURTEEN

JORDAN

Skintight, seductive, little black dress: check.

Tits galore: check.

Smooth legs, tantalizing perfume, soft curls halfway down my back: check, check, check.

I could tell Chico had no idea what he'd gotten himself into as we hailed the taxi and crossed town to the address in Union Square. His eyes roamed the length of my legs a time or two. When he reached for his phone, I touched his wrist.

"Hey. Who are you going to call?"

"Nobody." He paused. "I just wanted to check in."

"No need for that. We're perfectly fine, and Seven needs a night off. We should let the man enjoy his time. He needs a break from my presence, *trust me.*"

Chico nodded and slipped his phone back in his pocket. *Crisis averted.* The longer this went on, the more underhanded I felt. But jealousy was a powerful motivator. I hadn't felt this bratty and determined in...eons. Possibly ever.

All I could focus on was finding out whether he was meeting up with a woman. Possibly he'd had a girlfriend this entire time. Or maybe this was a dating app hook-up. Not knowing killed me. He was mine, even if he didn't know it. The thought shuddered through me, but it felt true. He'd grabbed my chin and offered to let me cry with him in a corner earlier that day. He'd even rescued my rescue cat. How could he be meeting up with another woman after all that?

I pulled my leather jacket tighter. Was I sending myself straight into a tangled mess? Both Seven and Chico would discover my scheming as soon as we arrived. But it didn't matter. I'd find a way to play it off.

We pulled up to The Chop, a steakhouse whose entrance looked weirdly similar to that of Gemstones with neon lights announcing the name and the formal awning over the door. Roxie waited for me outside, hopping from spiked heel to spiked heel in the chilly night air.

"There you are!" She held out her arms for a hug as I climbed out of the back of the taxi. She wore a tight-fitting red dress and big, golden hoops. I squealed as we hugged, her perfume mixing with the scent of cooking meat wafting from the restaurant. "This place looks nice. We thinkin' cocktails or—"

She trailed off as Chico appeared at my side.

"Why hello," she murmured, her gaze dragging up and down his body.

Chico stuck out a hand. "Nice to meet you..."

"Roxie," I supplied for him. "Roxie, meet Chico. He's just hanging around to make sure we don't get in too much trouble." I flashed him a pretty grin. "I work with Roxie and she's one of the good ones, so we gotta keep an eye on her, all right?"

"It's my pleasure," Chico said.

Roxie giggled, swatting at his arm. "I like this one more than the last one."

I rolled my eyes, linking my arm through hers. "Come on. Let's go in." I leaned in closer, my voice dropping to a whisper. "I think Seven is here on a date. I just came to spy."

Roxie giggled again, squeezing my arm linked through hers. "Are we detectives tonight?"

"Something like that. But this man offers up nothing about his personal life. So I decided to see for myself."

We pushed in through the main doors, taking a moment to acclimate to the moody red walls, dark wood floors and the cacophony of conversation and clinking glasses. Tables lined one side of the restaurant, and a long bar stretched along the other side. I could see a different seating area toward the back, but it seemed almost all the tables were spoken for. A hostess looked at me with a polite smile.

"Will this be for three?"

I scanned the area as quickly as I could, trying to spot Seven before he spotted me. If he was even here. I was just about to ask the hostess if we could grab a table so I could prowl the back of the restaurant—and then I spotted him.

The charcoal slacks, the white polo shirt I was dying to peel off him, the immaculately clipped dark hair that faded down into his cut jawline. I clenched my thighs together just imagining the way his attention would alight on me, the intensity of his dark gaze. I was suddenly so thirsty for it my tongue was dry. He was the only man who could look at me and both quench me *and* set me on fire.

Seven sat in one of the last seats at the bar before it curved around, obscured by some other patrons between him and the front of the restaurant. I couldn't see who was at his side, but I was so excited I blurted, "The bar. We just want the bar."

The hostess gestured sweetly to her side. "Go ahead, wherever you'd like is fine."

I thanked her and chose the closest set of seats to Seven and his date. Three customers separated us. My entire body vibrated with excitement as I slipped off my leather jacket and slung it over the back of my bar seat.

"God, this place looks nice," Roxie gushed as she plopped her tiny butt into the seat. "I've lived here for ten years and every day there's a new place to discover. I'm kinda thinking an app, what about you?"

Roxie was a transplant like me, but from Illinois rather than Kentucky.

"Oh, hell yeah." My gaze was stuck on the end of the bar. The seat to the right of Seven was empty—but featured a half-empty beer and wrapped silverware. *He's here with someone.* "You pick it and I'll share with you, sound good?"

"You think Chico wants something?" She leaned in closer to ask.

I shrugged, tipping myself closer to her so she could tell I was listening even though my gaze was fastened on the empty seat next to Seven. "Ask him. He's probably hungry."

A tall brute of a man appeared at the end of the bar, and I could almost hear the undertones of their conversation as he rejoined Seven in the empty seat. An easygoing conversation erupted, featuring genuine smiles from Seven and almost instantaneous laughter. The familiarity between them was striking—and extremely platonic. My heart beat a little easier as I realized this was probably Seven's friend.

He's just a friend, Jordan. He has friends.

I studied the man, something about his beard tipping me off. He seemed familiar, though I couldn't say why. His blue patterned flannel shirt sleeves were rolled up the forearm.

Seven's friend rubbed at the back of his neck, triggering my memory. I'd danced for him in the VIP room the other night. He'd pushed me about a special move while rubbing his neck in exactly the same way.

I stared at the menu in front of me, my vision going blurry as I mulled over this information.

"What's wrong?" Roxie nudged me. "Can't decide what to eat?"

I leaned close to her, keeping my voice a low whisper. "I'm just now realizing that Seven is here with someone I entertained in the VIP room the other night."

"Oh." Her mouth turned downward. "Are they friends?"

"I assume so, I mean they're having dinner together."

"So your bodyguard bought his friend a slot with you in the VIP room..." she trailed off, narrowing her eyes.

"Is this a nice gesture, or is it...something else?" I asked. Roxie didn't know that I'd all but fucked Seven in the VIP room a few days before that. I still didn't want anybody to know that I had *feelings* for my bodyguard, or that I'd coaxed him to cross that line at my workplace.

"Maybe he's just trying to show his friend a good time," she said with a dazzling grin. "You are the best, after all."

Bless her—she was trying to be helpful.

But this friend of Seven's had offered extra money if I'd do some physical stuff. It stuck out to me only because most of my customers knew better to ask for that. Or if they tried, it was quick, not persistent, like this guy had been. He'd asked like he knew a secret.

Seven had probably told him to come.

Because Seven knew what happened between us in the VIP room days before.

That left a couple different options: that Seven was sending me a prospective client for my fake new 'side gig'...or he thought that since he got something in the VIP room, that his friend could too.

That last option sank like the Titanic to the bottom of my guts. I pressed a finger to my forehead, suddenly feeling dizzy and sick. Any relief I felt at discovering Seven wasn't actually about to fuck some nameless blonde was replaced with humiliation and anxiety. Seven wasn't trying to pass me around to his friends...was he?

The bartender showed up, asking for drink orders. I interrupted Roxie mid-sentence to say, "Three shots of tequila, please."

"I can't drink right now," Chico reminded me.

"The extra's for me," I told him.

Roxie's brows shot up. "Oooh, tequila sounds great. Can we try the crabcake appetizer, too?" She slid the menu toward the bartender.

He collected all our menus and nodded. "Coming right up."

My skin prickled suddenly, an electricity gathering in my veins. I glanced over to see Seven coming our way—brows set, jaw flexing, looking neutral yet lethal. Desire fluttered through me, even though this was *not* the time. He approached Chico from behind, leaning to say something in his ear. Then he returned where he'd come from—walking right past me, not even sparing me a glance. Chico nearly tumbled off his seat in his haste to scamper behind him.

"Uh oh," Roxie said, leaning back in her seat to watch them depart, just as I was doing. "Your boyfriend doesn't look happy. Which one is your boyfriend again?"

"Neither of them."

"The answer could have been *both*, you know." She snorted, then her face grew serious. "Chico looks like he's getting in trouble. Well, I think our spy mission officially failed. Aren't you supposed to stay hidden as a spy?"

"Yeah, it turns out I'm not a really good spy." I exhaled, realizing I'd stepped right into more shit than I'd anticipated. I didn't know what I'd been expecting anyway—show up to his date and plop myself on Seven's lap, claiming him as my own? Pushing away his Tinder hook-up and threatening her with legal action? This was all so stupid. And in my quest to claim Seven as my own, I'd stumbled upon the most unnerving possibility as all: he saw me as just a stripper to pass around to friends.

Fuck, I needed that tequila.

"I fucked up," I muttered, my head dropping into my hands.

"Honey, it's okay. I've fucked up a time or two as well. I won't even tell you about the guy I dated who made me believe he was a French millionaire, but really was pulling an Anna Delvey. We're here, we'll have some crabcakes and get drunk. Sounds like a good night out if you ask me." When I didn't seem to be soothed, Roxie added, "Besides, we do crazy things when men look like *that*." She tipped her head toward the end of the bar. "I've seen the way he looks at you. I thought there was something there."

I perked up a little. "You did?"

"Yeah. I know he's like, making sure you're safe and all, but I dunno." She shrugged, toying with a lock of her platinum blonde hair. "Seems like he's got the hots for you too."

At the far end of the restaurant, Chico and Seven were locked in a tense conversation. Chico nodded on occasion, frowning.

"I think Chico might be getting fired because of me," I whispered, just as the bartender returned with our shots. Guilt cascaded through me.

"I'm sure we could convince him to reconsider."

"You don't know Seven like I do."

"But two pairs of tits are better than one," she said optimistically.

All I could do was laugh. Roxie had a way of easing life's stressors. I'd seen her do it with all the girls at the club. I squeezed her arm, sending her a warm smile. She made me think it might be okay to open up sometimes.

"You're really great, you know that?"

"Cheers to that," Roxie said. We clinked our shot glasses carefully, then tipped the tequila down our throats. Faces puckered, we both grabbed a lime slice on the plate left by the bartender.

"That was smooth," she said with a cough.

"Mm-hmm." I looked toward the end of the bar. Seven sliced a hand through the air, his jaw flexing. He and Chico exchanged a few more words, then Chico returned, looking perplexed. He slid onto the bar seat wordlessly.

"Everything okay?" I asked.

Chico expelled a sigh. "Sure hope so."

I rolled my lips in, determined not to let Chico take the fall for this. This was 100 percent my fault—my diabolical plan, my unexpected unraveling. I could practically imagine what Seven had told his friend:

Ask for the special move; she'll hump your dick and almost fuck you.

I reached for the second shot, offering to split it with Roxie, who declined. I took the whole shot, enjoying the warmth and buzz.

It wasn't long before the tipsiness took over. When the group of people sitting between me and Seven stood to leave, I seized my opportunity. I tapped Roxie's arm, tipping my head toward the end of the bar. She followed me when I shifted seats, leaving no chairs between me and Seven. Chico looked like he hated the idea almost as much as Seven did.

I gasped, bringing my hand to my chest in mock surprise. "*Seven?*" The tequila had bitch-slapped me now. I was equal parts drunk, hurt, and confused. I already knew this wouldn't end well. "I can't believe you're here! What a surprise!"

His friend's gaze slid between me and Seven's stony face. Seven's jaw flexed as he stared at the beer in front of him.

"And you brought a friend?" I stuck my hand out, right through Seven's field of vision. "I'm Jordan. You look so familiar though—haven't we met before?"

His friend shifted uncomfortably as he shook my hand. "I'm Trojan. Nice to see you again, Jordan."

"Ah!" I snapped my fingers, glancing at Seven. I estimated he was seething by now, but I couldn't stop this train. "You called yourself Troy. We had such a fun time in the VIP room, didn't we?"

Trojan coughed as he sipped at his beer, then he nodded. "Yep. Fun time."

I turned myself fully toward Seven. He dragged his gaze over to me, the fire in his eyes a warning. "That was so nice of you to buy a VIP room session for your friend," I said pointedly. "I bet you two always share things between each other, huh? Like just trading back and forth."

Trojan cleared his throat, signaling the bartender.

Roxie pinched my elbow. "Hey, the crabcakes are here. Eat 'em before I eat 'em all."

I turned away from Seven and toward the plate, heart hammering, palms hot. There was no way I could eat. I was too worked up. That damn tequila knew how to get into my head. Trojan's discomfort at Seven's side was all the proof I needed.

Roxie elbowed me.

"You should eat something," she said in a quieter voice. "You just took two top-shelf tequila shots back-to-back. And I don't know if you've seen yourself, but you're not the size of a football player. Come on."

I drew a deep breath through my nostrils, grabbing the fork Roxie offered me. I scooped the crabcake bite into my mouth, chewed, swallowed. It was food. That was all I could register. Two seats down, Chico rubbed at his face like he was desperate to teleport out of there. Poor kid. I'd ruined his chance to make a good first impression, but his sacrifice had been necessary.

I'd gotten what I wanted. I knew more about Seven. But I didn't like the new clues I'd found.

"Eat more," Roxie encouraged. I took another bite to placate her, dabbing at my mouth with the napkin. A bit of my burgundy lipstick showed on the white cloth, and I placed it neatly on the bar.

"You two are awfully quiet down there," I spoke up after a moment. My attempt at a lighthearted smile evaporated almost as quickly as it had arrived. "Don't let us kill the buzz."

Trojan rubbed at the back of his neck. He was just about to say something when Seven lifted his palm, silencing his friend.

Back to square one.

I huffed, sliding out of my seat. "I'm going to the bathroom," I muttered to Roxie. "I need to get my head straight." She nodded, offering me a hopeful smile.

I stormed off, followed the restroom signs down a winding back hallway. I needed to breathe through these emotions pushing me to the edge of a cliff I didn't want to tumble over. I was almost lost by the time the restrooms came into view. I burst into the dimly lit ladies room and pushed my palms against the granite countertop, drawing deep, cleansing breaths.

Tears threatened to join the pity party, but I forced them away. I would not cry over Seven. No fucking way. He couldn't even be bothered to speak to me out there, to clear the air. I gritted my teeth, letting the anger roll through me again. And again. And again. I stoked the flames only to calm myself down over and over. I did this through multiple rounds of customers using the restroom, washing their hands, and leaving. I had no idea how long I stayed there, only that I fucking needed it.

When I could finally draw a deep breath without wanting to scream curse words, I knew I was ready to rejoin the world. I strode confidently out of the bathroom, my head held high. A hand grabbed my wrist on my second step out of the restroom, yanking me to the side. I gasped, spinning like a ballroom dancer over the carpeted floor until my back was up against the wall.

Seven caged me in, his neck bent to bring our faces closer together, his bulging biceps blocking me at both sides.

"What the fuck are you doing here?" he growled.

I swallowed hard, searching his handsome face. He was so angry. But the mere sight of him calmed the desperate, raucous parts inside me. Looking at him felt *right*.

"I thought you were on a date," I admitted. His jaw flexed, the manly weight of his cologne settling around me like the most pleasant sweater.

This answer seemed to throw him off. He blinked a few times before he said, "Why did you come here if you thought I was on a date?"

I shrugged, unable to admit anything else. Especially after what I knew about him now. "I was curious about who she was. But I found out exactly what I needed to know."

"And what the fuck do you think that is?" The edge returned to his voice.

Hurt lashed through me. I studied the swirl pattern on the carpet, unsure how much I should let him know. "You tried to whore me out to your friend."

My voice broke on the last word and I covered my mouth with my hand, willing the emotion to stay inside. I drew a deep breath, forcing myself to plow ahead. I peeked up at him, finding real confusion wrought across his face.

"Do you know how degrading that is?" I asked, my voice pinched. I had mere seconds before I completely unraveled in front of him. Then he'd see that I'd actually developed feelings for him. I felt stupid enough around him—this was just the final nail in the coffin.

I tried to push past him but he didn't let me by. Instead, he took my chin between his thumb and forefinger, directing my gaze to him.

All of the anger had dissolved from his face. Now he looked torn. Distraught, even.

"You thought I was whoring you out to Trojan?" he repeated softly. I nodded, feeling my chin tremble under his thumb. He pressed harder, tenderness flooding his face.

"Jordan." He said it so softly I thought I imagined it. A tear escaped, rolling down my cheek, and he wiped it away with his thumb.

"I'm a little drunk," I admitted.

"I wasn't whoring you out. I was gathering information. I'm sorry if it seemed—" He stopped, his throat bobbing. He drew a breath. "I'm sorry if it seemed that way. But I needed to find out if you were telling the truth about...what happened in the VIP room."

I sniffed, searching his face as he spoke. Every word out of his mouth landed like a burst of aloe after the worst sunburn. Cool and refreshing, a godsend.

"I didn't think that you were testing a new routine like you said," he went on. "So I sent Trojan to test my theory. I never thought..." He shook his head, his gaze dropping to the floor. "I never thought you'd piece it together like you did. But I can see how, with you showing up here, recognizing Trojan..."

"I don't do that stuff for anyone," I admitted in a small voice. "Ever. I never have, and I never will. But... I couldn't help myself with you. I just made up the side gig story. I was trying to cover my tracks, because..." I couldn't say the rest. That I was falling for him. That I wanted so much more than I'd ever wanted from anybody else.

The corner of his mouth curled up. The warmth in his eyes sucked me in, and I was a goner. This, right here? This moment was what I lived for—Seven seeing me, wanting me, appreciating me. My body arched toward him, needing contact.

"So if you thought I was out with a woman... you showed up because you were jealous."

I pouted a little as the smug smile stretched wider across his face. "I just needed to know who you'd pick to date."

"You little brat." He said it triumphantly, like he was deeply pleased now that all the pieces had clicked together. "Well you can rest easy. I don't date."

My insides vibrated with need now. Being this close to him after reaching such highs and lows of vulnerability, I needed him to touch me. Kiss me. Fuck me. *Something.*

"Fine. You don't date." I huffed. "But I know you can kiss."

His gaze turned dark—almost predatory. "Are you asking me to kiss you?"

"You're off the clock." I reached for his chest, my fingers tripping over the contours of his chest through the soft polo shirt. I fisted the shirt, jerking him closer. "I haven't been able to stop thinking about those kisses in the VIP room, Seven. Please."

The cocktail of expressions that crossed his face fascinated me. His heated gaze dragged down my body, then back up to my face.

"You make it hard to say no when you're dressed like this." His other arm left the wall, sliding around my waist. Soon, the space between our bodies evaporated. I was flush against his rock-hard body. Every inch of me sighed with relief, but I wanted more. So much more.

"Then don't say no." I sought his lips, but he dipped his head away.

"You know I'm supposed to," he murmured.

"I don't care." I wriggled against him, squeezing my arms around his torso. I never wanted to leave this spot. I'd go to my grave cuddling with Seven at the back of this restaurant. He was worth it. "Don't you feel the same way?"

His gaze grew darker, hungrier. "You have no fucking idea."

"Then put us both out of our misery."

He cupped the side of my face with his hand, a rough, warm palm sliding over my cheek and around the back of my head. Every inch of my body ignited with pinpricks as he dipped down, claiming my lips with his own. A kiss so hungry, so needy, emerged that I almost choked on the passion. His mouth crashed against mine, our tongues seeking, teeth bumping, small noises emerging as we feasted on each other's kisses. Seven brought his other hand up, cradling my face, our kisses finding a sensual, desperate rhythm.

A rhythm that, if we were anywhere else, would send our clothes flying in mere moments.

His cock stiffened against my belly. I squeezed my arms tighter around his waist, rocking my hips in a slow circle against him. I was powerless to resist while he tongue-fucked me like this. I needed this and so much more. The chemistry between us threatened to level the whole building.

"Oh my God, Seven," I moaned between kisses, clawing at his low back. "Please. More. I need more."

He paused, smiling against my lips. The bathroom door creaked open further down the hall, causing him to jerk his head in that direction.

"Fuck, Jordan." He drew a deep breath, shaking his head. "Okay. That's enough." The man looked positively drugged, his gaze stuck on my lips. I could see him second-guessing himself.

"Is it?" I asked with a small laugh. "I thought we were just getting started."

"Don't even tempt me," he growled, his hands dropping to my waist, sliding down over my ass cheeks. He squeezed hard, eliciting a gasp. "That's not how this shit works."

"Then educate me"—I smoothed my hands along the collar of his shirt—"about how this shit works exactly."

He met my gaze, his eyes hooded. "You go back to your friend, and I go back to mine. You have your girls night. I have my guys night. And then you go back to the apartment with Chico when you're done."

When I started to protest, he interrupted me, pressing a finger to my lips. "This is how it has to go. I'm not going to show my ass to my new guy on day one, and you're not going to send me these pouty looks across the bar that have me ready to haul your ass over my shoulder and take you home myself."

I bit back a laugh. "I don't mind that last part of the plan."

"Jordan." He leveled me with a look. "Promise me."

I pouted, and he grunted.

"Not that look," he warned.

"Do I get more kisses tomorrow?" I asked hopefully.

He sighed, his jaw flexing. "That's something we have to talk about tomorrow."

It didn't seem entirely positive, but I didn't care. I knew the most important parts, which were that he fucking *wanted me too*, and he hadn't been whoring me out to his friend.

The rest of the details could come later.

"Fine," I whispered. "But you should stop by the bathroom first if you don't want to show your ass like you said. I left my mark, which is how I roll." I winked, enjoying the smear of lipstick across his lips one last time before I strutted down the hallway.

The last thing I heard him say before I turned the corner was, "Brat."

CHAPTER FIFTEEN

SEVEN

The buzzing of my phone on my nightstand was the first thing to bring me out of a catatonic state.

The splitting headache was the next.

I groaned, launching an arm toward my phone. I groped blindly until I connected with it and silenced it. I glimpsed the time as I did: *9:38 a.m.*

This was the latest I'd slept in years. Possibly a decade. All thanks to my good buddy Trojan and his arsenal of alcohol.

I rolled onto my side and sighed. I'd been awake for four seconds and already felt like warmed-over garbage. *Goddamn you, Trojan.*

When I rejected his offer to meet up with the sexy brunette he'd catfished for me, he'd turned to shots as a way to punish me. *We haven't drunk like this in years,* he insisted while dumping rum down my throat. There was a reason I hadn't drunk like that in years. Because the next day fucking sucked.

Trojan's stance was clear: starting shit with your client's little sister—and the person I was protecting—was a bad move. But he'd seen firsthand how enmeshed I was. I couldn't even lie and say I was upset that she showed up. Seeing her body packed into that skimpy black dress paired with her trademark leather jacket—eyes only for me—had more of an effect than I wanted to admit as a seasoned professional. If she'd been anyone else, I'd have been after her from the second she walked in the door.

But of course it had to be complicated. Trojan insisted I still needed to get laid—which was true. I needed to get laid four weeks ago. But I didn't need some unknown pussy and bland personality.

I fucking needed Jordan. In my arms. Wrapped around my cock. Lips locked to mine.

And I had no idea how to move forward from here. I'd slipped up twice with her. I couldn't let it happen a third time.

I hauled myself out of bed, needing something—anything—to dull the consequences of my night out with Trojan. I stumbled out of my bedroom, squinting against the sunlight flooding the apartment. The scent of eggs and bacon was the first thing I noticed, making my stomach turn. Not a good sign. Jordan turned to look at me from the stove, her eyes going wide.

"Warn a girl next time, why don't you?"

I squinted at her, stumbling toward the cabinet. "What?"

"You're...basically nude." She waved a spatula in my direction. "Jesus, Seven. You're just asking for it, looking like that..."

I ignored her as I rummaged through the medicine cabinet. I was wearing boxer briefs and nothing else. Big deal. Still, her gaze washed over me like molasses.

"Do you want some food?"

I grunted.

"How about a hydration drink?"

I nodded, struggling to open the ibuprofen. I couldn't make the cap come off in my disoriented state. Jordan was at my side a moment later, prying the bottle from my hands.

"Let me help you, Oh Drunk One." The lid popped off and she portioned out a dosage for me. Then she filled a glass of water for me. I swallowed the pills in a big gulp.

"Thanks," I rasped out.

"You should go back to bed." She flicked off the burner and grabbed my upper arms, navigating me toward my bedroom. "I'll get you all tucked in and then bring you some goodies."

I could only respond on the inside. Externally, I was unable to do anything but put one foot in front of the other. In my bedroom, I tumbled back into bed. Everything inside me hurt. Jordan went around tidying up: picking up my strewn clothes from the night before and slinging them over the back of a chair, plugging in my cellphone, and bringing me a Gatorade and more painkillers for later.

"All right, Seven. I think you're all set." She booped me on the nose before she left. I could only smile on the inside until my eyes closed and I drifted back to sleep.

When I awoke again, I could tell it was much later. This time, my phone read noon. When I tried to move, there was less screaming from my internal organs. I chugged the Gatorade, then swung my legs over the side of the bed. Progress. I rubbed my eyes, stood up, and pulled on some sweatpants.

The first time in my adult history that I'd skipped an early morning working during the week, and I had Trojan to thank. My phone screen showed plenty of missed texts from that lovable fucker, including a couple of missed calls. He had to know what he'd caused. The last text he sent simply said: *Alcohol poisoning or nah?*

I wrote back: *You tried your best but failed again. I'm alive.*

I pocketed the phone and headed to the bathroom to take a piss. Out in the living room, Jordan was in the kitchen again, now working on lunch. This time, I could absorb more details, like her messy bun and the wispy, sparkling strand of hair that had escaped next to her face. The simple black sports bra and boy short bottoms she wore told me she'd likely been practicing at the pole. Her little bare feet were adorable, toenails colored cerulean. Her luscious tops of her breasts in her skimpy lounge bra begged me to bury my face there, but instead I just lifted my fingers at her in a salute. *This is how it has to be.*

She looked delighted as I came into the kitchen. "Well, look at you! Wearing pants, like a real, live human."

"Humans can just wear underwear."

"Not when they're built like a Greek god."

I smirked, heading for the kettle. "That's sweet of you. Can I use that quote on my professional page?"

She laughed, knocking her hip into mine as I filled the kettle. "You feeling better?"

"1000%. Trojan almost fucking killed me last night."

"Sounds like a good friend." She offered wry smile. "I didn't even hear you when you came home. And I was up pretty late."

"I don't even remember coming home," I admitted. "I know Legs drove me, because he's the last outgoing call in my phone."

"You finally ready to eat?" She washed her hands in the sink, jerking her head toward the stove.

"Inherently prepared from the first day of life."

She smirked. "You must be feeling better. I made some paninis. But I also saved the breakfast burrito I made earlier. Your pick."

"Ooh. Panini sounds good."

She sent me a sexy smile as she brushed past me, knocking me with her hip again. "Why do you have to make it sound so seductive?"

"Panini is not a seductive word."

"You could say anything in your just-woke-up voice and it's seductive, okay?"

I reached for a teabag from the cabinet. "So I'm a Greek god and I've got a seductive voice. Anything else you'd like to share to boost my ego?"

"You're the best kisser I've ever met."

I fought a smile as I ripped open the tea bag and placed it in an empty mug. "Thanks. Ego officially inflated."

"Would you say it's at about a seven right now?" She looked at me expectantly.

"Higher."

"Then you're going to need to apply for a legal name change. I should have known—your name is referencing your ego, isn't it? Is your new name Nine now?"

I bit back a laugh. "Nope. You can call me Eleven."

"Better than Seven-Eleven."

My shoulders shook with laughter as I poured the boiling water over the tea bag. Once it was full, I moved to the kitchen island and slid onto a stool to watch Jordan finish the meal.

"How do you know that isn't my name already?" I teased.

"So this whole time I should have been calling you Mr. Eleven?" She sent me a doubtful look. "I want to see your license. That's the only thing that will lay this to rest."

I rose wordlessly, heading for my wallet. It had been on the kitchen counter all along; not only that, Jordan had been within stealing distance of this wallet plenty of times, yet to my knowledge, she'd never looked.

"You mean to tell me you never took a peek for yourself?"

"I'm weird about boundaries," she said, "as in I actually respect them."

"Unless it comes to date nights." I slipped my driver's license out of its laminated holder and handed it to her. She took it eagerly, gobbling up the information. A moment later, she gasped.

"No way." Her gaze slid up to me, looking awed. "You're Antonin Silva."

I nodded, sliding back onto my stool. "That's me."

"Why do they call you Seven?"

"Somebody misheard my last name in boot camp, and it stuck."

"So it isn't referencing what number in the robot production line you were." She pursed her lips, her gaze stuck on the license once more. "Six four, huh? And two hundred thirty pounds. I told you—Greek god."

"Now that you've received this confidential piece of information, I trust you'll tell no one."

"As long as you tell me where the names come from. Antonin *and* Silva both sound a little...foreign, but not the same foreign."

"My mother is from the Czech Republic and my father was from Guatemala."

Her brows lifted. "Do you speak either of the languages?"

"Nothing more than understanding the occasional outburst or bad word," I told her. "My lullabies were in Czech. But when I fucked up, I heard about it in Spanish."

She took one last look at the license and then pushed it toward me. "I bet your parents have an interesting origin story."

"My dad was military. Mom was a recent immigrant to the US. They met in California, got married, settled in Nebraska, and eventually divorced. Nothing wild."

"Nothing wild that they told *you*," she corrected, smiling down at the plates as she slid the paninis off the electric griddle. "So do my brothers know about Antonin?"

"Nope."

She gasped, touching her chest. "I feel so honored."

"Consider it your twenty-day reward."

"What does that—" Her eyes went to slits. "Is that how long you've been my bodyguard?" When I nodded, she added, "Feels like twenty years, Seven.

"Since you were born, then?"

Her mouth rounded, delayed shock and delight spreading across her face as she chucked a cherry tomato at me. "You jerk. I am not *twenty*."

"You sure act like it sometimes." I couldn't resist needling her. Last night unlocked something—I was showing her my legal name and sharing more with her than was necessary. But it felt good. It felt *natural*. "Crashing my guys night out because you were *jealous*."

She rolled her lips inward, a pretty pink staining her cheeks. "Here. You better eat before your Greek stature starts to shrivel. Or should I call you...Griego?"

"So you know some Spanish, too." I eyed the steaming panini hungrily before I took a bite, noting the warm, gooey explosion of mozzarella first, followed by roasted red pepper and seared chicken. She and I smiled at each other as we ate; I already had so many memories of us like this, one of us sitting on the stool, the other eating while leaning against the island mid-clean up, too eager to enjoy the food and too reluctant to break eye contact or step away from the moment.

"Holy shit, this is good," I mumbled between bites, inhaling the food in record time. Jordan was barely a third of the way done when I put my plate in the sink. "I win."

She laughed as she chewed, elbowing me.

"You take your time. Me and my tea are going to continue recuperating on the couch." I scooped up my mug and wandered into the living room. Our cohabitation had always been charged with sexual tension, but now, I realized that was only part of the picture.

I'd always felt buzzy and aware around her because somewhere inside, I knew the danger that lurked. That if I dove headfirst into her, I'd be swallowed whole. An effortless gulp that would dissolve me and any progress I'd made.

It was happening already. Our easy banter and teasing that transitioned into sharing secrets. Her taking care of me while hungover. That was just the beginning. I felt it deep in my bones. The electric excitement that Jordan inspired was a promise, but it was also a warning.

If you go deeper with Jordan, you will drown.

I settled onto the couch carefully, taking a sip of my tea. Perfect temperature. I drank it slowly while Jordan finished her food. After the sounds of a quick kitchen clean up, I felt Jordan's weight on the couch next to me. She'd curled up, head on the back of the couch, mere inches from me. Her angle was clear—but she wasn't overstepping it.

"So tell me, Greek god." She gestured at my bare torso. "When you're built like this, why on earth don't you date?"

I sighed, shaking my head. "I was just over here trying to enjoy my tea…"

"I think it's a fair question."

"Do *you* date?"

She blinked. "Well, no."

"See? Point made. Everyone has reasons. It's unrelated to perfect physique."

She smirked. "All right, now I'm gonna call you Eleven."

"You inflated me; this is what you get."

She bit her bottom lip. I could see the gears of her dirty mind turning. "I did inflate you, you're right. Especially the other night."

I dragged a hand down my face. This was a minefield. Every turn was going to be fraught with innuendos and tension. If I followed that path, then I'd have minutes, maybe only *seconds*, before I pulled her onto my lap and started grinding against her.

But the hangover, mixed with the light of day and plenty of time to distance myself from those back-of-the-restaurant kisses, had helped to knock some logic back into me.

"That's not what I meant. Jordan—" I drew a deep breath, setting down my tea on the coffee table. I turned to her, drinking in her tiny frame, her dark blonde ponytail, the fresh heart-shaped face of hers that felt like both coming home and the most insane turn on.

"What?" she asked.

"We can't…do this." I gestured at the dissolving inches of space between us. Her knee was against me, her warmth sinking into me. "Living together is just making this harder. But the truth is: I was hired to protect you. Not fuck to your brains out."

Her eyes lit up. "Was that an option?"

I gritted my teeth. As far as my cock was concerned, it was the *only* option.

"I want things to go smoothly," I went on. "Which means not ruining the most important business contact I've made in my entire professional career."

Her face softened. "I don't see how you and I could ruin anything for your career."

"You might not feel it yet, because I know you're unsure about them, but your brothers are crazy about you. If they found out that they hired me to protect you and I turned around and started fucking you instead? Jordan, that's not how I operate. I don't know how else to explain it to you. I do not fuck my clients. Not even when she's the most beautiful girl I've seen in my entire life."

Her gaze dropped, her lips turning downward. "Do you really mean that?"

"What part?"

"The last bit." Her voice came out barely a whisper.

"Yes. Trust me, Jordan—" I stopped myself, unsure how much I should admit. I'd already gone way too far. But that was par for the course with her. "If I was a normal man, and you were just someone I knew...then yeah, maybe this would make sense."

"What do you mean if you were a normal man?"

I reached for my tea again. But instead of drinking it, I stared into the murky depths, remembering all the reasons why getting close to someone was a bad idea. I could already feel the tug on my heart when it came to Jordan. The undertow, taking me out to sea. My heart couldn't withstand shattering a second time. It had been barely patched together, thumping but injured, after my fiancée's murder. Almost ten years later, I was mostly fine.

But if I ever experienced pain like that again, I wouldn't be fine. I'd be destroyed. And I didn't trust myself to limp out of the wreckage a second time.

"It's not worth getting into." I dipped my teabag a few times then set the mug back on the coffee table without drinking.

Jordan was quiet for a few moments. Then she sighed, pushing off the couch.

"Well, you make a good point," she said. "No use wading into something that neither of us even wants." She drifted toward the pole in the back of the apartment. "Unless you mean that fucking part. I'm pretty sure we both want that."

"Don't be a brat," I warned.

"How is telling the truth bratty?" She laughed, hanging on to the pole with one arm as she swung in a slow circle.

"Just make it easier on both of us and don't bring it up. How about that?" I sipped my tea testily.

Jordan stayed quiet as she climbed the pole. A moment later she was in the bat formation, her gaze bouncing around the room.

"What's the big deal about honoring my brothers anyway?" She let her arms hang slack toward the floor. "It's just work. You make more business contacts. You find new clients. Life goes on."

"Like I said, you might not get it, because you guys have some...family issues. But they mean a lot to me. They're not quite brothers but...they're not just my clients, either. They feel like family, somehow. And I know better than to throw something like that in the trash."

She didn't know just how small my circle was these days. I had Trojan at my side. My mother was in a nursing home. And the Fairchilds. That was it. Everyone else I kept at a distance. Jordan couldn't become an addition to that circle, even though it seemed impossible to keep her out. She needed to be transferred to a different officer immediately. But even if she was under the care of a different officer, it didn't give us the green light to be together.

Because letting her in would only lead to me falling in love with her. And I knew better than to go down that road a second time.

Jordan heaved a sigh, then reached up and grabbed the pole between her legs. She slid down a moment later, catching my gaze across the room.

"You done drinking that tea? Let's get started on your lesson."

I lifted a brow. "You have to be on drugs."

"The only thing I'm high on is the pole." She tipped her head. "Come on. Up and at 'em."

"Jordan." I tried my best to make my voice sound authoritative, because I was *not* getting on that fucking pole. "I'm hungover as shit."

"This will help."

"I disagree."

"You need to learn a basic move before I find my own place. The clock. Is. Ticking." She punctuated her final words with hand claps. "Now come on, don't make me activate your military competitiveness or whatever you Marines have dormant inside you at all times."

I admired her tenacity. That was the only reason I set my mug down and joined her. I paused at the base of the pole, crossing my arms. "I haven't stretched."

"You won't need to."

I sighed, joining her in front of the pole. She tipped her head back to look up at me, and for a split second, I saw how this could end: me, dipping down, catching her face in my hands again, coaxing those heartbreaking kisses from her lips.

I wanted that so badly. But I wanted my inner stability more. I wanted my future, unchanged and unbothered. I wanted the Fairchilds' respect. I wanted this all to be worth something, not just a humiliating chapter in my quest to expand and succeed.

The air buzzed between us. She felt it too. Jordan took one of my hands and placed it on the pole, smirking.

"Just grab this thick shaft right here and follow every instruction I give you."

A laugh rippled out of me. "I know better than to agree to that."

"You're probably right. The last time you did that, you and I ended up doing something we're not allowed to bring up anymore."

"Thank you for remembering the new rule." My skin prickled with anticipation as she positioned my other hand on the pole, about an inch above the first one.

"There we go. Just like that, Mr. Eleven." She placed her hands on my hips and adjusted my stance, bringing them closer to the pole.

"Once you see how good I am, you'll be calling me Thirteen."

"That ego just continues to grow."

I sniffed, squeezing the pole extra tight. "Your fault."

She sent me a heavy look before tapping my right knee. "Bring this up here." She showed me with her own knee. Once I did it, she showed me how to bring my other leg up.

The delight on her face once I was launched halfway up the pole had me smiling right back at her.

"You did it!" Jordan clapped. "The stiff body builder is officially mounting my shaft." She pushed onto her tiptoes, resting her hand on my thigh as she added, "And that's the most action either of us will get with each other, isn't that right, Eleven?"

The twinkle in her eye as she winked promised me nothing but bratty mischief.

CHAPTER SIXTEEN

JORDAN

I loved consecutive days off. The entire world stretched before me, unencumbered with annoyances like *shift times* and *handsy clients.* This was my second day off in a row, which made me feel like I wasn't a desperate, cash-strapped stripper, struggling to find a place to live that wouldn't drain her bank account within two months. No, I was a put-together professional with a two-day weekend, god-dammit.

At least, that's what I wanted to feel like on this momentous Tuesday.

Seven and I crossed paths early in the morning—after his workout and before mine—and he informed me that he had plans today. Before I could ask if they'd require me to scout out his location and hunt him down, he said, "Whatever you have planned for the day is fine. I'll call Chico to come over and be on call."

I sighed, rubbing my face. Somewhere between the family dinner and this morning, I realized how long it had been since I'd been *alone.* That was one of the perks of living by myself—*being alone.* At least for an introvert like me. "Can I just get some personal time? Or is that forbidden per the bodyguard laws?"

He dropped his chin, his gaze narrowing. "You promise you'll stay here?"

"Of course. What else am I going to do but swing around the pole and cook elaborate lunches?"

"You could always go hunt Pokémon," he said.

"Sure, but I don't feel like it today." I crossed my arms. Ranger sauntered into the room and sat equidistant between us, watching with mild interest.

Seven didn't seem convinced. "Are you sure?"

"Yes. I'll be good. *Promise.*"

He watched me for a moment longer before issuing me a curt nod. "Okay. But if you change your mind, let me know and I'll send Chico over."

"Thanks, Daddy Warbucks."

He shook his head as he walked toward his bedroom. "That's not a good one."

"I didn't realize you were scoring and judging my submissions." His bedroom door shut a moment later, and I drew a deep breath, dropping down to stroke Ranger's fur. Not only did I have an unexpected day off...I would have most of it to *myself*. And Ranger, of course.

This felt like luxury.

I was on the pole when Seven headed out for the day looking casual in dark jeans and a T-shirt, his laptop bag slung across his chest. My heart squeezed as I watched him go. I wanted to know what he was doing. What was he working on? Did he need any input? Was this more about the business that involved Chico?

I had so many questions, and I wanted to have none of them. Just like I wanted Seven, but wanted to not want him. The longer I practiced on the pole, the deeper my thoughts dove into the abyss. I was sick of this tangle my life had become. Nothing resembled anything I'd selected for myself. This wasn't my apartment. Not my furniture. Not my daily commute. Not my fucking neighborhood.

And Seven...definitely not my roommate. *Or* my boyfriend. Yet here we were.

I grunted as my positions became fiercer, my body whipping around the pole like I was exorcising the confusion. All this surveillance was getting old, too. I was sick of being tailed, treated like I couldn't go anywhere on my own. Sick of the confusion about what my next step should be, and more than sick of my attraction to Seven.

How was any of this right? How many more weeks or months or years would some armed bodyguard need to follow me before I could come home from work on my own?

I finished my practice in a blaze of aggression, my face flaming hot and my muscles aching by the time I flipped to the ground. My chest heaved for a few moments as I stared past the pole and out the window, unable to focus on anything but how constricted I felt.

My entire life right now felt like a swaddle—wrapped too tight, and no way to find the seam to unravel the whole thing.

I needed to get out of here.

Sure, saving on rent was nice. Living with a Greek god had its perks. Hell, I'd gotten a free pole out of the deal. But I couldn't keep pretending that not being in control of my own life was palatable. Who was I kidding? This entire arrangement had been doomed to fail, and I'd been too distracted by a pair of biceps holding me in the scary times.

I needed to remember what it felt like to be on my own.

Still struggling to catch my breath, I bolted for my bedroom. I'd pack a bag, take only the essentials, and see where I ended up. I could call Roxie if I needed a place to crash. Maybe I'd end up back here. I really had no idea. I just needed to prove to myself that I could hack it on my own again. Like I had from the beginning. Like I'd surely have to do again someday.

Once my bag was packed with a few nights' worth of regular clothes, work gear, and my stripped-down skincare routine, I popped on a T-shirt and leggings, slid on my leather jacket, and got the fuck out of there.

I moved stealthily at first, like Seven might be lurking in the stairwell, ready to jump out and call me a brat as if he could intuit my naughty moves. When he was nowhere to be found and I'd successfully strolled out onto Reade Street by myself, I knew I'd made it.

Free at last.

I spun like a top at first. Without Seven at my side, the freedom fizzed inside me, heady and disorienting. It might have been my first time in the city all over again, and I was a tourist without a map. I drew deep breaths of the crisp autumn air, unsure where to begin. My stomach rumbled within a couple of blocks, giving me my answer. Lunch first.

I picked up my pace, eager to get my butt to Chinatown and into the dining room of my favorite rice noodle joint. I hadn't been there since moving away, so this return to familiar territory seemed like a fitting celebration of freedom.

Hitting the pavement in Chinatown felt like coming home. I filled my lungs with the wafting scents of frying pork from a nearby restaurant mingling with street grit and exhaust. While I loved fresh air and forests, something about the big city kicked my senses awake. I wove my way through the heavy flow of pedestrians, and when I saw the neon sign of Yun Shin, a pang of sadness hit me in the solar plexus.

Seven would have liked to come along too.

But today wasn't about him. I was finally on my own, and I needed to remember that. I pushed inside the crowded restaurant, quickly snagging a small table in the corner. I didn't even need to look at the menu. I scanned the restaurant after I ordered, my mind drifting as I observed the other customers. Everything was hushed in here, moodily lit, serious and delicious. Just as I was debating whether or not I wanted to swing by my old apartment, my bowl of beef slices with rice noodles showed up.

There was no time for thinking then. Only eating. I inhaled my food in record time, only pausing to debate taking a picture to send to Seven. Not to tease him—just to let him know he needed to come here with me next time.

Could you stop thinking about Seven for once?

Once my belly was full and my spirits lifted, I rejoined the busy weekday outside, heading for my old favorite: Columbus Park. There was a chance Dustin would be there, but I was confident I could outrun him if he tried anything even remotely creepy. Still, I entered the calm greenspace with some hesitation, on the lookout for red hair and his worn-out khaki coat. I hated how nervous the idea made me—did this mean I couldn't survive without Seven now?

I'd confronted far scarier situations without batting an eye. I knew how to be aware, how to be *ready*. Seven didn't get to take that away from me.

I settled onto a park bench, sliding my duffel bag off my shoulder. I needed to sit with my thoughts. Everything inside me grew heavy with indecision and misdirection. And the worst part was that, if I was being completely honest with myself, I did want Seven at my side. As more than just my bodyguard.

But the thought terrified me. Even if he somehow stopped being my guard, even if there was some way to make this connection work without living together or him being around constantly, was I ready for something serious? With someone like Seven?

I watched the parkgoers as they drifted by, listening for an answer inside of me.

I was so used to hacking it on my own. But maybe I was ready for a new adventure. A new chapter. A new...approach.

A couple went up to the statue of Dr. Sun Yat-sen and sat at the base while they each ate their own container of sushi. Occasionally, the girl would offer a bite to her boyfriend, which he'd gratefully take. And then, a few bites later, he'd offer one to her.

Even *that* brought tears to my eyes. If I didn't know better, I'd think I was pregnant. But pregnancy was off the table, unless I was sorely mistaken about the mechanics of insemination. No, ever since my brothers had shown up in Black & Brewtiful, I was more sensitive and emotional than I'd ever been in my entire life.

You're just so tired of needing to be strong.

The thought resonated through me, prompting actual tears this time. I bent over my duffel bag, rummaging around as though I was searching for something. But really, I was just trying to hide my tears and not break down entirely in public. I was tired of always being on the defensive. Needing to look out for myself because nobody gave a god damn about me. I was tired of feeling like it was me against the world.

The last few weeks of being able to relax and stand down... I buried my face in my hands, suddenly overwhelmed by the revelation. This time had been a gift. One that my brothers gave me without realizing they were doing it.

My heart swelled, a warm mixture of both pain and tenderness. I didn't know up from down anymore. I missed Seven four hours after I'd last seen him; I was halfway crying from tender feelings about my brothers. This wasn't the Jordan I knew. What was I going to do next, start spilling all my life's secrets to Roxie and the other girls at work?

I drew a deep breath, checking my phone. No word from Seven yet, which meant he likely didn't know I'd broken my promise to him. I stared at the bright screen, fingers swiping across the apps before I had a chance to think better of it.

Suddenly I had a text to Damian open.

JORDAN: Are you guys home?

He wrote back immediately. Like he'd been waiting.

DAMIAN: I can be if you need me to be. What's up sis?

My chin trembled and I contemplated what to say. I didn't even know what I needed right now. Nothing felt quite right, but somehow, finding my brothers made the most sense.

JORDAN: Just wondering if I could swing by and we could talk.

DAMIAN: Of course. I'll be there in about ten minutes, is that quick enough? Are you near, or do you want me to send a car?

I was about to wave off his offer as usual. *I don't need help from you, or anyone. I can get there myself.* But something stopped me. A ride would be nice. A little softness, a little comfort...would be nice.

JORDAN: I'd love a ride. Thanks.

I sent him the address of the park. When I looked around, things felt a little calmer inside. I smiled at the group of older ladies practicing tai chi nearby. I even smiled at passers-by, which I knew was an implicit no-no in New York City, but I had the excuse of being a deranged out-of-towner who occasionally smiled at people.

When the sleek black sedan pulled to a stop near one of the main entrances of Columbus Park about ten minutes later, its flashers blinking, I knew it had to be the Fairchild vehicle. As I approached, the passenger window slid down and Legs grinned out at me.

"Your chariot awaits, Ms. Haynes."

"Legs!" I climbed into the front seat. His brows lifted.

"You comin' up front with me today?"

"Of course. Why wouldn't I?" I buckled in as he eased away from the park. "You're not in the SUV today."

"The ladies are using it, off with Harry somewhere." He side-eyed me, smiling to himself. "We're goin' to the Fairchilds, right?"

I nodded, surprised to find something like excitement prickling to life. My brothers were part of a special, elite world, and I knew the access code. This was the type of VIP feeling I'd longed for as a child.

"Yeah. I just wanna hang out with my brothers."

The words hung awkwardly in the air for me, though I'm sure Legs didn't notice. Kaylee didn't strike me dead from the great beyond for saying them either.

It's time for you to do what feels right. And reconnecting with your brothers is what's right.

I didn't doubt it anymore. And part of me suspected that Kaylee wasn't criticizing my choices from the Great Beyond. Hell, she was probably cheering this on. The Kaylee that would have been mad was the drug-addicted, traumatized teenager who'd led me to believe our brothers somehow chose to leave us behind. And while I still had questions I needed answered, there was no way Kaylee's version could be completely correct.

Legs and I chatted while he drove through slow midday traffic. I tinkered with the radio, until landing on Queen's "Bohemian

Rhapsody," which we both sang quietly to ourselves until it got to the end, which we belted out together. By the time we'd traveled a mile in about fifteen minutes, Legs felt like my best friend.

When he pulled up to the skyscraper known as my brothers' building, he said, "I'll be seeing you around, right?"

I shrugged. "Probably. I might be needing more rides soon."

"Good." He squeezed the wheel, smiling out ahead. "I'll be seein' ya, Jordy."

I'd gone from Ms. Haynes to Jordy in the distance of two neighborhoods. Somehow, it didn't bother me. I waved at Legs before entering the sleek, pleasantly warm lobby, heading to the center set of elevators as Damian instructed me via text. Since I wasn't with Seven, I didn't have his secret penthouse elevator key that went straight to the side entrance. Instead, I rode up a mirrored elevator by myself, staring at my slightly unrecognizable reflection. A messy ponytail, my most basic leggings and black tee, and my leather jacket, not an ounce of makeup or lip gloss. I nearly jumped when the doors slid open and my reflection split in two.

A gleaming, tiled hallway led to wooden double doors. Before I'd taken two steps, the doors opened, and my brother Damian filled the doorway.

"Hey, little sis." His warm smile softened whatever hard edges I had left.

I walked up to him, leaning against him in an awkward half-hug, before breezing past. "Hey."

"Quasi-hug status, huh?" He shut the door behind us.

"Yeah. For now." I looked over my shoulder as he joined me in the middle of the hallway.

"Cool. I can live with that." He gestured for me to follow him into the huge living room; low, boxy furniture sat expertly arranged and pristine, like he'd just held an interior design photoshoot moments before. Tall, skinny vases stood in clusters; sprays of exotic looking foliage bursting out of them. But the way he sank into the couch told me this furniture was here to be used, not just admired.

"Sit down," he encouraged, probably noticing my hesitation. "What have you been up to? You tired? Need a drink?"

I sat on the armchair facing the couch, unsure where to begin. I inspected my nails for a moment, caught between wondering if Seven was mad and whether or not I should just dive into childhood trauma.

"I'll take some water, actually. I was walking around the city a lot earlier."

"Of course. Where's Seven?" Damian got up, heading to a little wet bar tucked away near the huge span of windows. My gaze drifted to the light streaming through the glass, realizing it wasn't a picture—it was actually the fucking *city* I was looking at, not just a perfectly hung image.

"Oh, he had some things to do," I said. "He told me he'd be back later. I was supposed to stay at the apartment but...I left."

Damian grabbed a glass water bottle from a small stainless steel fridge hidden behind a sliding wood panel. He handed it over to me before sinking back into the couch. The bottle had a label in a different language—only after some squinting could I make out that this was bottled French spring water. *Classy.* I cracked it open and took a gulp. It was more refreshing than expected.

"God this water is good," I said, looking at the label again.

"We're obsessed," Damian admitted. "We buy it by the caseload from a French distributor. It's *le expensive* but worth it."

"Do you speak French?"

He laughed. "Hell no. Did I sound like I do?"

"No," I admitted, capping the bottle and setting it on the small table beside my chair. "In fact, that was a pretty bad accent, so I was worried you were trying."

He laughed, but my own smile faded more quickly. My thoughts had returned to Seven. "Hey, don't get Seven in trouble."

"For what?"

"He's doing his job really well," I said. "I slipped out on him today. If anything, I'm the one who should be in trouble."

"You can go and do things by yourself if you want..." he started.

"I know. I just...I've been feeling really lost." Here it was. The words I'd been struggling to bury and unearth in equal measure. My chest loosened, allowing some of the pain to pour out. "Ever since you and Axel showed up in the coffee shop, I've been really confused. I guess that's the only way I can put it."

"I've been feeling the same," he admitted. "Only because I was positive you were dead."

My brows furrowed, some of that anger I'd unleashed around Seven crawling back to the surface. "But how could you think I was dead? I don't understand."

"I've been scanning public records for mention of your name for years." He crossed a leg over his knee, a contemplative look in his green eyes. "I set up an automatic database scan pretty early on. It was crude, but it was able to sift through most local newspapers and county registries. I started that after we moved to New York for college, because by then I'd already lost track of you."

"My foster family moved," I said quietly. "I think the summer after you guys graduated. The lady found a bigger house, one that would let her accept more kids." I paused, a distant *thump thump thump* snagging my attention. It grew louder. Suddenly, Axel burst into the room at a run from the far end of the kitchen.

"Hey guys, I'm here." He took a deep breath. "I sprinted across this entire penthouse, too."

"I let him know you were coming," Damian explained.

"Couldn't miss a second with our little sister." Axel pinched the top of my ear as he passed by me and settled into the armchair angled in the corner of the area rug. He wore a navy business suit, tie and all.

"Where'd you just come from?" I asked.

"A meeting with some investors." He flashed me a smile. "They want to donate to your charity."

"My charity?" I echoed.

"We started a non-profit in your and Kaylee's names about six years ago," Damian filled in. "Between our collective childhoods, the way Kaylee died, and your disappearance, it was why we chose the foster system as the focus of our charity efforts."

"We want foster kids to suffer a little less in the hardest times of their lives," Axel added. "And we do what we can to root out the fucking sex traffickers."

"Though that is a black hole all its own," Damian said.

Damian's comment reminded me of what we'd been talking about before Axel came in. I sighed, gnawing on the inside of my cheek. "I still don't understand how you guys thought I disappeared or was dead."

"Well, I started doing those scans I told you about," Damian said. "It was basic, but more of a way to keep up the long-distance search efforts once we were in New York."

The second mention of them fucking off to New York—without me or Kaylee—sent my chest tightening again. I tried to tamp down the ancient feelings of abandonment and resentment swirling inside my gut.

"Then we found out Kaylee died," Axel said softly. "And it was like you just fell off the face of the earth after that."

"We were calling Kentucky CPS constantly," Damian added. "You'd been in the care of a household where a foster teen died from a drug overdose with suspected involvement in sex trafficking. It was really hard to swallow. And with being so far away..."

"You have to remember, Jordan, we had no money back then." Axel smiled grimly. "We were living day to day, mostly off dividends that Trace's earliest investments paid out."

"And *lots* of student loans," Damian said.

"And working non-stop when we weren't in classes," Axel added. "Point is, we weren't in a position to come home and poke around. We asked our adoptive mom to do some digging, but since she wasn't related to you, no one would talk to her. Even with us, it was like everyone clammed up. I think the FBI got involved with your foster family—"

"They did," I whispered.

"So nobody was giving up information."

"I was transferred to a new home after Kaylee died," I said, the words sticking to my throat. "It wasn't anywhere near Louisville. It was an emergency placement."

"They might as well have changed your name," Damian said. "And for a while, that's what I assumed happened. I couldn't get a lead on you. It was like you just vanished."

"But you never showed up again," Axel said. "We'd check constantly. Call the CPS office. I don't know if it was a bureaucratic fuck-up or what...but you were gone."

"And then I ran away from that final foster home when I was sixteen." I sniffed, grabbing the amazing French water for another sip. All this rehashing of the past had me parched. "I moved in with a boyfriend. For a while, I just drifted between jobs, working as a waitress or farmhand or whatever I could find."

"Under the table?" Damian asked.

I nodded. "Yeah. I always wanted cash the same day."

Axel shook his head, looking over at Damian. "Well that explains part of it."

"I've had under the table jobs for years. It wasn't until probably two years ago that I went on payroll at Black & Brewtiful," I told them.

Damian rubbed his face. "My god. And you were under our noses the entire time."

"I wasn't knowingly evading you," I said quietly.

"But you never reached out," Axel said, looking so bewildered that it felt like a blow to my body. "Why? We've been sharing the same city for how many years now? You had to have seen our names in the papers."

"Four years now," I admitted. I opened my mouth to add more, but I didn't know where to begin. The truth hurt so bad. But if I was ever going to say these words, to these men, it was now. It had to be now. Or I'd second-guess myself to the grave. "I didn't think you guys wanted anything to do with me. I never reached out because I figured Kaylee had been right about you two all along."

Both Axel and Damian seemed to scoot closer upon hearing this. "What do you mean?" Damian asked. "What would she say about us?"

"That you two abandoned us." I rolled the water bottle back and forth in my hands, enjoying the cool glass against my sweaty palms. "That you'd taken the better family and left us to rot in the foster system."

Axel leaned back in his chair. The edges of his tattoos peeked out from under the long sleeves of his shirt as he covered his face with his hands.

Damian rolled his lips inward, his gaze stuck on the ground.

"As we got older and she started using drugs, she said it more and more," I said. "After you guys left for New York, I believed her. Because you did what she'd said. Our brothers abandoned us."

My chin trembled, but at least the tears hadn't shown up yet. Damian pinched the bridge of his nose, his eyes squeezed shut.

"It wasn't like that," Axel said, sniffing hard. "Jordan, I promise you, that wasn't what happened."

The knot was growing in my throat. "Then why didn't you take custody of us once you turned eighteen?" I asked it on a whisper. The question I'd been too afraid to ask—and know the answer to—for so many years.

"They wouldn't let us," Damian said, his eyes shimmering. He cleared his throat, taking a deep breath before continuing. "I looked into guardianship. I was the only one who could have applied at the time of our graduation from high school, because Axel was still seventeen. They said with our permanent residence changing to New York and without any verifiable stable income or any legal residence, we weren't in a position to assume guardianship."

Silence thudded through the room.

Axel's jaw flexed, his ice blue eyes cutting through me. In a soft voice, he said, "We tried, Jordan. We did. But our hands were tied. Our only money was through these grants and student loans."

"Why didn't you stay in Kentucky?" I asked quietly. "Why did it have to be New York?"

"We all had big dreams; it just felt like the best decision," Axel said.

"And by the time we could prove that we had something stable in our lives…" Damian's breath whooshed out of him. "You were gone. Couldn't find you."

"And if you had, I don't think I'd have moved in with you anyway," I added with a sad laugh.

A tense silence stretched between us. I chugged more water, my heartbeat throbbing in every inch of my body. I never imagined how simple their side of the story might be. How honest and raw and real it would feel, coming from their lips. I supposed I thought, all this time, that they'd been hiding some malicious secret. That they never wanted Kaylee and me in the family, and their moving to NYC without us was their easy out.

What do you think Kaylee? I assumed—prayed—that she was sober now, up in Heaven, listening to us. And if that was the case, maybe she had a little more perspective. But I'd never know for sure if I was praying to Kaylee, or just listening to the sound of my own voice echo through my mind.

Maybe it didn't matter. Maybe now, it was for me to decide.

"I'm sorry you felt that we abandoned you," Damian said softly.

"I'm sorry, too." Axel shook his head, studying an unknowable point on the ground.

"I wish we could fix the past and erase all the suffering we endured. But we have time left in our lives. We still have a chance to enjoy what's left for us. I won't be woo-woo and say it happened for a reason. But it fucking happened, and it's up to us what happens next." Damian looked at me, the intensity in his green eyes feeling like both a hug and a promise. "Even if we get sent to prison for a decade after our trial next month…well, I want us to make the best of this next month together. Because that's what we have."

Axel nodded, his ice-blue gaze swinging my way, reminding me so much of my big sister. "I wish you and Kaylee had known how much we thought of you two. And after she died and you went MIA, we knew the only thing that made sense was dedicating the rest of our lives to trying to improve life for foster kids. In your names. It felt like the only way to atone for losing both of you."

"By doing whatever we could to help other families avoid a similar outcome," Damian added softly. "Even though it feels like an uphill battle. Money doesn't cure everything. Kids need loving guardians, foster parents, adoptive parents. There will always be bad seeds. But when counties and states have more resources—"

"Provided they don't mishandle them," Axel interjected.

"—then we're effecting a small bit of change along the way." Damian rubbed his palms together slowly, as though thinking. "We work with foster kids here in the city, too. Help them connect with educational opportunities and mentors, help fund college, things like that."

"Resources to find affordable housing," Axel added. "Whatever we can do."

I blinked back tears, but for a different reason now. "Wow. You guys are..." *Incredible.* I bit my tongue before it came out, because I still had Kaylee's resentment lurking inside me. But it didn't have such a strong grip anymore. Its power was dissolving. "You're doing so much."

"We have immense wealth," Damian said. "I think we're obligated to use the lion's share of it to help others. What do you think?"

I fumbled for an answer. It was something that hadn't ever occurred to me. Wealth wasn't on my radar as much as *making rent* and *scraping together an emergency fund* were on my radar. I planned for as far ahead as I could, but in New York, that wasn't much farther than six months.

"I don't know," I finally admitted. "I think if you've earned your money, that money is yours to do with as you want."

"Well, this is what we want to do with our money," Damian said.

"Give it away," Axel added with a laugh. "We take care of ourselves, of course. We lead a great life. But there's still so much left over. And no matter what the fucking SEC thinks, why shouldn't that go to feed people who need it? Kids who can't afford college? Friends back home who need a helping hand?"

"Or long-lost sisters who need a new apartment." A coy smile curled at Damian's lips.

CHAPTER SEVENTEEN

JORDAN

My afternoon melted away in that living room with Damian and Axel. We talked about everything and anything. Memories of our birth parents bled into random discoveries of how much we all equally detested green beans, which bled into a surprise cross-town visit to the building they'd purchased from Cora's family the year before and was now the headquarters for their charity efforts.

Kaylee's and my names were emblazoned on the lobby wall in steel letters, a dedication plaque turned art installation, reminding every person that passed through the doors what—and whom—this building was for.

As dinnertime approached, Damian and Axel insisted on a family meal. Back at the penthouse, they unleashed a flurry of planning—texting Trace, calling Jessa, leaving a voicemail for Cora, waiting for the chef to call back about the menu options. Watching them execute this together felt like observing a practiced dance. Businessmen, who were also in-tune brothers, availing themselves of their resources to make things happen at the snap of their fingers. Part of me still couldn't believe I was even here. And from the way they talked about it, I got the sense that they were desperate to relish every moment of freedom—because this upcoming SEC trial could very well take that away from them.

"I told Seven to come," Axel mentioned off-handedly.

I grimaced. "He's gonna be mad."

"I'm sure we'll be able to calm him down," Damian said.

"Whiskey and good food calms everyone down." Axel pinched the top of my ear again as he sauntered toward the kitchen.

I almost added more but wasn't sure what to say. I certainly didn't want to admit that Seven and I had shared earth-shattering kisses several times, or that I'd ground against his barely-covered cock in the VIP room at work. I pushed the limits with Seven, but I didn't want him to get fired—or lose his standing with his clients, my brothers. So I kept my mouth shut. It was better they didn't know. Hell, it would be better if Seven and I just forgot about the whole attraction thing altogether.

Except that was impossible, when Seven was a hulking, gorgeous, witty man who felt safer than any person I'd met in my entire life.

Cora arrived first, greeting Axel with a quick but passionate kiss before immediately gliding over to me for a hug. I embraced her, taking a deep inhale of her sweet clementine scent.

"I'm so glad you're here," she murmured, squeezing me extra tight before releasing me. I stared into her beautiful heart-shaped face. The sincerity radiated off her in waves. Her dark, glossy hair was pulled back in a low bun, and her sharp, black slacks and silk top suggested important appointments from the day.

"I'm glad I'm here too," I admitted. And I meant it. Deeply.

Jessa showed up a bit later, giving Damian the same quick greeting before immediately soldering to my side. "I was so happy when Damian told me we were having a family dinner tonight. I've been wanting to talk to you about making you a dress."

"A dress?"

"Yeah, ever since we met, I've been getting ideas for some cute dresses." Her auburn hair cascaded over her shoulders in soft waves as she looked me up and down, as if she could see something I couldn't.

"Jessa is a clothing designer," Cora explained. "She's been working with some big clients since moving to New York."

My mouth rounded. That explained the gorgeous dress she wore at the last dinner, and the one she wore today, belted and flowy with long sleeves. "You made this?"

Jessa nodded excitedly. "I sure did."

"If there's something you want to make for me, I'm ready for it."

Jessa clapped her hands, a grin lighting up her face just as Mercedes and Trace joined the party, a small blonde girl burrowing into Mercedes's olive green sweater. There was a commotion of greetings, the little girl clinging tightly to Mercedes as they said their hellos, heading my way.

Jordan wrapped me in a side hug, the little girl leaning away from me as we embraced.

"I'm hoping these family dinners become regular with you in the mix," she said warmly as Trace squeezed my arm with a smile. "This is Willow. Willow, can you say hi to your Auntie Jordan?"

Auntie Jordan. The phrase flashed through me like a lightning bolt. It was both endearing and terrifying. I could somehow play a part in the formation of a small child? It didn't seem possible, not after I'd come to terms with the fact that I'd roam this earth for the rest of my life single, childless, orphaned.

"Hi, Miss Willow," I said softly. She turned away harder.

"She's shy around all men and anyone new. But she'll warm up to you eventually. You have a knack for getting people warmed up," Mercedes said with a wink.

"Strange, considering I'm dead inside," I deadpanned. When Mercedes sent me a look that said *come on now*, I relented. "Okay, fine. I just pretend to be dead inside. Does she get along with Seven?"

"She's shy around all men except *him*," she said with a laugh, tossing her soft, blonde waves over her shoulder with a flick of her head. "She warmed up to him quickly. Just like she did Trace. Must be something about those two."

I shut my mouth before I could incriminate myself. I didn't need to tell *anyone* how quickly I'd warmed up to Seven.

While the room filled with the clamor of conversation and catching up, the chef arrived without much fanfare, other than my brothers shouting "Gaston!". While he unfurled his leather satchel of knives on the kitchen island and started preparing dinner, I almost missed the newest addition to the party.

Seven.

He lurked at the edges, broad-shouldered in his black T-shirt. He had a few inches on Damian, and with his deadly serious face, he looked like a hulking, brooding murder machine as he conferred with Damian. His eyebrows were straight lines, nearly touching as he frowned and listened to whatever my brother was saying. I knew it was serious when Seven looked up, his gaze landing on me.

The fire in his eyes suggested that whatever they were talking about had to do with me.

And as I'd suspected, Seven was *furious.*

CHAPTER EIGHTEEN

JORDAN

Seven and Damian's conversation seemed to drag on forever. They'd stepped away from the clamor of the gathering, retreating into the foyer to continue their discussion. I let myself be swept into the fervor, accepting glasses of wine and tiny cubes of cheese when presented with them. How could I not? Hors d'oeuvres were practically my love language.

My attention drifted back to the heated conversation on the fringes of the room. It couldn't be *that* serious...right? I mulled over the conflicting details while conversations floated around me. I told Damian it was my decision to slip away. I told him not to be mad at Seven. So what could they possibly be discussing over there for so long, and why did I feel like it was my fault?

Their eternal dialogue finally ended when Damian rubbed his forehead and drifted away from Seven, rejoining the party. Whatever passed between them dropped as soon as he reached Jessa's side with a smile. But Seven lurked in the shadows, his gaze burning through me.

He jerked his head toward the back of the penthouse, a signal for me to follow. I set my wine down, popped the cheese into my mouth, and hurried toward him. He stormed down a back hallway, taking long strides I struggled to keep up with. He pushed a door open, stepping inside and waiting for me to enter. My belly flipped, and I followed him into a spare bedroom, dimly lit from the waning evening light. Once the door was shut, Seven drew a deep breath, stuffing his hands into his pockets.

I leaned against the wall beside the door and nibbled on my lip, avoiding his gaze. I knew the lashing was coming. But he didn't say a word.

"Hi," I finally whispered.

"Don't fucking 'hi' me," he snapped, his anger leaking out in the sharpness of his words. His nostrils flared for a moment. "What you should be opening with is why the fuck you disappeared today after promising me you wouldn't."

I swallowed hard. I had no good reason that was easily explained. It was complex. It was deeply rooted. It was *personal*. I wasn't afraid to explain all that to Seven, but confronted this way, I couldn't form words.

I rolled my lips inward, my gaze stuck on the floor.

"Now, thanks to you, I look like a useless idiot who can't be trusted to perform the most basic task." His words were edged with a growl, and the way he advanced told me he needed to hear something—anything—from me.

"That wasn't my intention," I whispered, finally daring to meet his gaze. "I swear it wasn't. I just...needed to clear my head. I wanted to be alone."

"That's when you tell me what the plan is."

"I didn't know what the plan was," I shot back, some of my resolve returning.

"Then you give me a fucking heads-up." He stepped closer, that cologne reaching me again, making me weak. "You text. You call. You say 'I don't know where I'm going, but I'll be back later.'"

"Did you ever consider I'm used to living on my own?" I said, my voice rising. "Maybe I just want to go somewhere on my own and have it be fine."

"You're not living in that world anymore," he shot back. "Not while you're in my care. Do you know how fucking humiliating it is to have my employer be the one to let me know I've lost track of his sister? Think about it. It's common decency, Jordan. Which maybe you'd see if you weren't so busy being a brat all the time."

I balled my fists, annoyed by the way that word could activate me to be even more of a brat. But I couldn't resist the urge. "It's a full-time job, Seven, didn't you know?"

"Just like my job protecting you is," he retorted. "But I don't make your life harder. I make it safer."

"It's a job I never asked you to do," I said, already knowing this conversation was on a downward spiral.

"Then go talk to you brothers and persuade them to take me off this assignment so you and I can both go do the things that we actually want to do," he growled.

My heart thumped against my ribs, conflicting emotions clamoring to be released. Half of me wanted to make sure he never did *anything* but be forced to protect me, just so he couldn't go do these other things he "actually wanted to do." But the other half of me wanted to crumple at his feet and ask him to hold me, to reassure me that he *did* want to be with me.

Because the truth was that if I didn't have Seven nearby, everything would feel wrong.

I hated to even admit it to myself. So it needed to never pass my lips.

"Maybe that's a good idea," I taunted, rediscovering my edge. "I'll recommend you for someone much less challenging. Seven needs an easy task. Can't handle the cool girls, the brats, the ones who actually know how to speak up."

He let out a dry, humorless chuckle, something dangerous sliding over his face. The sly confirmation that my arrows were hitting their target only egged me on.

"But until I go have that conversation with my brothers, there's an easier solution here." I ran my tongue along my teeth, weighing what I was about to say. Being hidden away in this bedroom, inches from his masculinity, his scent, his power and strength, affected me in the same way it always did. I was fucking clenching and desperate.

"And what would that be?" he asked flatly.

"You should fuck the brat out of me." I smirked.

His chin dipped, his eyes darkening. "I wouldn't fuck a brat when I know she's just doing it to prove a point."

"And what point would that be?" I challenged, hearing the desperation in my own voice as he started to turn away from me. I couldn't even stop myself from grabbing his hand. Now that he was so close, I only needed him closer.

His gaze dropped to my hand at his wrist, then up to my face. "You know better than anyone what your little game is about."

Everything was churning together inside me. Desperate need, repressed desire, the heady realization that I wanted Seven more than I wanted air.

"You can feel for yourself what it's about." I couldn't stop the evil curl of my lips as I watched the desire darken his features. Suddenly he wasn't pulling away. He drifted closer. "You must need me to spell it out for you, huh?" I rolled my hips in his direction. "I bet you can even feel it through my leggings."

Seven bridged the remaining space between us in one step, his palms pressed to the wall on either side of me. "You're wet. I get it.

I'm not surprised, since pushing buttons clearly turns you on. But here's a newsflash—I don't fuck brats, and I don't fuck people who don't have my back."

His words landed like a sledgehammer. And not because of the brat part.

"What do you mean?" I demanded. I could hear the real hurt in his voice, which had my alarms going off.

"You walked out on me, no heads-up, no nothing, putting both yourself and my work at risk. That's inexcusable, Jordan, and that's not the type of woman I go for."

I blinked rapidly, trying to digest this information in milliseconds. "What type of woman I am shouldn't even matter. You don't date."

"Don't act stupid," he growled. "You could put the entire female population of Manhattan in front of me, Jordan, and I'd only see you. Of course it fucking matters. Even if it shouldn't."

I felt like I had a concussion. Were we talking feelings? Attraction? Compatibility? Nothing made sense, yet somehow, this was the *only* thing that made sense.

"I do have your fucking back," I corrected him. "I told Damian exactly what I'd done the second I showed up here. I told him not to blame you. I told him this was my emotional bullshit and no fault of yours. Happy?"

His jaw flexed as he studied me, his dark gaze bouncing like a pinball across my face. "It doesn't matter," he finally bit out.

"I think it does," I added, suddenly terrified that he'd tear himself away from me and leave me reeling, cold and abandoned. "And for the record, if you put the entire male population of Manhattan in front of me, I'd only see you." I swallowed a knot in my throat. Should I confess even more? I drew a deep breath and went for it. "Your smile is, like, the best thing I've ever seen. I can't stand how long your eyelashes are, because every time I look at you, I feel like I go a little crazier from how much I want you. I would climb on your back like a koala if you'd let me. I've never wanted someone more than I want you, Antonin Silva, and it's just—"

Seven dipped down, cupping my face in his rough hands as his lips met mine. The rest of my accolades melted into heartbreaking kisses, tender and seeking and heated. I whimpered, clutching the backs of his hands as we kissed, more deeply and passionately than ever before. I writhed beneath his touch, desperate for unending amounts of him. Our tongues moved slowly together in a rhythm all our own.

When we broke for air, the drugged look on his face was enough to undo me. I collapsed against the wall, suddenly unable to use my legs. He bit his bottom lip, his gaze dragging up and down my body.

"So what's the plan now?" he asked, the corner of his lip curling up as he smoothed his hands over the dip of my waist and down the sides of my legs. "Just fuck you in here before dinner with your family?"

"As long as we lock the door, I don't see a problem with that..."

One of his hands drifted across my thigh and between my legs. His gaze went hooded as he swiped his fingers over the crotch of my leggings. The brief pressure against my clit made my knees buckle. He caught me before I slid to the ground.

"You're right," he whispered hotly in my ear. "I can feel it through your leggings."

A shiver raced through my body. I angled my head toward him, welcoming more of that gritty voice right in my ear.

"I bet you could feel it through my pants, too," he added, and then gently bit my earlobe.

I moaned low, bucking my hips in his direction, just as I heard a deep voice call out, "Jordan?"

His gaze snapped to the door.

"I'm in the spare room," I called out, as Seven took several steps' worth of distance. "Just arguing with my bodyguard."

"Oh, cool," Axel said, his voice much closer to the door now. "Hope you guys hash it out soon, because we're trying to do a toast."

"Be there in a second," I said brightly, watching as Seven arranged his cock through his pants. The ridge there was delectable—edible—swallowable. I licked my lips involuntarily.

"We need to go back out there," he told me, clarity in his gaze. "And you need to clarify one thing right away."

"What's that?" I asked, unable to rip my gaze from the crotch of his pants.

"I called them your family before, and you didn't object." He crossed his arms, satisfaction leaking out of him. "What happened today?"

Prickles of warmth spread through my body at the comment. The man saw me. He knew me. He *noticed* me. Not to mention he wanted me. I bit the inside of my lip, unsure where to begin or how to corral all the surging emotions.

"We talked some things over," I said softly. "I guess you could say we finally had the conversation I've been needing to have since I was fifteen."

A genuine smile lit up his face and he nodded. "Good. I've been hoping I'd hear that." He pulled open the door and held it for me, waiting for me to pass through to the hallway first. But as I slipped past him, he gave me one hard crack on the ass cheek.

"That's for being a brat."

The satisfied smile on his lips only made me fall harder for him.

I inhaled sharply, squinting through the darkness at my surroundings. I'd come out of a deep sleep like a bear emerging from winter hibernation. I had no idea where I was, where I'd been, or what my name was.

Sheets rustled around me. But these weren't my sheets. I struggled to orient myself in the shadowy room but couldn't find a feature that made sense. Where the fuck was I?

Fragments of memories returned to me. A toast to family. A ridiculously delicious meal. And *wine.* So much wine I couldn't even recall how the night ended.

I turned onto my side, a dark mass beside me causing me to recoil. But only until I made out the shadowy relief of Seven's broad, bare back.

I'm in Seven's bed.

I felt the shirt I wore. Not mine. Extra big, yet comfortable.

I'm wearing Seven's shirt.

I drew closer to him as if on instinct, nuzzling against his warm skin. The masculine scent of him filled my senses, making my eyes droop. Now *this* was the spot. But the drowsiness didn't last long, once my wandering hands found his thick forearms then the hills of his biceps. I stroked his arm, drawing in deep gulps of his scent. There was something about the darkness and the rustling of sheets that set me on edge, took me back to uglier times. But the visceral sensations, the hardness of him next to me, and the drugging scent of him combined to act a balm.

Maybe this is the time.

I clenched my thighs together. Part of the reason I'd drunk so much the night before was to ignore how badly I wanted Seven. Letting my brothers in on anything was a strict no-no, but in his bedroom, in his apartment, in the cobalt hues of morning? This was fair game.

Seven stirred but didn't face me. I could tell he was awake, or at least rousing. I placed a soft kiss between his shoulder blades, then along the top of his shoulder. By the time I got to the top of his arm, he was turning to face me.

I could catch the dim outline of a smile. "Good morning."

"Extra good morning," I murmured as Seven brought me against him. His arms fit around me easily; I felt comically small in his embrace. His radiator-grade heat sank into me, making me dizzy. I nuzzled into his neck, moving against him, making my wishes known.

This seemed like the only chance I had. Not because there wouldn't be other times, other opportunities. But because first times scared the fuck out of me, and there was something comforting about crossing that bridge the morning after a great night with friends and family.

I'd opened up so much to him—and him to me—that I'd gone nearly wild with desire. This had to happen. *Now.*

I pushed my hand down the side of his body until I found the waistband of his boxer briefs. I tugged on them gently. In response, Seven rolled on top of me, caging me against the bed. He looked even bigger in the shadowy room, a hulking giant on top of me. A twinge of panic erupted deep in my gut, but I ignored it. This was safe. I was safe. I *wanted* this.

"You want this, huh?" Seven's cock was fully hard—and pressed against the crotch of my panties. He rocked against me in a slow, controlled motion, his cock nudging my clit. The pleasure that erupted fizzled quickly. I squeezed my eyes shut, counseling myself through the bad memories that were clamoring for air.

I was safe. This was Seven's bedroom. This wasn't my ex-boyfriend's shitty apartment outside Louisville. I swallowed hard, dragging my fingers along his biceps, bringing myself back to the moment.

"I do," I whispered, praying my body would catch up once things progressed a little further. It had been so long since I'd tried to have sex with anyone, I felt like a virgin by default. But I was determined to see this through. He turned me on just by breathing in the same room as me. I didn't want the assholes of my past to still be robbing me of moments like this one with a man like Seven.

Come on. You can do this. This is the time.

I clutched his biceps, my nails digging in. Seven nuzzled the hollow of my neck, soft kisses trailing down my skin and over the T-shirt. He bunched the fabric up, his lips meeting my belly. I focused on how hot his lips felt against my skin, how much I'd been fantasizing about this moment. And here it was—happening. At last.

And all you can think about is how your fuckwad ex pinned you to a bed like this one, on a morning like this one, and had his way with you until you were sobbing and ruined.

I gritted my teeth as his kisses danced along the edge of my panties. I focused on long, even breaths. Seven wasn't going to pin me here.

Seven was sweet, he was aware…and he was removing my underwear in a forceful tug.

I felt his body weight shift. My panties were gone. And then he was back on top of me. When he tried to open my legs, I realized how rigid they'd become. Seven paused, dragging his fingertips over my hip.

"What's going on, Jordan?" Concern filled his voice. "Why are you so tense?"

The simple question felt like a rock against the aquarium glass of my emotions. My breath hitched, then suddenly the tears came. Shame flooded me, and I tore myself out from underneath him, racing to the bathroom. I shut the door behind me and stumbled over to the closed toilet seat, collapsing. My head fell into my hands and I cried, my entire body electrified and confused.

That wasn't how the first time between me and Seven was supposed to go. And now, I'd outed myself. My shameful truth. I was mortified—he'd discovered just how sensitive I was, what a phony I was. I spent my nights at the club acting liberated and powerful in my sexuality, when the truth was that I was still a teenager ruled by bad memories.

I could turn on any guy in the world, but I couldn't fuck how I wanted. What did that make me?

A soft knock sounded at the door. "Jordan?"

I sucked in a deep breath, trying to calm down even a little bit. "I'm fine."

"You don't sound fine."

"I'm just hungover," I said, my throat thick with tears.

The knob jiggled. A moment later, the door swung open. He stepped into the bathroom, an olive-skinned mountain of muscle with washboard abs and deep concern filling his brown eyes. For a moment, we were suspended in time, his crushing confusion nearly choking me.

Then time snapped, and he was at my feet. Scooping me into his arms, pulling me into his lap as he sank onto the bathroom floor against the wall.

"What's going on?" His voice was a reassuring murmur at my ear.

I buried my face in his chest, a few more sobs escaping. "I'm sorry. That's not how I wanted any of that to happen."

"You don't have to apologize." His big hand swirled comfortingly against my back. "I just need to know that you're okay."

I wrapped my arms around his waist, nuzzling against him. The tears still flowed, but some of my rational mind was returning. He was genuinely concerned, not just following me in here to finish the fuck. This wasn't about his pleasure or him getting off. He actually wanted to see that I was okay.

And if I hadn't been in love with him before, I was now.

I melted a little more against him, until I could hear his heartbeat. I listened until my breathing regulated and the tears were dry. He didn't prod me. He just held me.

"I have a hard time with first times," I whispered after what felt like an hour on the bathroom floor. "And I haven't had a first time in a long time, because of how hard it is."

He stroked my hair, not saying a word.

"Something about the room...and the darkness..." I swallowed hard, not wanting to immortalize the details. "I know we're nowhere near where the bad things happened, but I-I just..."

"It's okay." He placed a kiss on the top of my head. "You don't have to explain. You're safe with me."

"Thank you." I squeezed him as tightly as I could.

"I'm sorry for putting you in an unfamiliar room when you were drunk," he said a moment later. "I should have known better."

"There's no way you could have known I'd...react like that."

"Do you have any other triggers I should know about?" He asked it softly, as if he'd almost thought better of it.

I shook my head. "It's first times. And it's dark rooms. I just don't have a good track record with them." I swallowed hard, thinking back to the moment the fear clicked into place. "Your bedroom wall color is almost the exactly the same as my ex's."

"I'm so sorry." This time, he was the one to squeeze me in a tight hug. My eyes drifted shut. If it weren't for the painful awareness that we were cuddling on a bathroom floor, I could have fallen asleep against his warm skin.

A long time went by before he said, "Do you have names?"

"What do you mean?"

"For who hurt you. I need to know names."

I swallowed hard, touched by the gesture. "You don't have to—"

"Jordan, yes I do." He trailed this thumb along my jaw, until it pressed into my chin. "Because you're mine, whether you realize it or not."

CHAPTER NINETEEN

SEVEN

One and done was a laughable concept now. It had been my game plan—sample the forbidden fruit, get it out of my system, and move on with my life. But no. There was no "done" anymore. After finding her broken and vulnerable in the bathroom, hugging her knees to her chest, there was only "mine."

Mine to hold. Mine to protect.

Jordan got her shift covered at the coffee shop that morning, which allowed her to sleep off the rest of her hangover. I carried her to her bed, left her with some water and ibuprofen, and got to work distracting myself via exercise. I changed into gray sweatpants and opted for weights, crunches, and push-ups, then I opened up my laptop to find the quickest interior painting company I could hire. I needed to repaint my bedroom walls ASAP. I sent inquiries to a couple of places, then switched to business management mode.

Despite Jordan's best attempts to either haze or scare Chico off, he wanted to continue working for Silva Security. His first assignments were with the Fairchild brothers on various outings when additional security was needed, like trips back to Kentucky for Willow's court hearings. He was doing well, which meant I needed to start looking for the second new hire.

I still wasn't sure which protection officer would become Jordan's full-time companion. I'd now crossed the line I swore not to cross, which would make handing over her protection even harder—and more necessary. Not to mention I still had to *inform* Jordan of my plans, which scared the shit out of me.

But it was a no-brainer. I had to do this, if I wanted to keep my heart and my future intact.

Around three p.m., I finished all I had to do. Jordan still hadn't come out so I knocked gently on her door. I heard a faint mumble from inside, so I pushed the door open slightly.

"Hey. Do you need anything?" I asked, squinting into the darkened room.

"I'm good."

"Not hungry?"

"No," she said faintly, like she was still half asleep. I shut the door quietly and confronted my apartment. It was already clean; I had Jordan's lunch waiting for her, whenever she woke up. My work and workout were done for the day. What remained?

Spoon carving. I went back to my bedroom, tossing on a white T-shirt before rummaging through the depths of the closet to find my supplies. It was the only alternative when I was sexually frustrated and anxiously awaiting Jordan.

Prior to my move from Kentucky to New York, I'd batch cut a bunch of utensil outlines from some spare wood I came across, mostly aspen and balsa wood. I grabbed one of the precut spoons from my big bag of woodworking materials, along with a safety glove, thumb guard and some carving tools, and retreated to the living room.

I loved the repetition and focus of spoon carving. It helped soothe my mind—or in this case, my raging sexual desire. At this point, half my kitchen collection were tools I'd carved myself. This would be a more basic spoon, just for my own personal enjoyment.

Time flew by as I shaped and carved the spoon to my liking, wood shavings tumbling to the plastic covering I used on the floor. I smoothed the curves; added extra roundness at the base. I wasn't even sure how much time had gone by when Jordan's voice cut through my concentration.

"Playing with your wood, huh?"

She came around the sectional, a smirk on her face. My big T-shirt hung loosely from her slight frame, a gut punch I hadn't planned on. I'd slipped it on her last night simply so she wouldn't have to sleep in her regular clothes. But seeing her wearing my old gym shirt, wandering around my apartment, took my fucking breath away.

She climbed onto the couch next to me, snuggling in close as she assessed my handiwork. Ranger joined us a moment later, his purring immediate as he snuggled up next to my other side.

"You've discovered my secret," I told her.

She twisted to look back at the kitchen, then at the spoon in my hands. "Wait a minute. Did you make all those wooden spoons in the kitchen?"

I nodded.

"I've been in love with them since I moved in." Awe shone in her voice. "Can I see this one?"

I handed it off, looking at the imperfections while she turned it over in her hands. It was about 97% ready, though I never felt any project was truly done.

"This is so cool," she said. "And you're good at it. I bet this is really calming."

"It is. Though probably not as calming as climbing a pole."

She smirked. "That is great for zeroing out any thoughts you might be having. But I can see how this would pretty much do the same. Unless you intentionally wanted to cut your thumb off, that is."

I lifted my right hand and wiggled my thumb, which was encased in a mesh thumb protector. "That's why I've got this on."

"Looks like a tiny medieval hat." She handed the spoon back to me.

We shared a laugh as I gathered my tools and set them on the leather mat I'd laid on the coffee table. Spoon time was over.

Now it was time for Jordan.

I slung my arm around her, pulling her onto my lap. She giggled, settling against my chest.

"You feeling better?"

She nodded, tracing invisible patterns over my T-shirt. "The sleep helped."

"I've got food for you if you're hungry."

"Maybe later. I was still queasy a little bit ago."

I rested my chin on the top of her head, a pleasant silence settling over us. This felt right. Her in my lap, in my arms. My pint-sized, spitfire brat.

Is she yours, though? The question seared through me, but I pushed it away. I wanted to enjoy this, even if I *shouldn't* have. I squeezed my arms around her.

"Does this help?" I asked.

"Mmm." She nodded, a smile curling at her lips. "It does." She nestled deeper into my arms, letting out a contented sigh. "Thanks for, you know, being cool with my breakdown earlier."

"It's what I'm here for." For *her*, at least. Emotional investment during breakdowns—not to mention the slew of other lines I'd crossed—wasn't a standard interaction between protection officer and client, by any means. In fact, if she'd been a regular client, I'd have drawn the line that night Dustin attacked her. She wouldn't know my real name. She wouldn't know a damn thing about me.

But here we are.

She propped her chin against my chest, searching my face with her mesmerizing blue-gray eyes. "It kind of freaks me out how much I like you, Seven."

I wanted to say the same to her. But I couldn't. That reservation was the last shred of logic I possessed.

"I don't think I've ever liked anyone more," she went on. "And it scares the crap out of me, because now I'm worried you'll just see me as broken or...whatever."

I was shaking my head before she even finished her sentence. "That's not how it is. Trust me, I know a thing or two about being broken. I'd never see you that way. I know some of your story. When I look at you, I see someone who has had the shittiest hand dealt to her and still somehow made magic out of it."

A smile flickered at her lips.

"Besides, I think all you need is a little bit more attention." Now *that*, I could give to her all day and all night. I shifted beneath her, which caused her back to fall against my chest, her head propped against my neck. "You need someone who actually wants to make *you* feel good."

This time, when she smiled, it stayed. "Yeah, that doesn't sound half bad."

I pushed my palms down along the sides of her body, over her thighs. I squeezed the tight muscles there, exhaling low.

"Is it time to play with wood again?" she cracked.

"No." I nipped at her earlobe, unable to keep myself from getting hard with her body pressed against me. "What did I just say? This is about *you* feeling good."

"Oh, right. So, playing with *my* wood."

I moved my hands to her inner thighs, dragging up toward her pelvis. She wore the stretchy black boy shorts she always put on before pole practice. My palms glided over the silky texture. I swirled my fingers over her covered pussy, so gently. "Hmm. Not finding any to play with here."

She rocked her hips toward my hand. "Oh yeah? You better check again."

I dragged my fingertips over her mons, swirling slowly downward, until I found the heated slit of her pussy. She sucked on her teeth.

"Ranger is watching."

I elbowed the cat—gently, of course—and he rumbled low, wandering across the living room to find a new resting spot.

"Nope. Still no wood." I nuzzled her face, dragging my lips across her cheek. I could feel the bud of her clit through the workout shorts and I pressed my middle finger back and forth across it. She inhaled sharply, her entire body jerking.

"Are you sure you shouldn't check more?" Her voice sounded strained now, her nipples hardened to tight points beneath her sports bra. My free hand wandered up to cup a breast as she allowed her legs to splay open wider.

"I'll check as long as you need or want." I kissed the side of her cheek. "And tell me if you need me to stop. This is about you, Jordan. You call the shots."

She nodded emphatically. "Okay. Yes."

"I'm not going to do a single thing you don't want or ask for."

A shuddery breath slid out of her. "I like this game."

I chuckled low, dragging my tongue against her earlobe as I pushed my fingertips across her clit again. "I assure you, this is no game."

She whimpered as I rubbed circles around her clit, close enough to tease, but not close enough to give her what she really wanted. She bucked her hips, urging more from me, but I wanted to move slow. I didn't intend to spook her again.

"Do you want me to keep going?" I asked.

She nodded vehemently.

"Say it, Jordan."

"I want you to keep going." She arched her back, clamping her legs around my hand. She had thighs of steel; I appreciated her attempt to keep my hand in the place she most wanted.

"Only if you promise not to snap my hand off first," I teased.

She laughed, low and throaty. "I know how to keep something long and hard between my legs when I need it."

She loosened her grip on my hand, and I rewarded her by gliding my fingertips back and forth across her clit again. She moaned low, eyes fluttering shut. I'd had my fill of teasing. I wanted more.

I inched my fingers toward the waistband of her boy shorts, pushing my hand beneath the silky, stretchy fabric. My fingers immediately found the tightly trimmed patch of hair. No undies. Just warm skin and her molten pussy.

As my hand drifted downward, my fingertips grazed her swollen clit. I pinched it, already dying to bury my face between her legs and get a taste for myself. But that would come in time. For now, I just needed to show her I was safe....and how much fun we'd have together.

I rolled her clit between my thumb and forefinger. She cried out, clutching at my forearm.

"Jesus, Seven," she gasped out.

"I'm just getting started. Was that number one already?"

"Almost," she said with a weak laugh. I pushed my hand deeper into the heat, finding her swollen pussy lips and the drenched core of her.

"Just need to check everything out," I whispered, tugging at her earlobe again. She whimpered, moving against my hand. "You see, I'm not going to fuck you with my cock. Not for a while."

Jordan groaned. "Why not?"

"Because I need to make sure you're ready for it." I smiled as I said it. I meant it both seriously and as a joke. I had a sneaking suspicion that she was going to be tight as fuck. And I wasn't a small boy. She laughed weakly.

"I promise I am."

"In the meantime, I'll fuck you with whatever else I have on hand. Like my fingers. My tongue. And whatever else you can dream up." I slipped my middle finger into her slick channel then, discovering the silken, juicy tightness that I'd been fantasizing about for so long. I gritted my teeth, a grunt escaping me. I pushed my finger in and out slowly. If she was this tight around one finger, I knew she'd need plenty of foreplay before my cock went anywhere near her.

Good thing I didn't mind extensive foreplay.

"You're so fucking tight, Jordan." I moaned as I plunged my finger inside her, then out; slipped my fingers up to tease her clit, then back inside her. She bucked her hips against my hand, and I continued the motion. She clutched at my hand cupping her tit.

"Ohhh, Seven. Don't stop." She sounded so far away. Breathy, as if she might pass out. "Pleaaaase, don't stop."

She bucked more frantically then, my fingers growing slicker from her juices. Her clit was a hard nub when I pinched it on my next round. She swore loudly, arching against me as her nails dug into my hand. I plunged my finger back inside her, her pussy clenching around me in chaotic waves. Her whole body jolted, and then again. She'd had a hell of an orgasm.

I leaned down and kissed the tip of her nose before I slipped my finger out of her. But I left my hand stuffed beneath the fabric of her pants. Mostly because I'd been wanting to do this for too fucking long and I liked the way it looked with my hand buried in her shorts.

Mine.

Her chest lifted and fell quickly. Finally, her eyes drifted open, and she looked up at me with a lazy smile on her face.

"*That* was number one."

"First of many."

"Is it your turn now?" she asked lazily.

I shook my head. "No. Not needed." When she looked doubtful, I added, "Do you really want to?"

She blinked a few times, her gaze drifting out across the room. "I just want to lie here and let you touch me more."

I grinned, pressing a sloppy kiss to the side of her cheek. "Then that's what you'll get."

CHAPTER TWENTY

JORDAN

It was somewhere around the fifth orgasm that I realized I was living in Heaven.

Seventh Heaven.

Heaven with Seven.

Roxie was wrong. The man *did* know his way around a pussy. Because he played mine like a fiddle every single night.

I couldn't believe how often his fingers were inside of me. And on some occasions, his tongue. I went through the next few days permanently sexually satisfied yet clamoring for more, more, more. I'd never known such limb-melting, euphoria-defining pleasure. And the man wouldn't even stick it in. Not until I screamed my consent and he was satisfied that I was fully "ready".

Friday morning, I woke up about a half hour before my alarm. It wasn't typical for me, but neither was sharing a bed with my bodyguard or sleeping buried in his arms, which were all part of the new norm. When I came to, I realized Seven had moved his muscular thigh between my legs, gently moving it against my pussy.

I drew a deep breath, unable to prevent the cheek-splitting smile. Shit like this was unreal. I moved my hips in the same rhythm, watching his lips curl up, too.

"You don't waste any time," I murmured, burying my face in his neck.

"Let's start the day off right." He kissed my cheek, my lips, my chin, then threw the covers back. In the shifting gray morning light, I relished the view of him. He'd stopped drawing the room-darkening curtains at night, which meant more natural light filled the bedroom, allowing me greater clarity of this Czech-and-Guatemalan god. His chiseled torso, the jaw-droppingly enormous bulge in his boxer briefs. Maybe he was right to spend so much time with his fingers inside me. There was a scientific likelihood that our parts wouldn't fit.

Seven propped himself on his heels near the foot of the bed, tugging me toward him. I giggled as I slid effortlessly across his sheets. He clambered off the bed, knelt on the ground, and tugged me even closer. I could tell from the glint in his eye what he was going for, the way he eyed my panties ravenously. He tore them off me in a fluid movement, skipping hot kisses along my inner thigh until he found my core.

Next, he dragged his tongue over my clit, causing my whole body to spasm. He pressed little kisses down my pussy until his tongue pressed inside, swirling and searching. A jagged moan escaped me as he returned to my clit, flicking his tongue back and forth across it. Electric heat started swarming my limbs, warning me. I arched my back and pinched my eyes shut, welcoming the sensation.

"Look at me, Jordan."

His gritty command sparked new fires inside me. I inhaled sharply, doing as he asked.

"Watch me tongue fuck you." The smile he gave me was equal parts sexy and boyish. Then he dove in, lavishing my pussy with his fiercest yet most delicate attention. It was hard not to melt into a puddle of goo. But with eyes on him, I saw the way his right arm moved methodically, his hand obscured by the foot of the bed. His muscles flexing rhythmically. Desire sizzled through me. He was jacking off while he ate me out.

He slurped at my pussy, his head moving from side to side as he explored my depths with his tongue once more. When he came up for air, he sank his teeth into my inner thigh. My whole body jolted, and I cried out.

"Do you know what I'm doing down here?" he asked, his voice sounding strained.

"Playing with your...wood?" It was hard to form sentences, much less be cheeky.

He grunted. I could hear the wet slap of him working his cock. But I wanted to see, too. I wriggled impatiently. "Let me see."

He sank his teeth into my inner thigh again, and this time I could tell it was a reprimand. "Not yet. I don't want to scare you."

"Oh come on. Is it that big?"

He smiled evilly, nodding slowly.

I squeezed my thighs around his head, needing more of his tongue anywhere he'd give it to me. Between the sounds of him jacking off, that evil smile, and the buzz of my pending orgasm inside me, I felt ready to explode.

"More. I need more."

Seven dove in again—sucking at my clit, dragging his teeth against the needy nub, then dipping his tongue deep inside me. It was an orchestrated rhythm, one that had me writhing and mewling. I fisted the comforter on his bed, so fucking close to release. He scooped an arm around my ass, bringing me crashing into his face. His tongue assaulted my clit, sending me blasting past the point of no return.

My vision went white and bright, and for a moment everything ceased to exist except this blinding pleasure.

He groaned low and guttural. "Ohhhh, fuck, Jordan."

With my chest heaving, I saw his gaze drop to his hands. His body jerked a few times, then he looked up at me, desire clouding his dark eyes.

I couldn't even form words. My head cocked lazily to the side.

He pressed soft kisses along my inner thigh, then gently removed my legs from over his shoulders. He repositioned my limp limbs on the bed. When he climbed onto the bed beside me, his cock was still a thick ridge pressing at his boxer briefs. He arranged himself behind me, wrapping his arms around my waist.

His cock pressed at the small of my back.

"I thought you got off?" I asked with a small laugh.

"I did." He nuzzled my neck. "Still hard."

"Probably time for me to sit on it, then."

He chastised me with a bite to my shoulder. "I think we might be close."

I shivered with excitement. "Right now?"

"No. We need to get up." He propped himself up slightly, squinting at the bedside clock. "The painters are coming soon."

"What painters?"

"They're going to repaint my room." He settled back against me, taking a deep inhale of my hair. "Maybe you can pick the new color."

My mouth opened to ask why on earth he'd repaint only his room, then I remembered: I'd told him the other day the color looked like my ex's bedroom. I clamped my mouth shut, suddenly so overwhelmed with emotion I couldn't find words.

"You don't have to if you don't want to," he added a moment later.

I cleared my throat, nodding. "I'd love to."

I wriggled out of his tight grip and spun around to face him. Then I clutched his beautiful face in mine and kissed him harder and more deeply than I'd ever kissed anyone in my life.

Despite the mind-blowing start to my morning, it was still a double-shift day. Which meant I'd be seeing far less of Seven than I wanted. Even though he constantly lurked around the edges, I needed more than just seeing him. I needed to be on top of him. Preferably stretched around that cock he wouldn't let me play with yet.

Despite the long-game tease, I was enjoying myself. Probably too much. It seemed too perfect, too easy. *What's the catch?* This was the question on repeat in my mind. There had to be a catch, something waiting around the corner to ruin this whole thing. It couldn't last forever; that seemed certain, though I wasn't entirely sure why.

We took the subway to Black & Brewtiful much as we did every day I worked there, but this time, there was an extra buzz in the air. We knocked hips. I even laced my fingers through his once, and he allowed it. When I teased him, he smiled. We spent so much time gazing at each other with silly grins on our faces that I wondered if maybe we both had some sort of sudden mental illness.

What's the catch?

I needed to find out. Before we rounded the block to the coffeeshop, I stopped Seven and guided him out of the flow of the sidewalk traffic. While he was backed against the building, I pushed onto my tiptoes.

"I just need one last kiss before I go in there."

He slipped his hand around the back of my head, offering up a tender but passionate kiss that stole my air and my balance. When we parted, that dark desire swirled in his eyes, and a different question started to circulate.

What if there's no catch for once?

Once we entered the shop, it was business as usual. Seven retreated to a corner to do his own work, and I slipped into barista mode. It was a busy, fun morning, with a never-ending line of customers that meant I had almost no time to chat with my co-workers. I only realized my shift was ending because I spotted Seven packing up his laptop. I hadn't even taken a lunch break.

I clocked out, met Seven outside, and let out a big cleansing breath.

"You thinking rice noodles?" he asked.

I shook my head. "I wanna hit up a Pokéstop. I need the thrill of a catch to make this day even better."

He smirked, and we set off toward the subway station. "Okay. Where you thinking?"

"Highline. Then we can grab lunch there, too."

He nodded, smiling down at me. "Deal."

"Ready?" I asked him, preparing myself for the response of the day.

"I arrived in the world willing."

We raced through pedestrian traffic to see who could reach the end of each block first. The first person to reach the bottom of the subway station steps won—it was me—and I held this over his head until the lady with a live parrot on the train distracted us.

When we got out at 14th Street, we raced the two blocks to the Highline entrance, our footsteps thudding up the metal staircase. This time, Seven won. He held his fists up in victory, and I took that opportunity to squeeze my arms around him in a hug that was both a punishment and a celebration.

We wandered like this, teasing and playful, along the public park converted from a freight rail line. I checked my phone on occasion, looking for Pokémon. Seven joined along on his phone, and watched over my shoulder as I sent out a lure and caught one of the rarer spawns.

"There we go." I showed him my phone, displaying the latest catch. "Another one for the collection."

"It looks like a snake dragon," he muttered.

"Yeah. It's cute."

"I'm not doing a very good job at collecting them all."

"It'll come with time," I told him. "Just watching you try though feels like I've caught the rarest one of them all. So maybe that makes *me* the ultimate winner."

I relished the shy smile he offered me, my growling belly reminding me that lunchtime had come and gone. "You ready to grab a bite?"

"I was going to eat that Pokémon if you didn't suggest lunch soon." He stepped behind me, draping his arms around me, pressing my back against him. "You wanna hit those food kiosks over there?"

I looked in the direction he pointed out, spotting a sign for tacos. "Absolutely. Look, they have tacos."

Seven dipped down, nuzzling me before he whispered, "I already ate a taco this morning."

I giggled, swatting his arm. "Very funny."

"I could go for another one, though." He bit my earlobe gently. "Either type."

"Well, we're not trying to be put in jail for public cunnilingus," I reminded him. "So let's try the street tacos this time."

We walked hand-in-hand toward the kiosks, sharing heated glances. At this point, I *did* feel ready to mount him publicly, indecency laws be damned. But getting a hold on his cock seemed to require a complex combination of consent, horniness, and some other thing I wasn't aware of yet. Like he wasn't going to give it up until I presented him with a notarized letter of vaginal readiness. But I had an idea about how to change that.

The little Michoacan-inspired Mexican kiosk served up some tender carnitas tacos in a double corn tortilla. We each ate two, grinning at each other as the occasional spot of salsa dribbled onto the ground. Once our bellies were full, we wandered the length of the park and then back again, hunting Pokémon and having the most normal, wholesome afternoon I'd had in, well, in my entire life.

There might not be a catch.

I'd never felt as safe or secure as I did when I was with Seven. He promised that nothing could ever hurt me when I was with him, and I believed it. And that sense of safety acted as gasoline on top of my already raging attraction to this man.

By the time we made it to Gemstones, my body crackled with electric desire. It didn't matter that I was already five orgasms deep for the day or that I was sure to get off again once we got home. I needed him completely. *Fully.* It seemed the only appropriate way to cap off what was growing between us.

And I couldn't wait another second.

I booked the VIP room for Seven before I even hit the stage that night. I spent extra time doing my hair and makeup before my performance, thanks to our extended visit to the Highline. All I could see or think about was Seven. My heart pounded for him—the corniest yet truest thing. I knew that I wouldn't be able to survive my entire shift without getting what I needed. What we *both* needed.

My outfit for the shift was high-waisted garter shorts with a low-cut mesh top. Perfect for my rigorous pole routine *and* for looking sexy. When I hit the stage, Seven was the first thing I looked for. Spotting that muscular, boxy frame in the shadows, every bit of his attention on me, provided a high I didn't know I could experience. Not until Seven came along.

I moved and swung and danced for him. My entire body vibrated with anticipation once my set finished. I scooped up all the tips that lay scattered on the stage and chatted with a few men who stopped me on my path to Seven. I didn't flirt as much as I normally would, not when I had a prime directive like this one. I made it over to Seven, and the way he raked his eyes over my body sent a shiver through me.

"You've got the first reservation tonight," I told him, grabbing his hand. "Shall I lead the way?"

He didn't resist, merely fell in step with me. "I'm assuming this is another one of those mysterious clients who cancelled?"

"How did you know?" I pushed open the door of the VIP room, strutting inside confidently. Once the door clicked shut behind us, muting the bass thump of the music from the club, I wrapped my arms around his big chest. With the stripper heels, I was much closer to his lips than normal.

"I can't fucking wait another second," I murmured, brushing my lips against his. "Seven, please. Put me out of my misery."

He seemed equal parts confused and amused. "Misery?"

I pushed him. He didn't budge, but he had the good sense to back toward the couch and sit down.

"I need you," I said succinctly, resting my hands on his shoulders as I sank on top of him. I rolled my hips in a slow, meaningful circle on top of him, already finding the bulge of his cock waiting to greet my clit. I whimpered as I felt the hot friction where I needed it most. "We have all the time we need right now. Let me sit on it."

His big hands scorched a path up the back of my thighs, over my bare ass cheeks. He squeezed hard and then said, "And you think here is the best place to do it?"

I rubbed against him more desperately, eager to show him how serious this was. "I can't wait anymore. Seven, please. I'm begging you."

An evil smile tugged at his lips. "You look so fucking hot when you beg."

My insides turned to mush. I nuzzled his neck, biting gently before I moved to his full bottom lip. I sucked at it, which morphed into deep, desperate kisses that had me grinding against him with abandon.

I was liable to orgasm—number six—from that friction alone, but I wasn't here just to get off. I wanted to make his cock disappear, goddammit.

I ripped myself away from him, even though every cell in my body rejected the decision. Clambering off him, I undid the garter belt straps around my thighs, since I knew they might snap from the upcoming exertion. Seven watched me with a drugged look on his face. But he didn't make a single move.

To show how serious I was, I slipped my mesh top off, exposing my breasts. His eyes went hooded.

"Come on," I pleaded.

He wet his bottom lip, pressing the heel of his palm over the straining bulge of his pants. Then he said, "Jordan. Be real. I don't have any condoms with me."

In my crazed state, I hadn't even thought of that. It had barely registered as a concern with how solid and real Seven was.

"I don't fucking care," I breathed out, barely above a whisper. "I've had an IUD in since I was seventeen. We're safe." Then I slipped out of my shorts, tossing them to join my top.

His throat bobbed, and he cocked his head, raking his gaze over me in a way that felt almost dangerous. Like I'd unlocked a new level.

"Come here." He unbuckled his belt, making quick work of the zipper until slate gray boxer briefs were revealed, the ridge of his cock straining beneath. He pushed down the waistband of his underwear, finally revealing the cock I'd been fantasizing about.

Whatever I'd expected from him, the reality was ten times better. And larger. He fisted the base of his cock, waving it slightly at me, grinning with a look that said *I told you so.*

I'd drifted back to him, straddling him without even realizing it. My hand met hot, silky skin encasing what I then realized was the world's hardest, largest cock. My thumb and middle finger didn't even meet as I attempted to wrap my hand around his erection.

"Seven," I breathed. I squeezed my fingers tighter, trying to close that gap around his monster cock. I couldn't. He groaned softly, shifting his hips.

"You still want to do this?" he asked, his voice strained.

"Fuck yes," I answered without hesitation. But then I paused. "You are...*really* big."

"You can take it, baby." His hands scorched up the small of my back, bringing our bodies closer together. The head of his cock probed between my legs. The scorching heat of him met the folds of my pussy, and I moaned. "I've been getting you ready. You can take it."

I drew a shaky breath, propping my hands on his shoulders as I arranged myself on him. My slick core slid against his erection, the hot glide making my insides melt.

"Where do you want me to come?" he asked, cocking his head as his gaze raked up and down our bodies.

"Inside me," I said before I could even process the question.

"Jordan—"

"I need it." I rolled my hips in a slow circle, teasing his swollen cockhead. He grunted, fingertips digging into the flesh of my ass cheeks.

"You want me to fill you with my cum?" he asked, cracking a palm against my ass cheek. Then he squeezed hard at the stinging flesh. I nodded, pressing my forehead to his.

"Every single one of those men out there will notice." His voice was gritty. "They'll see my cum dripping out of your pussy, down your legs. Do you know why?"

"Why?"

"Because you're mine."

I nodded harder, rocking against him, the tip of his erection dancing dangerously close to popping inside me. "That's right. Let them see."

He grunted again, gripping me by the waist. His dark gaze left no room for doubt. "Eyes on me." He guided me down, his cockhead probing as my pussy sank down and claimed his cock. He eased inside me slowly, stretching me more than I expected.

I whimpered, tightening around him.

"Stay with me." His chest heaved, but he still had control. "You can take it."

The way he said it, reassured and so fucking dialed in, made my entire body warm and loose. He guided me down further, steering me by the hips.

His nostrils flared, but he never broke eye contact with me. "You're doing such a good job."

I sank lower, stretching to accommodate his girth. My entire body was alive with sensation. It felt so fucking good I thought I might pass out, and he couldn't have had more than a few inches inside of me. I rocked my hips in a small circle, eliciting a guttural noise from him.

"This feels...like..." I could barely even form thoughts, much less make the words happen now that he was inside me. I sank lower, unsure of how much of his cock I'd swallowed inside me. It seemed never-ending.

He ran his teeth across each of my nipples in turn. "Go on."

I let the thump of the bass from the music outside act as my muse. I wriggled my hips, claiming another inch or two of him. "Like we're running out of space."

He shifted his hips against me, grunting. "Found some more."

But then I could tell we *had* reached the end of the line, as far as his dick filling my pussy was concerned. The sensation of him inside me was incredible; in fact, it bordered on painful, a fullness I had never experienced but knew I craved more of. My eyes fluttered shut from the mind-numbing pleasure coursing through my limbs.

"Eyes on me," he said softly.

I forced myself to open my eyes.

"You took it so good, Jordan." His arms squeezed around my waist, that same dangerous, dark glint in his gaze. "Now I want you to fucking ride it."

CHAPTER TWENTY-ONE

SEVEN

It didn't matter how many times I'd beat off over the past week. With Jordan's silken vice of a pussy wrapped around my cock, I was a ticking time bomb.

She let out a breathy sigh. Her nipples had been hard as diamonds since she took that top off. I snagged each one between my lips as she rocked against me.

"Fuuuuck, Seven."

I tightened my hold around her little waist, making sure there wasn't an inch of unnecessary space between our bodies. "Ride me like you wanted to. I'm yours."

Her mouth parted, the sexiest, yet most tender look searing across her face. I didn't go bareback with anyone—much less the client's sister I wasn't supposed to touch—but all bets were off with Jordan. I'd known it the second I met her, even though I'd been in denial.

Jordan pushed up, revealing the length of my cock, then sank back down. We both groaned. She was juicier than fuck, a waterslide of desire, and I held on for dear life as she slammed down around my cock. I cupped her tits in my hands as she rode me, matching the rhythm of the bass undertones coming from the current performance in the club. Bathed in purple light, fully naked and riding my cock like a champ, she was a goddess. This was absolutely the shit of my dreams. Better than my dreams, even, because I'd never been able to dream up someone like Jordan.

"That's it, Jordan." I squeezed her tits as she rocked against me. Her thighs trembled, and I could tell she was close. "You like how I fill you up?"

She nodded vehemently, her eyes glued to mine.

"You want me to show you how much I like it, too?"

She whimpered, biting her bottom lip as she ground against me.

"Let me hear you say it."

"Sh-Show me," she breathed. Her eyes were the equivalent of exclamation points. A sheen of sweat glimmered on her skin, and I could tell she was struggling to hold it together. "Fill me up, Seven."

The breathy command undid my little remaining restraint. The way her hips moved against me, the way that vice of a pussy continually slipped up and down, consuming my cock with nothing at all between our slick, hot flesh...after so much prolonged teasing and delayed gratification, I was shocked I'd been able to last this long.

"Fuck, Jordan. You take it so fucking good." I buried my face in the hollow of her neck as I felt the warning pinpricks spiral into a full-body assault. Heat flooded me, bliss spreading from top to tail, as I pumped round after round into her. Jordan made every type of indecipherable sound, the way a woman sounds when she utterly and truly falls apart. I could feel the truth of it from the way her pussy spasmed around my cock, the way she went limp in my arms and eventually stilled against me, buried balls deep inside her.

I couldn't release my hold on her. I wasn't sure I could ever let her go. Not fully. She breathed as fast as someone who'd just finished running a marathon. My cock pulsed weakly inside her, damn near ready for round two.

I'd found my moment of bliss. Everything made sense, and nothing but this languorous pleasure existed inside me and between us.

Jordan shifted after a few moments, or maybe a few hours. Her voice was a raw whisper. "Holy shit."

I could already feel my cum beginning its hot slide out of her pussy, dripping out and down. I was a big man in all senses, and that included my output.

I nuzzled her neck. "You good?"

All I heard for a few moments was her breath at my ear. Then she said, "More than good."

"Good."

"What about you?"

"Paralyzed with pleasure." I pulled back so I could get a good look at her, finding a drugged expression on her face. I likely wore a similar one myself.

"That's probably a little closer to the truth," she whispered. "I might need to go to the hospital after this."

I smirked. "Well, all your vitals have been verified..."

"You technically impaled me."

"I think you'll be able to walk," I said. Though I couldn't say it would be easy right away.

"You rearranged my organs," she said.

"They needed to be freshened up," I claimed, "it's good to rearrange things every so often."

She snort-laughed, then collapsed against my chest again. My dick had softened slightly, but it waited at attention. I lifted her by the backs of her thighs slightly, until she slipped off me and came to her feet unsteadily.

"Whoa," she whispered, bracing herself against my shoulders.

"Good thing you waited until after your performance."

We watched each other for a few moments, grinning like idiots. Then she started to look for her clothes.

"I have no idea how to finish the rest of my shift," she said, stumbling toward the discarded white mesh top.

I made quick work of slipping my cock back into my briefs and zipping myself up. I could have stayed in here with Jordan for another twelve hours, solely to fuck, but she had things to do. Besides, I knew we'd celebrate round two the first chance we got.

"Well, if you need to bring me in here again to think about things, you know where to find me."

Jordan laughed as she tugged on her top. But when she bent over to replace her bottoms, she gasped, her hand going between her legs. "Oh my God."

That could only be surprise about how much she was *leaking*. "You asked me to do it," I reminded her with a grin.

"Seven." She sounded panicked. "I didn't realize you were going to go all Hoover Dam on me!"

I looked around—there was nothing in here to use. "Are there any towels in here? Otherwise I'll go to the bathroom, but then you'll be alone."

She seemed confused for a moment, then she pointed to my feet. "Right there. It's a little trap door with sanitizing wipes and paper towels. Can you pass me something?"

I felt around for the little trap door, tugged it open, and ripped off some sheets for her. Sitting on the couch, I beckoned for her to stand in front of me. I wiped up the dribble that had almost reached her knee, then gently cleaned off the moisture on her inner thighs. The purple light made everything different in here, but I could have sworn I caught a blush on her cheeks. I pressed a soft kiss to each thigh before I released her.

"Thanks," she said.

I stood and caught her chin between my fingers and coaxed a deep kiss from her. When we broke, I said, "I wasn't lying. Your customers *will* see my cum dripping down your legs tonight."

She lifted her chin. "I told you I wanted them to see."

I grinned, pressing my thumb into her chin. "That's my girl."

Once we were both put back together, she still walked unsteadily. I offered my arm. She looked up at me before she opened the door.

"You are just unreal."

The way she said it sounded like it could either be a compliment or a point of frustration. Maybe it was a little of both. When she pulled open the door, some of the hard edges of her persona clicked back into place. She sent me a flirty look and strutted out into the club. Only I could notice the little wobble in her step.

I liked that. More than I wanted to admit.

I resumed my post along the wall, waiting for Jordan to return from freshening up in the Gems lounge. When she sauntered toward the VIP room about ten minutes later, a smarmy-looking dude in tow, I tried to ignore the way my hands formed fist, the way my heart rate picked up, and the sudden urge to follow them both inside.

I took a deep breath, reminding myself she was just doing her job. Nothing would happen in there with this guy or any other.

But the fact that I already felt the licks of jealousy and possessiveness wasn't a good sign.

I knew better than to fuck the person I was protecting, but that didn't mean I was ready to lash myself with regret and shame. No, I was fucking reveling in what we'd just done in the VIP room. It would be a while before the regret could find me. Until then, I planned to conjure up the 364 other ways I planned to fuck her. While staying vigilant, of course.

I scanned the club as I normally did, keeping tabs on the patrons. Looking out for red flags, creepy vibes, and shady activity. Gemstones was surprisingly safe, given my expectations when I first walked in the door. Their clientele *was* wealthier and better behaved overall, which at least tended to mean the nefarious shit was saved for outside club walls.

But that didn't mean I let down my guard. Not here, not anywhere, not ever. Every new group that filtered in, I checked out and rated according to my internal security threat scale. Part of it was intuition, which was hard to back up with facts sometimes, but it hadn't led me astray yet.

Just as Jordan was transitioning from the VIP room to the champagne room for a group of bachelors who wanted drinks and a show, I spotted a group of new arrivals.

Five men, clustered near the front door, dressed in standard-issue designer duds: beige business casual suits, collared polos, enormous watches. They remained clustered by the front door, conferring with the doorman. For a moment, it seemed like there was an issue. The guard's brows drew together, and then one of the bartenders was summoned. I kept an eye on them as Jordan began entertaining the group of bachelors.

After some tense discussion, Eddie arrived to greet the group of men with a big smile and open arms. Now the group had VIP vibes, though the doorman and bartender still seemed on edge. I watched as Eddie conferred with the blond guy, who seemed to be the leader, then Eddie personally escorted them to a large open table in the middle of the lounge area, facing the stage. The five of them settled in, their smiles varying degrees of smug. They looked to be late twenties and early thirties, and even from my post halfway across the club, I could smell the stink of rich entitlement.

My intuition was pinging already.

Eddie chatted with them for a few moments, then one of the bartenders, Val, flitted over to take their drink orders. As soon as Eddie stepped away, one of the men reached out and squeezed Val's ass. She swatted at his hand, playing it coy, but I was put off by the groping.

The longer I spied on this group, the more they raised my hackles. I already knew groups like these for what they were: troublemakers; men who pushed the envelope until it ripped. Usually abnormally wealthy or abnormally famous. I kept an eye on them during my club-wide surveillance. At one point, Joss brought over a tray full of shots from the bar, handing out two each. They were clearly here to party.

Jordan wrapped up in the champagne room after about a half hour. Eddie approached her as the men filtered out, grinning like idiots. He pulled her aside, discussing something with her that prompted a frown to form on her face.

Her gaze found mine as Eddie continued speaking into her ear. She nodded. I wanted to march over there and ask what was going on, but I restrained myself. I trusted her to tell me. She nodded again, saying something I couldn't lip-read in the dim lighting, then Eddie flashed her a thumbs up and wandered off. Jordan ambled my way.

"Figures," she said, propping a hand against the wall beside me. "The one night we say it's a good thing I got my performance out of the way, Eddie asks me to do a surprise second show."

I smirked. "I can't say I'll mind. Are you going to be able to?"

She nodded, crossing her arms as she assessed the club crowd. "I'll be fine. He's switching up the programming since he got a special request or something." She turned toward me, shrugging. "My guess is someone out there wants more than just the regular pole routine from the other girls."

My mind went to the group of men I'd been keeping my eye on, but I pushed the thought away. A second show wouldn't change anything. Jordan knew how to handle herself, and I was only twenty feet away. Everything was fine.

But I couldn't fight the nagging worry that grew as Jordan sauntered away to the Gems lounge to get ready for the next show, which she claimed involved a new outfit and a different persona. I kept closer watch on the table of five. All the shots had been consumed, and Joss returned with another round. These guys didn't waste any time. Before the new round was tipped back, one of the men—the blond—excused himself and stood up, adjusting his watch and polo shirt before walking my way.

We made the briefest of eye contact as he passed me, en route to the bathroom. His blond hair was gelled in a swept back style. He was the living embodiment of what I considered a rich Hamptonite, minus an expensive sweater draped over his shoulders. Something unsettling lurked behind his gaze, something oddly familiar.

I worked through this dilemma until he returned. Maybe a fresh look would jog my memory. There were an incredible number of celebrities in New York City; I walked past a few A-listers on random outings around the city, and Jordan herself had pointed out a slew of reality stars and D-listers inside these club walls. It was more than likely that this guy was on TV or I'd spotted him somehow in the newspapers once upon a time. Who knew?

But when the man in question breezed past me again, his lips tugged down in a natural scowl that I could only assume was his resting bitch face, I had no further ideas about who the fuck he was.

I *needed* to know. My intuition was pinging like crazy, and I needed a damn nudge.

I headed for the bar, where Joss waited on some other men. She looked surprised when she saw me sidle up.

"Root bear! You need the usual?"

"I'm good tonight, Jade, thanks." I had to laugh at the nickname. Maybe one day, when I got magically black out drunk sometime, I'd give Jordan and Jade the show they wanted. But that day was a long way off. I leaned closer, inviting her to lean in too. "I need you to give me some info on that table of five over there."

Her gaze flicked over my shoulder toward the group.

"You brought them two rounds of shots already," I added, hoping this would clarify.

"Yeah. What do you need to know?"

"Who's getting the tab?"

She squinted over my shoulder, thinking, then she said, "The blond one. With the blue polo shirt."

Bingo. I knew that Gemstones required a credit card behind the bar to open a tab. "I need you to give me the name off his credit card."

She nodded, quickly accessing the POS system at the bar. She squinted at the screen, swiping her finger across it a few times before she leaned across and told me, "It says E. M. Rossberg on it. There's a huge Boeing on it or something. That's all I can really see before we process the transaction. That's where I'll get the full name."

"Thanks, Jade." I offered a small smile. This was something to go on, at least. I returned to my post along the back wall, a bit closer to the table of five. Bright pop music filled the club, an expectant air building as the lighting shifted, signaling that a show would start soon. Men shuffled around, claiming their tables, lifting their hand for a server. And while the rest of the club waited, I started my search.

Rossberg. I wracked my brain for any hits as the google search loaded. The name sounded distantly familiar.

Results flooded the screen. I thumbed through the top contenders, skimming for anything that might catch my eye.

And that's when the pieces began to click together. News articles mentioning *Cora Margulis-Rossberg*. Paparazzi photos of the man and Cora, leaving a restaurant in Midtown or entering the towering Margulis building I'd seen in SoHo. I clicked on an article, almost reading too fast to comprehend what I was seeing.

Eli Rossberg.

Cora's ex-husband.

Something heavy thudded to the bottom of my stomach and I looked up, making sure Eli was still where I'd last seen him. Having been primarily protecting Trace, Mercedes, and Willow since starting with the Fairchilds, we'd been focused on different threats during our time in Louisville. And during the weeks I'd been in NYC prior to being assigned to Jordan, I'd only gotten the bare minimum regarding Eli. He'd made Cora's life a living hell, he was a rich and powerful man who hated the Fairchilds, and he was safely in the past.

Until now, when he'd unwittingly elbowed his way into my present.

I read more in the article I'd selected. Eli was the heir to the Rossberg Aerospace company, which was currently testing unmanned rockets to Mars and other space technology that made it sound like the top scientists were eager to escape the planet in favor of another one. I switched to a different article, something less technological and more rag mag. The title read "The Margulis Explosion." It was dated a few months ago, reading like an editorial deep dive into the past and present reality of the Margulis family, including Cora's breakdown and separation from her family. It was far too complex for the thumping pop music and swarms of horny men around me, though. I needed bite-size information before I could execute a proper investigation on my own. I texted Axel.

SEVEN: What info do you have on Cora's ex-husband?

AXEL: Jesus Christ. Tell me you haven't run into that award-winning POS.

I looked up just as Eli threw his head back in raucous laughter. Jade was delivering yet another round of shots. How much did this guy fucking drink?

SEVEN: I'm seeing lots of people out and about. Just want to make sure I'm briefed on all aspects of the family history. For Jordan's safety.

AXEL: Appreciate that. Though I trust you're still keeping it secret that she's our sister?

SEVEN: Of course. Haven't told a soul.

AXEL: Thank you. Eli is the definition of shit bag. Abused Cora for years, gaslit her, fucked her Pilates instructor under her nose. Damian dug up a whole history of mistresses he's had, too. Even had to pay a few off. He's an alcoholic, probable pill popper, just one of the most condescending motherfuckers you'll ever have the displeasure of meeting. If you see him? Turn around.

SEVEN: Noted. Thanks for the intel.

I pocketed my phone, my gaze sliding back to Eli. Turning around wasn't an option. Waiting until he left and disappeared from our orbit forever seemed to be the only choice.

The lights dimmed, and the music changed. Jordan's show was about to start. When the first sultry thumps of a new song began, she emerged from backstage, practically gliding. Her hair was pulled into a high ponytail, streaked with neon colors. Her makeup was smokier than before, and she'd replaced the white mesh outfit she'd had on before with a shimmery teal outfit that was part corset, part bandages wrapped around her thighs and hips. She took to the pole immediately, hair flying, teal fabric flowing behind her. I'd just seen her twenty minutes ago, and she rode my cock a couple of hours before that, but somehow, she looked like a completely different person. One I'd never seen before.

A reverent hush fell over the club as she scaled the pole, and the music grew more intense. She was upside down and executing a controlled fall, slowly heading toward the ground, until the beat changed and she snapped her legs around the pole. When she spun around, seemingly clutching the pole only with her pussy, her arms splayed behind her and her tongue hanging out the side of her mouth, the entire club erupted in cheers. Eli sprang from his seat, cupping his hands around his mouth as he shouted something unintelligible. He rummaged around in his pockets for a moment, then stalked closer to the stage.

I drifted toward his table, keeping a close eye on him as he stood at the edge of the stage, head tipped back, to watch Jordan like an adoring fan. He hooted and hollered as she performed, throwing bills onto the stage alongside a few other men. But what he threw were fifties and hundreds, not singles or fives like the others.

Jordan enthralled and bewitched every horny motherfucker in the club as she danced. Hell, it was hard for me not to get caught up as well. But Eli needed to be monitored. If I had a good enough reason, I'd be escorting him off the premises by now. Simply being Cora's ex wasn't enough, unfortunately.

The longer Jordan performed, the more raucous Eli became. He'd thrown roughly a grand onto the stage by the time Jordan's show wrapped up. As the music faded and Jordan smiled out at the thunderous applause, Eli leaned over the stage and shouted something.

It was loud enough that I heard it, but I couldn't make out the words. Jordan's gaze snapped to him quickly, her brows knitting together. Eli waved her closer. She knelt down as he said something to her—she laughed a moment later, gave him a coy response, and began collecting her tips from the stage floor. Eli turned and walked back to the table, looking pleased with himself.

I wandered off once he plunked his ass back in the chair. When Eddie showed up a moment later, I already knew what was coming. After Jordan collected her take from the stage, Eddie met her near the small set of stairs leading to the floor. A whisper, a nod, and then Jordan followed him.

My gut plummeted as the table of five stood. Eddie and Jordan met the group in front of the VIP room I'd fucked Jordan in hours before. But instead of one trustworthy man in there with her, it was five douchebags who I wouldn't trust with a microwave oven, let alone with someone as special as Jordan.

Jordan disappeared inside the VIP room with the group before I could bolt over there to stop them. Not like it would matter. This was her job, one that I had to let her do, no matter how much the ensuing half hour to forty-five minutes felt like nails against a chalkboard.

I posted up right outside the door, leaning in close to listen for any signs of foul play. As far as Jordan knew, these guys were just her regular clientele. I didn't presume she knew the entire backstory of Cora, especially if she'd barely kept up with news on her brothers.

Every minute that passed took twice as long. Thirty minutes turned into forty-five. Every second that went over the usual limit sent me closer to the edge of no return, where I'd burst into the VIP room and start peeling men off her, one by one. When they hit the hour mark, the door finally swung open, and the first men began trickling out. Red-faced, happy, and a little off-balance. Eli walked by, finally not scowling. Well, good for him. Then he paused, turned back toward Jordan, meeting her in the doorway. He held a business card between his fingers, passing it to her with a whispered something in her ear. Then he strode off.

Jordan looked at me, flushed and ecstatic. Hundreds poured from her bra, the straps of her heels, the bottoms of her pants.

"Seven," she hissed. "I just made five grand!"

I blinked. "That's..." I couldn't say anything positive. If anything, it was a tolerable one-off occurrence. "What did that guy just hand you?"

She seemed confused for a moment. Then she held up her hand, producing the card. "Oh. I don't know." She studied both sides of it, then huffed. "His number. He wants me to call."

Hard pieces clicked together inside me, forming an image I didn't like to look at. "Do you know who that guy is?"

"Some wealthy dudebro who wants to give me all his money?"

"It's Eli Rossberg. Cora's ex." When her brows began drawing together, I added, "The one that physically abused her."

"Fuck." Her throat bobbed and she looked up at me guiltily. "I didn't realize."

"I know that. But you won't give him your number, will you?"

She gave me a *duh* look. "No. I know better than that." She flicked the card and it fluttered to the floor. "But if he comes back I have to do my job. Until he actually tries something, I can't refuse a client."

Across the club, Eli and his entourage were packing up and heading out. He looked back at us one last time, his gaze searching for Jordan's. Then he turned and one-by-one, they all shuffled through the doors.

Finally. My shoulders relaxed slightly. The night was over.

I wanted to believe this was a dodged bullet. But even though Eli was gone, my intuition was still sounding the alarm. Except now, I didn't know what it was trying to tell me.

CHAPTER TWENTY-TWO

SEVEN

I woke up extra early the next morning. I'd been doing that a lot lately. Maybe it was the mint green bedroom walls I now had, or maybe it was the fact that my subconscious just couldn't get enough Jordan. Now that she'd been sharing my bed for almost a week, my sleep was deeper and I woke up readier for the day.

And hornier.

So much hornier.

Jordan's chest rose and fell rhythmically. She slept with her hands in a prayer position beneath the side of her face, curled up in a ball. She was so cute I wanted to take a bite of her, but I'd wait until she woke up for that. I slid out of bed quietly, heading for the bathroom to take a piss and brush my teeth. When I slipped back into bed, Jordan was rousing. I pulled her into my arms, folding her into the space against my chest that seemed made just for her.

Almost nobody had ever folded against me so perfectly. Olivia was the only exception. Normally the mere thought of my late fiancée would cause a painful wrench in my chest, but right now, with Jordan in my arms, I didn't have the energy to get lost in that pain. For whatever reason, right now, I felt good. This felt good. That was all I knew.

Jordan woke up slowly, grinning instantly as she came to, and those pretty gray-blue eyes zeroed in on me. She booped my nose, wriggled out of my grip, and scampered off to the bathroom. When she returned, the minty freshness of her breath hit me as she covered my mouth with her own, coaxing a deep kiss from me.

I chuckled as she settled on top of me, draping her body along mine. "Good morning."

"Great morning," she corrected, her warm, smooth skin sliding against mine. Her thigh brushed my hardening cock, already ready for whatever she wanted from me, and she purred like a kitten. "About to be the best morning, actually."

I trailed my hands along her body. We'd opted to sleep naked last night, even though we hadn't had sex again after her shift at the club. She'd been too sore—totally my fault and totally not unexpected.

"Are you ready for more?" I asked, expecting her to say no. But instead she nodded, brushing her lips against mine.

"As long as you go slow," she whispered.

I teased her lips with mine, the velvety brush of her mouth sending any remaining blood in my body straight to my cock. Her hips splayed open, and my erection nudged for the sweet heat of her core.

"I can go slow," I promised.

She gave me a sloppy tongue kiss, then pulled back, pushing her hands against my chest as she sat up. Instead of sitting on top of me again like I expected, she scooted off me, coming to my side. Her gaze scorched over my stiff cock, which jutted out at an angle.

"I want to do something first," she said shyly, wrapping her hand around the base of my cock. My ass cheeks tightened as she tried to make her fingers touch—and failed again. "You've fingered me and eaten me out so many times. It's only fair."

I couldn't rip my eyes from her small hand wrapped around me as she ran her fingers from base to tip. Her head dipped lower, and she looked up at me just before her lips touched my cockhead.

"Can I?" she asked.

I grunted, flexing my hips so that my cock met her lips. "Fuck yes."

She bobbed and licked at the head, then wrapped her lips around me. Her hot mouth descended, swallowing me as far as she could...until she gagged. She pulled back, disconnecting with a *pop*.

"I think I only took like a third of it," she complained.

"Best third ever." I gathered her hair to one side, flexing my hips. "Try again."

Jordan dipped down, wrapping her lips around me again as she sucked and licked. My balls tightened, a low groan rumbling out of me.

Just when I thought it couldn't get hotter with Jordan, it did.

"That's right. Just like that." I pushed my fingers into the mess of her hair, knotting them slightly as she sucked me off. "Look at me, baby."

Her gaze soldered onto me, sending warning spirals through my limbs. I found the line of her bottom lip wrapped around my cock. "You suck me off so good. I feel like I could come already."

She popped off me, her lips swollen, looking stricken. "I'll drown."

I laughed. "Then how about we finish together a different way?" I nudged her back onto the bed, then covered her body with my own. Anxiety prickled at the edges—would my being on top, in my bed, trigger her again? Did she feel safe enough? I watched her carefully as I filled the space between her legs.

"What do you think?" I prompted, nuzzling the hollow of her neck.

She squeezed her thighs around me, locking her ankles behind my back. "I think hell yes."

My cock glided against the swollen, juicy entrance of her pussy. The brief contact made me jerk. Her lips parted, desire swirling in her gaze.

"I'll go slow," I reminded her. I eased myself in, finding her just as tight as yesterday's session in the VIP room. She sucked in sharply, but I held her gaze, nodding.

"You got this, baby."

She relaxed slightly, searching my face as I eased myself in, more slowly than I'd ever done in my entire life. My back was tense from the restraint. The urge to plow her dripping core was intense. But I was a man, not a heathen.

Jordan stretched around me, a soft sigh passing her lips as I sank deeper, inch by inch.

"How does that feel?" I could hear the grit of my own restraint in my voice.

She blinked lazily, already in another world. "Like perfection."

She curled her nails into my chest, arching her back while a low, mewling moan escaped her. I studied her closely as I began moving against her at a glacial pace compared to what my body craved. I didn't want to scare her or hurt her, much less break her.

"Too much?" I asked.

She shook her head. "I love it."

"You love my cock, huh?" I slipped my arm along her right thigh, lifting her leg up against the side of my body. I found another inch of space this way, unable to prevent a deep groan. I rocked against her, looking down at the union of our bodies. The way we folded together, tangled limbs becoming one.

"Maybe I do," she breathed, smoothing her palms against the wide expanse of my chest. "How could I not? It defies science."

I smirked, pulling out of her all the way and then easing back inside. My cock glided into her more easily now that her pussy was dripping and primed. "Well I haven't gotten a call from the Guinness Book of World Records yet. I'm sure there are bigger ones out there."

"I can't even understand how it fits." She inhaled sharply as my cock filled her once more. Her eyes fluttered shut, and I dipped down, dragging my teeth against each of her nipples in turn.

"But it fits so well." I growled against her collarbone. Jordan was heavenly. If I were a different man, I'd dedicate poems to her pussy. I guided her other leg up, urging her to lock her feet behind my back. My vision went spotty from this angle. Borderline *too* good. I thrust into her again. She reached for me, and I could tell that she wanted me closer. I lay down so that our bodies came together at all possible points. The heat and feel of her plastered against me set every inch of my skin prickling with awareness. If I could have melted into her, I would have.

Each time I sank back into her, I made sure to grind up against her, give that swollen clit plenty of attention. Judging from the way she panted against me, clutching desperately like I might somehow float away, told me it was a good move.

She cried out, but it was unintelligible. I brushed my lips against hers.

"What was that?"

She laughed, and tipped her head back, a guttural moan floating past her lips.

"Noted," I said.

"Fuuuuuuck."

"Mm-hmm." My mouth was on her neck, her jaw, her chin. "Doing that right now."

"Seven, I'm so close," she panted.

"Me too, baby." I slid into her again, grinding up against her until she arched her back and let out the most pornographic moan I'd ever heard from her. That was my cue.

"Ohhh, Jordan. I feel you coming around my cock." My voice scraped past my lips, the sudden lightning bolt of pleasure shooting from head to toe. My whole body jerked as the orgasm barreled through me, then faded.

I grunted through the final waves, sinking down on top of her to capture her lips in a kiss. She was already grinning like crazy, her eyes half-lidded and drowsy with satisfaction.

"That," she whispered between kisses, "was fucking epic."

Epic was one word. *Addictive* was another. I buried my face in her neck, taking a deep inhale of her scent. I didn't want to leave this spot. This moment in time. This *situation*. Whatever it was, it was deeply fulfilling living with Jordan, accompanying her everywhere, protecting her and somehow along the way growing this close to her. She started as a job, but now it was so much more.

I rolled off her, the last thought settling awkwardly inside me. But I didn't want to think about it now.

"I'm not sure I can move for the rest of the day," she said, eyes barely open.

"Luckily, you have some time to kill before the club," I said, coming to my feet. "Let me get you cleaned up."

"Now that's VIP service," she said as I walked to the bathroom. I grabbed a washcloth, running it under warm water. She grinned at me as I eased her legs open and gently wiped at the cum dribbling down her thighs.

"Or is this just a perk because I admitted I love your cock?" she teased.

"Standard procedure if my cock's been inside you."

"How on earth are you still single, Seven?" Her tone was teasing, but I could sense the real question buried beneath. Now wasn't the time to go near that topic, though. I pressed a kiss to the inside of her knee once she was cleaned up.

"Stay here and rest if you want. I'm going to get dressed and head to the gym for a little bit before your shift tonight. I need to run some laps."

She sighed happily, curling up into a ball. "Sounds like a plan."

"You sure you don't need a cuddle buddy?" I was second-guessing my plan. I was all about the aftercare. And the pre and during care, for that matter.

She snuggled deeper. "You go work out. Those abs won't chisel themselves. Besides, a nap is sounding real good right now."

"Just promise me you won't sneak off again like last time."

She held up two fingers. "Stripper's honor."

"Not sure if that's supposed to make me trust you more or less."

She swatted at me, but I was already on my way to grab my pre-packed gym bag from the living room. This was the sort of thing I could get used to. Sexy mornings with Jordan in my bed. Work out breaks. And then hitting the city in whatever way the day demanded of me—close protection duties, meeting new clients, or backend office work.

If Jordan was in New York, then I could be in New York. Long-term, even. I'd never envisioned myself settling in a place like Manhattan, but life had a weird way of handing us unexpected twists and turns.

Except what the actual fuck are you talking about? Long-term with Jordan?

My phone vibrated against my thigh as I moved through pedestrian traffic on the sidewalk, distracting me from my thoughts. I power walked the three blocks to the gym as a rule—my warm-up—and didn't break stride as I checked my phone.

Incoming email: Re: Experienced CPO wanted.

Someone had responded to my latest help wanted ad. My gaze flicked between phone and sidewalk as I skimmed the email, trying to get a feel for who the new applicant was. I caught the most minimal details as I dodged between people and passed by slow-moving groups of tourists.

Liam Henderson. 29. Former NYPD. Marine.

This was sounding promising.

I pocketed the phone until I finished my trek to the gym. Once I reached the steel beamed, glass-walled fitness center, I paused outside the main doors, studying the rest of Liam's information.

He seemed just as qualified as Chico—possibly more.

Which meant Liam might be the protection officer to take over for me, as I'd planned.

If he works out, I reminded myself. *It will take a special new hire to take on your current caseload.* I surveyed the street in front of me, the thought settling heavily inside of me.

My current caseload was Jordan. Full stop. I had no higher priority than her right now, and the thought of passing her off to someone else had my gut doing strange flips.

I felt sick. I felt strange. I felt decidedly not well.

But this has been the plan all along. I pocketed the phone, taking slow steps in front of the gym as I mulled over whatever the fuck was happening inside my head right now.

The plan had always been to build the business. To step away from daily protection. To hand over Jordan's protection to someone else. Liam might be the guy, or someone would fit the bill, and I would continue building my business.

There's nothing wrong with that.

So why did it give me the weird churn in my gut?

I whipped out my phone again, knowing what I needed to do. There was no other option than to continue with the plan. The one that made the most sense for myself and for my future. I sent Liam a response to his application, expressing my interest in interviewing him further. I suggested a date, time and place, and hit send before I could think better of it.

I hadn't told Jordan much at all about the business. Mostly because it hadn't come up, but also because when it *had* come up, it hadn't seemed appropriate to divulge anything beyond the absolute necessary baseline.

But I suspected she wouldn't like the idea. I could already see her fighting back about me handing her protection over to someone else. Imagining it made me twitch, which only confirmed the deeper truth that circled inside me.

Jordan might be mine, but I could never claim her fully. Not when so much fear lurked in the shadows.

If we made this real—then I stood to lose her.

Whether from the hands of her brothers finding out about us and firing me, or from a cruel twist of fate a second time around.

I didn't know which it would be, but I was almost certain it would be one of them.

CHAPTER TWENTY-THREE

JORDAN

"You want me to do *what now* with my ankle?"

Jessa's disbelieving shriek prompted peals of laughter from me and Mercedes. Jessa was on the pole on a Tuesday morning, with Mercedes waiting in the wings to try next. I'd invited all the Fairchild ladies over for a little bit of pole dancing and caffeine, but Cora had a speaking engagement lined up somewhere out of town, so it was just the three of us. I was formally launching my *Teach My Entire Family How To Pole Dance* campaign. Even if they didn't win any awards and didn't end up on the stage at Gemstones, this was the best way I knew to spend time.

"You've got this," I coached Jessa, gently guiding her ankle where it needed to be on the pole. "Make sure you press your weight in here"—I squeezed the part of her leg to focus on—"and the rest of your body will compensate to keep you balanced."

"This is insane, Jordan!" Jessa said between laughs. Both Mercedes and I watched with huge smiles as Jessa followed my instructions and crept up the pole another few inches. She was a solid few feet off the ground now.

"Look at you!" I clapped. "You're on the pole!"

Jessa screamed, squeezing her eyes shut. "I shouldn't look down, right?"

"You're not *that* high up," Mercedes said.

The more time I spent with Mercedes, Jessa, and Cora, the more I began to see them as friends and even, kind of, sisters. It was so easy to be around them. So fun. So relaxed. They knew where I came from, so we didn't need to dodge any awkward topics. The truth was just out there, and they didn't judge me. They didn't *pity* me.

"You ready for the next move?" I asked Jessa.

"I guess!"

I laid out in a calm, level voice exactly what she needed to do next. These girls were beginners, which was so fun. Watching the shock and awe in new pole performers was a highlight for me. That moment when someone realized they really *could* do that crazy thing with their body. As I watched Jessa tentatively attempt the next progression on the pole, something warm and fuzzy spread through me.

I'd never tried to teach people like this; I'd only ever worked with novice strippers at the club, helping them learn some tricks that would translate better to the stage. But damn, this felt good. Especially as Jessa's face lit up with pride and she let out another peal of laugher.

"Mother clucker, I'm doin' it!"

I coached Jessa through another couple of steps before I could tell that her arms were getting shaky and she needed to come down. I snapped a few pictures before I guided her through the dismount. She had both feet on the ground and the three of us were high-fiving and clapping when Seven returned from his morning errands.

He wore his gym clothes but had his laptop bag along with his workout bag, which he set on a stool. His keys jangled on the coun-tertop, and he slid his coat off then came over to us, looking amused.

"Did I miss something?"

"Oh, nothing major. I just scaled a steel pole under the incredible guidance of this lady," Jessa said, knocking my hip.

"Is it pole lessons day?" Seven asked.

"Sure is. And if you stick around long enough, your second lesson will happen. Right after Mercedes takes her turn," I said, waggling my eyebrows at her.

"Oh, you've already started lessons?" Jessa looked over at Seven.

"More or less," Seven said with a boyish smile. It was hard not to melt on the spot, looking at him. He'd been trimming his hair less, allowing the top to grow the tiniest bit unruly while the sides remained shaved down. A hint of dark waves emerged, and paired with the dimple that flashed during these boyish smiles, and the broad expanse of muscles that both protected me and sent me flying to the heights of pleasure...

Playing it cool around Seven in front of other people was now the challenge of the century. I had no problem climbing him like a cat up a tree, but I didn't want everyone to know it, either.

"Jordan's a good teacher," Jessa said.

"She is," Seven agreed, leaning on the back of the couch. "Even when the student doesn't want to learn."

"Would that be you?" Mercedes asked with a giggle.

Seven cocked a heartbreaker smile, the type that sent a gush of warmth straight to my panties. I turned away from him; looking at him head-on was dangerous right now. I needed to focus on this girl time. "Mercedes, are you ready? It's all you, girl."

Seven retreated to the bedroom while we continued with lessons. Time melted away in a fun, laughter-filled, pole-gripping blur. Before I knew it, Mercedes was damn near the top of the pole, and I heard the knocking of a knife against the cutting board. Seven was starting lunch, which meant my girl date had to end soon so I could get ready for my pick-up shift that night at the club.

Jessa collected our used coffee mugs from the end table as I safely maneuvered Mercedes to the ground. "What's for lunch, Seven?"

"Turkey sandwiches, fresh veggies, avocado and mayo." He jerked his chin toward the high-fiber bread nearby. "You want one?"

"Sounds good, but I'm meeting Damian for lunch at the penthouse," Jessa said.

"What about you, Mercedes?" I tipped my head toward Seven's food prep in the kitchen. "You want one?"

She smiled shyly, red-faced and still ecstatic from her progress on the pole. "I need to go meet Trace and Willow, but thanks for the offer."

I realized, then, that I had extended Seven's offer. Because this apartment felt like my home, too. The thought thudded awkwardly through me as Jessa and Mercedes began picking up their things, slipping on shoes, finding coats.

Wasn't I supposed to be finding my own place? Moving out of here?

The coziness of this life at Seven's side, with my brothers and their significant others on the sidelines, was a lot more than I'd counted on. It made it hard to want to leave, now that I'd finally opened up a few inches of room in my heart for them all. I'd been ignoring all the most recent available apartment emails that were coming in from the rental search engine I signed up for.

But I needed to make good on the agreement with Seven: *this is an interim solution.* Even though my heart ached for it to be more permanent.

I tried to shove the thoughts away, focusing instead on giving big hugs to Jessa and Mercedes and seeing them out the door. Once all the goodbyes were said and loose plans made for another meet-up, Seven had my turkey sandwich plated and waiting for me.

"Lunch," he said.

That same creeping warmth and tenderness I'd tried to shove away earlier came slinking back. He took a bite of his sandwich, seemingly unaware of how sweet he was. How thoughtful. What a good caretaker and protector and lover.

"Are you crying?"

I wiped away a spilt tear, laughing softly. "I guess so."

"Everything okay?"

"I was just thinking about how wonderful you are."

He laughed as he chewed. "Yeah right."

I slid onto the stool facing the island. We were in our usual positions. I looked him dead in the eye. "I'm serious, Seven. You are wonderful."

He swallowed his food, pausing before the next bite. "So are you."

I picked up my sandwich and smiled at him before I took a big, crunchy bite.

My shift at the club started off low-key. I was getting ready in the Gems lounge, picking out my clothes for the shift and chatting with Roxie and Clara our House Mom about which hair style I should go with. We decided on soft waves, so Clara helped me curl my hair while I finished my makeup. Roxie went out to perform as I put the finishing touches on the night's style.

Just when my lips were the perfect shade of red to match my stretchy red boy shorts and bikini combo, Joss strode into the Gems lounge, beelining for me.

"Hey, lover," I said casually, giving myself a once-over in the full-length mirror. "What are you doing back here?"

"Looking for *Sapphire,*" she said with a smirk. "You've got an eager fan outside, waiting for you."

I snorted. "Already? I haven't even gone on."

"It's someone from the weekend. I recognize him. You danced for him and his friends in the VIP room I think, too."

I blinked a few times. "That doesn't narrow it down."

"Trust me—you'll remember when you see him. He's got money. I remember him because he left me a thousand-dollar tip that night. I'm sure you made even more off him."

My eyes rounded. "Ohhh, I bet I know who it is."

"There we go. Well, he's waiting for ya, sister. He seems impatient."

I fixed a few stray hairs before I straightened my back, ready to head out. "Did you let him know I charge $1,000/minute to come out early?"

Joss cackled as she strode out of the lounge. I followed her a moment later, my eyes adjusting to the dim, colored lighting of the club. I hadn't even taken two steps before he was at my side.

"Sapphire. There you are." The blond from last weekend filled my vision, almost too close for comfort. With the heels, we were roughly the same height. His hair was slicked back in the same upper-crust fashion I saw in wealthy circles, and he wore a similar business casual outfit. But with him standing this close, I could see the strain in his face. The lines around the eyes, the way he seemed both somehow dead tired and jacked up. An urgency radiated from him that nearly choked me.

"Hey." I tried to sound friendly, but I couldn't mask the surprise. Over his shoulder, I saw Seven standing at attention, mere feet away. He looked ready to pounce. I lifted my palm slightly so he could see: *Hang tight. Everything's fine.*

"Do you remember me?" the blond asked.

"Of course." I flashed a smile. But I couldn't think of his name, only that he was Cora's horrible ex. "Tell me your name again."

His face fell. "You don't fucking remember me."

I touched his arm, sensing a storm brewing beneath the surface. As a Hail Mary pass, my brain coughed up the name I'd seen on that business card before I lost it the other night: *Eli.*

"Eli. Don't be like that."

A smile curled at the corner of his mouth. "You know how to be slick, don't you?"

"Practically a water slide."

His chest hefted with a laugh, his gaze sliding over my face, down to my breasts. Everything inside me revolted at the attention; flirting with the clients was normal and expected, but the way he watched me felt wrong. I needed to figure out what he was after and whether those extra thousands of dollars would be accompanying him. Some guys wanted pure titillation, but other guys wanted a therapist. If Eli just needed a shoulder to cry on, well, putting up with a little unpleasantness was the name of the game in this industry—even if he was someone unsavory. And I could see a healthy savings account in my future if Eli crossed paths with me more often. Within these walls, I couldn't refuse a client just because they had bad blood with somebody else.

"You know I'm about to go do a show," I told him. "Are you going to stay to watch?"

"Of course. How could I miss my favorite?"

"I hoped you'd say that." I bit my bottom lip.

"Just wanted you to know I'm here," he told me. "I already talked to Eddie. Meet me in the VIP room straight after your show, okay, gorgeous?"

I sent him my sexiest wink, and he wandered off, occasionally looking over his shoulder to find my gaze. Seven's curiosity about the exchange was palpable from where he stood. And it was hard to miss his flexed fists as Eli strutted past. But I didn't have time to chat. The music had changed; the lights were dimming.

I sent Seven a reassuring smile and waited for my cue, adjusting my outfit one final time before stepping up on stage.

Seven stayed closer to the stage than normal. But he didn't need to worry. I met guys like Eli all the time. Entitled, as evidenced by his immediate demands on my time, and arrogant, seen in the way he glanced at those around him and even in the way he looked at *me*. Not to mention questionable histories regarding domestic violence. But most important: rich. Eli seemed to be leaking money. And he needed someone to catch the overflow.

I was happy to be that person. Eli would only ever exist as a part of my world within these walls. None of these men existed for me in the real world.

My show was intense and much more acrobatic than usual. I had extra energy I didn't know what to do with, which I could only attribute to the way Seven fueled—and filled—me. The stage was littered with bills by the time I took my bow, including plenty of fifties and hundreds that Eli himself had tossed to me.

Keep it coming, Eli.

I had barely made it off the steps before Eli's commanding gaze distracted me. He tipped his head in the direction of the VIP room, already impatient. I followed his quick strides, blowing kisses to some of my admirers as I breezed past. Nights like these, I did feel like a celebrity—in high demand, leaving behind a trail of heartbroken fans who wouldn't get their turn.

I liked to feel wanted, desired, lauded. Especially after a lifetime of feeling the opposite.

"You liked the show?" I asked breathlessly once we breezed into the VIP room. I shut the door, spotting Seven along the wall right outside.

"You're the best stripper on the East Coast," Eli said. "And you know it."

"So I'll take that as a yes," I purred, strutting toward the pole in the center of the room while Eli sank onto the couch. "Did you order any drinks? What can I get for you?"

"Just you. For now." Eli reached into his pocket and pulled out a thick wad of bills. Something else tumbled out along with it, a little baggie.

"Oh, you dropped your—" I started.

He seemed to notice the extra item at the same time I spoke. He smirked, stuffing it back into his pocket. "That wasn't supposed to come out. Unless you want some?"

That's when I caught the slight slur in his words. He was probably drunk as hell. Which meant he *needed* whatever was in that baggie to continue functioning. Cocaine would account for his strange energy. I swore half the city's elite snorted coke on a daily basis, based on what I saw in the shadows of the club. I shook my head, starting a slow spin around the pole.

"I'm good, thanks."

He huffed with a little laugh, returning to the wad of bills. "So. Sapphire." He thumbed through them, almost lazily. "Why didn't you call me after the weekend?"

I blinked a few times, calculating my response. I opted for the truth. "That's against stripper code."

His gaze snapped up to mine. "Oh come on. I'm not dumb."

"Well, would you be back here for me already if I'd texted?" I wanted to sound coy, not annoyed like I actually was. "You know girls worth their shit don't text or call back on the first try." I accentuated my statement with a slow, sexy drop down the pole, gripping it above my head.

He seemed pleased by this response—and maybe distracted by the view. He nodded to himself, lacing his fingers together. "Come over here, gorgeous. Let me look at you."

"You sure you don't want a show?" I came down until I was practically squatting, opening up my knees as far to the sides as I could, giving him a full-frontal view. He leaned back on the couch.

"We need to start getting to know each other a little better," he said.

"I'd like that." *Lie* flashed through my head.

"Then come over here."

I strutted toward him slowly, taking extra time to assess my game plan. I didn't think Eli was the type I'd need to use the panic button for—and I was relieved that Seven was right outside the door—but he had an undercurrent that was hard to grab onto and understand. His mood seemed like a riptide, invisible and powerful, with the potential to pull me under if things went sideways.

When I was within arm's reach, he grabbed my thighs. I tutted, stepping away. "We don't touch in here."

"Come on," he groaned.

"Club rules. Every girl will tell you the same."

"How much money do you want to change the rules?" He lifted his brow, clearly challenging me.

"No amount. I like my job and I intend to keep it." I pushed at his chest, sending him into a reclined position. "And if you let me do my job, you won't even need to touch me. Let me take care of things."

I started a sexy lap dance, making sure to brush and tease extra hard. He was the type who wanted more and didn't take well to hearing no. Again, not unheard of. Eli kept his hands to himself while I danced, letting out a satisfied noise once I returned to the pole to continue dancing.

"How did you get this sexy?"

"I swore to the witch I wouldn't share the secret with mortals," I retorted.

He hefted with a laugh, his gaze darkening. "So if I leave my number again, will you call?"

I shrugged.

"If you won't call *me*," he continued, "let me call you."

My belly constricted. An even *worse* idea. "I'm not in the habit of mixing work with my real life."

Eli thumbed through the bills again. "And I'm not in the habit of staying in seedy places like strip clubs long-term. So if we want to get to know each other, it needs to be in the real world."

We were suddenly negotiating, and I felt like I'd shown up unprepared. I swallowed hard, watching him count out twenty hundred-dollar bills.

"Here. Give me your number." He tossed the bills onto the floor. I didn't race to pick them up, but I knew there was two grand on the floor right now.

I gripped the pole above my head and started another slow slide to the floor. Strippers were ready for moments like these. Amongst us, we had a communal number to hand out when pressed by men. I rattled it off. Nobody checked that phone; it lived permanently in the back room, turned off. Eli nodded as he typed the number into his phone.

And then he called it.

He tutted a moment later, swiping it off. "It went straight to voicemail, and the voice wasn't yours."

"You're in the club, if you listen without bass thumping in the background you'll hear differently," I countered.

"Show me that it's a real number."

I blinked. "I can't. All my things are in my locker. I'm working—"

He cleared his throat loudly, annoyance seeping out of him. He reached into his other pocket, brought out another wad of cash, and then began thumbing through the bills. "Truthfully, I don't even think that number is real. But I'll give you the rest of this"—he held up the money—"if you can prove to me it is."

He must have caught me drooling over the cash, because he added, "You'll be leaving with ten grand total."

I swallowed hard, giving it one last shot. "Why do you want my number so bad, anyway? You look well connected. You're clearly wealthy. You can have whatever you want."

His grin turned a little evil. "And I want you."

"You flatter me."

"Sapphire, you're the woman of my dreams. I want to get to know you better." For all the yellow flags he'd been dropping, I did catch a note of sincerity in his voice. Except he didn't even know me. I was the woman of his *fantasies*—made up, not real, completely fictitious.

"Don't tell me no," he said in a low voice. "I'm a good person to have around if you need something. Not just money. I *am* well connected like you said. In fact, you have no idea *how* well connected."

"I'd love to find out," I said.

He chuckled softly. "You ever had someone you hated? Someone who did you wrong?"

I shrugged, walking back to the couch when he patted to the open spot beside him. I sank onto it, just a few inches of space between us.

"I can make those people suffer," he said, his voice going even lower, more threatening. "I can take care of you. Whatever you need done, I can do it for you, gorgeous. Do you believe me?"

I crossed my legs, pretending to think about it. I didn't need anyone to take care of me. Not when I had Seven. No, I needed his money. But the more he talked, the less I *wanted* it.

"If you'd do me the honor of spending some time with me"—he grabbed my hand, rubbing his fingers over my knuckles before lacing our fingers together—"I promise I'll take care of you. I just want to get to know you. And in return, I'll take care of whatever you need done."

"Like, bring down my foes?" I asked with a little laugh, trying to make a joke out of it.

He nodded. "I've brought down a foe or two. Three, actually." He snort-laughed to himself. "I've brought down people they told me were impossible to bring down. Including a special little band of brothers on Wall Street that nobody likes." The words dripped with condescension. "I could tell you some stories. But that's for another time, gorgeous."

Something about his comment struck a deep chord. There had to be plenty of brothers on Wall Street. Plenty of beef and warring factions among the elite.

But what if he's talking about your brothers?

I was suddenly desperate to find out.

"I'll give you my number," I blurted. It wasn't my *real* number. But it was a back-up number that redirected to my phone, with its own separate voicemail. I kept it around for emergencies like these – but had never used it until now. I struggled to remember the number I'd etched into my brain at the start of my career. "I like what you're saying, Eli. We *should* get to know each other."

"Figured you'd come around." He looked haughty as he swiped his phone on again. "Let's hear it. And this better not be another fake."

I rattled off the number. "It'll go to voicemail, but you'll hear my voice this time. I'll text you as soon as I get back to the lounge to show you it's mine." My heart pounded as I spoke. I couldn't believe I'd done it. But the intuitive nudge was there.

I didn't want to spend any more time than necessary around Eli. But he might know something that I should know too.

He tapped on his phone for a moment, then looked up at me with a smile. "We'll see, won't we?"

"We will."

"I'm gonna head to the bathroom. I'll look for your text."

I nodded. He'd come today just to lock me down, get a number. And he'd achieved it. He pocketed his phone, leaving all the money behind.

"All right, gorgeous. I'll be seeing you soon."

I blew him a kiss. He left the VIP room, and I made quick work of scooping up all the money. Seven stepped inside a few moments later.

"Everything okay?" he asked.

"More than okay." It was hard not to sound giddy.

"He came back." It wasn't a question, and it was more than just an observation, too. I scooped up a few more hundreds, stuffing them in my bra.

"He did. And today I made ten grand off him." A painful thud hit my ribs as soon as the words left my mouth. *But at what cost?* While I hadn't given him my real phone number, I'd given him my burner line, which directed straight to my phone via an app. I could cut it off or delete it at any time – but I felt like I'd crossed a line still. "I know he's an ex for a very good reason. But I told you—in here, I have a job to do."

Cora and I hadn't talked too much about her ex. I'd gotten the sense it was the last topic she wanted to bring up. And I could already think of a list of twenty-five reasons why she'd want to divorce Eli, after less than two hours in his presence.

And you've opened up the lines of communication with him. If he hadn't made that comment about three brothers on Wall Street, I'd have stuck with the communal phone number that led to nowhere. But I needed to see what else he had to say. Just in case.

But Cora's ex?

Shame flooded me. This was an unsettling situation of the highest order, and one that could affect my soon-to-be sister-in-law, a woman I deeply admired and respected.

Fuuuuuck.

"You gotta stay away from him," Seven said, standing with me once I'd scooped up the last bill.

"I can't exactly turn him away," I reminded Seven. "He requested me, and he got me. That's how it goes."

Seven didn't say anything more. I squeezed his arm.

"I hear you, though," I said. "My plan is to just milk him for money. That's what I'm here for. It's what I was hired to do. That doesn't change just because of who he used to be married to."

Seven nodded, looking like he wanted to add more.

"Besides," I went on, "I think he might have information that my brothers should know. He made a weird comment in there."

Seven's chin dipped. "Weird comment?"

"Not about me or anything. About...ruining three brothers on Wall Street or something." When I caught his doubtful look, I said, "I have no idea what it was about. But I want to see if he says anything else. Men confess things in the VIP room all the time. What if he was somehow involved in this whole mess my brothers are in?"

Seven let out a measured sigh. "The likelihood of that is...very small," he said.

"But if there's a chance? I want to find out."

Seven didn't look entirely convinced. But he had nothing to worry about.

Even though the mere thought of Eli sent my stomach churning.

CHAPTER TWENTY-FOUR

JORDAN

I awoke groggy the next morning, completely disoriented. I'd emerged from the deepest slumber of my life—no surprise, since Seven and I had fucked our brains out until three a.m. He wasn't in bed when I came to, and I looked around the room for a moment, struggling to place myself in the world. What day was it? What time was it? I looked at the bedside clock—almost eleven.

I yawned, collapsing back onto my pillow. I'd gotten my morning shift at the coffee shop covered, since I had a few more doubles on the schedule this week and even I had limits. One extra shift at the club more than made up for missing my coffeeshop shift, as long as I got it covered and didn't leave my coworkers high and dry.

At this point, you might not even need to keep working at the coffee shop.

The thought cycled uncomfortably through my body, reminding me of the reason why: *Eli.* He'd texted me immediately after our VIP session yesterday, as promised. And I'd responded, as promised, just to let him know it was a real number.

I unlocked my phone. Notifications were piled up on each other. All text messages from Eli.

Fuuuuuck.

I swallowed a bad taste in my mouth, shoving the phone back onto the nightstand. I didn't want to deal with him right now. I didn't want to deal with him ever again, actually.

I rolled out of bed, rubbing the sleep from my eyes on my way to the bathroom. Once I'd peed and washed my face and felt marginally more prepared for the day, I wandered into the living room. Seven was on the couch, carving wood. I couldn't stop the huge grin that broke out. I never thought it could bring me so much joy to see a man fondling wood.

But this man knew how to carve. And it just made him even more irresistible.

"Morning." I sauntered over to him, leaning over the back of the couch to give him a kiss. He smiled up at me as one kiss turned into two and then three.

"Good to see you finally woke up from your sex slumber," he said.

"Well, when someone fucks you into next week, you need a morning to recover."

"I couldn't sleep in. But then again, I wasn't the one walking on eight-inch heels for seven hours last night."

I grinned, wandering to the kitchen. "It's exhausting, that's for sure. Especially when I have to restrain myself from using said heel as a weapon for part of the night."

I could hear the *thwick thwick thhhhwick* of Seven's carving tool as I got things together for coffee.

"I assume that's in reference to Eli?"

"Mostly him. But you know how it goes. Most men are creeps."

He laughed. "Where can I apply for an exclusion?"

"You were automatically excluded on day three," I told him, filling the coffeemaker with water.

"Not even day one or two?"

"No, because that's when you *were* following me around like a creep," I reminded him with a laugh. I filled the coffee filter with grounds and hit the *start* button. "But when you broke into my apartment and didn't have your way with me, I started to think I could trust you."

"Ironic, considering how many times I've had my way with you since then," he added.

"Yeah, true. Good move, then, I guess. Do you use that one on all your female clients?" I teased.

He pinned me with a serious look. "You're the first. And the last."

Seven busied himself with his carving, and my mind wandered back to Eli. I needed to see what he'd been sending. I fetched my phone and returned to the kitchen.

Sixteen text messages, all with varying degrees of fawning, obsessing over my looks, and requests to come to his place. He'd started sending them around one a.m., and the most recent one was from nine. He had to have been up all night. Or was he just a night owl? My stomach churned uncomfortably.

A new text message came in, thankfully not from Eli.

AXEL: Hey baby sis! You got some time for your big bros? We wanna host a dinner to celebrate some exciting news

JORDAN: Oooh, what's the news? You know I'm down for one of your feasts. Gaston and I have a weird bat relationship going now and I gotta keep that alive.

AXEL: That is so fucking weird and I love it.

AXEL: Gaston, on the other hand...not sure. Gonna have to learn French to find out what he thinks.

AXEL: Anyway, Cora's divorce was finalized 2 days ago and we wanna host a Fuck You Feast dedicated to her ex tonight. You in?

I stared at the text for an abnormally long time. The uncomfortable churn from earlier had now turned into a dangerous storm. Cora wanted to celebrate being done with Eli forever, while I'd just given him access to me for ten grand.

Maybe it wouldn't pan out. But what if he did know something? If I'd driven him away, I'd never find out what it was.

I was just going to give him a little bit of what he wanted. The bare minimum. To see where it led. That was all.

JORDAN: I'd love to! Should I tell Seven to come?

AXEL: Of course. It's not a family affair without our big, muscled bodyguard.

I smiled at his text. My entire life was feeling more and more like a family affair. I'd never even remotely seen this as a possibility for myself...yet here I was. Living it. Kaylee hadn't struck me dead yet. And I was...happy.

Holy shit, I was happy.

"You must be reading an article about how rice noodles are made if you're smiling like that." Seven's voice jostled me out of my thoughts. I almost wanted to hide my screen, as if it held something salacious, but no. It was just my own sense of weirdness. It took a while to adjust to normalcy. Warmth. *Family.*

"Try again. I already know how they're made, anyway. But thinking about them *does* make me smile." I jerked my chin toward what he toyed with in his hands. "What did you make?"

He held up his newest creation, a three-pronged fork. "I'm about out of my starter wood. I'll have to go find some more soon."

"Can't you set up a real woodworking station in here?" I gestured to his vast living room, which was mostly empty, save the couches, TV, and his workout equipment.

"So it'll become a gym, a strip club, *and* a woodworking shop."

"Nothing wrong with that. One-stop hobby shop."

He grinned at me just as the coffee maker bleated that it was ready. My phone buzzed while I prepped my coffee, signaling an incoming text. As soon as I glanced toward my phone on the island, I saw Seven's gaze land on my phone screen.

"Probably Axel," I said, stirring creamer into my coffee. "He said they're planning a divorce celebration for Cora tonight. A fuck-you feast, he called it."

Seven said nothing. I blew gently on the top of my coffee as I crossed back to the island. I touched my phone to light up the notifications. Eli's name sat at the top of the list. My stomach sank.

ELI: Are you ever gonna write back?

My stomach twisted. When I looked up, I found Seven's studious gaze on me, concern wrought into his features.

"Who was that?" he asked quietly. "Definitely wasn't Axel, and there aren't too many people that make your face look like that when they text," he went on.

My shoulders sagged as I set my coffee gently on the countertop. "Eli."

The way Seven's brows shot upward made my stomach twist. "Cora's ex." He said it less as a question and more like a statement. Like he couldn't believe the words. "The one your brother wants to celebrate her divorce from."

"He asked me for my number. I told him no, because I never give out my number—"

"Then how the fuck is he texting you now?"

I winced—his words came out so sharp they nearly broke skin. "I gave Eli our communal throwaway number, the one we all give out to guys who won't stop pressing us. But he called me out on it. After he made that comment that sounded like it could be about my brothers, I decided to give him a different number that I access via an app on my phone. It's not my real number. I can delete it or get rid of it at any time."

"I told you to stay away from him," Seven said. His anger showed itself at the edges: the flare of his nostrils, the harsh hiss of his words.

"I am. When he comes into my workplace, we'll engage. But giving him this number will let me probe a little."

He shook his head. "I'm not buying it."

I scoffed. "Well when I'm making fifteen grand a day, I can afford to buy it."

"Don't be fucking sassy," he warned.

"I'm not being sassy. What's the downside here? Either I learn something that might help my brothers, or I make a shit ton of money that helps me."

Seven watched me for a moment, his nostrils flared. "He's a drunk, rich asshole who will say anything he can to impress the woman he wants to fuck. That's what I think."

I groaned. "Fine. Agree to disagree. But emptying Eli's pockets is the best way I can think of to help even the scales between him and my brothers. And he doesn't even fucking know it. It's like...secret alimony or something."

Seven seemed thoroughly unmoved by that.

"And you know what else? At the end of the day, I need to make money," I reminded him. "I need to get back on my own two feet. Remember? You told me this was a temporary place for me. So I need to find an apartment, start paying rent again. Move into a place on my own that doesn't have a door that lets some random guy just walk into my apartment while I'm working."

Seven said nothing, just studied the countertop while his jaw flexed and flexed.

And maybe reminding *him* was helpful to remind *me* as well.

No matter how sexy and fun this stay had been, it wasn't my home. It wasn't for me to stay in permanently. Seven had made that abundantly clear at the beginning, and I intended to make good on the arrangement.

"Don't you have anything to say?" I asked, when the silence became heavy.

"It doesn't matter what I say." He stood straight, his face a frighteningly neutral mask. "You've already made up your mind. You gave him access to you outside the walls of the club when you promised you wouldn't. It's done. There's nothing I can do except clean up the mess."

He started toward the bedroom, calling over his shoulder, "I'm gonna head out for a little bit. I'll be back in time for dinner."

He disappeared into the bedroom. Everything felt bloated and tense, and I had a sneaking suspicion his departure was directly related to *me.*

I frowned down at my coffee, stirring even though it was already perfectly mixed.

A moment later, he strode back through the apartment, his laptop bag slung over his shoulder. He grabbed his jacket on his way out.

"Text if you need anything," he said curtly.

And then he was gone.

I stood indignantly for a few moments, looking around the empty apartment, watching Ranger wander by. So Seven was mad—okay. Understandable. He needed some time to process. Also fine.

But now he'd ruined my day by walking out on me and putting up the brick wall again. I expected more from him; after so much intimacy and openness, his shutting down felt alien and cold.

I drained my coffee while roaming the apartment like a lost fruit fly. When I couldn't settle, I finally addressed Eli's texts.

ELI: I'm hosting a party tomorrow night. I NEED you there.

ELI: Come on gorgeous. Tell me you'll come.

JORDAN: I'm open. But I need to make one thing clear.

ELI: What is it?

JORDAN: I'm not your girlfriend, and I'm not a prostitute. I expect you'll want me to dance and entertain your friends. That's work for me. So I'm expecting to be compensated. And everyone keeps their hands to themselves.

ELI: Compensation is my middle name. Along with Perfect Gentleman. So you in?

JORDAN: One more thing.

ELI: Jesus.

JORDAN: My bodyguard comes with.

ELI: You don't trust me?

JORDAN: It's not that. He comes with me everywhere. This ass needs extra eyes...don't you agree? <kissy face>

ELI: I'm sure he doesn't hate his job. He can come too. Just promise me I'll get some alone time with you. I need you there.

My eyes fluttered shut. My entire body felt heavy. Seven was going to fucking *hate* this. And possibly hate *me*. But something deep inside, way past the trepidation, told me this was something I needed to see through.

JORDAN: Promise. See you tomorrow.

CHAPTER TWENTY-FIVE

SEVEN

"Liam, it was a real pleasure meeting you today." I stood from my office chair, extending my hand over the new, mahogany desk that had arrived a few days ago. Liam stood as well, giving me a firm handshake.

Our interview had gone well, and he'd passed the pre-interview background check with flying colors. I planned on hiring him immediately. My second new hire for the business, but the first one to occur within the walls of my new office, which I'd been putting together on the sly in my downtime.

"Likewise, Seven." Liam cast me an effortless grin. He had something of a boy-band aesthetic to him; he could become an A-list actor if the close protection thing didn't work out. "I appreciate you taking the time. I really like what you're building here."

I smiled as I came around the desk, heading toward the door of my office. I believed Liam, even though it could have been a line of bullshit.

"I hope you'll consider joining Silva Security," I told him, opening the door. "I'll be sending over the paperwork later today."

Liam tipped his fingers in a salute. "We'll talk soon, then."

I watched him stride through the sparse foyer of Silva Security, my new headquarters on the seventh floor of the Fairchild's charity building, the one they'd dedicated to Kaylee and Jordan. They'd given me the entire floor to use as I saw fit, even though I'd only asked for the suite. And, well, none of them wanted me to have any other floor but *seven*. Of course.

Excitement and urgency spread through me in equal measure as I returned to my desk. There was so much to do still. So much to take care of. *And you still haven't even fucking told Jordan.*

The thought haunted me more than I wanted to admit. In the beginning, I didn't tell her because it wasn't her place to know. I'd kept those lines drawn.

But now everything had changed. There were no lines anymore, just murkiness and poor decisions. I was in too deep, that was for fucking sure. Because now I was both dreading and celebrating the expansion of my business.

Liam or Chico would become my replacement. Exactly what I'd planned from day one, whether Jordan liked it or not.

And I already knew she wasn't going to fucking like it.

But there were a few things she was doing that I didn't fucking like either. So maybe this just leveled the playing field. My mouth turned downward as memories of her confession from that morning flooded me. I didn't have enough vocabulary to express how much I disliked the fact that she gave out her phone number—even an unofficial one—to fuckwad Eli.

But she knows he's a fuckwad, too. She's just doing it for the money.

That rationale grated on me. Her safety came first. Didn't she get that? There was no way to stop her from engaging with him that didn't include full-on control, and that wasn't my style. I could only protect a client as far as they'd allow it. I knew this. I'd lived it.

But I'd allowed myself to get way too intimate with my client. I'd fucked up. And now I was trapped in my own mess.

I huffed as I returned to the new hire process for Liam. I got together his paperwork, prepping the email with the formal proposal. But thoughts about Jordan kept cropping up, no matter how hard I focused on the computer screen.

The only way out of this mess was through. We needed to stick to the original plan. She needed to get her own place like she said. No matter how fun it was to play house, she wanted to move out, and I'd have to let her. Even though the thought made me queasy.

But what future do you see with her?

My confusion lay in the fact that I could see an amazing future with her; but it was roadblocked by all the snafus in front of us. Her brothers would never sign off on us as a couple, even if her protection was handled by Liam or Chico. And then if we did happen to find a way forward together...? I wasn't sure I could handle cracking open my heart again. I wasn't even sure there was anything left inside there after Olivia.

My frown deepened as I took care of a few administrative tasks I'd been putting off. My phone vibrated with a message.

AXEL: Hey Seven. Legs just picked up Jordan from the apartment for our celebratory fuck-you feast. You're coming, right?

My stomach had worked itself into knots by this point, but the idea of attending their dinner—and coming face to face with Jordan—set my gut twisting even more.

SEVEN: I've actually got a lot I need to finish at the new office. Just met with a new employee. If I'm not too tired afterward I might swing by. Chico's on hand tonight if you need him for anything.

AXEL: No problem. I hope we'll see ya, but if not, I totally get it.

I pushed my phone away, my face dropping to my hands. Two days ago, I'd been in paradise. And today, nothing felt right.

My intuition was pinging, and it told me something I didn't want to hear.

If you go any further, every day is going to be like this. And you know where that leads.

I stewed in the festering silence until my thoughts became so loud I needed an escape hatch. Deep down inside, all I could think about was the natural conclusion of this love affair: falling so deeply in love that I'd offer up my quivering heart on a platter, only for it to be shredded. I reached for my phone again and hit the speaker button, then speed dial. This was suddenly an emergency.

When Trojan answered, he sounded like he'd just been napping. "H'lo?"

"Hey, man. Did I catch you at a bad time?"

"Nah. I'm just in the spa."

I blinked. "Like...a nail salon sort of spa?"

"Sorta. I think they've got one of those places over there."

"Is this for you, or..." Some of my bad mood was lifting. All I could imagine was Trojan relaxing in a sauna by himself.

"Uh, sorta."

"And you give me shit about being cryptic."

"Listen, why don't you tell me why you called first and then maybe I'll tell you what I'm fucking doing at the spa," he countered.

I laughed into my hand. "I don't know. Why I called seems irrelevant now."

"Bullshit. What's up?"

"Nothing much." I rubbed my hands together slowly. Where to begin? Everything felt so jumbled.

"Okay, great. Thanks for the chat. I'll talk to you later—"

"Shut the fuck up." Laughter edged my words. "I'm calling because..." I let out a sigh, rubbing my face.

"I already know why. I just want to hear you say it," Trojan said.

"I just need some perspective," I finally summarized. "Things have...progressed with Jordan."

A loud groan ripped through the phone.

"You need a lot more than perspective, it sounds like," Trojan said.

"I don't know, man. It feels right with her. Like...indescribably right."

"You fell in love this quick?" He sounded incredulous.

"I never said that."

"I know how to read between the lines."

I scoffed. "Whatever. My point is, things are intense. I made a bad decision even starting this, and now she's making a dangerous decision that's got me freaking out, and I just..." My words faltered, my throat tightening. I hadn't shed tears over Olivia in years. But suddenly, I realized all my attempts to become a heartless monster had failed.

I still had emotions. I'd just bottled them up so tightly I'd forgotten they were there.

"Go on," Trojan prompted.

"What if we do fall in love and then something happens to her?" My heart raced as I spoke, my mouth suddenly dry. This fear had lain quiet and slithering inside me since the second I saw Jordan and realized I needed to have her. "Like what happened with Olivia."

Trojan's voice was softer when he spoke this time. "Seven, dude, that's not—"

"She's putting herself in danger. I can be there alongside her. I know this. But I can't prevent everything. I didn't prevent what happened with Olivia. I wasn't there. And I just feel like the closer we get, the better chance there is that something might...happen to her."

"Dude. First of all, you falling in love with someone does not curse them to getting hurt or worse. I promise you. History's not gonna repeat itself."

"You don't know that," I told him.

"You're right. I don't. But I do know there's no cause and effect there."

I sniffed, inspecting my hands as I rubbed them together. "I know we can't be together while her brothers are my employer. They made that clear. But I can't keep myself off her."

"You need space," Trojan said.

"Yeah." I needed it *desperately*.

"Assign her a different guard like you had planned," Trojan went on. "That's step one. Then stay busy. Focus on your business. You'll figure out how to fix this once you get some space. Just don't lose sight of the goal, my man."

I nodded, trying to plant Trojan's words so deeply they rooted and took over. I knew he was right. And part of the problem was that over the last couple of weeks, I'd secretly made Jordan my goal.

I'd lost sight of my real goals.

And that needed to change.

Now.

CHAPTER TWENTY-SIX

JORDAN

Thud thud thud.

I jolted awake, looking around me. This wasn't my bedroom. It wasn't Seven's room. It wasn't even my old bedroom. I rubbed at my eyes as the knocking returned.

"Rise and shine, cupcake!"

Axel's voice. Then the doorknob turned. Axel strutted in a moment later, bringing memories with him. The fuck-you feast from the night before. The vast quantities of wine consumed. The laughter, the fun, the bone-deep *warmth*.

I groaned, looking toward the nightstand. I grabbed my phone to check the time. Ten a.m. "Aren't you up early...?"

"Is ten early for you?" He strode to the curtains along the far wall, tearing them open like a museum director revealing his finest art. Sunlight streamed in, making me squint.

"Considering what time we went to bed last night...yeah."

He grinned, easing into an armchair along the wall. "Well, I've got a lot of annoying big brother activities to catch up on. The wedgies are coming next."

I collapsed back onto my pillow, laughing. My brothers were hilarious—a fact I was reminded of by the distant muscle pain I had from so much laughter the night before.

"Damian will handle the noogies," he went on.

"Then I'll have to make up for lost annoying little sister time somehow," I shot back. "I might hack your social media accounts and tell the world how much you love eating boogers if you're not careful."

Axel's eyes turned to slits. "Don't you dare."

Damian popped his head into the bedroom. "Morning, Jordan. You hungry?"

"I have no idea," I told him. "I'm either famished or repulsed by the idea of food."

"Sounds like a hangover," he said. "Trace and I made brunch if you want anything."

"Thanks, guys." I grinned over at Damian. "I'll just go wash my face and then be out."

Axel came to his feet, headed for the door. "I won't forget about the wedgie, just so you know." He sent me one last smile before he pulled the door shut behind him. I relished the comfortable, safe silence. I liked sleeping over at my brothers' penthouse. No, I loved it.

Just like I loved rebuilding these family ties.

I looked down at my hands, my chin wobbling as emotion found me so early in my day. Seven would be proud of all the progress we made last night as a family. But he hadn't shown up.

I tore myself out of the extra-comfy bed and slipped into the attached bathroom to get ready for the day. After washing my face and changing clothes, I found Axel, Damian, and Trace at the main island in the kitchen, munching on bacon. Zero sat at Axel's feet, perking up as I walked in.

"Morning, Jordan," Trace called out.

"Hey guys." I paused to pet Zero's glossy, boxy head, planting a kiss on him before settling on an open stool facing the spread they'd laid out. Zero stood and stretched, then repositioned himself at my feet. "Which cook should I be thanking today?"

"Mostly him." Damian jerked his thumb toward Trace. "Though I oversaw the bacon crisping."

"It looks exceptionally crispy," I said. "Just how I like it."

"Must be a Haynes thing," Axel mused. "If Trace had his way he'd serve it half-raw."

"Hey now," Trace said, lifting his palms. "I like it *softer*. Not still oinking."

"We need to enjoy the bacon *now*," Axel muttered. "Because who knows if we'll get it in prison?"

Damian wilted slightly. "Axel—" But he didn't say anything more.

My gut wrenched—there was darkness lapping at the edges of our conversation now, and I could feel how it threatened to pull them under. Me included.

"You guys don't know if you're going," I reminded them, reaching for the perfectly crisp bacon. "I think this is going to blow over."

"I appreciate your optimism," Damian said softly.

"We heard from the lawyer last week," Axel said, clearing his throat. "They've set the first trial date. It's in a month and a half. Our lawyer has been reviewing everything, and he says it's looking fifty-fifty right now. I don't know about anyone else, but fifty percent chance of prison is one hundred percent too high."

Trace studied his plate with deep ridges in his forehead. Damian pushed around the remaining eggs on his plate without eating anything.

And all I could do was grasp for something to reassure them.

"Do you know what evidence they have?" I asked.

"Yeah," Damian said. "It's all focused on our algorithm, the one that reinvests a portion of client profits back into the neediest areas of society."

"I think it really depends on how much of an issue the jury is going to take with our quasi-Robin Hood approach," Trace added. "If we get a bunch of penny-pinching assholes who couldn't give a fuck about the less fortunate, then we're probably screwed."

Silence thudded through the kitchen.

"How long would you go away for?" I asked timidly.

"It depends on the judge, and the verdict. But likely a decade," Axel said flatly.

My gaze dropped to my plate. I'd just started to get to know them. To feel good about having them in my life. And now they were potentially going to be disappearing for ten more years? It didn't seem fair. Life had ripped us apart for so many years already. Why were we facing the possibility of losing ten more?

"Is there a chance that someone...I don't know...framed you? Or something?" I'd asked the question before I even realized I was speaking.

There wasn't much of a reaction from the three of them. Only soft sighs and shaking heads.

"It's definitely true that our algorithm does syphon off money for charity," Damian said. "And that I set it up to do that on purpose."

"At the beginning, I thought we were being set up in some way. Specifically by Cora's father," Axel added distastefully. "But the more it's dragged on, the more I realize it's here to stay. Could he have cooked the evidence? Maybe. I don't know. I just don't fucking know."

My heart beat a little faster at the mention of Cora's father. I didn't know why. Only that it seemed like a window of opportunity somehow.

"What about Cora's...ex?" I chewed thoughtfully on the bacon, swallowed, and then said, "Could he have been involved too? I'm sure he doesn't like you very much."

Axel let out the driest laugh I'd ever heard.

"Understatement of the century right there," Trace said, his eyes twinkling.

"No matter how connected that turd-for-brains thinks he is..." Axel paused, seeming to mull over my suggestion. Then he shook his head. "I just don't think he's at the level of influencing finance fraud charges."

"He seems to be more focused on womanizing and...latex balloons," Damian said with a smirk.

"Latex balloons?" I blinked.

"Damian did some recon work on Eli—" Trace began.

"Don't say his name," Axel interjected.

"And he found out that he's into sex play with balloons. They're called looners." Trace laughed a little, scooping more eggs onto his plate. "Never pegged him for a balloon guy."

I wanted to add *me neither* but I kept my mouth shut. I didn't want them to know I'd been entertaining Eli, much less that I was going to his house tonight. Seven had reacted poorly, and I knew it would go over worse with these three. They actually had real, working knowledge of the man, firsthand experience outside of a strip club, with Cora at the center of it. No, I needed to keep this my shameful little secret. At least while I probed deeper and figured out if I was absolutely crazy for thinking Eli might have actually been talking about *them* the other night.

"Sounds like a winner," I offered, eager to change the subject. Not just away from Eli, but away from the storm cloud hanging over them and all that it entailed. "Hey, do you guys wanna see the short list of apartments that I've been looking at?"

"You know it," Damian said. "The one you're going to let us pay for, right?"

I elbowed him. "I still wanna do that part myself. But thank you. I appreciate the offer."

"How about we compromise and I connect you to our insider real estate guru?" Axel tugged on my earlobe. "And as an added brotherly perk, I'll have them hold whatever apartment you like best so that you don't have to worry about it going to someone else?"

I couldn't fight the grin. This sounded like help that I could accept on my terms, but making good on their connections. In my hunt, I'd found the perfect place—a one-bedroom with a huge living room drenched in natural sunlight in the Lower East Side that could easily be turned into a practice space. Plus, it had closets, and a bathroom that didn't form part of the kitchen. I'd gladly welcome their ability to snag it in this cutthroat market. I hadn't dared hope it would last on the market long enough for me to even look at, so I had a few others on the list that were fine enough.

"All right, big brothers. I'll let you hook me up with your connections."

The three of them whooped and exchanged high fives.

"You think Seven's gonna be sad when you move out?" Axel asked as I navigated to the browser to show them my saved apartment selections.

My stomach twisted. I tried not to think about that too much. I hated how much I dreaded the moment I'd move out and what it might mean for what had blossomed between Seven and me.

"Eh, he'll probably be relieved for me to be out of his hair." I tried to sound casual, lighthearted, when I was anything but. My insides clenched.

"He's been good with you, right?" Damian asked.

I nodded, focusing harder on my screen. "He's great. You hired a good one."

They didn't just hire a good one. They hired the best. The best man I've ever known.

My brothers and I hung out in the penthouse until almost lunchtime, then I caught a ride back to Seven's apartment from Harry, their other driver. Seven was washing dishes when I walked in, and he barely looked at me as I entered.

"Hey there," I called out, sounding abnormally cheery. I headed for the island, sliding onto the stool facing him, determined to make things feel normal. "We missed you last night."

"Yeah? Did you guys have a good time?" he asked, his voice sounding hollow. He snapped the water off and reached for a dish towel.

"I did. Just thought it was odd my close protection officer was nowhere near me yesterday and today."

He didn't flinch, or even react, to my barb. "Your close protection officer was advised of your whereabouts and safety, which falls under the protection plan that's been outlined for you."

His words felt like nothing but friction. "Well you were invited as a friend, too, you know. Why'd you bail?"

He finished drying his hands and set the towel down. "Thought you might want some time alone with your brothers. I thought I was being considerate."

I gnawed on the inside of my lip, unsatisfied in the extreme. Seven walked away from the kitchen, toward the hall. His sudden departure felt like a cold slap. So that was it? No conversation, no catching up, no nothing? Not even a kiss. I'd sensed that things were frosty, but now they were just downright weird. Ranger mewed from the living room as I stormed after Seven, stopping in the threshold of his bedroom.

"So that's it?" My heart beat a mile a minute.

"What do you mean?" He stood in front of his closet, rummaging through clothes.

"You're just gonna leave me hanging like that? Not even a 'what did you guys do' or, I don't know, something more?"

He blinked a few times, sliding hangers along the rod. "What do you want me to say? I asked you if you guys had fun. I was under the impression that qualified as conversation."

"Yeah, but..." I jerked in a quick breath, unsure how to express what was bothering me. I wasn't in the habit of expressing anything with *anyone.* I just knew that it felt weird, and that Seven had to feel it too. "You got really weird yesterday," I finally blurted. "And I feel like you're still weird."

He pulled out a button-up shirt from the closet, inspected it, and then put it back. "I'm not sure what constitutes 'weird' for you. I had things to do yesterday, I did them, and then I came back to my apartment so you could have some quality time with your brothers."

My stomach knotted up, and I didn't know how else to make my point. Maybe I didn't even have one. After all, what were we? We'd never talked about it. He was my bodyguard turned fuck buddy. I knew it was destined to dissolve. Not just because of the circumstances here, but because nobody ever stuck alongside me for the long-term. And I knew better than to expect it.

This was why I didn't let people in. Because they hurt me along the way. Whether it was with their hands, their words, or their actions, something always happened that showed me why it was better to stay on my own.

And Seven was showing me again that I'd been right.

I examined my nails, trying to conjure an air of indifference. "Well, do you have any plans tonight? Because I have something I need you to help with."

"I do have plans." He pulled out a pair of pressed black pants and laid them on the bed. "But I can get Chico to tag along no problem."

I dragged my eyes up to his face, preparing myself to drop the bomb. Everything inside me clenched. "Okay. Let Chico know we'll be going to Eli's tonight."

Seven stared at the pants on his bed for a moment before turning to face me slowly. Lethally slowly. His face was a mask of neutrality that told me it had to be hiding a storm. Silence pulsed between us, heavy as lead.

"No." He sniffed, turning toward his closet. "Absolutely not."

"I *am*," I told him. "I've already got clearance for a bodyguard, because I'm being smart. You know why I'm doing this. Why not just let me do it?"

His jaw flexed as he assessed the interior of his closet, hands on his hips.

"You think a couple extra thousand dollars is worth going into that den of vipers?" His voice came out a bark as he turned to me, real frustration finally tugging at the edges of his composure.

"I think that den of vipers is worth securing my future if that's what I need to do, yes," I spat, crossing my arms.

"That's not how you secure your future." His voice was an angry rasp, and if we weren't in the middle of a blossoming argument, I'd have collapsed at his feet in a needy puddle from how sexy he sounded. "The price of making it in this world does not include putting yourself in harm's way."

"Are you kidding me?" My voice came out more like a shriek, and I hated that I couldn't hide the emotion welling up in me. "That's the only price I know how to pay, *Seven.* I've been paying it my entire life. I lost my big sister to sex trafficking and a drug overdose. I lost my brothers to the foster system. I lost a lifetime with my parents due to a drunk driver. I lost my virginity and all my fucking dignity along the way, too many times to even mention. I've lived through it all. Besides, I'm not just talking about my financial future. I've finally found something I'm afraid of losing—I have my family back—and I'm not going to let this overly wealthy airline industry douche take it away from me."

He watched me for a long moment, clenching and unclenching his fists. "All money aside, you're risking too much on a bet that has almost zero chance of paying out. You think you've seen it all but you haven't. You're not naïve, but you're still young. It can get worse. Don't tempt fate, Jordan. Don't ask it to deliver more heartache to your doorstep."

I shook my head, but Seven wasn't done.

"These guys have their own dark side. You might recognize some of it, but it's different when there's so much money involved. They can get away with whatever they want. They can do more and worse than you realize. You shouldn't get involved. Please, Jordan."

I recognized the real pleading behind his words, and I softened for a moment. But lowering my defenses only allowed the emotion to flood in. My throat got tight, and I began to shut down. It was more than just the money, though that was a big part of it. My gut was telling me to go. To check it out. And Seven would never understand, much less approve.

I tore myself away from him, beelining for my bedroom. I spent a long time pressed up against the wall, drawing deep, cleansing breaths that did nothing to calm the storm inside me.

And I waited. Waited to see if Seven came to talk. To console. To hold me and just enjoy our togetherness. But he never did.

Because I was on my own. Just like I always had been.

CHAPTER TWENTY-SEVEN

SEVEN

SEVEN: You okay if we move the dinner to another night? Something came up and I can't go. We'll meet soon to talk about protection for Mercedes's sister-in-law, I promise.

I fired off the text to Trace then threw my phone on my bed. *Fuck.* There was no way in hell Jordan would go to Eli's with anyone but me at her side. I wouldn't allow it. So I didn't tell Chico shit. Instead, I focused on getting ready for this unexpected adventure.

I cleaned my guns. I loaded them. I got dressed in the standard black-on-black attire. I grabbed a bite to eat from the fridge before giving myself a once-over in the long mirror in the hallway. Then I knocked on Jordan's door.

Silence.

I knocked louder. "Jordan?"

No response.

She was probably still mad. She'd been right—I was acting weird. Only because I was still committed to proving to myself I wasn't in love with her. We needed space, both physical and emotional, for everyone's best interests. So why did it sting so much to put space between us?

I knocked again, and when there was no answer this time, I tried the knob. Unlocked.

The door swung open and I stepped inside, assessing her dark room. The bedcovers were rumpled but made, like she'd sat on the side of the bed. Everything looked in order. But there wasn't a trace of Jordan. I jogged to the hallway.

"Jordan?" My voice sounded like a bellow. She wasn't in the bathroom. Not in the corners of the living room. She wasn't in the fucking apartment. I swore to myself, whipping out my phone.

I called her first. It clicked over to voicemail almost immediately. Probably ignoring me.

I knew who to call next. Chico. If she wasn't here, it was because she'd snuck out early. I prayed she'd called Chico to tag along with her. If she'd gone there on her own, there was no telling what would happen—or if she'd even give me an address to send some protection her way. My heart hammered in my chest as the phone rang.

Just when I thought it was going to voicemail, Chico answered. "Hello?"

"Are you with Jordan?" There was no time for niceties. Not when my tension was skyrocketing by the second.

"Yeah," he said brightly. "She's right here with me. She said you'd assigned me to help out with an event she's going to tonight—"

"Do not let her get out of the fucking car until I get there," I snapped. "Send me the address and hold her until I get there."

"Okay..." Chico sounded unsure.

"Send me the address. And remember—she stays in the car."

I hung up, a string of curse words escaping my lips as I called both Legs and Harry—whichever one was carrying Jordan, I'd tell them to start picking detours. And whoever was free needed to come get me *ASAP*.

Once both drivers were up to speed, I checked the address that Chico had sent through. Plugging it into the GPS, it looked like a brownstone in SoHo. Not terribly far away. It might almost be faster to run there than wait for Legs to come. I went to the lobby, watching the blue dot of Legs' car get closer to my apartment building. Was he coming fast enough? Or should I start sprinting? If I sprinted, I'd save about ten minutes—but I'd arrive a sweaty mess. And running while packing wasn't the easiest.

Fuck it. Run anyway.

I checked Legs' location one last time. He was a block away. I pushed out onto the sidewalk, peering down the street to spot him. Instead of running to SoHo, I'd at least run to the car. I met Legs in the middle of traffic, weaving between cars as I navigated to him. I slipped into the sedan while he looked on, bewildered.

"Jesus, ya in a hurry?"

"Sort of an emergency situation." I checked my phone. I could see that Harry was about three blocks from Eli's house. I typed out a quick text to Harry.

SEVEN: Make another lap around the block. I need you to stall. Almost there.

"All right," Legs said, flipping on his blinker to merge into a different lane. "Where we going?"

I gave him the address, compulsively checking my phone as we crept closer. No word from Harry, but Chico occasionally updated me on their distance. *Two blocks away. Pulling toward the house.* When his message read *Pulling off to park,* I had the brownstone in sight. But Harry parked first. I saw a flash of blue sequins as Legs pulled up. I had my door open before he'd even slowed to a stop, hitting the ground running.

Jordan was halfway to the door when I spotted her, Chico close behind. I quickened my pace, easily doubling her stride.

"Jordan," I barked.

She slowed to a stop about five feet from the door. A sky-blue sequined dress hugged her in all the right ways; her calves shimmered and flexed as she walked in black heels. If I weren't determined to get her in line, I'd take a moment to let her know how stunning she looked. She turned slightly toward me, her mouth a thin line.

"Chico, you can wait for me in the car," I told him. Once he'd slid into the backseat, I turned my attention to Jordan. "Do you really fucking think you're going in there without me?" I filled the space in front of her, using every inch of my height. She didn't even flinch.

"I waited, didn't I?"

"You snuck off without saying a goddamn word."

"You said Chico would be my tagalong," she retorted.

"That was before I knew your fucking plan," I spat. "You're not going in there with anyone but me. Got it?"

Her brow lifted. "Oh. So you *do* care."

"I do. Deeply. When did you get the impression that I didn't?"

She didn't say anything to that, but she held my gaze, the challenge still in the air.

"I need to go talk to Chico. Wait for me here. Do not move a fucking inch. We'll go in together."

"Fine." She crossed her arms, her gaze drifting away.

I headed for the car she'd come in, pulling open the back door. "Hey." I nodded at Harry too. "Can we talk out here?"

Chico slid out of the back seat. I shut the door behind him, frazzled from the way this situation had ballooned. I was now consuming all of the Fairchild personal driver resources, which meant I'd need to add an additional driver to my new hire roster. And now I had to cover my ass *yet again* with the new hire.

"Sorry for the confusion today. Can you stick around here? I'll be accompanying her in, since this is a high-risk situation that she informed me of at the last-possible second. But I'd like you to be on hand in case anything escalates."

"Of course." Chico straightened his back, his curious gaze flitting over my shoulder to the brownstone.

"And we don't need to mention this to the Fairchilds, if it comes up," I added. I planned on sharing a similar note with Harry and Legs. They didn't need to know that their little sister was heading to Eli's brownstone. Even if they didn't put two and two together, I didn't want anything to jeopardize the blossoming relationship between Jordan and her brothers.

"Got it," Chico said, crossing his hands behind his back.

"Great. I'll let you know if we need you." I returned to Jordan, who looked bored as she watched me approach.

"All set, Daddy?" she deadpanned.

"Don't call me Daddy," I warned.

"Well you're certainly acting like one."

"Whatever. Let's get this over with." I gestured toward the front door. Each step closer to Eli's party my stomach clenched harder. "After you, brat."

"There's the sassy Seven I remember," she murmured. We strode up to the front door in step. I smoothed down the front of my shirt as we approached the door.

"Anything else you need to tell me in advance of tonight's plans?" I snapped.

"He knows this is work. I told him I'm not his girlfriend, and that I'd be bringing a guard. That's it."

"How long do you plan on staying?"

"Until it's time to leave." She sniffed, adjusting the corset top of her dress. "Can we go in now and get this over with?"

"What's the safe word?"

She lifted a brow, looking over at me with amusement. "Oh, you want that now?"

"Don't be stupid," I warned her. "We need a word if you need to escape, or if something goes wrong. It can be whatever you want. Just pick one."

"Fine." She drew a sharp breath, looking up to the sky. "Greek."

"Funny."

"It was the first thing I thought of," she hissed, her nostrils flaring, turning slightly my way. Of course her little nickname for me had to crop up again. Just as I opened my mouth to mention the *Greek god* reference, the door swung open.

Eli stood before us, smirking in a sky-blue seersucker. A marbled foyer stretched behind him, dotted with enormous vases, sprawling palms, and the rush of an indoor waterfall.

"Look at you." He punctuated each word with a hard ending, his gaze sliding over Jordan from top to bottom.

"We match," Jordan said with a little laugh.

"This your bodyguard?" Eli asked without looking my way.

"Sure is," she said.

His gaze slid to me. "God, don't you just love your fucking job? Following this tight little body around everywhere?"

Something dark and liquid slid through me, causing my fists to clench behind my back, where I had my wrists crossed. Jordan giggled, swatting at his chest. If she took any issue with his disgusting tone, she didn't show it.

"Oh, stop," she teased. "It's a boring job, I promise."

"Well come on in, you two. The party's just getting started." Eli offered his arm, which Jordan happily took. He led her inside and I followed, but he stopped short in the foyer. Where we stood was empty, but the sounds of a party wafted in from deeper in the house. The clamor of voices; the occasional laugh; a champagne cork popping.

Once the door swung shut behind me, Eli lifted a finger and said, "One quick thing. You"—he pointed at me—"can hang around but not at her side. Stick to the sidelines where you belong. And before we go any further, I'll need you both to sign an NDA."

A man appeared from one of the hallways as if on cue. I couldn't tell if he was hired help or just a friend with impeccable timing. He produced a clipboard that held a small stack of papers and got a pen ready for us.

Jordan glanced my way. "What's an NDA?"

"A non-disclosure agreement. Listen, you might not get it yet, but I have powerful friends, gorgeous." His slick grin was borderline sociopathic, but the words that came out of his mouth grated on me like sandpaper against a wound. "My guests like to know they can expect privacy. Who knows who you'll meet here tonight? The mayor, a former president, some senators, an actor or five; they all come to my parties."

"Sounds fine by me," she said brightly, reaching for the pen.

When her gaze lingered over the text, Eli rushed to add, "It's all standard stuff, gorgeous. I promise. Whatever you see or hear tonight, you *didn't* see or hear tonight."

I could tell Jordan was rushing to read more. He jostled the clipboard in front of her.

"Come on. We've got to make the rounds. Chop chop."

She scribbled on the contract, then handed the pen to me.

"Does he speak English?" Eli asked Jordan about me, without even looking my way as I took the clipboard from the helper, flipping to the next page.

"Of course he does, he's just very focused on work. That's why I hired him." Jordan's voice faded slightly as they started for the party. I noticed Jordan had signed her stage name, Sapphire, in near chicken scratch. I made my signature as close to a straight line as possible and gave the clipboard back to the assistant.

Eli and Jordan were halfway into the front room when I caught up with them. Through the open French doors, a bustling party was underway. Guests littered the room, sitting in clusters on large, overstuffed couches or chatting in corners with heads bowed together. The vibe was refined debauchery, like a modern, high-class opium den—mostly men in suit coats or business casual attire, and everyone held cocktail glasses or tumblers. The small handful of women in attendance clustered together, wearing skimpy dresses or form-fitting bodysuits. On the coffee table nearby, a long mirror was dusted with white, remnants of lines visible. Eli led us through the front room and into the next, toward two men standing in the corner, beginning his rounds with Jordan as promised.

I clung to the nearest wall, scoping out the room. This looked like a boys club, though I hadn't spotted any celebrities or senators yet. Servers flitted around, carrying trays full of empty glasses or fresh drinks. Once, it looked like a server carried smeared drug trays, though I wasn't sure if they were going for a wash or a refill.

Jordan shone like a diamond on Eli's arm, laughing as she interacted with the other guests, swatting Eli's arm, playing the sweetest, coyest little flirt. If I could relax even slightly, I'd have joked that she deserved an Emmy. But with Eli's arm wrapped around her, his hand creeping closer to her ass, or draping along her shoulders, I found it hard to do anything but fume.

Eli paraded her around like a new toy. Everyone seemed taken by Jordan; I caught plenty of laughter and enthusiastic conversation as they made the rounds. When they slipped into another room, I followed, scoping out the new scene. Lather, rinse, repeat.

We'd made it through the entire first floor, and Jordan had already drunk a full glass of white wine—poured directly from a newly opened bottle—when an imposing older man came into the great room, surrounded by a few underlings. He scanned the room distractedly, leaning closer to a companion to whisper something, who then disappeared a moment later. Eli noticed the man, shouting out a whooping greeting.

"Allan! My god, you're finally here!" He headed toward Allan, finally dropping his arm from its position around Jordan's waist. Eli and Allan conferred briefly, too far away for me to hear. Chatting, laughing people filed between me and the small group. The longer this party went on, the louder it got. Eli nodded severely, clapped Allan on the back, then made introduced him to Jordan. A moment later, Allan and his small entourage were gone.

Eli led Jordan to the enormous blue velvet couch in the middle of the room. They sank onto the cushions, joining a few other men who'd been sitting already. All eyes turned toward Eli as he launched into another self-important monologue. How the fuck had Cora been married to this douchebag? I spent some time trying to mentally unravel the logistics of such an unlikely marriage. No way had Cora married him for his good-naturedness or humility. I couldn't make it make sense.

Eli's arrogant voice carried through the room, above the din of conversation and music, so grating I couldn't tune it out. I could tell Eli lapped up the attention of his guests like a starving kitten. I'd wanted to punch him from the first second I'd seen him and would die happy if I never saw him again.

Please, Jordan, let this be our last time at Eli's.

The crowd in this spacious living room was constantly shifting, but the audience that Eli entertained on the blue velvet couch didn't change. Their heads seemed to grow closer together, the conversation lowering, as though they didn't want anyone to overhear.

Jordan suddenly looked away, searching the room for me. Relief flooded her eyes when she finally spotted me along the far side of the room.

Her eyes widened and she nudged her head to indicate I come closer. Whatever it was, I could tell it was urgent.

Wordlessly I relocated to the wall on the other side of the couch, taking the shortest route—right past the couch itself. I paused behind Jordan, dipping down to whisper in her ear.

"You okay?" I asked.

"Listen." Her voice came out an urgent hiss. I remained at her side, acting as though I was telling her something, while I shifted my attention to the conversation swelling around her.

"No, man, it came through completely because of Allan's connections," Eli was saying.

"And the charges stuck?" someone in the group of about six asked.

"Their trial starts this fall." The smugness emanating from him made my fists curl behind the back of the couch. "Sounds to me like they stuck."

A couple of the other guys chuckled, starting a slow clap. "Too fucking smooth, man."

"I told you I'd make sure those Fairchild assholes were out of here," Eli said, leaning forward to grab his tumbler off the large coffee table. When he sat back, he seemed to notice me, jerking to look at me. "What's going on here?"

"Mandatory check-in," I said gruffly, straightening. I smoothed the front of my shirt as Eli's words formed a tornado in my head. *...Make sure these Fairchild assholes were out of here.* I didn't have much to go on, but it seemed to involve the brothers. Unless there was another group of brothers he dealt with named the Fairchilds who faced a looming trial. Maybe Jordan had heard more of use than I had.

"Do you know who we've been talking about?" I heard Eli ask Jordan as I walked away.

Jordan reached onto the snack tray on the coffee table, popping a strawberry into her mouth. "I wasn't even listening. Fairmont somebody?"

One of the servers approached with a coke plate, offering it to Eli. He pulled out a personal scoop from his pocket and took a hard sniff at the plate. Eli smirked, satisfied, and leaned back onto the couch as the server made the offer to the rest of the people chatting with Eli. "Anyway, where were we?"

"Talking about how hard you fucked the Fairchilds," said one of his guests in an armchair facing the velvet couch. He looked like an investment banker from a reality TV show. At the very least, having relocated to along the other wall, the thumping bass from the other room wasn't angled directly at the side of my face. I could hear more snippets of their conversation.

Eli let out an exaggerated groan that bordered on orgasmic. "I can't *wait* until the Fuckchilds are behind bars where they belong. Ten years is what they're up for. If you ask me, a decade won't be long enough."

I clenched my teeth just in case any hint of a reaction threatened to spill out. I didn't dare slide my gaze to Jordan, for fear her face would show the same shock and horror I felt.

"So, are you taking requests?" A man in a taupe seersucker sport coat lifted his tumbler to his lips. I wondered if the man always dressed as though he was Eli's twin demon spawn. "I know a few guys I'd like to get out of my sight."

Eli laughed raucously. "Depends on where you want them to go. And whether my network reaches that far. But all signs point to yes."

Their conversation drifted into chatter about a political campaign. Apparently their close friend was running for senator somewhere, and another friend had convinced the right people to secure the votes needed for his election. Jordan been sitting quietly, popping strawberries while refusing the occasional coke plate that cycled around, when Eli suddenly turned to her, saying something in a low voice. Jordan blinked demurely, swallowing her berry before I saw her shrug and say "Sure."

Only Eli and Jordan stood. He began to lead her out of the room, and I followed a few paces behind. We reached the foyer, the sounds of music and conversation fading slightly. Their footsteps thumped up the steps of the wide staircase.

"I've been dying to get you on my own." Eli's arm was draped around her shoulders.

"Well, I've been waiting for you to get me on my own," she answered with a hollow laugh.

Eli rounded the corner at the top of the stairs, heading for a door. He pushed it open, gesturing for Jordan to enter. She sauntered inside what looked like a dimly lit bedroom.

I surged forward, inserting myself into the doorway. "I'll need to be inside as well," I said.

He swung his coke-drunk gaze my way. A smile curled at the corners of his mouth, and when he spoke, the tang of whiskey reached me. "Oh, you like to watch, huh?"

My stomach turned to acid and I gritted my teeth, reminding myself to keep my fist out of his face. No matter how good it might feel. "This was part of the arrangement."

"We're just gonna have some quiet time," he insisted.

"Hey, boys, I need to go to the bathroom, anyway." Jordan suddenly burst back through the doorway, grabbing my hand. "Eli, I'll have a word with him." She started dragging me away down the hallway before she called over her shoulder, "Where's the bathroom up here?"

"Third door on the right," Eli said behind us.

Jordan led me to the bathroom, pulled me inside, and slammed the door shut behind me. We stood watching each other for a while. I didn't even know where to begin.

"Did you…" Her wide eyes told me she was referring to what we'd overheard downstairs.

I nodded. "But we can't talk about it right now."

She went to the vanity, arranging her hair in the mirror. "I know."

I approached her from behind, meeting her gaze in the reflection. "You're not going in there with him alone."

She huffed, turning to face me. Our bodies nearly touched, and I had a hard time keeping my frustration at bay.

"But what if he says something else in there? I need to hear it."

"Let me rephrase. You're not *fucking* going in there alone with him," I repeated. "He's so high, my being there won't stop him from talking if he's going to talk."

"He's too drunk to try anything. Besides, you'll be right outside," she said softly, finally tipping her head back to meet my gaze.

I dipped my chin, unable to resist making contact. I touched her arms, lifting her butt onto the countertop so that our faces were closer to the same level. "You're not going in there alone, because you don't go anywhere without me. You're mine. Or have you forgotten?"

She tipped her head, curiosity swarming her gaze.

"Or do I need to make cum drip down your leg again to remind you?" I asked, dipping even closer. Our lips were inches apart now.

Her throat bobbed. "I didn't know you still felt that way."

The innocence and vulnerability behind her words sliced me in two. I was lost in a sea of conflicting emotions. The only thing I truly knew was that I wanted Jordan—consequences be damned.

"How could I not?" I grabbed her chin between my thumb and forefinger, lifting her head until our lips connected. A soft, sweet, hungry kiss erupted. But she cut it short.

"Nothing sexual is going to happen with him," she insisted. "You know this. This place is like the club for me. It's work. I'm going to dance for him in there. He knows that, and we agreed to that. Sex isn't just off the table with him—it's off the table with every man who isn't you. And it's been that way since the day I met you."

My heart raced faster even though her words had a calming effect deep inside. Probably because they spoke to the greater truth that I was desperate to ignore.

You've fallen in love with her. What happens now?

"Just let me keep my eyes on you," I told her. "It's not that I think you're going to do anything with him. I don't trust him, even if I'm right outside the door."

She couldn't hear how fast my heart raced, couldn't see how tense my shoulders were or how hard my stomach twisted.

She nibbled on her bottom lip and then nodded. "Okay. I'll let him know you have to come in."

Letting her out of my sight in a place like this felt like throwing her to the wolves. She thought he was too drunk to try anything, but

I knew the types of terror that lurked in the shadows. The types of things that could ruin a life, even when prepared and ready. I was in too deep to let her go like that. And God knew I couldn't suffer another heartbreak like the one I'd endured eight years ago.

There was no way I'd survive that a second time.

But the deeper I went with Jordan, the less sure I was that I'd survive falling in love a second time either.

CHAPTER TWENTY-EIGHT

JORDAN

We got back to Seven's apartment building just after one a.m. We hadn't spoken a word in the car in front of Harry, per Seven's instructions. He didn't want anybody knowing we'd been inside Eli's drug den, and neither did I.

Our walk to his apartment was quiet. I'd been trapped in my thoughts the entire car ride, and now I had no idea where to begin. Sleep sounded best. A long hug also sounded great. But I was still confused about where things sat between Seven and me. I knew there was more to the story, but he wasn't offering up details, and I was too confused to pry.

He reached to unlock his door, and his hands trembled. I touched him gently.

"Are you okay?" I asked softly, looking up at his face. He wore a hard mask of neutrality, his brows drawn. He nodded.

"I'm fine."

"Have you eaten?" I pressed, watching the shake in his hands as he pushed the door open and stepped inside. I followed him to the island, where he dropped the keys on the counter. He sniffed hard, propping his hands on his hips as he stared at the floor.

"I might eat later," he said distractedly.

"Are you sick?" I asked, reaching for his hand again.

He gave me a heavy look, one that carried the weight of the world. Then he opened up his arms and scooped me into his embrace. I melted against him, my body more than ready to comply. But on the inside, I had a million questions. What was going through his head? Why was he so jittery? What the hell was actually going on?

My eyes drifted shut, and I closed my arms around his neck. This felt nice. No, better than nice. Being in his arms was the deepest, most cleansing sigh of relief. I'd missed this during his brief period of distance.

But there was more behind this hug. It wasn't for my benefit. It was for his. And I hated how warm and comfortable and safe he could appear, only to dig deep and find this brick wall waiting for me underneath.

"Tell me what's wrong," I whispered.

He was quiet for an eternity. Then he rasped out, "I can't."

I pulled back, searching his face for an answer. Something lurked beneath the surface. But if he wouldn't tell me, I couldn't pry it out of him. I wouldn't beg him to share his secrets. I hoped by this point he wouldn't want to keep any from me. I'd shared all of mine with him, and I didn't like that there was something he couldn't share with me.

Before I could sink into my thoughts, he dipped down and captured my lips in a kiss. But it wasn't soft or tender. It was hungry, possessive. Like we hadn't kissed in years.

He walked me backward, cupping the sides of my face as his tongue traced the contours of my mouth, tangling with mine. Each time we broke for air, he dove in for double. I whimpered through the kisses, clutching the backs of his hands until my ass bumped up against a windowsill at the far side of the apartment. His warm hands slid behind my thighs, hoisting me onto the wide ledge of the bay window overlooking the street. The exposed skin of my back touched the cool glass, sending shivers through me.

"Seven," I breathed, grabbing his wrist, reaching for his torso to bring him closer. He filled the space between my legs, but the short, tight fit of my minidress prevented him from getting as close as we needed. He looked down, dazed, then yanked the skirt up around my hips. He grunted, his gaze drifting over my dress.

"How upset would you be if I ruined this dress?"

A bunch of questions sprang to mind, and I couldn't quite find words. "Uh...I mean..."

"I'll buy you a different one." Then he tugged at the hem of the dress, tearing it up the middle with a loud *rrrrrrriiipppp*. Sequins popped off as he tore the dress from bottom to top until it hung off both arms as useless scraps. My mouth dropped open, and I stared down at my thong panties and bare belly.

"Wh—why did you..."

"I don't ever want to see this dress again," he whispered into my ear, nipping at my lobe. My nipples were tight points as he tugged the rest of the fabric off me until it crumpled to the windowsill. "And next time you do anything with that creep, wear a bra." His rough hands cupped my tits, his thumbs tweaking my pebbled nipples. "These are mine. He doesn't deserve you going braless for him."

The headiest thrill raced through me as Seven pushed between my legs, capturing my lips in a punishing kiss. When he spoke to me like that, I'd do anything he wanted. I was so turned on I felt like I could get off on his words alone. I hooked my ankles behind his back, rocking my hips in a circle against him. The thick ridge of his cock already strained against the zipper of his pants.

"So you get jealous, too," I murmured between kisses.

"Try spending six hours at a house party watching me on someone else's arm," he bit out. "Then let me know how you like it."

I smoothed my hands over his biceps while he claimed the hollow of my neck. Then I got to work undoing his shirt buttons, though I could barely concentrate on what I was doing. He yanked at his belt buckle, pants crumpling to his feet a moment later, followed by another *rrrip*.

Panties, destroyed.

"Ok, so destroy everything that was in the same room as Eli. Noted."

Seven freed his cock from the dark briefs he wore, then his hands slid beneath my ass cheeks. His silky hot erection glided against my needy core, nudging for entrance. I inhaled sharply, digging my nails into the ridge of his shoulders as he dragged his drugged gaze up to find mine.

"Ruin the clothes," he corrected. "Don't want to see them ever again."

I exhaled shakily as his cockhead eased inside me. I was turned on immensely, but the few days without extensive foreplay or fucking made me worry my pussy had forgotten how to handle him. My head dropped to the windowpane with a loud thunk.

"Careful," he rumbled, his eyes on his cock sliding into me.

I squeezed his biceps as he pushed himself inside me. My lips parted as I welcomed the hot glide of his skin. There was nothing more perfect than this: his steel heat filling me, the warmth of his body around me. Safe. Protected. Turned on. Cherished.

My eyes fluttered shut.

"Eyes on me, Jordan."

I forced my eyes open, finding his hungry gaze waiting for me. Desire prickled through every inch of my body. Fuck, I loved this man. I loved everything about him. The way he held me. The way he fucked me. The way he honored me but also commanded me.

"You are so fucking sexy, Seven," I said, the guttural edge to my voice surprising even me. "I want to explode."

The corners of his lips curled up. "I plan on making you do just that."

"For all of Manhattan to see?" I teased. My bare ass was smashed against his window.

"No. Only I get to see that." He looked smugly satisfied as he pushed himself in deeper, so slowly despite the urgency I could feel in his kisses and behind every movement. "They just get to see what they can't have."

His rough hand cupped the side of my face, claiming my lips in a deep kiss as he sank deep, burying himself until there was no space left. I squeezed my legs around him, needing even more, and he rocked against me, never breaking eye contact. With a free hand, he ran his thumb gently back and forth across my clit while he plunged into me, filling me, completing me. The slick sounds of our lovemaking mingled with my whimpers and his grunts. The cold window at my back warred with the furnace heat between our bodies. Seven scooped me tighter against his body, pinching my clit and pounding into me as I rode the waves higher and higher.

His dark gaze was more intense than I'd ever seen. And I gladly got lost in the abyss. All I could feel was my love for him. I don't know if it was the friction of his fingers combined with being stuffed with his cock, or whether his penetrating gaze really pushed me over the edge. But fireworks lit up, heating me from my toes all the way to my scalp. I clung to him, a strange, mewling moan piercing the air as he plunged into me over and over, driving me even higher.

"Ohhh, Jordan." The grit in his voice rubbed me in all the right ways. "Do you know how hot it is when you come around my cock?"

My entire body shuddered against him in lieu of a response. He groaned low, tightening his arms around me and stilling. Then his shoulders shook, and his hips jerked one last time. His lips were on mine instantly, coaxing more kisses from me.

He pressed his thumb into my chin as we kissed, over and over again, until his dick softened slightly and he slipped himself out of me.

The words were at the tip of my tongue. *I love you.* I'd never said it to any man and meant it. But it seemed right—and *time*—with Seven.

I love you.

I pressed my forehead to his, trying to pry the terrifying words from my throat. The sweet drug of our passion still wound through me, making me sluggish. But when I looked into his eyes, I saw the same depth swirling there. It was like we'd said it, anyway. I could feel the love coursing through him; he showed me without saying it.

I stroked his cheek, unable to tear away my gaze.

"You want to go somewhere more comfortable?" he asked, hoisting me into his arms.

"I'll go wherever you take me." I giggled as he carried me toward the bathroom, where he set me down and gently cleaned between my legs with a warm washcloth. After that was done, he turned on the shower, the rush of water filling the bathroom.

"Let's wash the Eli's house off us," he suggested. "Permanently."

"Good idea. But just warning you: if that's how you plan to fuck me after going to Eli's house..."

He laughed, pinching the bridge of his nose. "Don't even fucking say it."

I traced my index finger along the indents of his abs and up to his pecs. "Well, you have to admit, you being on edge led to an excellent time on the windowsill."

"I'll admit that much."

A comfortable silence settled between us as I relished the closeness, the intimacy.

"As unpleasant as it was going there, I think it was worth it," I squeezed my arms around his waist as the air slowly grew more humid from the shower. "You were able to hear what he said, right?"

He let out a slow exhale. "Yeah. That's fucking crazy, though. Do you think he's serious?"

"I do. I don't know all the details, but he's bragging about it enough to connect the dots, don't you think?"

Seven loosened my ponytail holder, allowing my hair to spill over my shoulders. He pushed his fingertips through the hair at my temples, searching my gaze. "I didn't hear as much as you did, but even that seems like enough details to throw this whole case into question."

Excitement nipped at me through the fog of my orgasmic haze. "Exactly! I mean, he's pretty much admitted that he used his connections to bring somebody down. How can this not be taken somewhere and used somehow?"

He arched a brow. "We signed an NDA. And it's not like we can bring your brother's lawyer or the SEC into Eli's house the next time he invites you to a house party."

I sighed testily. "You're right. But this just seems unfair. We have confirmation that the case against my brothers is a load of crap. We have to *do* something."

Seven nodded, his gaze drifting as he sank into thought.

"And it's not like we can tell them what we found out at Eli's house," Seven murmured. "Axel would flip."

"He'd be that mad?"

"Jordan, he would murder me." His serious gaze cut through to my core. "After he fired me, of course, and dismembered me limb by limb. If there's one thing your brothers can't know, aside from the fact that I fucked you on my windowsill, it's that I allowed you to go anywhere near Eli Rossberg."

I nodded, swallowing hard. "Okay. So this stays our little secret. I get it. But can't we at least...probe further?"

Seven sighed heavily, pinching his eyes shut like he just remembered something he'd rather have forgotten. "I might have an idea."

"Yeah?"

"It's probably a long shot. But Trojan has some connections with the FBI."

My eyes widened. "Really?"

"The man is well connected, what can I say? If there's anybody who can figure out a viable next step, it's him and his contacts." He swallowed hard, seeming almost hesitant to go on. "Like I said, this might lead absolutely nowhere. Don't get your hopes up. But I'll see who I can get ahold of tomorrow, and we can go from there."

I squealed, tackling Seven until he fell flat on his back. "God, sometimes I feel like I love you, Seven." My words hung throbbing and strange in the air. I shouldn't have said that. But there it was. It was the closest I could get to admitting my true feelings out loud.

"Only sometimes?"

"Maybe all the time." I tried not to make it seem like I was confessing the biggest thing lurking in my heart. Which I absolutely was.

He watched me with so much tenderness I thought I'd explode. I wanted him to say the same back to me. God, I wanted it so badly.

He ran his fingers through my hair and said, "I think it's time for shower and bed. A brat needs her beauty sleep."

CHAPTER TWENTY-NINE

SEVEN

However sweet things were between us when we went to bed, I woke up with a storm brewing in my mind in the morning. It didn't matter that I'd claimed Jordan for my own again, or that she'd fallen asleep in my arms. It didn't matter that I'd almost told her *I love you.*

Everything was still a mess, no matter how sweet it felt.

I was keeping a secret from the brothers about what was happening between us. I was keeping multiple secrets from Jordan: my business details, Olivia, how long I'd continue being her guard. Assigning Liam or Chico to her protection officer wasn't enough to clean up the mess. I needed to come clean to her brothers, as well.

It could very well ruin my career—or at least my employment within the Fairchild family. I just prayed that once they found out, my indiscretion with Jordan wouldn't become a stain that followed me for the rest of my professional life.

That didn't even touch what I viewed to be the biggest risk in front of me: bringing Jordan into the folds of my heart forever. *Can you live through it if something happens to her?* I didn't have an answer. I just knew I was in too deep.

And then we had the storm cloud of Eli to contend with. I moved through my morning workout with a cancerous knot in my gut. Jordan was scheduled for a shift at the coffee shop, so we headed that way by seven a.m., bleary eyed and on edge. I could feel it in her, too, though I wasn't sure she had half the hang-ups that I did about what was growing between us.

Once we got to Black & Brewtiful, I paused outside the main doors with Jordan. She shivered in her leather coat, pulling it tighter around her in the chilly morning air. Another reminder, beyond the red and gold leaves plastered to the shop windows, that fall was peaking and winter was right around the corner.

"I'll stay with you for a little bit," I told her, squeezing her arms. "But Chico will come and stay for the rest of your shift, so I can get in touch with Trojan's contact."

She nodded eagerly. "Awesome. I love it. And I promise I won't scare off Chico this time."

There was a warm but painful wrench in my chest. I wanted her for my own. I really did. But I didn't know how to make that become a reality without losing my balls, my business, or Jordan herself. Every path forward seemed to include too many traumatic obstacles. The storm cloud was endlessly brewing.

Something needed to change, immediately. But I couldn't figure out what.

She pushed onto her toes, searching for a kiss, and I was too soft to reject it. I cupped the side of her face, kissing those velvety lips of hers once, then twice, then three times. Part of me wanted to stay there for an hour, locked in the goodbye kiss, but she pulled away, giggling.

"Time to go clock in," she reminded me.

I pushed at her hip. "Go do it."

I followed her inside a moment later. I took my usual place in the back corner—perfect for keeping an eye on both her and the front doors. A call to Trojan was up first. He was expecting it after I'd texted him earlier that morning.

"You're lucky I'm not in California right now," he muttered in lieu of a greeting.

"You would have to answer at four a.m. even if you were," I told him. Jordan arrived at my table with a grin a moment later, dropping off a steaming Earl Grey tea. I winked at her before she returned to the front counter.

"Because I'd never risk missing some other completely batshit crazy idea you have," he scoffed.

"Listen, I haven't even *told* you my newest idea," I reminded him, unable to contain my grin, "so don't get too cocky. It could be perfectly level-headed for all you know."

"Something tells me it's not."

I paused. "You might be right."

"Jesus Christ. Let's hear it."

I looked around the small alcove where I was seated. A few other patrons sat at tables nearby, focused on laptops and steaming mugs of coffee. I was probably safe here. But I'd need to tone things down, just in case.

"We met someone recently who has some interesting information." I cleared my throat. "Related to her brothers."

"Okay...good guy or bad guy?" he prompted.

"Bad."

"Hm. What type of information?"

"The sort that could destroy the SEC case against them," I said softly. "And expose it as completely corrupt."

Trojan heaved a sigh, staying quiet for a moment. "Okay. And I'm assuming when you texted me earlier about connections, you had Federico in mind."

"Yep." My heart rate picked up. Federico had been working for the FBI as recently as three months ago. He was a walking true crime documentary, and that was only based on the shit he was allowed to talk about. I didn't know him half as well as Trojan did, but if anybody had a shot at pointing us in the right direction, it was this dude.

"Let me reach out. The best you could hope for is a phone call."

"That would make my day."

Trojan and I chatted for a few more minutes, catching up on my business progress and his general whereabouts—Paris, out on a new assignment with a celebrity he couldn't name per contract stipulations but could assure me I'd seen in plenty of movies over the past five years.

Before we hung up, he asked, "You still bangin' the client or what?"

I sighed heavily.

"Jesus. Well, you can't say I didn't at least try to knock some sense into you."

"I don't need your shit," I told him.

"Yeah, well, just trying to help. Pretty sure that's why you keep me around."

"I'm trying to get smart." My gaze drifted across the coffee shop, landing on Jordan, mid-laugh with a client. The sight of her sparkling made a smile come to my face. "I plan to step down soon. But that won't solve everything. Her brothers made it clear that any funny business with their sister would terminate my contract. So I have to figure out how to handle that."

"And then what?" he challenged. "Get married? Go have kids?"

"Also things I need to figure out."

He laughed. "Okay. I gotta go."

"Love you," I said in my sweetest voice. Trojan hung up grumbling while I cackled to myself. I did love that fucker—a lot.

I busied myself with some administrative tasks while I awaited the hoped-for phone call. I reached out to Chico, got him set up for Jordan's protection today, then got ahold of Liam to set up his first assignments. He'd start with basic stuff, just to test the waters, like accompanying Cora to her former residence to pick up some personal items, and a planned outing with Willow and Mercedes.

Within a couple of hours, I got a text from Trojan. Federico would talk to me on my secure line in the Fairchild building at noon. I checked my watch—an hour to go.

Once Chico was on site and I'd briefed him about the plan, I caught Jordan's attention on my way out. She looked a little sad to see me go, but she waved brightly regardless. I took the subway to the Fairchild charity headquarters building, where my office was located. Except I was the only one to enjoy the oddities of the day on this leg of my trip, which involved an old man with too many tiny birds in a cage, and a group of strangers who discovered a bottle of wine underneath their seat and decided to open it and share it straight from the bottle—all before noon. The next item on my to-do list was to find another personal driver to add to the roster—but that was *after* things were settled with Jordan's ongoing protection.

My heart wanted to remain her close protection officer, out of fear that something would happen while I wasn't there, like what happened with Olivia. But I wanted to grow my business, too. Like I'd planned since before I'd ever met her.

What if she kept living with you? Then you guys could stay together. Placate the brothers. Grow the business.

But we'd be together in secret, and that wasn't sustainable either.

All I could think about was the brothers' warning to me when Jordan first moved in. The way I'd promised them that I'd never engaged in inappropriate contact with any of my clients or their siblings, and never intended to. All of that had flown out the window. Damian had promised to end my contract if any funny business emerged—well I was certain Jordan and I were in the midst of the funniest business possible right now.

I couldn't imagine the conversation where I admitted to Axel and Damian I'd been fucking their little sister for weeks. Didn't even *want* to imagine it. They hadn't been in touch for years, but I knew that didn't exempt them from feeling that brotherly protective urge. They'd dedicated an entire business—and an entire building—to Jordan and Kaylee. I absolutely believed they'd fire me and beat my ass into the ground if they found out the man they'd hired to protect her ended up fucking her. Even if she'd asked—no, begged—for it.

And worse yet, I wouldn't think they were wrong if they beat my ass to the ground.

I deserved it. I knew better. And I was battling this shame every step of the way.

But then what happens when you go all the way? Fall in love? Ask her to marry you?

I couldn't see past that inevitable tangle. I'd never gotten a future with Olivia—what made me think I'd have one with Jordan?

I was fucking terrified of what Jordan represented—to my heart, to my future, to my stability. I wanted to end things as much as I wanted to run off into the sunset with her and get married.

Inside the office building, I got to work preparing for Federico's call. At noon on the dot, the landline rang. I picked it up and tucked it under my shoulder.

"This is Seven," I said.

"Trojan said you needed some intel." Federico's voice was heavy, immediately serious. I imagined he was like this all the time, even during Christmas parties. But the FBI and Homeland Security guys were a different breed. Not always in a good way, but at least Federico had Trojan to vouch for him.

"I do." I gave him a detailed rundown of the situation involving Eli—the history with the brothers, the current charges, and the things that Eli admitted in our presence that had the potential to upend the case.

Federico let out a low hum once I finished explaining the situation. He took a deep breath. "I know that man personally."

I blinked. "Eli?"

"I met him and his family once during a covert mission. It was linked to a political campaign that I was staking out. He is very well connected, but it's mostly due to his parents. On his own, I don't think he could pull this off. If what you're alleging is true, he's likely acting alongside someone."

Alleging. I appreciated his neutrality.

"It's becoming more and more apparent that he has a pretty far-reaching network." I paused, thinking back to the odd introduction that happened during the party between Jordan and someone named Allan. "He was hunted down by a man named Allan during the house party. He seemed important."

Federico paused, and I heard the clacking of keys through the phone. A moment later he offered, "Allan Margulis?"

All I heard was the last name. *Cora Margulis.* My stomach sank to the core of the earth. "Probably."

"I'll make a note. Listen, you have a real shot at collecting evidence, based on who these people are and what you're hearing already. But it's not going to be simple. It's going to be risky, and you need to keep a tight lid on this if you decide to do it."

"We have to do it," I said. "I already know Jordan will want to do whatever it takes, if it means she can help her brothers."

"The first step is to tell absolutely no one. You need an intel team, and that's it. This mission *cannot* leak. If there's any interference in the evidence gathering aspect, the entire thing could be thrown out by a court. It's easy to toss evidence when the intel being gathered is by someone related to the defendant. Trust me on this one. If you want this to succeed, the brothers cannot in any way know that you are gathering information. In fact, I'd get comfortable right now with the idea that this has a higher likelihood of failure than success."

"Got it."

"If they're being prosecuted by the SEC and their trial is set to start later this fall, then you'll need to act quick. Your most likely route is to convince the Office of the Inspector General that there's been sufficient corruption and misconduct to warrant a mistrial. They'd likely throw out the case. But that's only if they accept your evidence."

I drew a slow breath, nodding. "Understood."

Federico went on to suggest some methods for clandestine recording—top of the line devices that only he knew how to source, along with some ideas about how to coordinate all of this in a short amount of time. By the end of our call, I felt like a full-blown operative—mostly because Federico said he'd be express shipping me a selection of devices that had proven to work well with small dresses in loud situations. Suddenly, I was a part of the operative network, and now I needed to assemble the intel team.

My head spun by the time we ended our call. I sat for a while massaging the bridge of my nose, going over the immense amount of information I'd just received. This would become a full-blown operation...right when I was planning to assign someone else to her full-time protection.

What the fuck are you supposed to do now?

One thing was certain: I didn't like all the deceit that awaited me in the near future. Keeping a budding relationship with Jordan from the Fairchilds was one thing. Maintaining that secretiveness amid this covert spy mission? Way too much. Something had to give.

I didn't know how to resolve this moral conflict without removing myself entirely. Making someone else in my business her primary protection officer was never going to be a solution, since the fact remained that I'd fucked her *and* fallen for her while she was on my client roster.

I needed to resign. Immediately.

It wasn't an ideal time, but we'd figure out the next steps with a clear conscience and the truth out in the open air.

My palms sweated as I called Damian. *Here goes nothing.* I tried to practice what I'd say while the phone rang. Nothing came to mind except *I'm sorry* and *you're really not gonna like what I'm about to say.*

"Hey, Seven." Damian's greeting jostled me out of my thoughts. "How's it going?"

I let out a low breath, thinking over all the insanity of the last few days. "Pretty normal, I guess. Took Jordan to her shift this morning, now working on a few things." I paused, wondering how to segue into what I'd really called about.

"You guys haven't noticed anything strange lately, have you?"

"Strange?"

Damian sighed. "I don't mean to derail whatever you were calling about. It's just that Axel and Trace and I were talking today about how we've been noticing more...attention on us. Since the trial is right around the corner."

"Hm." I frowned, clicking into assessment mode. "Have there been any physical incidents? Threats? Do you feel like you're being tailed?"

"The amount of commentary on our case is increasing again. News outlets are running the story more; we're getting lots of requests to appear on TV, give statements, things like that. We're getting more hate mail than usual. I know Jordan hasn't been visually identified as our little sister yet—but I'm worried the extra scrutiny in advance of the trial could lead to something we don't like."

"You're absolutely right," I said. "People are going to be digging. We've done a good job of keeping her separate from you in public but that doesn't mean the wrong people won't be eager to find out whatever they can."

"That was our thought too." He sighed heavily. "I don't know what to expect with this trial. I feel like it's going to be a shit show. Things are ramping up before it's even started—so what will it be like when it starts?"

Guilt flooded me. And here I'd been thinking about resigning. Leaving them high and dry when shit was about to blow up. I pinched at the bridge of my nose, weighing my options while the seconds ticked by.

"I'll ramp up security," I told him at last. "We've got Chico on hand, and Liam is onboarding. I'll make sure Jordan stays out of the public eye as much as possible. And all planned excursions for you and your brothers will be accompanied."

"Good. Yeah. That sounds like a plan," Damian said, the relief thick in his voice.

"Forward me all the hate mail you've been getting," I instructed. "Along with any threats. I'll use those to assess if we need to modify the plan at any point along the way."

"Thank you, Seven. I know we made the right decision going with you."

I rubbed at my forehead once the call ended. I wasn't sure if I fully agreed with Damian. There was so much he didn't know right now, and the guilt from *those* omissions was just as raw for me. But one thing was clear: I couldn't abandon the Fairchilds in their time of need.

But continuing with the Fairchilds as my employer meant I needed to end things with Jordan.

If I wanted to keep this job, keep her safe, and do right by her brothers, I needed to execute a clean break. And if she wanted to move forward with this evidence-gathering mission, I'd help her craft a plan. As a colleague. Not as her confidante and lover.

The plan already tasted sour. But I couldn't afford to fuck this up. My love affair with Jordan was not the priority here—the safety of the entire family was most important. Making it through this spontaneous covert mission *alive* was most important.

She and I could figure out our tangled love story later. Right now, I needed to re-focus in the worst way.

Who else could be at her side when she went back into the lion's den to collect evidence from Eli? I sure as fuck wouldn't be sending Chico or Liam in there with her. No, nobody would protect her well enough. The only person I'd trust even slightly would be Trojan, and he...well...

My gaze drifted back to my cell phone.

He was already used to me calling him with some crazy-ass ideas. What was one more?

If there was anybody I'd pick for my intel squad, it would be him. I just needed to figure out a way to convince him to say yes.

CHAPTER THIRTY

JORDAN

My phone chimed with a text during my shift at the coffee shop. Axel sent me a picture of himself holding a key between his thumb and forefinger, accompanied by the text: *Got your keys little sis. When do you want to move in?*

Chico and I went straight to the penthouse when my shift was over. Cora and Axel were both there, beaming. After a lot of hugging and shrieking and jumping, Axel formally handed me the key.

"Want to go see it?" he asked.

"Yes!" I shrieked. "How did you make that happen so fast? It was my top pick, too!"

"I told you. Connections." He tipped his head toward Cora. I almost broke down in tears. "I might have paid your security deposit for you, too. I know you didn't want anyone paying your way, but consider it a housewarming gift."

I swallowed a knot in my throat, pocketing the key. "Thanks, big bro. I appreciate that."

He tugged my ear. "Anytime, Jordan."

"And thank you, Cora, for all your help."

Cora stepped forward, and I bridged the distance, hugging her tightly.

"It's the least I could do," she said. "I'm so excited for this new chapter in your life. And I can't wait to see how you decorate it." She squeezed the sides of my arms as she stepped back. "Just let me know if you need any help. I know a few interior designers who you'd love. We could just consider it another housewarming gift."

While her words warmed my chest, my stomach felt a particular type of sick chill. Because her generosity was occurring at the same time as my deceit. Even though it was for a greater good...it didn't sit right. I shoved the thoughts aside, determined to enjoy this family moment without anything bringing me down.

Damian and Trace joined us, all six of us piling into the SUV with Legs. As we crossed town, my entire body buzzing with happiness and *belonging*, the conversation turned to Seven.

"Where's Seven today?" Trace asked good-naturedly, turning to face Chico and me in the third row of the SUV.

Chico glanced at me first before answering. "Not sure. Had some other business to attend to."

"Probably at the office," Axel said, his eyes on the world flashing past the windows.

I snorted. "What office? Is that code for *the bathroom*?"

Damian laughed. "No. It's his actual office."

Confusion made slow steps throughout me. "Wait, for real?"

"Yeah. He rents one from us," Trace said helpfully. "In the same building as the one we dedicated to you and Kaylee."

"The building that started it all," Axel said quietly, nudging Cora, who giggled in response.

My brows trekked slowly toward the center of my face. There was no way he had an office and hadn't told me. "Why on earth does he need an office?"

"It's the headquarters for Silva Security," Axel said. "I think that's the name. What does *Silva* mean anyway?"

My heart was beating more rapidly now. "Has he had a security company since...you met him?"

"No, he just started it not too long ago." Axel rummaged in his pockets for something, glancing down as he hunted.

"I was his first hire," Chico supplied with a smile.

I stared at him, trying my best not to react. I wasn't supposed to care about what Seven did with his life, in his free time, or with his purported *business.* In front of everyone here, I was supposed to be a regular client. Not some broken-hearted little girl who fell in love with her bodyguard.

"Are there more?" My voice came out strained as I tried to maintain some degree of lightheartedness.

"Yeah, he just hired a new guy, I think." Axel swore to himself. "I had the business card here, and I cannot fucking find it."

"Which one are you looking for?" Damian asked from the front.

"Seven's!" Axel grunted in frustration and gave up. "Whatever. I had his card, but now I don't. Metaphor for life."

"Oh, I have it," Damian said. "I took it off your desk."

Axel sent me a flat look. "Damian has it. He took it off my desk."

I laughed but it died quickly. Not only was there something happening that everyone knew about but me, it was serious enough that Seven had his own headquarters, employees, and personalized *business cards.* The news settled like a boulder in the ocean. I'd been fucking this man for weeks. Why were my brothers and the *back-up guard* the ones to break this news to me?

I wanted to stew. I wanted to fester. I wanted to scream my head off. But nobody in this car was supposed to know that I cared what Seven did with his life, so I crossed my arms and forced myself to stow it away where I could deal with it after this momentous visit to my new apartment.

I drew a few deep, cleansing breaths as my brothers chattered about something else. And then we were in the whirlwind of checking out the apartment: testing the locks, opening the windows, examining the doorframes, discussing wall colors, imagining where the furniture would go. With my brothers—including Trace— and Cora at my side, things moved at light speed. They had the vision *and* the resources to make whatever they wanted happen. Whatever *I* wanted happen. Before we concluded our visit, a delivery person arrived with things that Axel ordered on the down low. Cleaning supplies, pantry staples, cookware.

"I'll work on getting the rest of your things brought over," Axel promised me. "You could be living here by tonight if you wanted. What do you think?"

All I could do was look at Axel, Damian, and Trace with watery eyes and hug them each in turn.

I was finally starting a new chapter of my life. With my family at my side.

And no matter how good it felt, I couldn't keep myself from wishing Seven were there, too.

****

Chico and I arrived at Seven's apartment around dinnertime, much later than I'd expected. I found Seven in the kitchen, chopping onions at the island.

"Hey, guys," he said brightly.

But his tone and general hotness were no match for the bombshell revelation in the SUV earlier. Just from looking at him, all those bad feelings came back. The secrecy. Keeping me in the dark. Everyone else knew but *me.*

How fucking dare you.

"How'd your day at the office go?" The question erupted from me like a geyser. There was no dancing around the issue.

Seven looked between me and Chico a few times. "It was fine."

"Building something big over there, huh?" I crossed my arms, maintaining my stance near the door. Chico backed away slowly.

"Well, I'll hand this back to you," Chico said.

"Thanks, Chico. I'll touch base with you later." Seven watched as Chico slipped out of the door. Once it clicked shut behind him, his gaze returned to me. "What's going on?"

"I should ask you the same fucking question!" My voice was nearly a shout, and I couldn't contain it. I was furious. Humiliated. *Depressed.* "Turns out everyone and their brother—including my own brothers—knows about this business you've started. Axel even has a business card! Yet somehow, conveniently, you forgot to mention it to me?"

He set down the knife he'd been using and faced me slowly. "I've been waiting for the right time."

"It takes literally ten seconds to mention the fact that you started a business," I shot back. "Oh look, I just said the words. Less than ten seconds actually. Maybe it took three."

"Building a business of my own has been the plan since before I even met you," he said slowly, in a measured tone. "It didn't come up earlier because I wanted to keep that line drawn with you. I didn't think you needed to know. It seemed irrelevant. Those aren't the type of things I talk about with my protection clients—business ideas, future plans. But then things...changed."

I scoffed. "Yeah. They sure fucking changed, didn't they?"

He watched me heavily for a moment. "Listen, I have news from my meeting with Federico. This is important. Do you want to hear what it is?"

I sighed, nodding, still not completely satisfied about the whole business-hiding thing. Seven pushed aside the cutting board, gesturing for me to sit. This time, as I sat in the stool facing him, I realized I felt farther away from him than ever before. There was a cutting loss in finding out that somebody you trusted, let get so close to your heart, had been withholding important details. It made me look back on everything we'd shared the past few weeks with suspicion.

"Federico thinks we have a shot at building a portfolio of evidence," Seven said. "He's fast-tracking some recording devices for us to use, and he says we need to build a top-secret intel team. This is, for obvious reasons, something that cannot be shared with anyone. Not even your brothers. So it would just stay between whoever is on the team. But he seems confident that if you get some admission of guilt from Eli, that we could use it to cause a mistrial or have the case dismissed completely before the trial even starts."

Excitement flooded me. "Okay. So...we can move forward."

Seven nodded slowly. "Yes. But with precautions. And...awareness. This might not work out. There's a higher chance of failure than success, according to Federico. But I'm willing to help if you want to do it."

"Of course I want to do it," I blurted. "I can't let something like this go unaddressed. Especially when my brothers are facing a decade of prison time."

He smiled, pulling the cutting board back into position so he could resume chopping. "I figured you'd say that."

But the prickles of my discontent returned, reminding me of what I was still so angry about. "In fact, Eli is planning to pick me up from my new apartment in a few days." It wasn't entirely true—while Eli was begging to see me again after our last visit, I hadn't told him where I lived, much less asked him to send a car for me. But what was an argument without poking the bear a little? "We can do the first set of recordings then."

Seven's gaze hardened into stone. "Excuse me?"

I smiled sweetly. "What part didn't you understand?"

"There's a few things you're going to want to go over." His voice felt like a slap. "One: new apartment. Two: Eli visiting any residence of yours at all. Three: additional plans with him. When did that happen?"

"I signed on the new place this afternoon," I said simply. "And Eli's been begging for more of me since the second I left last night. He wants me at some gala in Midtown, which is happening this Friday."

Seven's gaze slid slowly back to the cutting board. "Why wouldn't you have told me about the new apartment?"

"I thought that's how you preferred to play the game," I shot back. "Not too much different than a new office. Except the difference is, you knew all along I was apartment hunting. Well, one panned out. I would have celebrated with you, if I hadn't found out today just how much you've been hiding from me."

He drew a slow inhale through his nostrils but said nothing.

"Who knows? Maybe there's more I don't know about. Secret wife on the West Coast? An entire family you failed to mention? Maybe this isn't even the first business you've started since we met. Maybe you've got offices all over Manhattan."

"Jordan—"

"It doesn't matter. I'm going to go pack up some things. I'm planning on spending the night in my new place." I headed for my bedroom, calling over my shoulder, "All alone!"

I shut the bedroom door hard, pressing my back up against it as I fought tears and listened to the frantic beating of my heart. I only knew how to press forward on my own. Even though I was desperate for someone to fight for me.

Waiting for Seven. Waiting for...something. An explanation that felt good. A plea to stay. Maybe even just a long hug and deeply felt apology.

But none of that came. Only silence.

So I got to packing.

CHAPTER THIRTY-ONE

JORDAN

I woke up the next morning abnormally early, assaulted by sun shining directly on my face. *Curtains.* That's what I'd forgotten in my first-night-in-the-apartment haste. My brothers had sent over *yet another* brand-new king-size bed, which was already waiting for me in the bedroom, when I returned later that night. With a bed, the cookware, and the other basics Axel had bought, I felt ready to begin this new chapter.

I was just missing an assortment of wooden spoons. And Ranger. The thought crashed through me, dampening my new-apartment bliss.

I'd brought over everything I'd been living with in that small bedroom in Seven's apartment, which helped things feel slightly less sterile and vast. But the place needed a lot of furniture, not to mention my mug collection.

I was off from both jobs today, which meant I had plenty of time to work on the new place and coordinate delivery of the things I'd stored from my last place. By lunchtime, I had everything dropped off, minus the coffee mugs. At two p.m., I got my first text from Seven.

My heart leapt into my throat when I saw his name on the notification screen. Maybe he took the night to cool off. Recalibrate.

Personally, I felt more ready to talk things over now. Start mending fences and figure out how to move forward together—with Ranger.

SEVEN: Chico will be on hand if you need to go anywhere. Update him with your schedule when you can.

SEVEN: We'll need to meet before Friday to go over the plan.

I stared at the screen for what felt like an eternity, a frown growing deeper by the second.

No *I miss you* or *how was the first night*. Just business-as-usual. Back to bodyguard square one. I swallowed a knot in my throat and looked around my empty apartment. I'd wanted to share this with him, and he didn't even care. How did I misread him so terribly? How had I fucked this up?

Seven was the only man I'd truly fallen for, and he was going to act like this? I'd bared my soul to him, and this chill was what I got?

Tears brimmed in my eyes as I struggled to not cry. I never used to cry, not until I met my brothers. Now my emotions were in full view and constantly spilling over. I'd lived for so many years frozen, terrified to emote or get too close to anyone. And lately, I'd had so much warmth that it had melted the frozen casing from my life.

But Seven was showing me maybe I should never have warmed up to him, or anyone else.

There was still plenty of opportunity for me to get hurt, even by the good guys.

JORDAN: Where should we meet?

SEVEN: You can come see the new office if you want.

Was that an olive branch, or a pity twig? I knew nothing anymore. If we'd been together before, this had to mean that we were broken up now. I should not have spent my first night in this apartment without so much as a check-in text from him. I knew this in my bones.

And the stupidest part was that I craved Seven, even though the hurt lashed through me.

JORDAN: Just send me the address and when I should be there.

Seven's next text held the address and a meet-up time for two days later. I didn't write back. And neither did he.

Not that day.

Not the next day.

Not even the next.

Chico accompanied me on all my coffee shop and Gemstones shifts. By the morning of the office meet-up, I was so confused that I wasn't sure how to act around Seven. We'd gone from living together to cold distance. He didn't ask about the apartment. And now Ranger was caught in the middle. I wanted my cat, but I worried that going there to collect him would be the last time I ever saw the inside of Seven's apartment.

I'd shared pictures of the progress with Jessa, Mercedes, and Cora in our girl group chat, as well as Damian, Axel, and Trace in my brothers group chat. Hell, Chico had seen the inside of my new apartment multiple times, and Seven had yet to *ask*.

It hurt more than I wanted to admit even to myself.

When Chico delivered me to the office building, he lingered under the dedication plaque where my and Kaylee's names were emblazoned, allowing me to visit Seven's headquarters on my own. When I walked into the stark office area, decorated with only a potted palm set directly in the sunlight streaming in through a big window and an overstuffed chair that formed the waiting area, Seven stepped out of his office to greet me.

The sight of him nearly disabled me. He filled the doorframe, looking somehow completely different than the last time I'd seen him, even though it had only been three days. He wore a light blue button-up with navy slacks, and his hair was slightly shorter and styled just a bit differently. Altogether, he resembled a strange replica of the Seven I'd known. This was Seven the CEO. Equally as hot as the old one, though. He smiled when I approached.

"Hey, Jordan."

I sized him up, still undecided on how to proceed. I crossed my arms, nibbling at the inside of my lip. "Hey."

"I've been wanting to show you this."

"Oh, I bet." There was my answer for how I'd handle this: *snark.*

He led me into the office, which was a large space with gray vinyl plank flooring, lots of windows, and a big wooden desk. It was sparse, but neat. Exactly as I knew Seven preferred things.

"Looks nice," I said, sinking into the chair facing his desk. "Good for you."

"Thanks." His smile was genuine. "How's the new place?"

"Good. It's coming along." I intertwined my fingers in my lap, focusing on my nail beds as I spoke.

"I'd like to see it sometime," he said.

I pursed my lips together. "Could have fooled me. You haven't even done a security check on it."

"I have," he answered coolly. "I couldn't break in."

I turned this information over in my head. So he'd visited the apartment—without telling me. Without asking to come up. Without even *wanting* to see me. Just further proof of how distant we'd become. My chest cracked in two, though I wasn't sure how to explain it to him.

"Well, let's see this recording equipment," I said suddenly, shifting forward. I needed to focus on anything other than this overbearing elephant in the room. Seven refusing to acknowledge how drastically things had changed only made me more upset, and I wanted to be out of this place as quickly as possible.

He brought out a small box which contained an assortment of threads and cords that looked like anything *but* recording devices. He picked up a small capsule, the size of a paperclip.

"These are the ones Federico recommends most," he said, turning it back and forth between his fingers. "You could even sew them into your top, he said. They're voice activated, last for up to ten hours on a full charge, and can recharge completely in an hour. Plus, it can store up to ninety hours of recordings."

"Wow," I murmured, unable to rip my eyes from the tiny thing. "That would be really easy to hide."

"There are others." He pulled out something that looked like a necklace. "Each strip on this is a recording device, but the quality isn't as good as the first one. It's an option depending on your costume for the night."

The mention of my *costume* made me think back to when he'd ripped my dress off after our last outing, since he couldn't stand the fact that it was associated with Eli. We'd gone from fucking on his windowsill to this? I worried at my lip.

"Okay," I said.

Silence thumped between us. Seven watched me curiously, his face creasing with tenderness. "Are you sure you want to do this?"

I nodded without a second of hesitation. "I do. I want to make a difference in somebody's life. Three people's lives, actually. No, even more, because if we can pull this off, it'll affect more than just Axel, Damian, and Trace. My brothers have been working their whole lives in honor of me and Kaylee. It's time somebody tried to honor them."

His lips curled into a small smile. For how mad I was at him, I could tell he was proud of me. Especially compared to where we'd started.

"Even if this fails," I went on, "at least I tried. That's all I can do."

"But what if it does fail?" Seven narrowed his eyes. "If Eli finds out and turns on you? He was violent with Cora."

His question was the uncomfortable beast lurking at the back of the whole thing. I didn't have a good answer for him. It was a possibility, but one I was willing to confront.

"I guess I'll just have to figure it out when I'm there," I said softly. "When *we're* there. Because you'll be there with me, after all."

His chair creaked as his gaze dropped to the desk. An expectant pause filled the air.

"Jordan—" he started.

Dread coated my insides. I already knew he was preparing himself to deliver some bad news, though I couldn't say how. "What?"

"This is something else we need to discuss." His throat bobbed, and for the first time, I sensed real nervousness pouring from him. "I've decided to excuse myself from your full-time protection. Chico will be your regular guard from now on."

I nibbled on the inside of my lip, avoiding his gaze as his words cycled through me.

"To be honest, I should have excused myself a long time ago," he went on. "Based on how things progressed between us. This decision has been a long time coming. We crossed some lines. Too many lines. And it just...that's not how I operate."

I studied the contours of my hands, my nails, the bone in my wrist. Anything to avoid looking at him.

"Chico will handle daily, business-as-usual stuff," Seven added. "For any time you're with Eli, Trojan will accompany you. He's the only person I'd trust in an environment like that. Honestly, he's even better than me."

I mulled over his words for a few moments, focusing all my energy on appearing unaffected. Inside, though, everything was crumbling to dust. When I finally lifted my head, I still couldn't look him in the eye.

"So when will we meet next?" I asked, too afraid to ask the actual question in my heart. *Are we really done?*

"I have some things to set up to process the recordings and to perform general surveillance outside the house during your next event with Eli," he said. "So...Friday?"

I nodded, the truth sinking into my bones. Everything inside my head was loud and raucous, pushing me toward the one question burning inside my chest.

"Why haven't you called or come over to see me?" I could hear the quaver in my own voice, and I hated it. Something inside Seven crumpled at the question, which was a slight relief at least.

"You walked out," he said. "I thought me coming over was the last thing you wanted."

I folded my hands in my lap, rubbing at a knuckle. All I wanted from him was a fucking hug. A soft touch. A reminder of what we'd shared. "I was mad."

"Besides, do you really think that's a good idea right now?" Seven asked. When I didn't answer right away, he added, "We both know where that ends up."

"What's wrong with it ending up there?" I sniffed, wiping at my eye. It had only been the warmest, safest, most special spot I'd ever known. I thought he'd felt the same. A tear spilled, despite my best intentions.

"Your brothers are my employers. You are my client. We are in the middle of an extremely tense and important operation." He paused, exhaling sharply. "I don't know what else to say. I can't cross that line again, and I won't."

I nodded, his words hammering home exactly what I feared: *You're the idiot. You fell in love, and he was just having a moral lapse.*

"So all that talk about 'mine' was just..." I started, unable to even finish my sentence. The tears were coming for real now, and I needed to leave.

"Jordan, can we please just get through this?" He sounded testy now. And I didn't need to stick around for yet another round of humiliation and rejection.

"Yep." I surged to my feet, snapping up the box of recording devices. "I'll need you to send Ranger to my place when you can. Thanks." Without another word, I spun on my heel and stormed out of the office.

That was the last time I put my heart on the line.

Because after this, there wouldn't be any heart left.

CHAPTER THIRTY-TWO

SEVEN

"Oh my God, you're working out *again*?" Trojan's incredulous voice broke through my mid-afternoon workout session. Admittedly, it was a new addition to my routine.

But a week after that horrible, cringe-worthy meet-up with Jordan in my new office space, I needed some extra oomph in my routine. There was a lot I wanted to distract myself from. A lot of thoughts I needed to stop haunting me.

"I'm just keeping things interesting." My breath came out wispy as I did sit-ups clutching a fifty-pound weight to my chest. "Trying new combinations."

"You're obsessed. You need to work out once a day, five days a week, like the rest of the civilized world. But what you're doing is like, double that." He flopped onto the couch, heaving a sigh. He'd been occupying Jordan's old bedroom for almost a week, since his protection gig with the celebrity wrapped up. Now, he was officially on my payroll as a drop-in officer, on duty whenever Eli came into the picture, twice since he arrived in New York.

I grunted, dropping the weight and collapsing back onto the floor. I stared at the ceiling as I took a few deep breaths.

"Pretty sure you're trying to distract yourself from how miserable you are," Trojan went on.

"I'm not miserable."

"You're fucking miserable," he affirmed. "And I know exactly why, but I'll pretend I don't if that's what you want."

I sighed, pushing up onto my elbows. "I have no idea what you're talking about."

Trojan groaned. "Sure. You know, I really did think that you were being dumb by sleeping with your client, but you're being dumber pretending this whole avoid-and-ignore approach is going to work."

"I needed a clean break," I reminded him. It was easier than admitting I was a breath away from losing this job, this apartment, this *life* because of this hole I'd personally dug. "She walked out. I took my opportunity. It needed to happen. You told me yourself."

"Yeah, but that was before you guys became all..." He jumbled his hands around in the air in front of him. "*Enmeshed.* Now you're both just moping around like sad birds."

"Is she sad?" I asked sharply, looking back at him.

"Seven, you're the first thing she asks about whenever I see her."

I swallowed hard. I had daily reports on her coming in from Chico and Trojan, but it still wasn't enough. I didn't need to know how she was doing, officially, but I couldn't help asking. Though it didn't even scratch the surface of what I wanted.

"And do you tell her?"

"I haven't told her how bad you're getting. But the next time she asks, I'm going to tell her you're a moping dodo bird." Trojan sent me a pointed look. "Because you are."

"Well, it makes the most sense to stay the course. It might hurt for now, but that's better than it hurting for the rest of our lives."

Trojan squinted at me. "Did you tell her about Olivia?"

I exhaled heavily, popping to my feet.

"Seven." His voice held a warning.

"What?"

"You fucking heard me. Did you tell her?"

I put my weights back on the rack, loud *clangs* ringing through the apartment. "No."

He groaned, covering his face with his hands. "Okay, well, that might be a good place to start."

I had a few comebacks ready for him, but my phone rang, interrupting my plan of attack. I snatched up my phone from the coffee table, finding Damian's name on the screen.

I swiped it on, grateful for the distraction but worried he might have yet another suspicion to confront me with. "Hey, Damian. What's up?"

"Hey, Seven. Got a couple things I wanted to run by you."

"Shoot."

"First of all, Axel and I are planning a dinner for Jordan. To celebrate her new apartment and everything. Would you like to join?"

My insides went cold. "When is it?"

"Tomorrow night."

I pinched the bridge of my nose, grappling for some excuse. I *did* want to go. But I wanted to maintain this clean break more. To prove to him I *didn't* have anything going on with his little sister. "Damn. My friend is in town, and we had some plans for tomorrow night."

"Mmm. Okay." Damian tutted. "Well, moving along. I'm going to send something to your phone. Could you look at it for me?"

"Sure. What is it?"

Damian cleared his throat, and a prickle in my gut warned me what was coming. "It's a picture I stumbled across. Take a look."

I pulled my phone away from my ear and waited for the picture message to finish loading. When it was ready, a high-resolution image of Jordan showed up on my screen—on Eli's arm.

My mouth parted. I needed a few extra seconds for things to click into place.

But when they did, all I could think was *fuuuuck.*

"Did you get it?"

"I did." I pressed the phone to my ear. "It's Jordan."

"Yes, it was taken two days ago in Midtown." Damian said. That had been one of the excursions Trojan accompanied her on. Something like a PR/shopping trip that Eli insisted Jordan attend.

"You know who that man is," Damian said it more like a statement, but I could tell it was also a question.

"Um..." I started.

"You've been looking into his history. That's Cora's ex-husband, Eli Rossberg."

"That's right," I said slowly. "I knew I recognized him."

"Why is Jordan with him?"

I swallowed hard, my hands going clammy. I had nothing prepared. No response at the ready. I'd foolishly assumed that Axel or Damian discovering Jordan's activities was impossible.

But I'd underestimated Damian's sleuthing skills.

"I wasn't accompanying Jordan in this picture," I finally said, trying to sound confident, like there wasn't a massive plot going on under his nose. "I do know that she has crossed paths with him at the club a time or two." I swallowed hard. Was I making things better or just condemning us both?

"And you're both aware of his place in our family history, correct?" Damian's voice held an edge I didn't like. An edge I knew to respect.

"I never briefed Jordan on who he was." I wanted to take some of the blame here. As much as I could, anyway. "That was my fault.

I was under the impression that you or Axel spoke with her about him. Did his name not come up at the divorce celebration dinner?"

Damian cleared his throat. "We don't speak his name, especially not around Axel. Apparently, we need to have a direct conversation about it."

"I did think that Cora might have mentioned him as well, given how close she and Jordan have become." I was pacing the living room now, ignoring Trojan's curious looks.

"Is she seeing Eli?"

"That's not my understanding." I rubbed my forehead, desperate not to push Jordan any deeper into this sticky misunderstanding. "He's a strip club patron who wants to blow his money on the best dancer."

Damian sighed softly. "But they're not in the club here. They're on Fifth Avenue."

I had nothing for him on that point. "You're right."

"I'll talk to her about it. But I want you and I to be on the same page: she's not to see him again. At all. I get the club is different, she can't control that. But beyond those walls, she needs to stay away from him. For her own safety. That's a non-negotiable. Make sure all your employees understand."

There was no room for argument. I simply responded, "Understood. It'll be handled."

I hung up the phone with a sick dread cycling in my gut.

"I take it that wasn't a great call," Trojan said, grimacing.

"No. It wasn't." I let out a terse exhale as I set my phone down on the coffee table and sank into the armchair facing Trojan. "The brothers caught wind of Jordan's outing the other day with Eli. It looked like a paparazzi photo."

"Shit. I was keeping an eye out for media, too," Trojan muttered.

"They say she can't go near him outside of the club again," I said, that dread taking root and blossoming into something much more dangerous. "Non-negotiable. I took that to mean that if she's near Eli again in public, the consequences will be severe."

Severe was an understatement. I'd lose my job and any chance of a referral to other clients. And Jordan would lose whatever healing and rebuilding she'd managed to cobble together thus far. After so much pain and struggle to get to this point...I didn't want to see her lose this connection with her brothers.

But what was more important here?

Trojan sat up, clearing his throat. "So what's the plan? Scrap the mission?"

I shook my head. I knew Jordan wouldn't want that, though I planned on briefing her about this, regardless. If she canned it, I'd go along with it. But if she wanted to continue, we'd have to get craftier. And if I knew that stubborn spitfire, she'd do whatever it took to give back to her brothers.

"I'll let Jordan know about this. It'll be her decision. But ultimately, if she wants to stay the course, we keep going," I said. "We'll just need to get more discreet. It's only a little bit longer. We can make it through, right?"

My friend didn't look entirely convinced.

Whatever risks we were taking, they'd just gotten a little more dangerous.

CHAPTER THIRTY-THREE

JORDAN

"Come on, gorgeous. Let's go shopping." Eli's voice over the phone made my stomach lurch. The man called *all the time,* and I did my best to only answer sparingly.

"Eli, I'm really tired...." I looked at the clock. It was eleven thirty a.m. Clearly, I was running out of excuses.

"I have the perfect powder for that," he said with an evil chuckle.

"You know I don't do that stuff."

"Fine. Take a nap. Then can we go out to dinner?"

I tried to keep our public outings to a minimum, especially since Seven told me about how my last outing with Eli had leaked. Damian and Axel called me personally to impress upon me the severity of Eli's crappiness. Not like they needed to tell me. I'd done my best to play it off as a money grab, just a chance to sock away some money for the rainy day fund. But when my brothers not only offered to replace whatever Eli was giving me, but double it? I had no reasons left to give them.

I couldn't be spotted with Eli again. That was absolutely *not* how this whole undercover mission was supposed to go. I was terrified that Cora would find out, too. I'd just started to gain some sisters—I didn't want to lose *them,* too. But Axel promised me he wouldn't tell her—he just didn't want me to associate with Eli anymore, unless he came into the club.

"Can't we just have a cozy night in?" I asked. That would be better than being out and about on the town. I *needed* to get closer to him, on the off chance he revealed something damning about the SEC case. The last couple of times we met, I'd picked up an errant statement or two about his involvement. Juicy tidbits, for sure, but nothing like what he admitted in front of me during that first house party. Maybe if I got him alone, I could steer the conversation back in that direction.

"I have things to do, people to see, gorgeous," he replied coolly. "I need you *out* with me."

"Fine. Let's do lunch. Maybe eating will perk me up," I said. Already, my stomach was in knots. Eating would be impossible while I wondered at every turn whether someone would snap a picture that could somehow make it back to my brothers. I hadn't spotted the camera the first time.

"I know just the place," Eli said. "I'll send you the address."

Lately, he'd been pushing for more alone time, for kisses, for things I didn't want to give him. I'd figured this would happen eventually. I just prayed I could continue finding the perfect excuse to dance around it whenever it came up.

I called Trojan, who already felt like my big lumberjack brother after over a week of him following me around. His gruff voice answered, "Hello?"

"You busy?"

"Not if you're calling."

"Can we do a lunch thing with Eli? I'll try to make it quick."

"Yeah. I'll come pick you up. Hang tight."

I got ready while I waited for Trojan, slipping into a bodycon dress that I paired with my leather jacket. Sexy, but simple. I worked on my makeup next and put my hair into a sloppy topknot to finish it off. When Trojan texted that he was outside, I double checked that I had all my recording devices in my handbag, then hurried downstairs to the waiting SUV. My bare legs turned to goosebumps at the chilly air as I slipped into the backseat, pulling the door shut.

Trojan smiled down at me, hulking and bearded at my side. "Sup, Jordy."

I smiled, sinking back into my seat. "Oh, nothing much." To the front, I called out, "How are you, Liam?"

I'd found out from Trojan that Seven had purchased this vehicle for close protection use only. No more Harry and Legs for these trips. I could only assume that Liam, as the new hire, was being hazed by doing chauffer duty.

"Doing fine. Living the dream." He squeezed the wheel, squinting ahead of him as he merged into traffic.

"That's a lie," Trojan informed me. "He hates driving. But Seven's the boss."

"I guess he is." I crossed my arms, looking out the window. I didn't want to think about Seven, much less talk about him. But the fact that he sat so heavily on my mind every day, despite my best intentions, didn't help much with moving on.

He was all I could think about. Especially while we waded deeper into Eli's treacherous world.

I wanted him at my side. As my partner. My confidante. My lover. My *Seven*.

But he was able to step away so cleanly, so *easily*, that it made me wonder if I'd been the stupid little infatuated girl who was blind to the fact that he'd never been invested at all.

The ride to the lunch spot passed quietly. I was dying to ask the same question I asked every time I sat at Trojan's side. I made sure my wireless recorders weren't turned on before I asked.

"How is Seven doing?" We were a block away from the restaurant, so I knew I could just dart out if I didn't like the answer.

Trojan cleared his throat. "He's, uh, just doing his thing. Working himself to death, in all senses."

I turned slightly. "What does that mean?"

"With the business. In the gym. He's just nonstop. He gets like this when he's trying to not think about something. And I think there are a few things he's trying not to think about, if you know what I'm saying."

My gaze shifted to Liam in the front seat. He pulled up to the valet lane in front of the restaurant and flashed his blinkers. It was my time to leave...but I wanted to probe a little deeper with Trojan.

"Explain," I said softly.

Trojan sighed tersely. To Liam, he said, "Can you give me a minute to brief Jordan? Step outside, I'll let you know when we finish."

Liam nodded and slipped out of the car. When it was just the two of us, Trojan assessed me heavily. "My friend is going crazy, Jordan. Because of *you*. And I need him to fucking snap out of it soon."

I blinked rapidly. I had not seen *that* coming.

"He's crazy about you, and he's suffering without you. But he won't fucking admit it because he's a stubborn asshole."

My throat tightened. It was what I'd been dying to hear, but it didn't make things easier, or better. If he refused to do anything about his feelings, I certainly couldn't convince him to change his mind.

"Well, he knows where to find me." I reached for the door handle. "And he's had plenty of time."

"He's had a hard time opening up since Olivia," Trojan blurted. The new name made me pause, turning to look at him.

"Olivia?"

"His late fiancé," Trojan said, emotion creasing his features. "She was murdered eight years ago. They were engaged to be married, living off base in California. Seven was out on duty one night, and a serial killer broke into their house and murdered her." His throat bobbed, but he didn't look away. I was pinned to my spot. "I thought you should know."

"Oh my God," I whispered, too stunned to even blink. "I...that...I can't even imagine what that must have been like for him."

"I've known this guy since we were nineteen. You two are cut from the same cloth," Trojan said. "You've both lived through some serious shit. But what happened with Olivia turned him into a brick wall. When shit gets tough, he shuts down, builds the wall. It's happened between him and me, too. It just means you need to get handy with a pickax from time to time."

I mulled over this information. My heart broke for Seven. But it broke for what he was letting die between us, as well.

"I can't force him to be open with me," I finally said. "He's kept so many things from me. His business. His plans. Olivia. I just...I can't..."

"I get it. But know this. I could tell he was in trouble from the first time I heard him mention your name. The way he talked about you...shit, Jordan, I haven't heard him talk about anyone like he talks about you. Not even Olivia."

"In trouble?" I asked with a small laugh.

"Yeah. Code for *in love*." He shook his head, rubbing the back of his neck. "I don't know. Just think about it. I want you both to be happy. You guys deserve it."

I touched his arm. "Thanks, Trojan. You're really sweet and a good friend. But I can't make him change his mind. And neither can you."

I opened the door, signaling the end of our conversation. Trojan knocked on the window for Liam to reenter, then gave him directions on what to do during our lunch date. Once I turned on all my recording devices, I slipped out of the car. Trojan followed me, the two of us gliding along a dark carpeted runner leading up to a swanky gold-plated set of doors beneath the scripted metallic font broadcasting the name: Adobe.

Inside, Eli was waiting for us. I spotted him almost immediately, waiting at a round table in a corner, no windows nearby. Two cocktail glasses were already on the table; one drained, and one that he sipped. I went to Eli while Trojan posted up at a different table nearby—the common bodyguard protocol inside restaurants. Along the way, I glanced around as furtively as possible, looking for cameras, curious gazes, anything that told me this meet-up wasn't safe.

I tried to blend in as much as possible, but Eli welcomed me with a long, sweaty hug and only spoke in tones a half decibel below shouting. Lunch was a tremendous bore, made tolerable only by the amazing lump crab cakes and beetroot salad. Acquaintances of his cycled through constantly, always when I was mid-bite, and I got the sense that he just wanted to be seen out with me.

Our conversation was stilted and basic. He wasn't in the mood for shit-talking the Fairchilds, and this wasn't the place for me to pry. Once the plates were cleared, the check paid, and his third cocktail emptied, I was ready to escape out the secret back door, lest anyone discover me here with Eli.

"When am I going to get you to myself?" he asked, his gaze sliding past my shoulder, presumably toward Trojan, then back to me. "You've been toying with me long enough."

I offered him a coy smile, but on the inside, panic threaded through me. "You want more?"

"I always want more." He reached across the table, scooping my hand up between his clammy palms. "And you know it."

"You know how we arranged things..." I started, unsure what else to add. The truth was plain to see. He wanted more, and I didn't know how much further I could tease things without trapping myself in a spot I didn't want to be.

"I just thought I'd be getting a little higher return for my money." His gaze sharpened to a knifepoint, and I could hear the insinuation weighing heavily in his tone. "But maybe I just need to look elsewhere."

I batted my eyelashes. "Don't be like that, Eli. You just need to tell me what you want."

He leaned closer. "Kiss me."

My heart started pounding. On a list of the least desirable activities in the world, kissing Eli rang in at the number one spot. I tried to survey my surroundings without looking like I was disintegrating from panic. "In public?"

"I want them all to see," he murmured. The legs of his chair scraped across the floor until we were inches apart. "Kiss me and prove you're serious about where this is heading."

I laughed, but I could tell it sounded nervous. "Geez, is that all you want?"

"Now, Jordan."

I leaned into him, every inch of my body wanting to lean in the opposite direction. He caught the back of my head in his hand and pulled me into him, laying a sloppy kiss on my lips. His sweat-tinged cologne sank into me, making my insides revolt. I never wanted to be this close to this man again—and I was crying out for Seven on the inside.

I tried to school my reaction when he pulled away. All I could see was his look of deep satisfaction.

"I'm having another house party," he said when we parted. "I need you there."

"Just tell me when." I tried to keep my voice casual.

"This weekend. You'll have to call off work. But I'll make it worth your while." He grinned evilly as he adjusted his navy-blue jacket. I was dismissed, made evident by the way he stood and sauntered off, ready for the next portion of his day. I twisted in my seat, searching out Trojan's familiar boxy shoulders and powerful frame. He watched me with a worried look but surged to his feet.

We hurried out of the restaurant. Humiliation clung to me, and I didn't speak for a long time, even after we were in the SUV and heading back to my apartment. Once Liam pulled up to my building, I turned to Trojan and said, "Can you not tell Seven?"

His handsome face crumpled. "Jordy, I have to. Besides, he's gonna know. He reviews all the audio."

Seven would for sure hear that muffled kiss.

"Then just tell him...I didn't fucking want to," I grumbled.

"Trust me. It was obvious." He squeezed my shoulder before I slipped out of the SUV and headed up to my apartment.

Once inside, I contemplated burning my outfit again, since Seven couldn't tear it off me, but I opted for a long, hot shower. I didn't have to work at the club that night, so I pampered myself for the rest of the day—face masks, decadent lattes, comfort TV running constantly in the background. Just when I thought I might pop out to the nearby park to hunt some Pokémon and grab some rice noodles for dinner, Axel called.

"Hey, big brother," I said cheerfully once I swiped the call on.

"Hey, Jordan." His voice sounded strained. "Listen, you got a minute?"

"Yeah, sure." I plopped onto my couch, muting the current movie, which was the most recent remake of *Baywatch*. "What's up?"

He sighed heavily. "I don't even know what to say, honestly. I'm just...confused."

"About what?"

"Jordan, you and Damian and I talked last week about Cora's ex. Remember?"

My heart sank to my feet. "Yeah, I remember."

"Then why the fuck did Cora get sent a picture of you and Eli kissing at Adobe today?"

I pressed a fist to my forehead, gritting my teeth as I tried to contain the shriek of frustration that threatened to spill out. *Fuck fuck fuck fuck.*

"Who sent it to her?" I squeaked out.

"Her friend. Someone who was having lunch there and recognized Eli. Does it matter? Jordan, what the fuck are you doing? Why are you dating Eli?"

"I'm not dating him," I rushed to say.

"Aren't you? You're fucking kissing him in public. Jordan, Cora is *devastated*. I thought we could keep her from needing to know about this, but...dude. What are you doing?"

My insides felt like a ringing bell on the brink of shattering. I didn't know what I was doing, I just knew that I needed to keep it going, for *just a bit longer*. "Axel, I told you—he pays so well—"

"And I told you that I'll double whatever you're making from him," Axel snapped. "That man is scum. Unless this is some sort of payback or something?"

"Payback?"

"Yeah, are you mad at me and Damian still? Is this your way of getting back at us or something? Fuck, Jordan—this is fucked up, ya know?"

"Axel, it's not like that, I *promise*." My voice quaked now. This had spiraled out of control, and I felt like everyone was slipping out of reach.

"Just end it with him." Axel sounded like he was pleading. "That's all I ask. I don't want this to break Cora's heart again. You deserve so much better than him. It breaks my heart, too, to see you with an asshole like that. Please, Jordan. Please."

I gripped the phone so hard I thought it would snap in two. I had no idea what to say. Other than "Okay."

Axel's desperation lingered in the air even after we hung up. I texted Cora after I'd disassociated for a while, eager to begin repairing what I could.

JORDAN: Hey Cora. Can we talk?

By the time I went to bed, she still hadn't responded.

And in the morning...still nothing.

I needed to get this intel to save my brothers, but going through with it just might ruin everything.

CHAPTER THIRTY-FOUR

SEVEN

"You're such a stud, Eli...this party will be the perfect chance for us to slip away."

The staticky sound of Jordan's words rang through my head like a gong. I heard every breathy thing she whispered to him on their outings over and over in my head. As the self-appointed data sifter for our undercover mission, I listened to every minute of every "date." And after almost six hours of sifting through files today, I needed to pack it up.

I might physically disintegrate from how badly I needed Jordan back in my daily life, if I didn't.

I pushed away from my computer desk and stood, stretching. It was damn near dinner time, and I'd been in this office since eight a.m. I was ready to eat, and I was ready for my second workout of the day. I was also ready to put my fist into Eli's face so many times he could never kiss anyone again.

So far, my workaholic plan to distract myself showed only limited success. But it was the only way forward. I couldn't get close to Jordan now, because if things went south, it would all come crashing to the ground. Her brothers were mad at me; they were mad at her; and if we couldn't prove that this had been for some greater good, then what was the fucking point?

She'd end up an outcast; I'd end up jobless.

We'd all be miserable and broken.

I returned to my apartment with a heavy heart. All day every day, I waited for some call or text from Damian or Axel that would deliver the final *you're fired*. It hadn't come yet, but I knew it had to be around the corner. After Cora was sent that picture by her friend in Adobe, I wasn't sure how much further we could push the envelope. The shit was hitting the fan in every way possible and all at once, including my burning need to ask Jordan for a second chance.

I was scared of losing you. I didn't think I could fall in love again. But I'm already there. I imagined pulling her into my arms, feeling her tightly packed frame against my body, the delicious heat of her. *We'll find a way to make it work. Because none of what comes next is worth it if I don't have you at my side.*

I played around with what I might say, even though I had no idea when I'd get a chance to say the words. At this point, I doubted she'd even let me near her long enough to get out three words. I'd have to send a written letter via Trojan or Chico. And maybe it was better to wait until this thing with Eli ended. I was torn up with indecision and anxiety as I went back to my apartment, finding it empty and dark. I flipped on the lights and started prepping dinner, a good old-fashioned rib-eye and baked potato.

My stomach growled as I cooked. My metabolism was hard to keep up with these days. And I hadn't even knocked out my second workout of the day.

Trojan barged into the apartment just as I pulled the potato out of the oven. The steak was sizzling on my cast-iron grill, sputtering and making my mouth water as it cooked.

"Hey, buddy," I said over my shoulder as he stomped up to the island. He heaved a big sigh, dropping a bag on the kitchen island.

"Don't you 'hey' me," he grumbled.

"Wow." I turned sharply, lifting my brow. "Is somebody hangry?"

He scowled at me. "Maybe. But I'm also annoyed with you. They're unrelated."

"But you *are* hungry," I said, already reaching for another potato to start cooking. I popped it into the microwave so it would be quicker, though not nearly as tasty.

"Yes. Insanely." He harrumphed and sat down, massaging his temples. "Listen, you and Jordan need to figure your shit out."

Now it was my turn to sigh testily. "Just save it. Now's not the time."

"You could fucking talk to her," he snapped.

I pulled open the oven, removing the potato with an oven mitt. I set it on the waiting plate, then snapped off the stovetop.

"It's not the time." I moved the rib-eye to the plate, grabbed a knife and fork, and pushed it across the island. "Here. Eat my dinner and shut up."

He narrowed his eyes, but I could see the start of a smile on his lips. "You're sweet, you know that? For being a total jerk, you're also sweet."

I glared at him before turning back to the fridge to grab another steak. My own dinner would have to wait a bit longer, and with the subpar microwaved potato. But I was prepared to make these sacrifices for my best buddy. "I'm not being a jerk." I started salting the next rib eye. "I'm being practical. It's too risky to go after Jordan."

"Well you need to make something happen. I live with you, and I'm with her all day, so I'm getting this shit from both sides. You're both miserable, you're both moping, and honestly, I don't even know how you've kept yourself away from her this whole time. You couldn't keep yourself off her in the beginning. And now you're just..."

I turned to the sink, washing my hands. "I'll tell you why. It's because I got reckless. One of the Fairchild drivers started getting suspicious and passed those suspicions along to Damian. If I go near her again and take what I want? I *will* be fired. I can promise you."

Trojan cut his potato open, a puff of steam emerging. "Then tell her that."

"I will. Someday."

"*Now*," Trojan corrected, sending me a sharp look. "I know you've been out of the game. I know you're scared because of Olivia. I know it's hard for you. I really do understand all that. But a real man would be there for his woman. Maybe I've just become a little Jordan fanboy since trailing her all over Manhattan, but that hard-assed brat is exactly what you need in your life. And she deserves to know why you're being such an asshole."

He wasn't wrong. In fact, it hurt to hear how *right* he was. Because it showed just how much I'd been deluding myself.

"She's smart as fuck. She loves you to pieces, and she's as loyal as they come. Look at what she's doing for her brothers. You think that she wouldn't do the same for you?"

"I'd beg her not to."

"I know. Because you're her protector. But we both know she'd do it anyway." He cut into the steak and took a bite. He hummed happily. "You cook it just the way I like it. Medium-raw."

"Well, I'm glad you want me to ruin my brand-new business," I muttered.

"Your business is already on the brink of collapse with this risky operation," he said as he chewed. "What's it hurt to add on a little illicit relationship with your client?"

"Maybe I'm just the only one not wearing rose-colored glasses anymore." I returned to the stove, flipping the steak as it started to brown. "Seems to me I should spread my disasters evenly over time, not invite them all in at once."

"Yeah, well, you're too damn practical," Trojan said, his knife scraping against the plate as he forked another bite into his mouth. "It's your greatest strength in work, but your biggest flaw in love."

I laughed, in spite of how annoyed I was with everything in my life right now. "When did you become a love guru? Last I checked, you haven't had anything but a booty call in years."

"Well, I'm avoiding love for very practical reasons," he said haughtily. "I have no home base. I'm a workaholic. I'm too terribly good-looking to be tied down."

"And extremely humble," I added.

"That too," he said, chewing thoughtfully. "Anyway, this about your flaws, not mine."

"Thanks for keeping us on task."

"That's why you hired me. And that reminds me of why I'm mad at you. Bro, I've gotta leave by next week, no matter where we're at in this spy mission clusterfuck. I got offered a new protection gig, and I took it. So you and Jordan need to figure your shit out, because I'm not going to be able to run point for you for much longer. Please, for the love of God, end this bullshit."

I turned back to the stove, staring at my cooking steak. My best friend had a point. One that I agreed with entirely.

I just needed to figure out a way to get back into Jordan's heart and prove to her that I was serious about a second chance.

CHAPTER THIRTY-FIVE

JORDAN

"I got my small recorder...the tiny recorder...the anal beads recorder..." I muttered to myself as I rushed around my living room, checking and double checking that I had what I needed for Eli's party. The anal beads recorder wasn't *actually* for sticking up someone's ass, but the way they hung on the slender cord looked a lot like a gift in somebody's sexy toy party bag. I slipped them around my neck, opting to mask them among my other silvery, glittering necklaces.

Perfectly hidden.

Trojan sent Liam to pick me up, planning to meet up with me in front of Eli's house before we went in. I checked my phone—it was almost eight p.m. Instead of heading to the club on a Friday night, I was heading into the lion's den. Nervousness churned inside me. I was worried about what "more" he would request from me tonight and whether I'd be able to dodge it and still get the information I wanted.

My brothers were a common conversational topic in elite circles, but it was mostly gossip and speculation. Eli hadn't blatantly confessed to interfering in their case since that first party that Seven attended with me. I tried not to get too frustrated that Eli hadn't opened up with the same amount of detail since then, especially since I'd been recording every breath, grunt, and fart. I knew it was just a matter of time. And I hoped tonight's house party would be the turning point.

Even though Seven won't be there with you.

I had grown to love Trojan—but he was no Seven. My body and my heart still craved Seven, even if he was content to act like nothing ever happened between us. I hated how much it hurt me. I hated that I'd let him in at all.

Trojan said Seven missed me, too. But talk was cheap. If Seven really missed me and believed we had something, then he'd have shown me by now.

I tried to push these thoughts out of my head before I got into a sadness spiral. I needed to be on point for this evening at Eli's, and starting it off moping about Seven was not the way to shine. I made one final assessment of my purse—microphones, lipstick, and phone in place—and headed downstairs to meet Liam in front of my building.

Outside, it was already dark. Liam was in the SUV at the curb with his hazard lights flashing. My teal heels clicked against the sidewalk as I hurried to slip into the back seat, tugging my curve-hugging slate gray dress down over my thighs.

"Hi, Liam." I buckled up as he pulled into traffic, then smoothed my high ponytail, a strategic choice, in case Eli wanted me on the pole tonight. "Back on chauffeur duty, I see."

"Yeah, yeah." He grinned at me through the rearview mirror. His charming good looks were always a mild surprise when I saw him. "Just doing my time before I get a fun assignment, like guarding you."

"Oh, you think you'll be assigned to me?" I executed a haughty hair flip. "Gonna have to train a little harder to keep up with this mess."

He laughed as we worked our way through the stop-and-go traf-fic. "I wouldn't mind the excitement."

"I'm sure Seven won't keep you doing the boring stuff for long." I settled back into my seat, watching the world creep past the tinted window. "The Fairchilds always have something interesting going on."

The mention of my brothers made me think about Cora. She had left my text unanswered for two days now. I could physically feel the rift that had cracked and spread between us. And that unexpected distance between my bonus sister and me was even harder to deal with since I'd also lost Seven.

My phone vibrated with a text. I slipped it out of my handbag. *TROJAN: I used the pickax.*

I frowned down at the screen for a minute then stuffed my phone back in my purse, mulling over his comment. I was so tired of miss-ing Seven, of thinking about him, of *craving* him. Even if I wanted to try to force Seven to let me in, when would I have the chance?

Liam pulled up in front of Eli's house. Per protocol, I waited for Trojan to escort me from the car to the front door. I unclicked my seatbelt, giving myself a once over before heading out.

The back seat handle clicked; the door swung open. I slipped out of the car, swinging my gaze up to Trojan. But as I did, a few things registered as off.

The hand waiting for mine was rougher than Trojan's. The stature, much taller. The outfit, much sleeker.

It took a few seconds for my brain to catch up with my eyes. I tipped my head back, drinking in the dark gaze of the man I'd been longing to lay eyes on.

My mouth parted, and my voice completely evaporated.

"Jordan." Seven's deep rumble lit a fire inside me at the same time it soothed my every aching nerve. I used his offered hand to step onto the sidewalk. He pushed the door shut behind me, tapping it once. Liam pulled away.

I swallowed hard, looking around us on the sidewalk. Trojan was nowhere to be found. I pulled my leather jacket tighter around me. And that's when I found my voice. And my anger.

"What are *you* doing here?" I snapped.

"There was a change in plans," he said simply, his heavy gaze not wavering from me for even a second. I couldn't tell what he was thinking behind that neutral mask he wore. But I ached to know.

"Where's *my* guard?" I asked, glowering at him. "I'd hate to waste your time with something so frivolous as me."

"I told you. Change of plans. I'm on duty tonight. Can we proceed?" His voice held an edge, which tasted like honey to me. God, it was a relief to be near him again and basking in this energy that pulsed between us, even when I was angry, even when we were distant.

"Besides," he added, "you're not frivolous." He gestured toward the front door, and I walked alongside him, crossing my arms over my chest, like the gesture might contain the emotion inside that was desperate to burst out.

"Well, if that isn't the most romantic thing I've ever heard in my life," I muttered.

He sent me a sharp look. "You're the most important thing there is, Jordan. Not just to your brothers. To me."

I rang the doorbell, looking over at him quickly before it swung open and Eli's attendant greeted us. I gave him an air kiss—Eli's staff were what I liked best about his place—and glided into the foyer, spotting Eli through the crowd in one of the front rooms.

"Oh, I see Eli," I announced, to no one in particular. My act was beginning for the evening. I slid my leather coat off my shoulders and handed it to an attendant nearby. "I'll go say hi."

I didn't make it two steps before a strong hand caught my wrist. Seven stilled me, leaning in close.

"Can we talk?"

I shook him off. "Not now. I'm busy."

He angled himself in front of me, looming in my path. "Let me rephrase. We're going to talk."

"*Not now*," I hissed, glaring at him before brushing past him, adding, "Your time to talk came and went."

I hurried into the party, lifting my hand to catch Eli's attention. He grinned across the room at me, his green eyes already glassy. I rushed over to him, throwing my arms around his neck.

"There you are," I murmured into his ear.

"Been waiting for you, gorgeous." I felt his hand at the small of my back and, for the first time, I didn't care. I just hoped Seven was watching extra carefully. Not because I was in danger. Because I wanted to piss off Seven in every way possible.

"I'm finally here," I purred before kissing his cheek. I could feel a portion of the breathable air in the room disappear, likely Seven's fists tightening as he watched us, though I couldn't see him to confirm. Eli smiled even wider, slinging an arm over my shoulders.

"Let's make the rounds," he said. "And we need to get you a drink..."

I tagged along, tucked under his arm, as we drifted through the party, much like last time. We mingled with politicians, paused to chat with Eli's friends, and I watched as he took occasional lines from passing mirrored trays, downing whatever drink or shot a server handed to him. I drank my white wine slowly, taking as many peeks at my bodyguard as I could.

Seven stayed stoic and looming against the far wall of whatever room we were in. A couple of times our gazes met, and my body was consumed with shivers. I hated how his being here was exactly what I'd been desperate for. He wanted to talk. Well, so did I. But only after he suffered first.

I stuck *extra* close to Eli. When he came in for a peck on the cheek or more, I didn't shy away. I played up the bubbly lover part as needed, and from Eli's constant grin, I could tell he was lapping this shit up.

After an hour or so at his side, I needed to pee. I disentangled myself from him, slipping away to the bathroom. Seven stepped out after me, keeping his distance as I hurried down the hall to the bathroom. Before I could shut the door, Seven was in the doorframe.

I frowned. "Worried I forgot how to pee without you?"

He stepped inside, causing me to stumble backward. He caught me by the wrist.

"I need a few minutes with you. Alone."

"Does it have to be when I'm on the brink of emptying my bladder?"

He pushed the door shut behind him then leaned against it with a smirk. "I'll wait."

"Oh. Inside. Thanks." I huffed, shuffling over to the toilet as I lifted my skirt.

"Not like I haven't seen it before," he replied coolly.

"Yeah, well, I'm not in the habit of peeing in front of my *close protection officers*," I snapped as I sat on the toilet and did my business. The tinkling filled the bathroom air, seeming aggressively loud as his attention sizzled on me. It sounded like I was peeing off the top of a building, for God's sake. I sighed, willing this to be over. I'd never had such intense focus on my urination before.

"Do you have to stare at me?" I finally asked, tearing off some toilet paper.

"Just getting you back for all that staring you liked to do in the mornings."

My cheeks flushed at the intimate mention. I shouldn't have been surprised. I was trapped in a bathroom with him, peeing. This could only be intimate.

I stood, rearranged my dress, and stepped to the sink, careful to avoid his eyes. As I washed my hands, his gaze burned through me. I saw his approach in the mirror.

"Don't worry, I know proper handwashing procedure," I muttered as he filled the space at my side. I dried my hands on one of the disposable hand towels set out, tossing it in the trash can. When I turned, I found the brick wall of his chest.

"Please, Jordan. Let's talk."

In one swift movement he had me backed up against the edge of the countertop. I tipped my head to look at him, both eager to deny him whatever he wanted, and desperate to fall headfirst into him. This close, it was hard not to touch him. To seek a kiss. To remember all the reasons I'd fallen so hard for him in the first place.

"About what?"

He rested his palms on the countertop on either side of me, angling himself slightly so we were more eye level. He opened his mouth to speak, then closed it. Then he did it again. He was struggling to speak. He was *nervous*. I'd never seen him like this before.

"I'm sorry," he finally blurted.

"Oh, God, are you about to give me more bad news?" He watched me heavily, something foreboding in his gaze. "Don't tell me. Trojan is leaving me too, now. Or maybe Chico quit?"

He shook his head, searching my face. "No. It's not that. I'm sorry for how I treated you. For acting like a total jerk."

I blinked hard, almost unable to process his words. "What?"

"I'm sorry that I rejected what was growing between us." He drew a shaky breath. His nervousness was so endearing I wanted to take a bite of him. "I didn't do it because I didn't want you. I promise. I...have never wanted anyone more than I want you, Jordan."

Want. Present tense. He still felt the same way. I sat, stunned, as he went on.

"I rejected the idea of us because I...I was terrified of where it would lead. Because I knew it would...could...lead to something...huge."

My fingers curled under the ledge of the countertop in an effort to stop them from curling into the front of his shirt. Emotion clamored for release, tightening my throat, making my vision go a little blurry. I was waiting for the "but." There had to be one.

"I'm a man of my word. I promised a certain level of conduct to your brothers, and I fell short. Your brothers made it clear from the beginning that there would be consequences if anything happened between us while you were living with me," he added. "So I thought the solution was to resign. Then we could be together. But Damian came to me and asked for heightened security before the trial, and I realized I couldn't ditch them in their time of need. It was a moral clusterfuck. And I was terrified. It's just made me shut down."

He squeezed his eyes shut for a moment, and when he opened them again, the clarity there seared through me. "I just felt like if I opened up and told you about everything, including what happened with Olivia, then it would be over. I'd lose my job, lose my business, lose my heart a second time, ruin everything. But I see now that if I *don't* have you, I'm still going to lose my heart and ruin everything. Because you already have my heart. And I...I don't know, I'll figure out what comes next. I never planned on meeting you or falling in love with you. But that's what happened, and I'm done denying it. Please, Jordan. Will you give me a second chance?"

I was so stunned I forgot to breathe. I watched him with wide eyes until my brain started working again. Brattiness front and center.

"Well, I don't know about that, Seven," I tried to be defiant, but even I could hear the quake in my voice. "You'll probably need to ask my handler, Trojan, for permission."

"I already have," Seven shot back. "Trojan would die a happy man if we admitted everything and made it official. He's been begging me to stop being a miserable asshole for weeks."

I tried not to show how much I relished every word that came out of his mouth. Internally, I was turning into a puddle of goo for this man. I could never forget the intensity of his dark gaze on me, the way he drank me in. He only saw *me*. Only wanted *me*.

And however defiant I acted, he was the only man for me.

I sniffed, straightening my back. "Well, I need to think about it."

He dipped his chin, gritting his teeth. "Jordan." That wasn't what he wanted to hear, and I *loved* knowing this.

"I'll have an answer for you tomorrow," I flipped my ponytail over my shoulder, trying to signal the end of this conversation. But he didn't back away. He only drew closer.

"Don't be a brat."

I couldn't fight the evil grin. "Only way I know how to be."

He leaned closer, his lips a breath away from mine. "Then let me rephrase. Don't be a brat without me. Be *my* brat."

His words sank into me like caramel drizzle in foam, the sweetest treat that had me dizzy and flying high. His lips were against mine then, slow and seeking. The masculine heat of him sank into me. My head tipped back, and suddenly his warm, rough hands were at my face. One hand slipped down my neck, resting against my collarbone. My body arched closer to him, needing to close the small distance between us, as our tongues danced and our kisses grew deeper, hungrier.

I curled my fingers into the front of his shirt, a deep shiver of satisfaction winding up my spine. When we broke for air, I looked up drunkenly at him.

"Trojan's on data review tonight, isn't he?" I whispered.

Seven nodded, biting back a silly grin.

"Hi, Trojan," I said with a laugh, to the thin air. "Hope you enjoyed that make-out session."

"He wants us to have another," Seven said, dipping down again.

I tilted my head, pressing a finger to his lips. "Hey. Rules are rules. I said I'd let you know tomorrow. You've made me miserable for weeks. I need the next twenty-four hours to assess whether I need you in my life."

He wrapped his arms around my waist, pulling me flush against him. I gasped softly, the steel heat of him overwhelmingly, unbearably *right*.

"Twenty-four hours," he whispered. "Not a second more."

CHAPTER THIRTY-SIX

JORDAN

Back in the party, I glided back up to Eli. He lifted a brow. "What took you so long?"

I sighed. "Just woman stuff."

He crumpled slightly. "Oh. Well that changes my plans."

I didn't like that comment at all. "No big deal, though. I took care of it." I shot him a breezy smile. "Besides, I needed to have a word with my guard."

Eli's gaze hardened as he looked over my shoulder then back at me. "Do you want me to get rid of him?"

"He's been so overbearing." I paused, a flimsy idea forming in my head. "In fact, I...want to talk to you about something. Kind of related to that idea. Maybe we can go have a dance and chat about it? And then we can see where the night takes us."

Eli wet his bottom lip, guiding me by the small of my back. "Let's go upstairs, gorgeous."

I stuck to his side, my skin prickling as I sensed Seven following. Eli paused near one of the attendants at the base of the stairs, whispered something into his ear, and then led me up. Our footsteps thumped softly against the carpet until we reached the landing.

"You can stay out here," Eli said to Seven as we neared the bedroom with the pole area.

"I'll be coming inside," Seven said gruffly.

"No, Seven, I think you need to stay out here," I spoke up, putting a little extra emphasis into my tone. I had to convince him somehow, without admitting my half-formed plan. "Eli and I have something we need to discuss in private."

Seven looked at me sternly. "Not allowed."

"What, do you think I'm speaking *Czech*?" I looked at him pointedly. It wasn't the safe word, but maybe the small clue would give him an idea that this plan was intentional. Once I got Eli inside, I could work him for more information. But it wouldn't work if Seven was there.

Seven backed down slightly. "Half hour."

"How generous of you," Eli said condescendingly, "but we'll be taking all the time we want, thanks." He pushed opened the door, gesturing for me to enter first, then sauntered in after me. He shut the door loudly behind him, exhaling a sigh of relief.

"Finally. I get you to myself." He ran a hand through his blond hair, knocking the finger wave at the front askew, and rolled his neck in a slow circle. "Only took me how many weeks and how many thousands of dollars?" He led me over to the minibar.

"You know what they say about the best." I kept my handbag clutched close as I came up to him, sliding my palm along his shoulders. "It's fucking worth it."

He cocked a smile, pulling open the fridge. "You better be."

I pushed down a wave of revulsion. He pulled out a bottle of wine, then hunted down two glasses.

"Go sit over there," he said brusquely. "I'll get these ready."

Alarms were going off again. No way in fuck I'd let him prepare my drink. I needed to get some intel, *immediately*. "I need your help, though. And I thought you wanted me to dance?"

"You'll get my help. And the dance can wait. Just go sit on the bed and get comfortable."

I drifted toward the bed, a bad feeling flowering in my gut. I glanced back at him a few times, watching him pour the wine. He angled his body suddenly, reaching for something else out of a cabinet. A few uninflated balloons tumbled out and to the floor, alongside whatever he'd been looking for. The drink preparation was taking too long. Something was off.

Just go along with it. Get the intel.

"Here we go." He came toward the bed, his half-lidded gaze stuck on the cups. He held out the one in his left hand straight to me. "Drink up."

"I'm not really thirsty right now," I said, leaning to set the cup down.

"Come on," he said sharply. "Let's have a toast. To wonderful moments." His smile was unsettling, laced with tension. I clinked my glass against his, and he watched me as I brought the drink to my lips.

Fake it. Just fake it.

"Come on, it's your favorite wine," he chided when I didn't take a sip. "I bought it just for you."

Fear trembled through me. If he'd put something in it, I had a small window of time before I passed out. Trojan was on data review, which meant he was listening live as I recorded. Surely he'd notice if something sounded amiss. At least, I prayed he would.

I did my best to take the tiniest sip possible. At the last second, he jostled into me, spilling my drink into my face. I gasped, getting way more of it down my throat than I'd intended.

"Sorry," he said.

I grabbed a tissue from the nightstand and cleaned myself up. "Well, cheers to that." I tried to sound lighthearted, but I could hear a ticking clock. If he'd laced it, I had limited time. But maybe it was fine. Maybe he was just already drunk and acting weird.

I knew better. I needed to act fast. *This will be worth it if the information you get will save your brothers.*

"Listen. This is about my guard. I need to do something." My whole chest grew tight as I struggled to get back on track. "I can't get rid of him. And I remembered what you told me about the...fuck, what was their name?"

"The Fairchilds," he supplied for me.

"*Yes*. Those guys. What did you do again?"

"I fucked them in the ass so hard they won't be able to walk again for the ten years they're going to prison." A Cheshire Cat smile stretched across his lips. "Is that what you're trying to do to that guard out there?"

"I need him off my back," I insisted, the weight of my clutch in my lap reminded me of the recorders inside.

"Why don't you fire him?" Eli asked.

"I *can't*," I blurted, my mind whirring in overtime to concoct enough believable details on the fly. "I didn't hire him to begin with. I'm in a conservatorship. It's just...it's so fucked up. My parents, they never trusted me, and they put me into a mental institution when I was sixteen, and somehow they got their hands on all this money I made from my acting career—"

"You used to act?" His smile went wider.

"Just in Disney shit," I lied. "Anyway, I can't get a judge to dissolve this stupid conservatorship, and, it's just—" I wracked my brain for more details from the celebrity news outlets that I liked to read on occasion "—all I'm trying to say is, it's not my choice. I can't fire him. But someone like *you?* You could help me."

"Well this explains why he's aways been tagging around." Eli leaned closer.

"Tell me again what you did to those brothers," I whispered. "I love to hear this story."

My pulse throbbed beneath my skin as he launched into his hero's tale. *Please let the recorder work perfectly. No issues. No hiccups. I need this recording.* "It's all about the connections, gorgeous. And I've got plenty of them. Nobody liked those assholes, so I had an insider do a little digging. Allan and I were motivated to get them out of our sight, so we used the intel, took it to a friend at the SEC, and the rest is history."

"So can't you do something like that for my guard?" I asked.

He laughed. "I don't think my contacts in the SEC are going to be able to help with your bodyguard unless he owns an investment firm or has been doing insider trading. But I'm sure I could cook something else up."

I wilted against him. "Oh, thank you Eli."

"Anything for you, gorgeous." His hand was at my back.

"I just want you to do something that could put him in jail," I went on. "Get him away from me. Like you did to those brothers."

"The Fairchilds are going away for ten years," he said haughtily.

"And they wouldn't have gone without you working your magic, right?"

"Hell no." He laughed. "What do I always say? It's about the connections, baby." He leaned close, pressing a kiss to my cheek. "How are you feeling?"

"Fine." I assessed the state of my organs, my responses, my mobility. Everything seemed normal. Or maybe...a little sluggish. "I do have to pee."

When I stood up, he grabbed my wrist. "You just went."

"It's the wine."

He tightened his grip on me and jerked me backward. Hard. I tumbled back onto the bed, panic streaking through me.

"Maybe you should just stay where you are," he suggested, draping his arm around my shoulders. His heat coated me like slime. Deep inside, revulsion sputtered to life. But much closer to the surface was a desire to rest. Sluggishness coated my veins, prompting me to relax deeper into his embrace.

"Hmmm." Now that I thought about it, I *was* tired. I didn't need to pee. But the tiredness set off more alarms. I needed to get up. Get out. Tell Seven. I struggled to stand, but his grip around me tightened. My shoulders were crushed together, and I whimpered against the pain. But I couldn't fight him.

"Hmm?" He laughed, and even through the descending haze I could hear the sarcasm. "Say it again Jordan. Louder this time." Somehow, in my half-awake state I could tell that he was oozing with accomplishment. The prey was his.

"I can't..."

"Didn't think so." He shoved my shoulder, and I flopped backward.

Eli's unsettling smirk was the last thing I saw before my eyes drifted shut, and I welcomed the softness and the quiet.

CHAPTER THIRTY-SEVEN

SEVEN

"Dr. Tutlow....paging Dr. Tutlow..."

The intercom jostled me from my light sleep. I'd been dozing, sitting upright in my chair in the hospital waiting room. I inhaled sharply, straightening and rubbing my eyes. The people who'd been the seats around me earlier that morning were gone. How fucking long had I been here?

I tried to find some clarity, looking around, searching absent-mindedly for my phone. I found it in the pocket of my coat, but I hissed as my hand brushed against the wool.

That's right. My knuckles. Completely busted.

I inspected my hand. I'd washed off the blood sometime around two a.m., once Jordan had been admitted to the hospital for over-dosing on a drug cocktail that included Rohypnol. The only thing I was worried about now was whether she'd wake up or not. I had no idea how much she ingested, what the long-term effects were, or what the risks were right now. The staff wouldn't tell me because I wasn't family.

The only thing I knew for certain was that I'd left Eli a bloody, broken mess in that bedroom. I came into the room just before Eli pushed his bare dick into her. The sight of him half-naked, settled between her legs, her dress bunched up to her waist, was a sight I might never forget. Rage lashed through me again, and my fingers curled into fists.

I hadn't decided to maul him, I simply acted. I heard the crunch of bones as he hit the wall. Made sure I broke his jaw, left both his eyes bruised, and broke his nose. And that was only the start of what he deserved.

I escaped with Jordan's deadweight over my shoulder before anyone realized what I'd done to Eli. And now, I waited for the police to show up or someone from his "connections" to swoop in and take me out. I didn't doubt he'd try—if he was even conscious yet.

I checked my phone. It was time to call the brothers. I'd meant to do it a couple of hours ago, but I'd nodded off. I dialed Damian.

He answered, sounding groggy.

"Sorry for the early call," I said.

"Is everything okay?"

"No. Jordan's at New York-Presbyterian Hospital. I'll send the exact address and room number."

Damian inhaled sharply. "Wait...*what*?"

"I'll explain everything when you get here," I said. "Just come. She needs her brothers."

"We'll be there right away."

The phone went dead, and I heaved a sigh. I wasn't looking forward to this conversation. I'd failed the brothers at every turn. I hadn't kept Jordan safe. I'd let her walk right into Eli's house party, for the second time. And at her urging, I'd been complicit in her taking a stupid risk.

My knee bounced as I waited for...something. Anything. I wasn't leaving until I had some news about her, that was for damn sure. I rubbed my eyes again, thinking back on the past twelve hours. She'd been so insistent on going in there alone. But why?

My brain was exhausted from poring over the details.

Axel, Damian, and Trace filed into the waiting room less than a half hour after I'd called. They looked bleary-eyed but determined. I stood.

"Have you been in there?" Axel asked, in lieu of a greeting.

"They won't let me in since I'm not family," I said. "Visiting hours are starting soon, so I was hoping you could get the updates from the doctor."

"What happened?" Damian asked, his gaze dropping to my hands. "And who did you murder?"

I clasped my hands behind my back. I couldn't admit to them who I'd subdued...much less *why*. "I accompanied her to a party last night. It got a little wild. She had an admirer who spiked her drink and took things way too far. I intervened before he was able to act on his desires, and I made sure he couldn't act on them again for a very long time."

Axel pinched the bridge of his nose. He looked like he was about to say something, then he shook his head. "Okay. Let's get in there."

The brothers gathered at the nurse's desk nearby, speaking in hushed tones with the woman on duty. Axel and Damian were led back through secure double doors a moment later, and Trace returned to my side.

"Only allowed two at a time," he said, sinking into the chair beside me. He paused. "Did you spend the night here?"

I nodded, unable to look at him.

"You want some coffee?"

"I wouldn't say no," I told him.

He squeezed my shoulder. "Let me go hunt down some caffeine. Then maybe you and I can go back next."

Trace returned to the nurse's station then strode off in the direction she pointed out, leaving me alone in the waiting room once more. I stared at the doors leading into the ICU, worrying over what came next. I needed to assume, for my own sanity, that Jordan would wake up at some point. It was too easy to entertain the worst outcomes, but I wanted to focus on the best-case scenario, in which she woke up and everything was fine and there was no long-term damage.

But the likelihood that I could avoid the brothers finding out that we went to Eli's house seemed nil at this point. My stomach knotted up as I contemplated what I might say to defend our decision. Everything that came to mind sounded crazy, delusional even. But I couldn't admit the one piece of information that would allow it all to click into place.

Trace eventually returned with two lidded cups of coffee. I thanked him and sipped tentatively, still watching the ICU door. He eased into the chair next to me.

"So who was the attacker?" Trace asked. So much for casual conversation. "Anyone we know?"

My heart sank. I sipped again, thinking about how to answer.

"Someone I'd like to never see again." It seemed honest enough.

Trace rotated the cup back and forth between his hands. "Why did she want to go to that party last night?"

I shrugged. "I don't know exactly. I just wanted to make sure she was safe."

Trace nodded, a heavy silence filling the air between us.

Damian pushed through the double doors from the ICU, his face drawn. He offered a grim smile as he approached.

"She's awake," he said softly.

I covered my face with my hands, trying to mask the surge of relief. They'd see how much she meant to me, how close we'd gotten, on my face, so I took a second to compose myself before I cleared my throat and straightened.

"Thank God," I said.

"She was roofied," Damian went on, studying something on the floor as he spoke. "But they found traces of another drug that accelerates the effect of Rohypnol. So she got a double whammy. They want to keep her in the hospital tonight too for observation."

Trace let out a long, slow exhale. "Shit. Any long-term effects?"

"There shouldn't be," Damian said. "But I told them to spare no expense in making sure."

I wrung my hands together, my next words forming a logjam inside me. I didn't know how to ask to go back there to see her, because there was no *asking*—there was only *informing* them that I *would* be going back there.

"Do you, uh..." I cleared my throat, deciding to start over. "Would I be able to..."

Damian smiled softly. "Would you like to go see her?"

I nodded.

"She asked about you. Seems like she'd like to see you too." Damian led the way to the nurse's desk, informed her of who I was, then I was buzzed in. Everything inside me was drawn tight as violin strings, waiting to lay eyes on Jordan.

Axel was sitting with an ankle over one knee in a chair beside her bed. I blinked, and then I was at Jordan's side, my arms scooped around her slight body.

"I'm so fucking sorry, Jordan," I murmured into her hair as she clung to me. "I'm so sorry. Please forgive me."

"Don't apologize." Her voice was hoarse. She wrapped her arms around me tighter. "This wasn't your fault. I swear."

I took a few deep breaths with her in my arms, then I pulled back, brushing kisses across her forehead. "I'm so happy you're okay."

"I'm okay because you were there," she said.

Axel cleared his throat. He'd seen all of that. There was no graceful exit after a display like that, and I didn't care. I straightened, keeping Jordan's hand in my own. If there was ever a time for them to find out, this was it.

"I'll give you two some time," he said, a hard glint in his eye. He narrowed his eyes at me before he stood, looking like he wanted to say more. Then he excused himself from the room, leaving Jordan and me alone.

"How do you feel?" I asked.

"Exhausted," she said with a weak laugh.

"I heard they want to keep you here for another night."

"Yeah. I guess because of the other drug they found in my system. I already forget the name." She sighed, her gaze drifting off. "I'm so tired I could sleep the rest of the day."

"Then do that. I'll be here."

"Seven, you should go home and actually sleep," she said, admonishment in her tone despite her hoarseness. "My brothers told me you spent all night in the waiting room."

"I'll do it again."

She laughed. "There's no need."

"Yes there is," I insisted. "My beautiful brat might need me."

She smiled so warmly I was ready to call the hospital chaplain and marry her on the spot.

"Do you remember anything that happened?" I asked softly, squeezing her hand.

She shook her head. "He gave up a lot of great information, but insisted I drink with him. It was the only way to move forward, so I was going to pretend to take a sip, but he knocked the glass, and I choked on it. Within fifteen minutes, I was passing out. That's all I remember."

I nodded, the image of his pasty white ass between her legs still seared through my mind. Now was not the time to get into all that.

"I take it you took care of Eli on your own?" Her gaze fastened on my knuckles.

"I did. He might sue me as a result, but I have no regrets."

She laughed softly. "I wish I could see how you left him."

"Pretty boy is no longer pretty."

A comfortable silence settled between us. I scooped her hand between mine, pressing a kiss to it.

"I love you so much, Jordan."

Her blue-gray eyes went watery as she watched me, a smile drifting across her lips. "I love you more."

I nuzzled her hand, feeling so full and complete while simultaneously ready to dissolve. "Has it been twenty-four hours yet?"

"Nope."

"Fine." I couldn't fight the grin. Even in the hospital, she found a way to be the brat I loved.

"Promise me you'll go home and at least take a nap," she said. "I'm about to pass out."

"I'll do that. Only for you." I leaned forward and pressed a soft kiss to her lips.

As soon as I pushed through to the waiting room, I could tell something was wrong. The three brothers watched me approach, varying degrees of tightness in their faces. I could only assume Axel had shared what he'd seen.

"She's ready to sleep again," I said, opting to break the ice with an update. I sank into the chair next to Trace, facing Axel and Damian in the opposing line of chairs. Nobody said anything.

"How long have you two been together?" Damian's question sliced through the air like a knife. He watched me curiously, and I couldn't entirely read him. He sounded genuine, though the question also felt like a test.

I cleared my throat. "Not long. It sort of only came up...recently."

Axel ran his tongue over his teeth, studying me closely. "There's always been something between you two though, hasn't there?"

I squeezed my eyes shut, unable to lie. *Unwilling* to lie. "There has. Even though I ignored it for a long time."

"Don't you find it a little...inappropriate?" Damian asked. "Especially after all the times you've insisted that it was against protocol."

I studied the floor, nodding. "I do. It's not how I conduct business. It's not something that's ever happened to me before. But believe me—this was completely unexpected. I never once dreamed that we would...feel this way about each other."

The brothers regarded me heavily. I wasn't sure if they were impressed by my words or disgusted. But whatever their response was, I was relieved to have this out in the air. No longer a secret I had to hide behind.

"Will this impact the quality of your protection?" Trace asked suddenly.

"No. And for what it's worth, her full-time protection has been transferred to a different guard." I looked over at Damian. "Like we discussed more recently."

Axel leaned forward, resting his elbows on his knees. He seared me with a look. "Be honest with me, Seven. Were you two at Eli's last night?"

I clenched my teeth, everything inside me sinking down, down, down. I didn't know a way past this question.

"Think carefully about your answer," Damian added, "because whatever you tell me, I have ways to verify."

I studied my knuckles, remembering the way they'd cracked against Eli's jawbone. I braced myself for the fallout once the words passed my lips. "We were."

Axel sighed testily. Damian's gaze grew edged with something I'd never seen before, and Trace sank back into his chair, rubbing his face.

"Seven, did we not just fucking talk about this?" Axel spat out.

"We did," I said.

"Then why the fuck would you take her there? Next you're gonna tell me that he's the one who almost raped her."

I squeezed my eyes shut, willing myself to hold the line. I couldn't share the investigation with them. Not now. Not like this. We needed to complete the steps, hand over the evidence, and see what happened. That's how it had to go.

"I'd like to view it as I protected her despite decisions that led to us attending that party," I finally bit out.

"You'd *like* to view it that way." Axel laughed, crossing his arms. "Jesus Christ. Well, I'd *like* to hire a close protection officer who makes good on his word."

I clenched and unclenched my jaw, suddenly wary of where this was heading. "I promise you, I followed all appropriate protocols—"

"Like you followed the protocol about beginning a relationship with your client?" Damian interjected.

I clamped my mouth shut. The shit had officially hit the fan.

"You had *one job*," Axel spat. "One place to keep her away from. One person to keep out of her life. And look where the fuck we are right now."

"She's a grown woman," I said, but my rationale withered in the wake of their righteous anger. "I can't influence decisions. I can only protect given the circumstances."

Axel laughed dryly. "That's bullshit and we both know it."

"I'm sorry." I didn't know what else to say. I'd fallen headfirst into the most complicated situation of my life, and I didn't know where to go from here but *through*. "I can't change how I feel about Jordan, but—"

"Would you rather resign or get fired in the middle of a hospital waiting room?" Damian asked, sniffing. His question caught me off guard. All the delirium and anxiety from spending the morning sleep-deprived in the hospital made me shaky. Off-balance. Absolutely prone to collapsing from within.

That's what was happening to my insides. Utter destruction. All of the worst-case scenarios, wrapped up into one little brick launched off the skyscraper rooftop of my brain, where it would explode on the floor at my feet.

"You guys," I sputtered, "this isn't how I wanted—"

"I have zero qualms with firing you right here," Axel said. "In fact, at this point, I think it would be fitting."

"Please." I looked at each of them in turn, trying to turn this ship around. "Let's talk about this later. After we've calmed down."

Axel shook his head, his blue gaze searing through me. "Consider your work with the Fairchilds terminated immediately."

CHAPTER THIRTY-EIGHT

JORDAN

"You wanna press the button?" Seven's teasing question made me laugh as we entered the elevator in my building. He'd been so doting and sweet to me since I'd been discharged from the hospital that morning.

Given what went down between him and my brothers, I needed to escape. We'd snuck out together in the early hours, before my brothers had a chance to come pick me up. Damian and Axel were also furious with me, but they still wanted to help. I could feel the frostiness in our interactions, though. The suspicion. The growing distance. And after a decade of distance followed by so much warmth, I never wanted to feel that coldness between us again.

"I'd rather *race* you," I told him, pressing the button for the fourth floor. "But I don't want to make you feel bad for losing after you just lost your job, too."

He bit back a smile, wrapping me in his arms as the doors closed. "That's very thoughtful. For a brat."

I laughed and looked up at him, clutching his thick forearms wrapped around me. Everything was a total mess, but in his arms, I could find a little sanity and stability.

And we both needed it.

At my floor, he leaned against the doorframe as I hunted for my key.

"I've been dying to see your new place," he said, his eyes on me rummaging through my purse.

I glanced up at him, and my mouth parted. His bicep bulged where he leaned against the doorframe, his looming, powerful frame an aphrodisiac I wasn't prepared to behold.

"Can you not stand like that?" I ripped my gaze away from him to re-focus on the task at hand. "That sexy lean is *dangerous*. I don't want to alienate my neighbors this early. I've only lived here for a few weeks. That's far too little time to start fucking in the hallway."

"Mm." He only leaned harder. "If you hadn't just gotten out of the hospital, I'd make good on the last part of that sentence."

I couldn't fight the grin as I finally found my key and opened the door. It swung open, showcasing my brightly lit, wood-floored paradise. I took it in with new eyes, after my surprise hospital stay. The newest potted plant additions—a fern, an enormous snake plant, and a baby fig tree—all stood bathed in sunlight in the kitchen, not even drooping like I feared they would. I glided in, gesturing around. "Here we are. Home sweet home."

He clicked the door shut behind us, taking a few moments to look around and absorb everything. Then he nodded.

"It's perfect."

"It's been a slow process settling in. But I think this could be home for a long time. I'm gonna need some wooden spoons as a finishing touch, though." I smiled up at him as he strode over to me and squeezed the sides of my arms.

"I can handle that," he said. "Specially carved, just for you. Though I might have already started on your kitchen collection." His phone vibrated, and he sneaked a peek at it. "You okay if Trojan swings by for a visit? He just turned the evidence into the SEC, and he wants to say bye."

I slumped a little. A lot happened while I was in the hospital. Not only did Seven lose his job, leaving him adrift and scrambling to pick up the pieces, but he and Trojan had been preparing the evidence we'd gathered over the last couple of weeks to submit it to the Office of the Inspector General. They were under the strict guidance of Federico at every turn to ensure the highest chance of success. And now Trojan was off to his next assignment in Louisiana. I felt like I was losing a friend.

"Yeah. I'd love to say bye to him before he leaves." I drifted to the coffeemaker, ready to prepare my brew and Seven's tea. "And to thank him for all his help with this. I can't believe he's turned everything in already."

"You okay if I have him bring my bag?"

Seven's question hung oddly in the air. I looked over my shoulder at him, surprised to find him looking so vulnerable.

"You mean...to stay with me here?" I asked.

He nodded.

"Of course." Another grin broke out. I'd done nothing but smile since we'd left the hospital, and it felt wrong to be this happy when the rest of my life was slowly disintegrating. I had a stable, safe apartment. I had a stable, safe partner. *Holy shit.*

If this were me three months ago, I would have called this the unattainable dream. But now, I knew there were more components of the perfect life worth fighting for. And it involved my *family*. I'd reunited with Axel and Damian, and my bonus brother, Trace. I'd gained three almost-sisters. I didn't want to lose them all just when I'd begun to count on them as part of my future.

"It's cute you thought you had to ask," I said, returning to my task at the coffee machine. He approached from behind, wrapping his arms around me as I loaded the grounds.

"Didn't want to assume," he murmured into the top of my head. Just then, a knock on the door sounded. Seven's face lit up. "Let me get that."

He hurried to the door, revealing a delivery person holding a bouquet of flowers in a glass vase. After a quick thank-you and a tip, Seven was back at my side, presenting me with the bursting bouquet of dahlias.

"These are for you. My very overdue housewarming gift. One of many to come."

I fought tears as I accepted them, admiring the gorgeous blooms. "You're the first man to ever buy me flowers."

"Now that you said that, I'll have to make this a frequent occurrence," he said.

"Did my brothers kick you out of your place?" I asked as I set the vase on the countertop, selecting the perfect location

"No. I'm renting it on my own now. But I thought we both might like sharing an apartment again, for a little bit at least."

"You're the only person in the world I can say that about." I turned around to face him. He hooked his hands beneath my thighs, hoisting me onto the kitchen countertop. I giggled, wrapping my arms around his neck. "That didn't take long."

"I planned on doing it in the hallway until you ruined the vibe," he teased, nuzzling my neck.

Laughter cascaded out of me as his mouth drifted higher, our lips finally meeting in soft, exploratory kisses. He pushed at the hem of my sweatshirt, bunching it around my waist as his hands slid hot and seeking underneath. I'd had my brothers bring a few basics to me in the hospital—not even a bra. Seven's hands coasted over my bare chest, leaving sparks in their wake.

"Mmmm." He grinned through a kiss as he massaged my breasts, running his thumbs over my tight nipples. "God, I've missed you."

"Don't lie. You staged this whole spy mission just so my brothers would fire you and you could fondle my naked breasts without issue, right?" I wiggled my hips against him as he filled the space between my legs.

"Guity." His deep laugh rippled through me, filling me with something so simple and satisfying that I hardly knew how to share it with him. It was like his mere presence filled all the places inside me that ached for acknowledgement. There was no other way to feel around Seven but *complete*. I shivered through our kisses, ready to say the three words that I felt in my heart every day for this man.

But he spoke first, breaking the kiss. "Jordan, what do you want?"

"You," I blurted.

A sexy grin curled at his lips. "I mean, do you want to eat? Do you want to sleep? Do you want me to fuck you senseless in the morning light?"

"I love all of those options, but I'll take C, please. And let's do it in the shower. I want to wash the hospital off while we're at it."

He scooped me into his arms, heading for the nearest door.

"That's the pantry," I whispered.

"Oops. I'll try the next one." He redirected to the actual bathroom door, and I giggled the whole way. Inside the bathroom, he delicately undressed me, removing every piece of clothing with a reverence I'd never experienced before. My sweatshirt. My leggings. My panties. When all the clothes were crumpled at our feet, he undressed himself. I got the water ready, then we both stepped in.

He traced the curve of my waist with his hand as the warm water beat against his back.

Then he washed every inch of me with my washcloth and soap. It was as serious as it was sweet. When he washed my legs, he sank to his knees, lifting each leg in turn to soap up my calves, ankles, and feet.

Then he turned his attention to the V between my legs. He sent me a heated glance, then pressed a kiss against my inner thigh. Then another one, higher. I spread my legs for him, aching for more. I watched with bated breath as he nuzzled between my legs, his lips grazing my pussy. And then his tongue darted out, flattening against my clit, sending an electric spasm of pleasure through me. My entire body jolted, and I fisted his hair for balance.

"Oh, Seven." My eyes drifted shut, head lolling against the shower wall as he took what he wanted from between my legs. His tongue danced mercilessly over my clit, while he eased one finger inside me, and then another. After he'd licked me almost to my peak, he hoisted me by the backs of my thighs, hooking my legs over his shoulders, trapping me against the wall as he finished me off.

I screamed his name as the white-hot fireworks spread through me. He stood slowly, kissing each of my nipples in turn as he came to his full height in front of me. Then he lifted me again. My ankles crossed behind his back, and we found the perfect position instantly. His cock nudged for entrance at my slippery folds, my clit still throbbing but desperate for more.

"You came so fast." His gritty voice only turned me on more. I cinched my arms around his neck as he began to sink slowly into me, his cock filling every inch of space.

"It's not hard when you eat me out like a demon." My voice was shaky as I focused on the divine sensation of him filling me, stretching me, completing me.

"I'll take that as a compliment."

I laughed throatily, but it disappeared as he sank deeper. He groaned, capturing my lips in a kiss.

"You feel so fucking amazing, Jordan," he bit out when the kiss broke. "You take it so good."

"Give it to me," I breathed. "I need it. I need it so bad."

He grunted, palming one of my breasts while he eased himself out of me, then back in again. The slick slide of him, in and out, deeper than I'd ever been penetrated in my life, sent me spiraling again. He never looked away as he fucked me, the intensity of his caramel gaze only lifting me higher.

"That's right." His voice was gritty, strained. "Take it. Take all of it. Mmmm, you really needed this, huh?"

"I've been dying for you since I moved out," I whispered as the tornado of pleasure began to swirl deep inside again. "Ohhh, Seven!"

"That's right, let me feel you coming on my cock." He skated kisses over my cheek, up to my forehead. His steel heat filled me, crashing into my throbbing clit. My thighs began to tremble. My head pitched back, and a low, guttural moan escaped me.

His fingertips dug into my ass cheeks as I came, sending the message: *Mine.* Warmth flooded my body, and for a moment, I couldn't see anything at all. My chest heaved as he began to groan and slow his movements. His belly jerked, then a moment later I could feel the hot gush of his cum inside me.

He kissed my lips softly as the warm water beat down on us.

"I love you, Jordan."

Kiss.

"I love you too, Seven."

Kiss.

I needed this man in my life, more than I needed air. And I needed my brothers in my life, just as badly. As Seven turned off the water and dried me off, I sent up the most urgent prayer I'd ever prayed in my entire life.

Please let my family come together, once and for all. Make all of this worth it.

CHAPTER THIRTY-NINE

SEVEN

Trojan wasn't even gone two days before he called with good news: the SEC promised to review the information in earnest.

We didn't know what that meant, or what would come of it. But it felt like a small victory.

So we waited.

The week after Jordan left the hospital felt like suspended animation. She took a leave of absence from work—under the guise of recuperating from an injury, but really she wanted to avoid the possibility of running into Eli at the club. Or anywhere else, for that matter. I approved of this idea—had suggested it to her, actually—and we found our pocket of bliss amid the weirdness.

Roxie came over for a girl's night one night. Jordan didn't want me to leave, so I contented myself watching spy movies in the bedroom while I worked on more of Jordan's wooden kitchen collection. In my brief visits to the kitchen for snacks and drinks, I overheard Jordan confessing everything to her friend. Who her brothers were. Why they'd hired me. What her childhood had been like. It almost brought tears to my eyes. My beautiful brat was opening up.

And Roxie opened up too: she'd met a new guy, but he hated the fact that she was a stripper. He wanted her to quit. He wanted her to dress differently. He kept poking holes in the condoms. It warmed my heart to hear Jordan emphatically tell her friend how fucked up all of that was and to leave him, under no uncertain terms.

Roxie reported that Eli had been coming around the club looking for her, looking a wreck. Healing black eyes, drunk as shit. He'd even gotten himself kicked out of Gemstones once in his hunt for Jordan. That part didn't exactly placate me, though, since I knew Eli's pockets were deep and his connections were sinuous. If he wanted Jordan, I worried that he'd make sure to find her. Someday. Somehow. Especially now that we knew about Eli's involvement with the brothers' charges.

I decided to move my headquarters for Silva Security elsewhere. The break with the Fairchilds was too painful, and they'd made it clear that I was no longer welcome in their sphere. Part of me wanted to wait it out, to hope for the best, to see them backpedal once the truth came out. But I also knew that I needed to act *now*. Axel, in particular, was still seething about what I'd allowed Jordan to do while in my care. I didn't even try to reason with that type of big brotherly protection.

Chico and Liam were still on board with me as I actively recruited new contracts, but it wasn't the type of sustainable work that would allow me to keep the lights on for very long. Expenses had to be cut.

I went to the office exactly a week after Jordan was released from the hospital to take my last boxes with me and lock up. Trace showed up to receive the key just as I was turning the light off and shutting the door.

"How's it look?" he asked in lieu of a greeting.

The fact that I'd lost my job in the name of trying to protect him and the others didn't prevent the humiliation from lapping at my feet. I offered a small smile. "Better than I found it. I cleaned every crevice so you wouldn't have to."

Trace stuffed his hands into his pants, his dark hair trim and impeccably styled. He looked like he'd come straight from the office across town. And at eleven a.m. on a Tuesday, he probably had.

"Well, I'm glad it got some use," he said.

"Yeah. It was great. I would have loved to continue…" I trailed off, not sure how far I wanted to wade into those waters.

We watched each other awkwardly for a moment.

"How are Axel and Damian?" I asked.

He shrugged. "Pretty pissed."

"They haven't talked to Jordan too much lately," I commented.

Almost every night Jordan flirted with the idea of calling Axel and admitting everything. She was dying to begin mending fences, but I always talked her down, because I wanted to do things exactly as Federico laid out. If we had a chance, it would come from following the rules.

"Yeah. Not sure how those relationships are really going to evolve from here, but…" Trace shrugged again. "I guess that's for them to figure out."

I nodded. What else could I possibly say to make things better?

"Is Jordan still seeing Eli?" Trace asked abruptly.

I couldn't school the shock from my face. "No. Not at all. She was never 'seeing' him to begin with."

"Then what was she doing on his arm, kissing him, all of that?" Trace challenged.

I sighed. Backed into the corner again. "Exploiting him. Trying to take him for all he was worth, in whatever way she could."

I held out the key just as he got a call. He frowned down at his phone, leaving my hand hanging in the air for a moment or two before he remembered and grabbed it from me.

"I need to take this," he muttered quickly before swiping the phone on. Into the phone, he snapped, "What is it?"

In the near-silent office, I could hear the other end of the conversation. It was Damian.

"We got a call from our lawyer. Something about the investigation being fraudulent? There's an emergency hearing, and our lawyers are filing a motion to have the case dismissed."

Did I mishear somehow? Trace looked just as bewildered as I felt.

"Wait, what? You mean our trial? That's coming up in a couple weeks?" Trace asked.

"Yes. There's been some type of evidence that was found at the last minute."

Trace's eyes went wide, and he looked up at me. I returned the look, hope crackling to life inside me.

There was some faint laughter. "I have no fucking idea. But he thinks someone on the inside was working against us when otherwise they wouldn't have pursued the charges. Like, someone paid off an agent or something."

Trace's voice was whisper thin when he spoke. "Holy shit. Are you serious?"

They exchanged a few more words before Trace hung up and pocketed his phone. He looked dazed.

"I wasn't trying to listen," I said after a moment of silence, "but I could hear..."

Trace moved his bewildered gaze to me. "I don't even know what to think. I'm scared to get my hopes up."

I reached out and squeezed his shoulder. "I sincerely hope it means something amazing for you and your brothers. You guys have been nothing but generous with me. You all deserve the best."

They deserved that and more. They deserved to have the truth exposed. They deserved to live a full life with their sister at their side.

I held on to the seeds of hope that had sprouted, desperate to see them turn into something real and tangible...a future for the Fairchilds.

CHAPTER FORTY

JORDAN

"Where did you say it was again?" I hissed at Seven as we poked our heads down yet another hallway in the labyrinth of the lower Manhattan federal courthouse.

"I have no fucking idea anymore." He looked behind us, then down the sprawling corridor that gleamed to our right. He checked his watch. "But this thing starts in ten minutes."

"This thing" was the last-minute hearing that would hopefully resolve what my brothers had been fearing for almost a year. I'd been able to get the time and date details out of Damian during some brief text messages earlier that week, even though he and Axel remained frosty. I didn't blame them. They had every right to feel the way they did about how they perceived my relationship with Eli. I was just chomping at the bit to set the record straight, no matter what today's outcome was.

I had a whole confessional planned. I needed my brothers back in my life.

"Wait. I think it's this way." Seven spun on his heel, returning down the hallway we'd just come from. "You said courtroom thirty-six, right?"

"I think." Courtroom numbers blurred past us as we speed walked down the corridor. There were over forty courtrooms in this granite behemoth of a building. Entirely too many courtrooms for one city block.

"We need to go down a level," he said suddenly, then pushed open the door to the stairwell. We raced down the stairs, though it wasn't as fun as usual. When we burst through to the other floor, we nearly crashed into Jessa, Mercedes, and Cora.

I sucked in a sharp breath as their gazes swung our way. Mercedes and Jessa smiled—strained, sad, but still a smile. Cora stiffened at the sight of me. They all wore various takes on business-formal black—which Seven and I had chosen as well—which meant we all looked like we were attending a fancy funeral.

I just hoped that whatever happened beyond those doors today wouldn't truly be the death of my brothers' empire.

"Hey. We were just trying to, uh..." I swallowed hard as the door clanged shut behind us, echoing in the quiet hall. "Find the court-room."

"It's right here," Jessa said, "but they haven't opened the doors yet."

"The brothers are inside already," Mercedes said softly, her gaze swinging toward the closed doors in front of us. "With the lawyer."

I nodded, looking up at Seven for some sort of guidance. Not only was this the heaviest, most anxiety-ridden day for all of us, the tension brimming between Cora and me resembled a festering wound. She hadn't responded to a single text or call since the news broke about Eli. The most I'd gotten out of Axel was that Cora was relieved I wasn't hurt.

I couldn't stand being in her radiant presence and feeling this weight between us. I drifted her way. "Cora, do you think we could step aside for a second?"

Her mossy green gaze flicked my way, her brows furrowing. "Jordan, I don't think that's a good idea right now. We're about to go inside. I can't think about anything except what's going to happen inside those doors."

"I know," I said, "I just want you to know how—"

"Please, let's just focus on the brothers." She brought out the knife-edge business voice, which told me to shut the hell up. And I listened. I clamped my mouth shut, nodding.

The double doors of the courtroom jostled, then swung open a moment later, revealing multiple rows of dark wooden benches, like church pews facing an impressively high judge's bench. At the front of the courtroom, I spotted the backs of Axel's, Damian's, and Trace's heads, bent together as they conferred with their lawyers. Huge windows overlooked the city, the sunny November day filling the courtroom with a brightness and positivity that felt at odds with the heaviness in the air. Seven grasped my hand as we followed Cora, Jessa, and Mercedes into the courtroom and toward a row near my brothers and their lawyer. A few other people, some of whom I assumed were reporters, took their own seats. By the time the hearing was set to begin, the courtroom was a little under half full, a murmur of hushed conversation buzzing through the air.

"All rise."

The *whoosh* of people standing filled the room as the door to the judge's chambers opened. My heart pounded as an elderly, dour-looking judge stepped into the room and assumed his position at the front of the room. Judge Barton and his clerks underwent some official procedures then, initiating the day's docket, as everyone returned to sitting. After a bit of formal recordkeeping, Judge Barton called out, "The United States versus Fairchild Enterprises."

A shiver ran up my spine. I looked over at Seven, who watched the proceedings with drawn brows. I reached for his hand, and he squeezed it softly.

Please God. Let this work.

My brothers' lawyer was the first to speak. "In light of new evidence that has emerged after our standard pretrial and discovery period, I am submitting a motion to dismiss. As both Your Honor and the SEC have been made aware, startling details have emerged recently that raise serious accusations about the legitimacy not only of the charges but the investigation itself."

The lawyer went on, explaining the details of his motion. *Unprecedented breach of trust. Unconscionable corruption with life-altering stakes and consequences.* Documents were delivered to the judge. Materials were reviewed.

"There is no way that this courtroom can consider the charges against my clients when it was discovered that the SEC has a corrupt agent who was paid off by high-profile businessman and rival, Eli Rossberg. As anyone who follows the news will be aware, Mr. Rossberg has reason to feel a certain animosity for one of my clients," the lawyer said, going on to name the corrupt SEC insider. "The submitted evidence demonstrates that these charges would not have been brought up if the corrupted official had not been paid to do so. Any evidence collected in this case must also be suspect."

Then it was the prosecution's turn. I couldn't follow all the legalese, but I think it boiled down to "We're fucked, but we have to pretend to still want to prosecute these terrible people who didn't let rich people get *quite* as rich as they otherwise might have. But whatever you say, Judge, is fine."

Emotion washed over me. The entire room was drawn tight, waiting.

The judge cleared his throat, his deep, rumbling voice reaching the entire courtroom. "I have reviewed all documentation presented, and rule in favor of the defendant, Fairchild Enterprises, and all parties connected thereto. Motion to dismiss sustained. Case dismissed."

The gavel slammed. Conversation erupted in the courtroom as the judge retired to his chambers.

Axel turned around in his seat. His watery, red-rimmed gaze immediately landed on me as his lawyers clapped his back. I blinked rapidly, too stunned to fully process what was happening.

"It's over?" Mercedes squeaked at my side.

"Did they really..." I started, turning toward Seven.

The world around me slowed to half speed. Sunlight from the windows highlighted Axel's and Damian's faces as they stood and rushed our way. My limbs grew heavy, confused; all I could do was gape as the crowd parted, time lurched, and then suddenly Axel's arms were around me in a bear hug, squeezing the air from my body.

"Is it really dismissed?" I asked in a daze.

Axel let me go and cupped my face in his hands, looking at me with tears in his eyes. "It is. And answer me something now. Is my lawyer on drugs, or did you really go through all of that for us?"

My chest hitched. I nodded, a mass of emotion arriving like a gut punch. Then Damian's arms were around me, too, Seven mashed against my side.

"How the fuck did you two pull this off?" Damian asked, his voice hoarse. Trace joined a moment later, adding to the group hug.

I clung to Axel, sobbing. I hadn't fully processed what was happening, but I was making small steps.

"How did you—"

There was a commotion of voices. I heard Cora, Jessa, Mercedes, and a few unknown voices. Axel whooped. Our hug disbanded, and Seven guided me out of the courtroom into the echoey hallway. I rummaged through my purse for a tissue as people filed out past us.

"I can't believe this," I whispered, dabbing away my tears. The rest of my *family* gathered around, all eyes on me and Seven.

"What did I miss?" Cora asked, her eyes wide as she looked between Axel and me.

Axel propped his hands on his hips as he looked at me, tears filling his eyes again. He watched me with wonder as he said, "That whole time Jordan was hanging out with Eli, she was wired and gathering evidence against him to throw the case." He looked over at Cora, pulling her into his arms. "My baby sister saved us."

Trace wiped at his eyes before slinging his arm around Seven. Everyone had red-rimmed eyes as we formed a little circle. Damian brought me into his arms next, squeezing me. "How did you pull it off?"

"He came into the club as a client," I whispered, everything spinning and euphoric. I had barely imagined what success could look or feel like, in an attempt to protect myself against the worst-case scenario. And now we'd achieved it, the feeling was so powerful and overwhelming, I thought I might choke. I was grateful for Damian holding me down—it seemed likely that I might float away if not tethered.

"I didn't know who he was at first, but he brought you up once in the VIP room," I went on. I gave the short version of how we'd proceeded from there, knowing they'd want the full story later. But this wasn't the time or place for details.

"The only way any of this worked was because of what Jordan was able to get recorded while she met up with Eli," Seven added, his voice thick with emotion. "She got drugged that night because she had a hunch that if she gave Eli what he wanted, alone time, then she could get information out of him that might seal the deal."

"And I was right," I said with a little laugh, that turned into more tears. I covered my face with my hands, trying to compose myself. These were happy tears. Shocked tears. Relieved tears.

Arms squeezed around me, and the sweet clementine scent that settled over me told me it was Cora. I looked up, folding into her embrace.

"I'm so grateful for you," she whispered into my ear. "I'm so sorry that you had to be anywhere near that awful man. I promise I'll do whatever I can to make sure you find justice."

"It was worth it," I told her. "Look what we achieved."

"We will never not be in your debt," Cora said, squeezing my arms. "You and Seven saved this family. *Our* family."

"And I'd do it again," I said, looking around at the shining, incredulous, tear-stained faces. I met Axel's then Damian's eyes. "If that's the price I have to pay to make sure I keep my brothers in my life forever, well, I gladly paid it. I've lost you too many times. I didn't plan on losing you again."

"You'll never lose us," Damian promised.

"And I hope you keep us forever, too," Mercedes added, rubbing my back.

Damian pulled me into his arms, and everyone crowded around us again. At this rate, we'd never make it out of the courthouse. Stuck forever outside room 38, embracing until our bones turned to dust.

I laughed to myself amid the bliss, relishing the warm embrace of family.

It's what I'd been missing since entering the foster system. What I'd been craving throughout childhood, after Kaylee's death, and all through my listless, wandering young adulthood. A family surrounding me. A true love at my side.

After everything we'd been through, it seemed like this would be the end of the story. But for me, it felt like the beginning of a brand new life.

The one I'd been too scared to hope for.

EPILOGUE

JORDAN

"Are we ready for the performances?" I had to speak so loud over the din of voices in Seven's apartment that I was nearly shouting. A few heads turned. I'd never seen so many people in Seven's apartment before, but we'd never thrown a Christmas party like this before, either.

Not just a Christmas party. This was a pole dance exhibition, employee banquet, and family get-together all in one. But Axel had insisted we go all out, so that meant a professional holiday decorator had come in the day before to spruce the place up with fancy wreaths, enormous ornament displays, and so much gorgeous, sparkling garland that every corner of the apartment could have become an Instagram backdrop.

My brothers were in attendance with their beautiful counterparts, as well as Willow, Legs, Legs' wife Harietta, Harry, Chico, Liam, Trojan, Jessa's friend Kendra, and Roxie. Mercedes' ex-sister-in-law, Maddie, was in town with her daughter Grace, visiting New York City for the first time for the holidays. Zero was here with

Axel and Cora. He'd been on-and-off tailing Ranger, who seemed to enjoy the brief chases that ensued.

I'd been training Jessa, Cora, and Mercedes on the pole for almost a year, and my brothers finally joined the lessons about six months ago. Tonight, they would showcase their talents and have some fun. Even Seven was going to do the routine I taught him.

They were my first students, but hopefully not the last. Not if everything went according to plan over the next year. I was currently collaborating with my brothers to bring something new to the seventh floor of their charity building—a pole dance studio and classroom. Teaching Cora, Jessa, and Mercedes showed me how much I loved teaching. And how much I loved showing women the power of their own bodies, the inherent strength they held between their legs and in their femininity. It gave me a shiver every time I thought of their journeys and all the journeys that were yet to be discovered.

Eventually, everyone stopped chattering and looked my way. I smiled brightly at the familiar faces. "Who wants to go first?"

When nobody raised their hands, I pointed at Seven. "Thank you for volunteering, honeycake."

Laughter rippled through the room. I sent him a shit-eating grin. "You ready?"

Seven sent me a smirky-smile and put his beer down. "I entered this world equipped. Make me set the tone, why don't you?"

A year later, and still finding creative ways to say *born ready.* "I'm not gonna go easy on you just because you're sleeping with the instructor," I called out. More laughter, but Axel and Damian groaned.

"Can we not do the sex jokes?" Axel asked me in a withering tone.

"You're only going to get *more* of them since you said that," Damian warned him.

I cackled. "You are *so right.*"

Roxie operated the Bluetooth speaker set up near the pole. Electronic music sprang to life. With a sexy look back over his shoulder at me, Seven tore off his shirt, and then ripped off his performance-ready sweat pants like Magic Mike.

"Oh God, he even gave her bedroom eyes," Axel muttered.

Clad in just his performance undies, as we called them, he grabbed the pole and began his routine.

"Look at how he works that pole," I said, internally counting the beats as he went through the routine. Everyone started cheering as he scaled the pole. "Almost as good as I work his."

Trace snort-laughed. Damian fought a grin, while Axel just sent me a glare.

"You are being such a snotty little sister right now," Axel informed me.

"Still trying to make up for all those years you missed," I said with a laugh. When Seven extended his hands away from the pole, clinging only by his muscular thighs, I cupped my mouth and hollered. "That's my man! Root Bear!"

"Root Bear!" Roxie shouted, our gazes meeting across the room.

"Root Bear!" Trojan echoed, clapping loudly for his best friend.

Chico and Liam were hollering too. Over the past year, the three of them had formed quite the security team at Silva Security. Of course the Fairchilds hired Silva Security back immediately after the hearing. Seven even resumed his prior headquarters space in their building. I loved seeing him as CEO—watching all the ways he handled hiccups, worked with clients, and navigated business issues. He was on track to hire three new close protection officers this year. Watching him not just start this business but grow it was inspiring—I hoped to draw inspiration and guidance from him as I launched my own pole business.

Once Seven wrapped up his performance, sliding gracefully down the pole with only minimal thigh-squeaking, he lifted his fists in victory. The crowd went wild.

"How the fuck is anyone supposed to follow that act?" Axel muttered.

"So I take it you'd like to go next?" I asked him.

"I'm still training," Axel said. "Maybe next year's Christmas party."

Jessa was the next to volunteer. She shimmied out of her jumpsuit, revealing a black spandex bodysuit. Roxie changed the music, and Jessa's routine began. Seven leaned against the kitchen island beside me, dipping down for a kiss.

"How'd I do?" he asked, sweat glistening on his chest.

"The best you've ever done," I told him.

"Thanks to my awesome teacher," he replied.

I cupped the side of his face, getting lost in his caramel gaze. "I love you, you know that?"

"I do know that. Are you aware that I love you?"

I laughed. "I'm aware."

"Endlessly and forever and through the eons?"

"I suspected that, based on how many wooden cooking utensils I've acquired over the past year, yes."

His heartbreaking grin nearly split me in two. I pushed onto my tiptoes for another kiss. If we didn't have a full party in swing, I would have snuck off with him to the bedroom.

Cora crossed the room, heading straight for me. Axel grabbed her hand and brought it to his lips before she started speaking. "Jordan, listen to this! I just got a text from my assistant. Eli's been convicted in one of the cases brought against him." Excitement poured out of her, her green eyes brimming. "He'll have to register as a sex offender."

I gasped, my hand shooting to cover my mouth. After we'd over-turned the case last year, Eli had gotten into some trouble regarding his involvement with the SEC scandal. Mostly fines, unfortunately. Cora and I worked together to get him arrested for what he'd done to me at his house party. In the process, other women came forward with their own stories involving Eli. It ballooned out of control—so much larger than we'd ever imagined. My own case against him didn't make it too far, but a few were very solid. And finally, *justice*.

Seven wrapped an arm around me, pressing a kiss to my temple. "That's music to our ears." He spoke the words I was thinking in my head. We were *that* kind of couple now.

Axel pumped his fist in the air. "Fuck yes! The looner goes down! That was the last square on our bingo card."

Cora sent him a satisfied look. "I think we'll all be breathing a little easier from here on out."

The entire Margulis brand went down in flames after the Fairchild SEC trial was dismissed; they were still a functional busi-ness, but with almost zero influence after all the damning exposés had come out about Allan's alleged involvement with federal cor-ruption. It must have been too much for old Allan to handle, be-cause he passed away from a heart attack about four months after the trial concluded. Cora didn't attend the funeral, and she still hadn't spoken a word to her mother since their initial fracture when Cora separated from Eli.

Through all of our excitement, we'd missed most of Jessa's per-formance. I cheered extra loud as she finished up.

She dropped to the floor, red-faced and beaming, and then let out an ear-piercing whoop. "I was made for the pole, mothercluckers!"

Everyone applauded. Near the front, Mercedes leaned down to point something out to Willow and Grace, who both watched the pole transfixed. Maddie clapped gleefully at her side. It was nice having another Kentucky girl in the mix, though I sensed she might become another northern convert after this visit. It sounded to me, based on what Mercedes said, that there wasn't much for Maddie in Kentucky anymore after her contentious split with Mercedes's brother Jericho. I was just about to call up the next performer when I spotted a too-sweet sight: Zero and Ranger cuddling in the corner. Zero had laid down to take it all in, and Ranger was tucked up against Zero's glossy coat, looking too comfortable.

"Look at those lovers," I whispered to Seven.

"They couldn't be more different, but on the inside, they're just the same," he said. "Even though one is clearly taller and built like a Greek god, and one is roughly ten years younger and very good at climbing things, they're made for each other."

I looked up at him. "Trying to say something profound?"

His ear-to-ear grin was contagious. "Maybe. Metaphors are one of the few things I'm not good at."

When I had recovered from the side-splitting laughter we shared, I drew a deep breath and turned to Trace. "Should Mercedes go next?"

He looked over at me, something heavy in his gaze. He opened his mouth to say something, but stopped. Then he said, "You should ask Mercedes if she thinks that's a good idea."

An odd response. I called out for Mercedes, waving her toward the kitchen. She and Willow came our way.

"Do you want to go next?" I asked her.

Her brows dipped together. "I really did want to perform today. But I found out something a couple weeks ago that I…" She glanced at Trace, rolling her lips in as she handed Willow to him.

"Tell them if you want to," Trace said softly. "It's up to you."

Mercedes looked back at me, her cheek twitching from the effort of hiding a smile. "I'm pregnant."

I gasped, covering my mouth again. Cora shrieked, wrapping Mercedes in a hug. Jessa showed up a moment later. "Don't tell me I missed some big news."

"Congratulations, Mercedes!" I gushed, claiming the next hug. Jessa heard the news from Cora, and she also shrieked. Soon, we were all hugging. Axel, Damian and Seven all clapped Trace on the back. He beamed as he looked over at Mercedes.

"Our little Christmas present," he said.

"It's so early," Mercedes said, "but I want to be extra safe. I had a loss before this, so…"

"I completely understand," I told her. "Maybe Willow can go up there and do a little dance in your place?" I suggested. "If not, I'll just send Roxie up there. She's champing at the bit, anyway."

Axel appeared at my side, glancing around the room. "Okay, I'm ready."

"Oh, you're going to perform after all?" I asked.

He shook his head, his gaze not wavering from the front of the room. Then his meaning clicked into place. We'd talked about the possibility of this. "You mean…for the…" My gaze drifted to Cora, who chatted with Mercedes.

He licked dry lips, nodding. "Totally."

I gave him a gentle push toward the front of the room. "Go for it, big bro."

Axel headed for the pole, but instead of beginning a routine, he called out a quick, "Hey, guys" over the din. The chatter in the room quieted, all eyes turning to the front. "I just wanted to thank you all for being here. Big thanks to Seven for hosting this unconventional Christmas party. It's the only kind of party we'd have, as Fairchilds, I suppose." Laughter trickled through the room.

"I mostly just wanted to share how much you all mean to me. I'm so thankful you're all in our lives, that we've come through to the other side together." He shifted his gaze to Cora, who had started to drift closer to the front of the room as he spoke. "Cora, come here, I need to touch you while I'm being sappy."

She laughed and drifted his way. Axel slid his arm around Cora's waist, smiling out at everyone. "There we go. Now I can think properly. We've had a crazy ass couple of years. And now that we are officially out of our financial fraud chapter, I'd like to propose the start of something new: wedding season."

Laughter swelled as Axel tipped his chin down to gaze at Cora. Electricity snapped between them as Axel reached into his pocket, pulled something out, and then sank down onto one knee.

"I wanted to wait until our family was around us." Axel spoke more quietly now, which caused us all to step closer and listen in. Between his thumb and forefinger, he held a sparkling ring. "Our chosen family. And I wanted to wait until everything was resolved with the storm clouds that have been following us around the past couple of years. This is a decade overdue, babe, but everything's in place now for us to enjoy the rest of our lives in peace and bliss. There's never been anyone else for me, since the day I laid eyes on you our sophomore year of college." Axel paused to brush away a tear, which made me tear up as well.

"It's always been you, Cora," he went on. "We're ready for the best times of our lives. Let's finally do this right. The way we could only dream of before everything got derailed during grad school. Will you marry me?"

Cora watched him with her hands clasped over her mouth, eyes watering. In lieu of a response she sank down onto the floor in front of him and threw her arms around his neck. She clung to him, and I could tell from the way her body trembled that she was sobbing. After a few moments, she pulled her head out of the crook of Axel's neck and said,

"I said yes, by the way!"

The room erupted into cheers. I spotted Seven rummaging in the cabinets in the kitchen. A moment later, champagne popped, which started another round of cheers. Axel slipped the ring on Cora's trembling finger, and they hugged again.

I helped Seven pour and pass out champagne flutes to celebrate. Once Cora and Axel had stopped crying and hugging, we all began our rounds of congratulations.

"There's a lot to celebrate in this room," I told Seven, knocking his hip, just as an unexpected peal of laughter grabbed my attention. *Maddie.* She had Grace in her arms, bouncing her, as she chatted with Trojan. She was the tiny blondie next to his burly, lumberjack beefcake. I tilted my head, watching as Trojan grinned endlessly at her.

I jerked my chin in their direction, leaning toward Seven. "You think that Trojan might be...I dunno..."

His gaze followed mine. He assessed them for a moment, then said, "Hm."

"Yeah. That's what I thought."

"Trojan is a self-proclaimed bachelor, Jordan," he finally said. "Maddie is the epitome of sweet, loyal schoolteacher. I bet she decorates her house for every single holiday. I don't think we can expect anything to happen there."

"That's probably what you told yourself when you met me, huh?" I elbowed him. "Just a sassy little stripper, ten years younger than you, your client's little sister. Nothing's gonna happen there."

He dipped his chin, that dark gaze of his drinking me in, turning desirous. "You may have a point."

"I know I do." I grinned up at him, loving the twinkle in his eyes, the energy that pulsed between us, and, more than anything, the fact that he was still in his performance undies. "Are you gonna stay in the boy shorts all night?"

He shrugged. "They're pretty comfortable. Now that he's finally come out to play, Root Bear wants to stay awhile."

I tipped my head back as laughter cascaded out of me. I wrapped my arms around Seven's warm torso and hung on for dear life.

I never wanted to let this life go.

I'd lived through hell and rebuilt from nothing...and discovered paradise on the other side.

Now that I'd found it—and fought for it—it was mine. *Ours.* All of ours.

Forever.

THE END

How do we feel about the end of the Fairchilds? What if I told you it...wasn't quite over? Stay tuned by signing up for <u>my newsletter</u> (h ttps://bit.ly/EL-newsletter) so you won't miss updates about what's coming next.

Need more brothers? I happen to specialize in that.

Check out my Winter Harbor series and get to know the alpha Winters brothers as they settle their father's estate and confront a fractured family dynamic. Start with The Bastard Heir (http://books2read.com/the-bastard-heir).

Check out my rom-com series, set in small-town Bayshore in Ohio. Five stubborn, alpha, hyper-competitive brothers reconvene in their idyllic, lakeside hometown to collect their inheritances and confront their fractured family. What could possibly go wrong? Get to know the Daly brothers in book #1, Make Me Lose (http://books2read.com/make-me-lose-el).

ACKNOWLEDGEMENTS

This book would not have been possible without my awesome beta squad, who stepped up even in a time crunch! Big thanks to Whitley Cox and Elisabeth Nelson for helping me plot and plan this series for what feels like three years.

Huge thanks to my husband for giving me the time and space to complete this beast of a book, including all those daycare and school runs so I could stay glued to the laptop. I could NOT do this without your help!

Thank you to Katrina DeHart for supplying the name of Trojan/Troy in my reader's group when I asked for suggestions!

And last but never least, enormous thanks, hugs, and kisses to everyone who's read this book and enjoyed the world of the Fairchilds. Your support means THE WORLD to me!!

HAVE YOU READ THE BAD BOYS OF WALL STREET PREQUEL?

You can read *The Price of a Promise* (Axel & Cora's back story) **for free** when you sign up to <u>my newsletter</u> (https://bookhip.com/ZBGRSRB)! By joining, you'll also receive information about upcoming releases, sales, and other exciting news. Score!

Or join my reader group, EMBER'S BLOSSOMS , to hang out up-close and personal! Early looks at new covers, exclusive access to ARC sign-ups, and more.

FACEBOOK

INSTAGRAM

GOODREADS

BOOKBUB

http://www.emberleighromance.com/

And before you go...
Please consider leaving an honest review about this book! Even just a few words or a line mean so much to us authors.

ALSO BY EMBER LEIGH

THE BAD BOYS OF WALL STREET
The Price of Revenge
The Price of Passion
The Price of Infamy
The Price of Forever

WINTER HARBOR
(co-written with Whitley Cox)
The Bastard Heir
The Asshole Heir
The Rebel Heir
The Matchmaking Heirs

THE BAYSHORE SERIES
Make Me Lose
Make Me Fall
Make Me Yours
Make Me Choose
Make Me Hot
Make Me Smile

THE BREAKING SERIES

Breaking the Rules
Changing the Game
Breaking the Sinner
Breaking the Habit
Breaking the Fall